Nina Singh lives just outside of Boston, USA, with her husband, children, and a very rumbunctious Yorkie. After several years in the corporate world she finally followed the advice of family and friends to 'give the writing a go, already'. She's oh-so-happy she did. When not at her keyboard she likes to spend time on the tennis court or golf course. Or immersed in a good read.

Michelle Major grew up in Ohio but dreamed of living in the mountains. Soon after graduating with a degree in journalism, she pointed her car west and settled in Colorado. Her life and house are filled with one great husband, two beautiful kids, a few furry pets and several well-behaved reptiles. She's grateful to have found her passion writing stories with happy endings. Michelle loves to hear from her readers at michellemajor.com.

Also by Nina Singh

Miss Prim and the Maverick Millionaire
The Marriage of Inconvenience
Snowed in with the Reluctant Tycoon
Reunited with Her Italian Billionaire
Tempted by Her Island Millionaire

Also by Michelle Major

Second Chance in Stonecreek
Falling for the Wrong Brother
Coming Home to Crimson
Sleigh Bells in Crimson
Romancing the Wallflower
Christmas on Crimson Mountain
Always the Best Man
A Baby and a Betrothal
Her Soldier of Fortune
A Fortune in Waiting

Discover more at millsandboon.co.uk

CHRISTMAS WITH HER SECRET PRINCE

NINA SINGH

A STONECREEK CHRISTMAS REUNION

MICHELLE MAJOR

MILLS & BOON

First Published in Great Britain 2018
by Mills & Boon, an imprint of HarperCollinsPublishers,
1 London Bridge Street, London, SE1 9GF

Christmas With Her Secret Prince © 2018 Nilay Nina Singh
A Stonecreek Christmas Reunion © 2018 Michelle Major

ISBN: 978-0-263-26542-2

1118

MIX
Paper from
responsible sources
FSC® C007454

This book is produced from independently certified FSC™
paper to ensure responsible forest management.

For more information visit: www.harpercollins.co.uk/green

Printed and bound in Spain
by CPI, Barcelona

CHRISTMAS WITH HER SECRET PRINCE

NINA SINGH

To my two very own princes.
And my two princesses.

CHAPTER ONE

PRINCE RAYHAN AL SAIBBI was not looking forward to his next meeting. In fact, he was dreading it. After all, it wasn't often he went against his father—the man who also happened to be king of Verdovia.

But it had to be done. This might very well be his last chance to exert any kind of control over his own life. Even if it was to be only a temporary respite. Fate had made him prince of Verdovia. And his honor-bound duty to that fate would come calling soon enough. He just wanted to try and bat it away one last time.

The sun shone bright and high over the majestic mountain range outside his window. A crisp blue stream meandered along its base. The pleasant sunny day meant his father would most likely be enjoying his breakfast on the patio off the four-seasons room in the east wing.

Rayhan found his father sitting at the far end of the table. Piles of papers and a sleek new laptop were mixed in with various plates of fruits and pastries. A twinge of guilt hit Rayhan as he approached. The king never stopped working. For that matter, neither did the queen, his mother. A fact that needed to be addressed after the events of the past year. Part of the reason Rayhan was in his current predicament.

This conversation wasn't going to be easy. His father

had been king for a long time. He was used to making the rules and expected everyone to follow them. Particularly when it came to his son.

But these days the king wasn't thinking entirely straight. Motivated by an alarming health scare Rayhan's mother had experienced a few months back and prompted by the troublesome maneuverings of a disagreeable council member, his father had decided that the royal family needed to strengthen and reaffirm their stability. Unfortunately, he'd also decided that Rayhan would be the primary vehicle to cement that stability.

His father motioned for him to be seated when he saw Rayhan approach.

"Thank you for seeing me, Father. I know how busy you are."

His father nodded. "It sounded urgent based on your messages. What can I assist you with, son? Dare I hope you're closer to making a decision?"

"I am. Just not in the way you might assume."

Rayhan focused his gaze on his father's face. A face that could very well be an older version of his own. Dark olive skin with high cheekbones and ebony eyes.

"I don't understand," his father began. "You were going to spend some time with the ladies in consideration. Then you were to make a choice."

Rayhan nodded. "I've spent time with all three of them, correct. They're all lovely ladies, Father. Very accomplished—all of them stunning and impressive in their own unique way. You have chosen well."

"They come from three of the most notable and prominent families of our land. You marrying a prominent daughter of Verdovia will go far to address our current problems."

"Like I said, you have chosen well."

The king studied him. "Then what appears to be the issue?"

Where to start? First of all, he wasn't ready to be wedded to any of the ladies in question. In fact, he wasn't ready to be wedded at all.

But he had a responsibility. Both to his family and to the kingdom.

"Perhaps I shall choose for you," the king suggested, his annoyance clear as the crisp morning air outside. "You know how important this is. And how urgent. Councilman Riza is preparing a resolution as we speak to propose studying the efficacy and necessity of the royal family's very existence."

"You know it won't go anywhere. He's just stirring chaos."

"I despise chaos." His father blew out a deep breath. "All the more reason to put this plan into action, son."

The *plan* his father referred to meant the end of Rayhan's life as he knew it. "It just seems such an archaic and outdated method. A bachelor prince choosing from qualified ladies to serve as his queen when he eventually ascends the throne."

His father shrugged. "Arranged marriages are quite common around the world. Particularly for a young man of your standing. Global alliances are regularly formed through marriage vows. It's how your mother and I wedded, as you know. These ladies I have chosen are very well-known and popular in the kingdom."

Rayhan couldn't argue the point. There was the talented prima ballerina who had stolen the people's hearts when she'd first appeared on stage several years ago. Then there was the humanitarian who'd made the recent influx of refugees and their plight her driving cause. And finally, a councilman's beautiful daughter, who also happened to be an international fashion model.

Amazing ladies. All of whom seemed to be approaching the king's proposition more as a career opportunity than anything else. Which in blatant terms was technically correct. Of course, the people didn't know that fact. They just believed their crown prince to be linked to three different ladies, and rumors abounded that he would propose to one of them within weeks. A well-calculated palace publicity stunt.

"As far as being outdated," the king continued, "have you seen the most popular show in America these days? It involves an eligible bachelor choosing from among several willing ladies. By giving them weekly roses, of all things." His father barked out a laugh at the idea.

"But this isn't some reality show," Rayhan argued. "This is my life."

"Nevertheless, a royal wedding will distract from this foolishness of Riza's."

Rayhan couldn't very well argue that point either. The whole kingdom was even now in the frenzied midst of preparing for the wedding of the half century, everyone anxious to see which young lady the prince would choose for himself. Combined with the festivities of the holiday season, the level of excitement and celebration throughout the land was almost palpable.

And Rayhan was about to go and douse it all like a wet blanket over a warming fire.

Bah humbug.

Well, so be it. This was his life they were talking about. He wanted to claim one last bit of it. He wouldn't take no for an answer. Not this time. But this was a new experience for him. Rayhan had never actually willingly gone against the king's wishes before. Not for something this important anyway.

"Well, I've come to a different decision," he told his father. Rayhan made sure to look him straight in the eye as he continued, "I've decided to wait."

The king blinked. Several times. Rapidly. "I beg your pardon?"

"I'd like to hold off. I'm not ready to choose a fiancée. Not just yet."

"You can only postpone for so long, son. The kingdom is waiting for a royal wedding… We have announced your intention to marry. And then there's your mother."

Rayhan felt a pang of guilt through his chest at the mention of the queen. She'd given them all quite a scare last year. "Mother is fine now."

"Still, she needs to slow down. I won't have her health jeopardized again. Someone needs to help take over some of the queen's regular duties. Your sisters are much too young."

"All I'm asking for is some time, Father. Perhaps we can come to a compromise."

The king leaned toward him, his arms resting on the table. At least he was listening. "What sort of compromise did you have in mind?"

Rayhan cleared his throat and began to tell him.

"Honestly, Mel. If you handle that invitation any more, it's going to turn into ash in your hands."

Melinda Osmon startled as her elderly, matronly employer walked by the counter where she sat waiting for her shift to begin. The older woman was right. This had to be at least the fifth or sixth time Mel had taken the stationery out simply to stare at it since it had arrived in her mailbox several days ago.

The Honorable Mayor and Mrs. Spellman request
the pleasure of your presence...

"You caught me," Mel replied, swiftly wiping the
moisture off her cheeks.

"Just send in your reply already," Greta added, her
back turned to her as she poured coffee for the customer
sitting at the end of the counter. The full breakfast crowd
wasn't due in for another twenty minutes or so. "Then
figure out what you're going to wear."

Melinda swallowed past the lump in her throat before
attempting an answer. "Greta, you know I can't go this
year. It's just not worth the abject humiliation."

Greta turned to her so fast that some of the coffee
splashed out of her coffeepot. "Come again? What in the
world do you have to be humiliated about?"

Not this again. Greta didn't seem to understand, nor
did she want to. How about the fact that Mel hadn't yet
moved on? Unlike her ex-husband. The ex-husband who
would be at the same party with his fashionable, svelte
and beautiful new fiancée. "Well, for one thing, I'd be
going solo. That's humiliating enough in itself."

Greta jutted out her chin and snapped her gum loudly.
"And why is that? You're not the one who behaved
shamefully and had the affair. That scoundrel you were
married to should be the one feeling too ashamed to show
his face at some fancy-schmancy party you both used to
attend every year when you were man and wife."

Mel cringed at the unfiltered description.

"Now, you listen to me, young lady—"

Luckily, another customer cleared his throat just then,
clearly impatient for a hit of caffeine. Greta humphed and
turned away to pour. Mel knew the reprieve would be
short-lived. Greta had very strong opinions about how

Mel should move along into the next chapter of her life. She also had very strong opinions about Mel's ex. To say the older woman was outraged on Mel's behalf was to put it mildly. In fact, the only person who might be even angrier was Greta's even older sister, Frannie. Not that Mel wasn't pretty outraged herself. A lot of good that did for her, though. Strong emotions were not going to get her a plus-one to the mayor's Christmas soiree. And she certainly was nowhere near ready to face the speculation and whispery gossip that was sure to greet her if she set foot in that ballroom alone.

"She's right, you know," Frannie announced, sliding into the seat next to Mel. The two sisters owned the Bean Pot Diner on Marine Street in the heart of South Boston. The only place that would hire her when she'd found herself broke, alone and suddenly separated. "I hate to admit when that blabbermouth is right but she sure is about this. You should go to that party and enjoy yourself. Show that no-good, cheating charlatan that you don't give a damn what he thinks."

"I don't think I have it in me, Frannie. Just to show up and then have to stare at Eric and his fiancée having the time of their lives, while I'll be sitting there all alone."

"I definitely don't think you should do that."

Well, that was a sudden change of position, Melinda thought, eyeing her friend. "So you agree I shouldn't go?"

"No, that's not what I said. I think you should go, look ravishing and then confront him about all he put you through. Then demand that he return your money."

Melinda sighed. She should have seen that argument coming. "First of all, I gave him that money." Foolishly. The hard-earned money that her dear parents had left her after their deaths. It was supposed to have been an investment in Eric's future. Their future. She had gladly handed it to him to help him get through dental school. Then it was supposed to be her turn to make some kind of investment in herself while he supported her. Instead, he'd left her for his perky, athletic dental assistant. His much younger, barely-out-of-school dental assistant. And now they happily cared for teeth together during the day, while planning an extravagant wedding in their off-hours. "I gave it to him with no strings attached."

"And you should take him to court to get some of it back!" Frannie slapped her palm against the counter. Greta sashayed back over to where the two of them sat.

"That's right," Greta declared. "You should go to that damn party looking pretty as a fashion model. Then demand he pay you back. Every last cent. Or you'll see him in front of a judge."

Mel sighed and bit down on the words that were forming on her tongue. As much as she longed to tell the two women to mind their own business, Mel just couldn't bring herself to do it. They'd been beyond kind to her when she'd needed it the most. Not to mention, they were the closest thing to family Mel could count since her divorce a year ago.

"How? I barely have the money for court fees. Let alone any to hire an attorney."

"Then start with the party," Greta declared as her sister nodded enthusiastically. "At the very least, ruin his evening. Show him what he's missing out on."

Nothing like a couple of opinionated matrons double-teaming you.

Mel let out an unamused laugh. "As if. I don't even have a dress to wear. I sold all my fancier clothes just to make rent that first month."

Greta waved a hand in dismissal. "So buy another one. I tell you, if I had your figure and that great dark hair of yours, I'd be out shopping right now. Women like you can find even the highest-end clothing on sale."

Mel ignored the compliment. "I can't even afford the stuff on sale these days, Greta."

"So take an advance on your paycheck," Frannie offered from across the counter. "We know you're good for it."

Mel felt the immediate sting of tears. These women had taken her in when she'd needed friendship and support the most. She'd never be able to repay their kindness. She certainly had no desire to take advantage of it. "I can't ask you to do that for me, ladies."

"Nonsense," they both said in unison.

"You'd be doing it for us," Greta added.

"For you?"

"Sure. Let two old bats like us live vicariously through you. Go to that ball and then come back and tell us all about it."

Frannie nodded in agreement. "That's right. Especially the part about that no-good scoundrel begging you for forgiveness after he takes one look at ya."

Mel smiled in spite of herself. These two certainly knew how to cook up a good fantasy. Eric had left her high and dry and never looked back even once. As far as fantasies went, she was more likely to turn a frog into a prince than receive any kind of apology from her exhusband.

"I don't think that's going to happen anytime soon." Or ever. Mel reached down to tighten the laces of her comfortable white tennis shoes. She had a very long shift ahead of her, starting with the breakfast crowd and ending with the early-evening dinner guests.

"You won't know unless you go to this ball."

She couldn't even tell which of the ladies had thrown

that out. Mel sighed and straightened to look at them both. Her bosses might look like gentle, sweet elderly ladies, complete with white hair done up in buns, but they could be relentless once they set their minds to something.

"All right. I give."

They both squealed with delight. "Then it's settled," Frannie declared and clasped her hands in front of her chest.

Mel held a hand up. "Not so fast. I haven't agreed to go just yet."

Greta's smile faded. "Come again?"

"How about a deal?"

"What kind of deal?"

"I'll go out after my shift and look for a dress." Though how she would summon the energy after such a long day was a mystery. But she was getting the feeling she'd hear about this all day unless she threw her two bosses some kind of bone. "If, and only if, I come across a dress that's both affordable and appropriate, I'll reconsider going."

Frannie opened her mouth, clearly about to protest. Mel cut her off.

"It's my only offer. Take it or leave it."

"Fine," they both said in unison before turning away. Mel stood just as the bell for the next order up rang from the kitchen. She had a long day ahead of her and it was only just starting. She was a waitress now. Not the young bride of an up-and-coming urban dentist who attended fancy holiday balls and went shopping for extravagant ball gowns. That might have been her reality once, but it had been short-lived.

Little did the Perlman sisters know, she had told them something of a fib just now when making that deal. She had no expectation that she'd find any kind of dress that would merit attending that party in a week.

The chances were slim to zero.

His driver-slash-security-guard—who also happened to be a dear childhood friend—was very unhappy with him at the moment. Rayhan ignored the scowl of the other man as he watched the streets of downtown Boston outside his passenger-side window. Every shop front had been decorated with garlands and glittery Christmas decorations. Bright lights were strung on everything from the lamp poles to shop windows. Let his friend scowl away, Rayhan thought. He was going to go ahead and enjoy the scenery. But when Saleh took yet another turn a little too fast and sharp, he found he'd had enough. Saleh was acting downright childish.

To top it off, they appeared to be lost. Saleh had refused to admit he needed the assistance of the navigation system and now they appeared to be nowhere near their destination.

"You know you didn't have to come," Rayhan reminded the other man. "You volunteered, remember?"

Saleh grunted. "I clearly wasn't thinking straight. Why are we here, again? At this particular time, no less."

"You know this."

"I know you're delaying the inevitable."

He was right, of course. Not that Rayhan was going to admit it out loud. "I still have a bit of time to live my life as I see fit."

"And you decided you needed to do part of that in Boston?"

Rayhan shrugged, resuming his perusal of the outside scenery. "That was completely coincidental. My father's been eyeing property out here for months now. Perfect opportunity for me to come find a prime location and seal the deal."

"Yes, so you say. It's a way to… How do the Americans say it? To kill two birds with one stone?"

"Precisely."

"So why couldn't you have come out here with the new soon-to-be-princess after your engagement?"

Rayhan pinched the bridge of his nose. "I just needed to get away before it all gets out of control, Saleh. I don't expect you to understand."

Not many people would, Rayhan thought. Particularly not his friend, who had married the grade-school sweetheart he'd been in love with since their teen years. Unlike Rayhan, Saleh didn't have to answer to nor appease a whole country when it came to his choice of bride.

Rayhan continued, "Everywhere I turn in Verdovia, I'm reminded of the upcoming ceremonies. Everyone is completely preoccupied with who the heir will choose to marry, what the wedding will be like. Yada yada. There are odds being placed in every one of our island casinos on everything from the identity of the next queen to what flavor icing will adorn the royal wedding cake."

Saleh came to a sudden halt at a red light, a wide grin spread across his face.

"What?" Rayhan asked.

"I placed my wager on the vanilla buttercream."

"I see. That's good to know." He made a mental note to go with anything but the vanilla buttercream when the time came. If he had any say on the matter, that was. Between his mother and the princess-to-be, he'd likely have very little sway in such decisions. No doubt his shrewd friend had made his bet based on the very same assumption.

"I don't understand why you refuse to simply embrace

your fate, my friend. You're the heir of one of the most powerful men in the world. With that comes the opportunity to marry and gain a beautiful, accomplished lady to warm your bed. There are worse things in life."

Saleh overlooked the vast amount of responsibility that came with such a life. The stability and prosperity of a whole kingdom full of people would fall on Rayhan's shoulders as soon as he ascended. Even more so than it did now. Few people could understand the overwhelming prospect of such a position. As far as powerful, how much did any of that mean when even your choice of bride was influenced by the consideration of your position?

"How easy for you to say," he told Saleh just as the light turned green and they moved forward. "You found a beautiful woman who you somehow tricked into thinking marrying you was a good idea."

Saleh laughed with good-natured humor. "The greatest accomplishment of my life."

Rayhan was about to answer when a screeching noise jolted both men to full alert. A cyclist veered toward their vehicle at an alarming speed. Saleh barely had time to turn the wheel in order to avoid a full-on collision. Unfortunately, the cyclist shifted direction at precisely the same time. Both he and their SUV were now heading the same way. Right toward a pedestrian. Saleh hit the brakes hard. Rayhan gripped the side bar, waiting for the inevitable impact. Fortunately for them, it never came.

The cyclist, however, kept going. And, unfortunately for the poor pedestrian woman, the bicycle ran straight into her, knocking her off her feet.

"Watch where you're going!" the rider shouted back over his shoulder, not even bothering to stop.

Rayhan immediately jumped out of the car. He ran

around to the front of the SUV and knelt down where the woman still lay by the sidewalk curb.

"Miss, are you all right?"

A pair of startled eyes met his. Very bright green eyes. They reminded him of the shimmering stream that lay outside his windows back home. Not that this was any sort of time to notice that kind of thing.

She blinked, rubbing a hand down a cheek that was rapidly bruising even as they spoke. Saleh appeared at his side.

"Is she okay?"

"I don't know. She's not really responding. Miss, are you all right?"

Her eyes grew wide as she looked at him. "You're lovely," she said in a low, raspy voice.

Dear heavens. The woman clearly had some kind of head injury. "We have to get you to a doctor."

Saleh swore beside him. "I'm so terribly sorry, miss. I was trying to avoid the bike and the cyclist was trying to avoid me but he turned right toward you—"

The woman was still staring at Rayhan. She didn't acknowledge Saleh nor his words at all.

He had a sudden urge to hold her, to comfort her. He wanted to wrap her in his arms, even though she was a complete stranger.

Rayhan reached for his cell phone. "I'll call for an ambulance."

The woman gave a shake of her head before he could dial. "No. I'm okay. Just a little shaken." She blinked some more and looked around. Her eyes seemed to regain some focus. Rayhan allowed himself a breath of relief. Maybe she'd be all right. Her next words brought that hopeful thought to a halt.

"My dress. Do you see it?"

Did she think somehow her clothes had been knocked off her upon impact? "You…uh…you are wearing it still."

Her gaze scanned the area where she'd fallen. "No. See, I found one. I didn't think I would. But I did. And it wasn't all that pricey."

Rayhan didn't need to hear any more. Unless she was addled to begin with, which could very well be a possibility, the lady had clearly suffered a blow to the head. To top it all off, they were blocking traffic and drawing a crowd. Kneeling closer to the woman sprawled in front of him, he lifted her gently into his arms and then stood. "Let's get you to a hospital."

"Oh!" she cried out as Rayhan walked back toward the SUV with her embraced against his chest.

Saleh was fast on his heels and opening the passenger door for them. "No, see, it's all right," she began to protest. "I don't need a doctor. Just that gown."

"We'll make sure to get you a dress," Rayhan reassured her, trying to tell her what she clearly needed to hear. Why was she so focused on clothing at a time like this? "Right after a doctor takes a look at you."

He gently deposited her in the back seat, then sat down next to her. "No, wait," she argued. "I don't need a doctor. I just want my dress."

But Saleh was already driving toward a hospital.

The woman took a panicked look out the window and then winced. The action must have hurt her injuries somehow. She touched a shaky finger to her cheek, which was now a dark purple, surrounded by red splotches.

Even in the messy state she was in, he couldn't help but notice how striking her features were. Dark, thick waves of black hair escaped the confines of some sort of complicated bun on top of her head. A long slender neck graced her slim shoulders. She was curvy—not quite what one would consider slim. Upon first glance, he would never consider someone like her his "type," so to speak. But he had to admit, he appreciated her rather unusual beauty.

That choice of words had him uncomfortably shifting in his seat. He stole a glance at her as she explored her facial injuries with shaky fingers.

Now her right eye had begun to swell as an angry, dark circular ring developed around it. Rayhan bit out a sharp curse. Here he was trying to enjoy what could very well be his last trip to the United States as a free man and he'd ended up hurting some poor woman on his first day here.

Perhaps Saleh was right. Maybe this whole trip had been a terrible idea. Maybe he should have just stayed home and accepted his fate.

There was at least one person who would be much better off right now if he had.

CHAPTER TWO

SHE WOULD HAVE been much better off if she'd just ignored that blasted invitation and thrown it away as soon as it arrived in her mailbox. She should have never even opened it and she definitely should have never even considered going to that godforsaken party. Her intuition had been right from the beginning. She no longer had any kind of business attending fancy balls and wearing glamorous gowns.

But no, she had to go and indulge two little old ladies, as well as her own silly whim. Look where that had got her—sitting on an exam table in a cold room at Mass General, with a couple of strange men out in the hallway.

Although they had to be the best-looking strangers she'd ever encountered. Particularly the one who had carried her to the car. She studied him now through the small window of her exam room door. He stood leaning against the wall, patiently waiting for the doctor to come examine her.

Even in her stunned shock while she lay sprawled by the side of the road, she hadn't been able to help but notice the man's striking good looks. Dark haired, with the barest shadow of a goatee, he looked like he could have stepped out of a cologne advertisement. Though there was no way he was some kind of male fashion model. He carried himself with much too much authority.

His eyes were dark as charcoal, his skin tone just on the darker side of dessert tan. Even before they'd spoken, she'd known he wasn't local.

His looks had taken her by surprise, or perhaps it had been the blow she'd suffered, but she distinctly remembered thinking he was lovely.

Which was a downright silly thought. A better description would be to say he looked dangerous.

Mel shook off the fanciful thoughts. She had other things to worry about besides the striking good looks of the man who had brought her here. They'd called the diner after she'd been processed. Presumably, either Greta or Frannie was on her way to join her at the hospital now. Mel felt a slight pang of guilt about one of them having to leave in the middle of closing up the diner for the night.

She would have frowned but it hurt too much. Her face had taken the brunt of the collision with the reckless cyclist, who, very rudely, had continued on his way. At least the two gentlemen out there hadn't left her alone and bleeding by the side of the road. Though now that meant she would be saddled with an ER bill she couldn't afford. Thinking about that expense, coupled with what she'd paid for the evening dress, had her eyes stinging with regret. In all the confusion and chaos right after the accident, her shopping bag had been left behind. Mel knew she should be grateful that the accident hadn't been worse, but she couldn't help but feel sorry for herself. Would she ever catch a break?

A sharp knock on the door was quickly followed by the entrance of a harried-looking doctor. He did a bit of a double take when he saw her face.

"Let's take a look at you, Miss Osmon."

The doctor wasted no time with his physical examination, then proceeded to ask her a series of questions—everything from the calendar date to what she'd had for breakfast. His unconcerned expression afterward told her she must have passed.

"I think you'll be just fine. Though quite sore for the next several weeks. You don't appear to be concussed. But someone will need to watch you for the next twenty-four hours or so. Just to be on the safe side." He motioned to the door. "Mind if I let your boyfriend in? He appears to be very concerned about you."

"Oh, he's not—they're just the—"

The doctor raised an eyebrow in question. "I apologize. He took care of the necessary paperwork and already settled the fees. I just assumed."

He had settled the bill? A nagging sense of discomfort blossomed in her chest. This stranger had paid for her care. She would have to figure out how to pay him back. Not that it would be easy.

The physician continued, "In any case, if he's the one who'll be watching you, he'll need to hear this."

"He won't be watching me. I have a friend—"

Before she got the last word out, Greta came barreling through the door, her springy gray hair still wrapped tight in a kitchen hairnet.

"Yowza," the older woman exclaimed as soon as her gaze landed on Mel's face. "You look like you went a couple rounds with a prizefighter. Or were ya fighting over a discounted item at The Basement? Their shoppers can be brutal!"

"Hi, Greta. Thanks for coming."

"Sure thing, kid. I took a cab over as soon as we heard. You doin' okay?" She'd left the door wide-open behind her. The two strangers hovered uncertainly out in the hallway, both of them giving her concerned looks.

Mel sighed. *What the heck? May as well make this a standing room–only crowd.* After all, they were nice enough to bring her in and take care of the processing while she was being examined. She motioned for them to come in. The taller, more handsome one stepped inside first. His friend followed close behind.

"The doctor says I'll be fine," she told them.

The doctor nodded. "I also said she needs to be monitored overnight. To make sure there are no signs of concussion or other trauma." He addressed the room in general before turning to Mel directly. "If you feel nauseous or dizzy, or if over-the-counter medications don't seem to be addressing the pain, you need to come back in. Understood?"

"Yes."

He turned to the others. "You need to watch for any sign of blacking out or loss of balance."

Greta nodded. As did the two men for some reason.

The doctor gave a quick wave before hastily walking out.

Mel smiled awkwardly at the two men. It occurred to her she didn't even know their names. "Um… I'm Mel."

They exchanged a glance between them. Then the taller one stepped forward. "I'm Ray. This is Sal." He motioned to his friend, who politely nodded.

More awkwardness ensued as all four of them stood silent.

"I'm Greta," the older woman suddenly and very loudly offered.

Both men said hello. Finally, Greta reached for Mel's arm. "C'mon, kiddo. Let's get you dressed. Then we'll call for a cab so we can get you home."

Ray stepped forward. "That won't be necessary. We'll take you anywhere you need to go."

Ray sighed with relief for what must have been the hundredth time as the old lady directed them to the front of a small eatery not far from where the accident had occurred. Thank goodness that Mel appeared to be all right. But she was sporting one devil of a shiner on her right eye and the whole side of her face looked a purple mess.

For some inexplicable reason, his mind kept referring to the moment he'd picked her up and carried her to the car. The softness of her as he'd held her, the way she'd smelled. Some delicate scent of flowers combined with a fruity shampoo he'd noticed when her head had been under his nose.

"This is our stop," Greta declared and reached for the door handle.

Ray immediately got out of the car to assist Mel out onto the street. After all, the older woman looked barely able to get herself moving. She'd actually dozed off twice during the short ride over. Ray hadn't missed how Mel had positioned herself to allow Greta to lean against her shoulder as she snored softly. Despite her injury. Nor how she'd gently nudged her friend awake as they approached their destination.

Who was taking care of whom in this scenario?

How in the world was this frail, seemingly exhausted older lady supposed to keep an eye on her injured friend all night?

Ray would never forgive himself if Mel had any kind of medical disaster in the middle of the night. Despite his reassurances, the doctor had made it clear she wasn't completely out of the woods just yet.

"My sister and I live in a flat above this diner, which

we own and manage," Greta informed him around a wide yawn as the three of them approached the door. She rummaged around in her oversize bag for several moments, only to come up empty.

"Dang it. I guess I left my keys behind when I rushed over to the hospital."

She reached for a panel by the side of the door and pressed a large button. A buzzer could be heard sounding upstairs. Several beats passed and…nothing.

Mel offered him a shy smile. Her black hair glistened like tinsel where the streetlight hit it. The neon light of the diner sign above them brought out the bright evergreen hue of her eyes. Well, the one that wasn't nearly swollen shut anyway. The poor woman probably couldn't wait to get upstairs and lie down.

Unfortunately, she would have to wait a bit longer. Several more moments passed. Greta pressed the button at least half a dozen more times. Ray wasn't any more reassured as they continued to wait.

Finally, after what seemed like an eternity, the sound of shuffling feet could be heard approaching as a shadow moved closer to the opposite side of the door. When it finally opened, they were greeted by a groggy, disheveled woman who was even older than Greta. She didn't even look fully awake yet.

It was settled. There was no way he could leave an injured woman with the likes of these two ladies. His conscience wouldn't allow it. Especially not when he was partly responsible for said injury to begin with.

"I'm glad that's over with." Saleh started the SUV as soon as Ray opened the passenger door and leaned into the vehicle. "Let's finally get to our hotel, then. I could use a long hot shower and a tall glass of something strong and aromatic." He reached for the gearshift before giving him a quizzical look. "Why aren't you getting in the car?"

"I've decided to stay here."

Saleh's eyes went wide with shock. "What?"

"I can't leave the young lady, Saleh. You should see the older sister who's supposed to watch Mel with Greta."

"You mean Greta's the younger one?"

"Believe it or not."

"Still. It's no longer our concern. We've done all we can. She'll be fine." He motioned with a tilt of his head for Rayhan to get in the car.

"I'm going to stay here and make sure of it. You go on ahead and check us into the hotel."

"You can't be serious. Are you forgetting who you are?"

Ray bit down on his impatience. Saleh was a trusted friend. But right now, he was the one close to forgetting who he was and whom he was addressing.

"Not in the least. I happen to be part of the reason that young lady is up there, sporting all sorts of cuts and bruises, as well as a potential head injury, which needs to be monitored. By someone who can actually keep an eye on her with some degree of competence."

"Your Highness, I understand all that. But staying here is not wise."

"Don't call me that, Saleh. You know better."

"I'm just trying to remind you of your position. Perhaps I should also remind you that this isn't an announced state visit. If these ladies were to find out who you are, it could leak to the rest of the world before morning. The resulting frenzy of press could easily result in an embarrassing media nightmare for the monarchy. Not to mention Verdovia as a whole."

"They won't find out."

Saleh huffed in exasperation. "How can you be sure?"

Ray ignored the question as he didn't really have any kind of adequate answer. "I've made up my mind," he said with finality.

"There's more to it. Isn't there, Rayhan?"

Ray knew exactly what his friend meant. The two had known each other their whole lives, since they were toddlers kicking around a sponge soccer ball in the royal courtyard. He wouldn't bother to deny what his friend had clearly observed.

"I saw the way you were looking at her," Saleh threw out as if issuing a challenge. "With much more than sympathy in your eyes. Admit it. There's more to it."

Ray only sighed. "Perhaps there is, my friend." He softly shut the car door.

Ray was asleep on Frannie and Greta's couch. Mel popped two anti-inflammatory pills into her mouth and then took a swig of water to swallow them down. Her borrowed nightgown felt snug against her hips. It belonged to Greta, who could accurately be described as having the figure of a very thin teenage boy. A description that didn't fit Mel in any way.

The feel of her nightwear wouldn't be the only thing bothering her tonight, Mel figured. The man lying in the other room only a few feet away would no doubt disrupt her sleep. Had she ever felt so aware of a man before? She honestly couldn't say, despite having been married. He had such a magnetism, she'd be hard-pressed to put its impact on her into words. Everything about him screamed class and breeding. From the impeccable and, no doubt, expensive tailored clothing to the SUV he and his friend were driving around in, Ray was clearly not lacking in resources. He was well-mannered and well-spoken. And judging by what he'd done earlier tonight, he was quite kindhearted.

Ray had feigned being too tired to travel with his friend to their hotel across town and had asked the Perlman sisters if he could crash on their couch instead. Mel wasn't buying it in the least. First of all, he didn't seem the type of man to lack stamina in any way. No, his true intention was painfully obvious. He'd taken one look at Frannie, studied Greta again and then perused Mel's battered face and decided he couldn't leave her in the care of the elderly sisters. None of them questioned it. Sure, Ray was barely more than a stranger, but he'd had ample opportunity if his motives were at all nefarious.

Besides, he hardly appeared to be a kidnapper. And he definitely wasn't likely to be a thief looking to take off with the Perlman sisters' ancient and cracked bone china.

No, he was just a gentleman who'd not only made sure to take care of her after she'd got hurt, he'd insisted on hanging around to keep an eye on her.

She crawled into the twin bed the Perlman sisters kept set up in their spare room and eyed the functional sleigh-bell ornament taken off the diner Christmas tree that Greta had handed her before going to bed. She was supposed to ring it to arouse their attention if she felt at all ill during the night. As if either sister had any chance of hearing it. Frannie hadn't even heard the much louder door buzzer earlier this evening. No wonder Ray had insisted on staying.

She felt oddly touched by his thoughtfulness. Not every man would have been so concerned.

She tried to imagine Eric going out of his way in such a fashion under similar circumstances. Simply to help a stranger. She couldn't picture it. No, Ray didn't seem at all like her ex. In fact, he was unlike any other man she'd ever met. And his looks! The man was heart-stoppingly handsome. She still didn't know where he was from, but based on his dark coloring and regal features, she would guess somewhere in the Mediterranean. Southern Italy perhaps. Maybe Greece. Or even somewhere in the Middle East.

Mel sighed again and snuggled deeper into her pillow. What did any of her speculation matter in the overall scheme of things? Men like Ray weren't the type a divorced waitress could count among her acquaintances. He would be nothing more than a flash of brightness that passed through her life for a brief moment in time. By this time next week, no doubt, he wouldn't give the likes of Melinda Osmon more than a lingering thought.

"So did she even find a dress?"

"I guess so. She says she lost the shopping bag 'cause of the accident, though."

"So no dress. I guess she definitely isn't going to the ball, then."

"Nope. Not without a dress. And not with that crazy shiner where her eye is."

What was it about this dress everyone kept talking about? Ray stirred and slowly opened his eyes. To his surprise it was morning already. He'd slept surprisingly well on the lumpy velvet-covered couch the sisters had offered him last night. Said sisters were currently talking much too loudly in the kitchen, which was off to the side of the apartment. Clearly, they didn't entertain overnight guests often.

His thoughts immediately shifted to Mel. How was she feeling? He'd slept more soundly than he'd expected to. What if she'd needed something in the middle of the night? He swiftly strode to the kitchen. "Has anyone checked on Mel yet?"

Both ladies halted midspeech to give him curious looks. "Well, good morning to you, too," Greta said with just a touch of grouchiness in her voice. Or maybe that was Frannie. In matching terry robes and thick glasses perched on the ends of their noses, they looked remarkably similar.

"I apologize. I just wondered about our patient."

The two women raised their eyebrows at him. "She's *our* patient now, huh?" one of the women asked.

Luckily, the other one spoke before Ray could summon an answer to that question. "She's sleeping soundly. I sneaked a peek at her as soon as I woke up. Breathing nice and even. Even has some color back in her face. Well, real color. Aside from the nasty purple bruise."

Ray felt the tension he wasn't aware he held slowly leave his chest and shoulders. One of the women pulled a chair out for him as another handed him a steaming cup of coffee. Both actions were done with a no-nonsense efficiency. Ray gratefully took the steaming cup and sat down.

The small flat was a far cry from the majestic expanse of the castle he called home, but the sheer homeliness and coziness of the setting served to put him in a comfortable state of ease, one that took him a bit by surprise. He spent most of his life in a harried state of rushing from one activity or responsibility to another. To be able to simply sit and enjoy a cup of coffee in a quaint New England kitchen was a novel experience. One he was enjoying more than he would have guessed.

"Damn shame about the dress," Greta or Frannie commented as she sat down across him, the other lady joining them a moment later after refreshing her mug.

He really needed one of them to somehow identify herself or he was bound to make an embarrassing slip before the morning was over about who was who.

"Can someone tell me what the deal is with this dress?" he asked.

"Mel was coming back from shopping when you and your friend knocked her on her keister," the sister right next to him answered.

"Frannie!" the other one exclaimed. Thank goodness. Now he just had to keep straight which was which once they stood. "That's no way to talk to our guest," she added.

Ray took a sip of his coffee, the guilt washing over him once more. Though technically they hadn't been the ones to actually run into Mel—the cyclist had done that—he couldn't help but feel that if Saleh had been paying better attention, Mel wouldn't be in the state she was in currently.

"She lost the shopping bag in all the confusion," Frannie supplied.

"I'm terribly sorry to hear that," Ray answered. "It must have been some dress. I'll have to find a way to compensate for Mel's losing it."

"It's more what she needed it for."

Ray found himself oddly curious. When was the last time he cared about why a woman needed an article of clothing? Never. The answer to that question was a resounding *never*.

"What did she need it for?"

"To stick it to that scoundrel husband of hers."

Ray found himself on the verge of sputtering out the coffee he'd just taken a sip of. Husband. Mel was married. It really wasn't any of his business. So why did he feel like someone had just landed a punch in the middle of his gut? He'd met the woman less than twelve hours ago for heaven's sake. Had barely spoken more than a few words to her.

"He's her ex-husband," Greta clarified. "But my sister's right about the scoundrel part."

"Oh?" Ray inquired. For the second time already this morning, he felt like a solid weight had been lifted off his shoulders. So she wasn't actually married currently. He cursed internally as he thought it. What bit of difference did it make where he was concerned?

"Yeah, he took all her money, then left her for some flirty flirt of a girl who works for him."

That did sound quite scoundrel-like. A pang of sympathy blossomed in his chest. No woman deserved that. What little he knew of Mel, she seemed like she wouldn't hurt another being if her life depended on it. She certainly didn't deserve such treatment.

"Before they got divorced, Mel and her ex were always invited to the mayor's annual charity holiday ball. The mayor's daughter is a college friend of both of theirs. This year that no-good ex of Mel's is taking his new lady. Word is, he proposed to her and they'll be attending as doctor and fiancée."

Frannie nodded as her sister spoke. "Yeah, we were trying to convince her to go anyway. 'Cause why should he have the satisfaction? But she had nothing to wear. We gave her an advance on her paycheck and told her to find the nicest dress she could afford."

Ray sat silent, taking all this in. Several points piqued his interest, not the least of which being just how much these ladies seemed to care for the young lady who worked for them. Mel was clearly more than a mere employee. She was family and so they were beyond outraged on her behalf.

The other thing was that she'd been trying to tell him right there on the sidewalk about how important the dress was, and he hadn't bothered to listen. He had just assumed that she'd hit her head and didn't know what she was talking about. He felt guilt wash over him anew.

"I still wish there was a way she could go." Greta shook her head with regret. "That awful man needs to know she don't give a damn about him and that she's still going to attend these events. With or without him."

A heavy silence settled over the room before Frannie broke it with a clap of her hands. "You know, I got a great idea," she declared to her sister with no small display of excitement.

"What's that?"

"I know she don't have anything to wear, but if she can figure that out, I think Ray here should take her." She flashed a brilliant smile in his direction.

Greta gasped in agreement, nodding vehemently. "Ooh, excellent idea. Why, he'd make for the perfect date!"

Frannie turned to him, a mischievous sparkle in her eyes. "It's the least you can do. You did knock her on her keister."

Greta nodded solemnly next to him.

This unexpected turn proved to take him off guard. Ray tried to muster what exactly to say. He was spared the effort.

Mel chose that moment to step into the room. It was clear she'd heard the bulk of the conversation. She looked far from pleased.

Mel pulled out a chair and tried to clamp down on her horror. She could hardly believe what she'd heard. As much as she loved the Perlman sisters, sometimes they went just a tad too far. In this case, they'd traveled miles. The last thing she wanted from any man, let alone a man the likes of Ray, was some kind of sympathy date. And she'd be sure to tell both the ladies that as soon as she got them alone.

For now, she had to try to hide her mortification from their overnight guest.

"How do you feel, dear?" Greta asked.

"Fine. Just fine."

"The swelling seems to be going down," Frannie supplied.

Mel merely nodded. She risked a glance at Ray from the corner of her eye. To his credit, he looked equally uncomfortable.

Frannie stood suddenly. "Well, the two of us should get downstairs and start prepping for the weekend diner crowd." She rubbed Mel's shoulder. "There's still fresh coffee in the pot. You obviously have the day off."

Mel started to argue, but Frannie held up a hand to stop her. Greta piped up from across the table. "Don't even think about it. You rest and concentrate on healing. We can handle the diner today."

Mel nodded reluctantly as the two sisters left the kitchen to go get ready for their morning. It was hard to stay aggravated with those two.

Except now she was alone with Ray. The awkwardness hung like thick, dense fog in the air. If she was smart, she would have walked away and pretended not to hear anything that was said.

Of all the...

What would possess Greta and Frannie to suggest such a thing? She couldn't imagine what Ray must be feeling. They had put him in such a sufferable position.

To her surprise, he broke the silence with an apology. "I'm so terribly sorry, Mel."

Great, he was apologizing for not taking her up on the sisters' offer. Well, that got her hackles up. She wasn't the one who had asked him to take her to the ball.

"There's no need to apologize," she said, perhaps a little too curtly. "I really had no intention of attending that party anyway. I hardly need a date for an event I'm not going to. Not that I would have necessarily said yes." Now, why had she felt compelled to add that last bit?

Ray's jaw fell open. "Oh, I meant. I just—I should have listened when you were trying to tell me about your dress. I didn't realize you'd dropped your parcel."

Mel suddenly realized her mistake. He was simply offering a general apology. He wasn't even referring to the ball. She felt the color drain from her face from the embarrassment. If she could, she would have sunk through the floor and into another dimension. Never to be seen or heard from again. Talk about flattering oneself.

She cleared her throat, eager to change the subject. Although this next conversation was going to be only slightly less cringeworthy. "I was going to mention this last night, but you ended up staying the night."

"Yes?"

"I know you paid for my hospital visit. I have every intention of paying you back." Here was the tough part. "I, um, will just need to mail it to you. It's a bit hard to reimburse you right at this moment."

He immediately shook his head. "You don't need to worry about that."

"I insist. Please just let me know where I can mail a check as soon as I get a chance."

"I won't accept it, Mel."

She crossed her arms in front of her chest. "You

don't understand. It's important to me that I pay back my debts." Unlike her ex-husband, she added silently.

He actually waved his hand in dismissal. "There really is no need."

No need? What part about her feeling uncomfortable about being indebted to him was he unable to comprehend? His next words gave her a clue.

"Given your circumstances, I don't want you to feel you owe me anything."

Mel felt the surge of ire prickle over her skin. She should have known. His meaning couldn't be clearer. Ray was no different than all the other wealthy people she'd known. Exactly like the ones who'd made her parents' lives so miserable.

"My circumstances? I certainly don't need your charity, if that's what you mean."

His eyes grew wide. "Of course not. I apologize. I meant no offense. I'm fluent, but English is my second language, after all. I simply meant that I feel responsible for you incurring the fees in the first place."

"But you weren't responsible. The cyclist was. And he's clearly not available, so the responsibility of my hospital bill is mine and mine alone."

He studied her through narrowed eyes. "Is it that important to you?"

"It is."

He gave her a slight nod of acquiescence. "Then I shall make sure to give you my contact information before I leave so that you can forward reimbursement at your convenience."

"Thank you."

Ray cleared his throat before continuing, "Also, if you'll allow me, I'd love to attend the Boston mayor's annual holiday ball as your escort."

CHAPTER THREE

MEL BLINKED AND gave her head a small shake, the action sending a pounding ache through her cheek straight up to her eye. In her shock, she'd forgotten how sore she was. But Ray had indeed just shocked her. Or maybe she hadn't actually heard him correctly. Maybe she really did have a serious head injury that was making her imagine things.

"I'm sorry. What did you just say?"

His lips curved into a small smile and Mel felt a knot tighten in the depths of her core. The man was sinfully handsome when he smiled. "I said I'd like to attend the ball with you."

She gently placed her coffee cup on the table in front of her. Oh, for heaven's sake. She couldn't wait to give Frannie and Greta a speaking-to. "You don't need to do that, Ray. You also didn't need to cover my expenses. And you didn't need to stay last night. You've done more than enough already. Is this because I insist on repaying you?" she asked. How much of a charity case did he think she was? Mel felt her anger rising once more.

But he shook his head. "Has nothing to do with that."

"The accident wasn't even your fault."

"This has nothing to do with the accident either."

"Of course it does. And I'm trying to tell you, you

don't need to feel that you have to make anything up to me. Again, the accident yesterday was not your fault."

He leaned closer to her over the table. "But you don't understand. It would actually be something of a quid pro quo to take me to this ball. You'd actually be the one doing me a favor."

Okay, that settled it. She knew she was hearing things. In fact, she was probably still back in Frannie and Greta's guest room, soundly asleep. This was all a strange dream. Or maybe she'd accidentally taken too many painkillers. There was no way this could actually be happening. There was absolutely nothing someone like Mel could offer a man such as Ray. The idea that accompanying her to the ball would be a favor to *him* was ridiculous.

"Come again?"

"Allow me to explain," Ray continued at her confused look. "I'm here on business on behalf of the king of Verdovia. He is looking to acquire some property in the Boston area. The type of people attending an event that the mayor is throwing are precisely the type of people I'd like to have direct contact with."

"So you're saying you actually want to go? To meet local business people?"

He nodded. "Precisely. And in the process, we can do the two-birds-killing."

She was beginning to suspect they both had some kind of brain trauma. Then his meaning dawned on her. He was misstating the typical American idiom.

"You mean kill two birds with one stone?"

He smiled again, wider this time, causing Mel's toes to curl in her slippers. "Correct. Though I never did understand that expression. Who wants to kill even one bird, let alone two?"

She had to agree.

"In any case, you help me meet some of these local business people, and I'll make sure you stick your ex-husband."

She couldn't help it. She had to laugh. This was all so surreal. It was like she was in a completely different reality than the one she'd woken up in yesterday morning. "You mean stick it to."

"That's right," he replied, responding to her laugh with one of his own.

For just a split second, she was tempted to say yes, that she'd do it. But then the ridiculousness of the whole idea made her pause. It was such a harebrained scheme. No one would believe Mel and someone like Ray were an actual couple. An unbidden image of the two of them dancing close, chest to chest, flashed in her mind. A curl of heat moved through the pit of her stomach before she squelched it. What a silly fantasy.

They clearly had nothing in common. Not that she would know with any real certainty, of course. She didn't know the man at all.

"What do you think?" Ray prompted.

"I think there's no way it would work. For one thing, we've barely met. You don't know a thing about me and I don't know a thing about you. I have no idea who you are. How would we even begin to explain why we're at such an event together?"

A sly twinkle appeared in his eye. "That's easy to fix. We should spend some time getting to know each other. Can I interest you in breakfast? I understand there's an excellent eating establishment very nearby. Right downstairs, as a matter of fact."

Greta seated them in a corner booth and handed him a large laminated menu. The giant smile on the older woman's face gave every bit the impression that she was beyond pleased at seeing the two of them at breakfast together. Though she did initially appear quite surprised.

Well, Ray had also surprised himself this morning. He'd had no idea that he'd intended to ask to take her to the mayor's ball until the words were actually leaving his mouth. Saleh would want to throttle him for such a foolish move. Oh, well, he'd worry about Saleh later. Ray's reasons were sound if one really thought about it. So he'd exaggerated his need to meet local business leaders, considering he already had the contacts in Boston that he needed. But Mel didn't know that or need to know that. And what harm would it do? What was so wrong about wanting to take her to the ball and hoping she'd have a good time there? Between the terrible accident yesterday and what he'd found out this morning about her past history, she could definitely use some fun, he figured. Even if it was only for a few hours.

Why he wanted to be the one to give that to her, he couldn't quite explain. He found himself wishing he'd met her under different circumstances, at a different time.

Right. He would have to be a completely different person for it to make an iota of difference. The reality was that he was the crown prince of Verdovia. He'd been groomed since birth to be beholden to rules and customs and to do what was best for the kingdom. He couldn't forget this trip was simply a temporary respite from all that.

This ball would give him a chance to do something different, out of the norm, if he attended as an associate of the royal family rather than as the prince. After all, wasn't that why he was in the United Sates? For one final adventure. This was a chance to attend a grand gala without all the pressures of being the Verdovian prince and heir to the throne.

He asked Mel to order for them both and she did so before Greta poured them some more coffee and then left their booth, her smile growing wider by the second.

"All right," Mel began once they were alone. "Tell me about yourself. Why don't you start with more about what you do for a living?"

Ray knew he had to tread carefully. He didn't want to lie to her, but he had to be careful to guard his true identity. Not only for his sake, but for hers, as well.

"You said something about acquiring real estate for the Verdovian royal family. Does that mean real estate is your main focus?" she asked.

Ray took a sip of his steamy beverage. He'd never had so much coffee in one sitting, but the Boston brew was strong and satisfying. "So to speak. I'm responsible for various duties in service of the king. He'd like to expand his American property holdings, particularly in metropolitan cities. He's been eyeing various high-end hotels in the Boston area. I volunteered to fly down here to scope out some prospects and perhaps make an agreement." Technically, he was telling her the complete truth.

Mel nodded. "I see. You're definitely a heavy hitter."

That wasn't an expression that made immediate sense to him. "You think I hit heavy?"

"Never mind. Do you have a family?"

"My parents and two younger sisters."

"What would you tell me about them?"

This part could get tricky if he wasn't careful. He hated being on the slim side of deceitful but what choice did he have? And in the overall scheme of things, what did it hurt that Mel didn't know he was a prince? In fact, he'd be glad to be able to forget the fact himself for just a brief moment in time.

"My father is a very busy man. Responsible for many people and lots of land. My mother is an accomplished musician who has studied the violin under some of Europe's masters and composes her own pieces."

Mel let out a low whistle. "Wow. That's quite a pedigree," she said in a near whisper. "How'd you end up picking such a high-profile career?"

He had to tread carefully answering that one. "It was chosen for me," he answered truthfully.

She lifted an eyebrow. "You mean the king chose you?"

He nodded. Again, it was the complete truth. "There were certain expectations made of me, being the only son of the family."

"Expectations?"

"Yes. It was a given that I would study business, that I would work in a career that led to the further wealth and prosperity of our island kingdom. Otherwise…"

The turn in conversation was throwing him off. Mel's questions brought up memories he hadn't given any consideration to in years.

She leaned farther toward him, over the table. "Otherwise what?"

He sighed, trying hard to clamp down on the years-old resentments that were suddenly resurfacing in a most unwelcome way. Mel stared at him with genuine curiosity shining in her eyes. He'd never discussed this aspect of his life with anyone before. Not really. No one had bothered to ask, because it was all such a moot point.

"Otherwise, it wasn't a career I would have chosen for myself. I was a bit of an athlete. Played striker during school and university. Got several recruitment offers from coaches at major football clubs. Though you would call it soccer here."

She blinked. "So wait. You turned down the opportunity of a lifetime because the king had other plans?"

Ray tapped the tip of his finger against the tabletop. "That about sums it up, yes."

She blew out a breath. "Wow. That's loyalty."

"Well, loyalty happens to be a quality that was hammered into me since birth."

"What about your sisters?" she asked him. "Are they held to such high standards, as well?"

Ray shook his head. "No. Being younger, they have the luxury of much fewer demands being made of them."

"Lucky for them. What are they like?"

"Well, both are quite trying. Completely unbearable brats," he told her. But he was unable to keep the tender smile off his face and his affection for his siblings out of his voice despite his words.

That earned him a small smile. "I'm guessing they're quite fortunate in having you as a brother." She sighed. "I don't have any siblings. I grew up an only child." Her tone suggested she was somewhat sad about the fact.

"That can have its advantages," he said, thinking of Saleh and the rather indulgent way the man's family treated him. "What of your parents?"

Mel looked away toward the small jukebox on the table, but not before he caught the small quiver in her chin. "I lost them about three years ago. They passed within months of each other."

"I'm so terribly sorry."

"Thank you for saying that."

"To lose them so close together must have been so difficult."

He couldn't help but reach for her hand across the table to comfort her. To his surprise and pleasure, she gripped his fingers, taking what he offered her.

"It was. My father got sick. There was nothing that could be done. It crushed my mom. She suffered a fatal cardiac event not long after." She let go of his fingers to brush away a tiny speck of a tear from the corner of her eye. "It was as if she couldn't go on without him. Her heart literally broke. They'd been together since they were teens."

Ray couldn't help but feel touched. To think of two people who had decided at such a young age that they cared for each other and stayed together throughout all those years. His own parents loved each other deeply, he knew. But their relationship had started out so ceremonial and preplanned. The same way his own marriage would begin.

The king and queen had worked hard to cultivate their affection into true love. He could only hope for as much for himself when the time came.

A realization dawned on him. Mel had been betrayed by the man she'd married within a couple of years of losing her parents. It was a wonder the woman could even smile or laugh.

He cleared his throat, trying to find a way to ask about her husband. But she was way ahead of him.

"You should probably know a little about my marriage."

"Aside from the knowledge that Frannie and Greta refer to him as 'that scoundrel,' you mean?"

This time the smile didn't quite reach her eyes. "I guess that would be one way to describe him."

"What happened?" He knew the man had left his wife for another woman. Somehow he'd also left Mel to fend for herself without much in the way of finances. He waited as Mel filled in some of the holes in the story.

She began slowly, softly, the hurt in her voice as clear as a Verdovian sunrise. "We met at school. At homecoming, our first year there. He was the most attentive and loving boyfriend. Very ambitious, knew from the beginning that he wanted to be a dentist. Husband material, you would think."

Ray simply waited as she spoke, not risking an interruption.

"When I lost my parents, I couldn't bear to live in their house. So I put it on the market. He invited me to live with him in his small apartment while he attended dental school. Eventually, he asked me to marry him. I'd just lost my whole family…"

She let the words trail off, but he could guess how the sentence might end. Mel had found herself suddenly alone, reeling from the pain of loss. A marriage proposal from the man she'd been seeing all through college had probably seemed like a gift.

"My folks' house netted a good amount in the sale. Plus they'd left me a modest yet impressive nest egg."

She drew in a shaky breath.

"Here's the part where I demonstrate my foolishness. Eric and I agreed that we would spend the money on his dentistry schooling after college graduation. That way we could start our lives together free of any school loans when he finished. I handed over all my savings and worked odd jobs here and there to cover any other costs while he attended classes and studied. When he was through, it was supposed to be my turn to continue on to a higher degree. I studied art history in my undergrad. Not a huge job market for those majors." She used one hand to motion around the restaurant. "Hence the waitressing gig. At the time, though, I was set on pursuing a teaching degree and maybe working as an elementary school art teacher. Once we had both achieved our dreams, I thought we would start a family." She said the last words on a wistful sigh.

Ray didn't need to hear the rest. What a foolish man her former husband was. Mel was quite a beautiful woman, even with the terrible degree of bruising on her face. Her injuries couldn't hide her strong, angular features, nor did they diminish the sparkling brightness of her jewel-green eyes.

From what he could tell, she was beautiful on the inside, too. She'd given herself fully to the man she'd made marriage vows to—albeit with some naïveté— to the point of generously granting him all the money she had. Only to be paid back with pure betrayal. Her friends obviously thought the world of her. To boot, she was a witty and engaging conversationalist. In fact, he wouldn't even be able to tell how long they'd been sitting in this booth, as time seemed to have stood still while they spoke.

"Frannie and Greta are sorely accurate in their description of this Eric, then. He must be a scoundrel and a complete fool to walk away from you."

Mel ducked her head shyly at the compliment, then tucked a strand of hair behind her ear. When she spoke again, she summoned a stronger tone. He hoped it was because his words had helped to bolster some of her confidence, even if only a little.

"I have to take some of the blame. I moved too quickly, was too anxious to be a member of a family again."

"I think you're being too hard on yourself."

"Enough of the sad details," she said. "Let's talk about other things."

"Such as?"

"What are your interests? Do you have any hobbies? What type of music do you like?"

She was trying valiantly to change the subject. He went along.

For the next several minutes, they talked about everything from each other's favorite music to the type of cuisine they each preferred. Even after their food arrived, the conversation remained fluid and constant. It made no sense, given the short amount of time spent in each other's company, but Ray was beginning to feel as if he knew the young lady across him better than most of the people in his regular orbit.

And he was impressed. Something about her pulled to him unlike anyone else he'd ever encountered. She had a pure authentic quality that he'd been hard-pressed to find throughout his lifetime. Most people didn't act like themselves around the crown prince of Verdovia. Ray could count on one hand all the people in his life he felt he truly knew deep down.

As he thought of Saleh, Ray's phone went off again in his pocket. That had to be at least the tenth time. If Mel was aware of the incessant buzzing of his phone, she didn't let on. And Ray didn't bother to reply to Saleh's repeated calls. He'd already left a voice message for him this morning, letting his friend know that he'd be further delayed.

Besides, he was enjoying Mel's company too much to break away simply for Saleh's sake. The other man could wait.

"So just to be sure we make this official." He extended his hand out to her after an extended lull in their lively conversation. "May I please have the pleasure of accompanying you to the mayor's annual holiday ball?"

She let out a small laugh. "You know what? Why not?"

Ray held a hand to his chest in mock offense. "Well,

that's certainly the least enthusiastic acceptance I've received from a lady. But I'll take it."

It surprised him how much he was looking forward to it. Even so, a twinge of guilt nagged at him for his duplicity. He'd give anything to completely come clean to Mel about who he was and what he was doing here in the city. Something shifted in his chest at the possibility of her finding out the truth and being disappointed in him. But he had no choice. He'd been groomed to do what was best for Verdovia and its people.

As Mel had phrased it earlier, though, the king had other plans for him.

CHAPTER FOUR

A LIGHT DUSTING of snow sprinkled the scenery outside the window by their table. Mel couldn't remember the last time she'd had such a lighthearted and fun conversation. Despite his classy demeanor, Ray had a way of putting her at ease. Plus, he seemed genuinely interested in what she had to say. He had to be a busy man, yet here he still sat as the morning grew later, happy to simply chat with her.

She motioned to Ray's plate. She'd been a little apprehensive ordering for him. He didn't strike her as the type who was used to diner cuisine. But he'd done a pretty nice job of clearing his plate. He must have liked it a little. "So, what did you think? I know baked beans first thing in the morning is an acquired taste. It's a Boston thing."

"Hence the name 'Boston Baked Beans'?"

"Correct."

"I definitely feel full. Not exactly a light meal."

She felt a flutter of disappointment in her stomach. Of course, she'd ordered the wrong thing. What did she know about what an international businessman would want for breakfast? She was completely out of her element around this man. And here she'd just agreed to attend a grand charity gala with him. Pretending she was his date. As if she could pull off such a thing.

"But it definitely—how do you Americans say it?—landed in the spot."

His mistake on the expression, along with a keen sense of relief, prompted a laugh out of her. "Hit the spot," she corrected.

"Yes, that's it. It definitely hit the spot."

His phone vibrated for the umpteenth time in his pocket. He'd been so good about not checking it, she was starting to feel guilty. He was here on a business trip, after all.

She also hadn't missed the lingering looks he'd received from all the female diner patrons, young and old alike. From the elderly ladies heading to their daily hair appointments to the young co-eds who attended the city's main university, located a shuttle ride away.

"I know you must have a lot to do. I probably shouldn't keep you much longer."

Ray sighed with clear resignation. "Unfortunately, there are some matters I should attend to." He started to reach for his pocket. "What do I owe for the breakfast?"

She held up a hand to stop him. "Please, employee privilege. It's on me."

"Are you sure? It's not going to come out of your wages or anything, is it?"

Not this again. It wasn't like she was a pauper. Just that she was trying to put some money away in order to finally get the advanced degree she'd always intended to study for. Before fate in the form of Eric Fuller had yanked that dream away from her.

"It so happens, Greta and Frannie consider free meals part of my employee package." Though she normally wouldn't have ordered this much food for herself over the course of a full week, let alone in one sitting. Something told her the two ladies didn't mind. Not judging by the immensely pleased smirks they kept sending in her direction when Ray wasn't looking.

"Well, thank you. I can't recall the last time I was treated to a meal by such a beautiful woman."

Whoa. This man was the very definition of *charming*. She had no doubt that had to be one doozy of a fib. Beautiful women probably cooked for him all the time.

"But you're right, I should probably be going."

She nodded and started to pile the empty plates in the center of the table. Waitress habit.

"Can I walk you back upstairs?" Ray asked.

She wanted to decline. Lord knew he'd spent enough time with her already. But a very vocal part of her didn't want this morning to end. "I'd like that," she found herself admitting.

He stood and offered her his arm. She gently put her hand in the crook of his elbow after he helped her out of the booth. With a small wave of thanks to her two bosses, they proceeded toward the side door, which led to the stairway to the apartment.

"So I'll call you tomorrow, then?" Ray asked. "To discuss further details for Saturday night?"

"That sounds good. And I'll work on finding a plan B for what my attire will be."

His mouth furrowed into a frown, causing deep lines to crease his forehead. "I'd forgotten about that. Again, I'm so terribly sorry for not paying more attention as you were telling me about your parcel."

She let out a small laugh. "It's okay. It wasn't exactly a situation conducive to listening."

"Still, I feel like a cad."

"It's all right," she reassured him. "I'm sure Frannie

and Greta won't mind if I do some rummaging in their closet. They might have something bordering on suitable."

He paused on the foot of the stairs right as she took the first step up. The difference in height brought them eye to eye, close enough that the scent of him tickled her nose, a woodsy, spicy scent as unique as he was.

"I'm afraid that won't do at all." His eyes looked genuinely troubled.

"It's all right. I'm very creative. And I'm a whiz with a sewing machine."

"That may be, but even creative geniuses need the necessary tools. Not to mention time. Something tells me you're not going to find anything appropriate in any closet up in that apartment." He pointed to the ceiling.

It wasn't like she had much choice. She'd already spent what little she could afford on the now-missing dress. All her closest friends had moved out of the New England area, so it wasn't as if she could borrow something. She was out of options. A jarring thought struck her. Could this be Ray's subtle way of trying to back out of taking her? But that made no sense. He was the one who had insisted on going in the first place. Could he have had a sudden change of heart?

"There's only one thing to do. I believe I owe you one formal ball gown, Miss Osmon. Are you up for some shopping? Perhaps tomorrow?"

Mel immediately shook her head. She absolutely could not accept such an offer. "I can't allow you to do that, Ray. Thank you, but no."

"Why not?"

She would think it was obvious. She couldn't allow herself to be this man's charity case. He'd done enough when he'd paid for her hospital bill, for goodness' sake.

A sum she still had to figure out how to pay back. Further indebting herself to Ray was absolutely out of the question. She opened her mouth to tell him so.

He cut her off before she could begin. "What if I said it was more for me?"

A sharp gasp tore out of her throat. He had to be joking. That notion was so ridiculous, she actually bit back a laugh. He didn't look like the type, but what did she know? Looks could be deceiving. And she certainly wasn't one to judge.

He responded with a bark of laughter. "I see I've given you the wrong impression. I meant it would be for me in that if I'm trying to make an impression at this event with various people, I would prefer to have my date dressed for the occasion."

That certainly made sense, but still, essentially he would be buying her a dress. She cleared her throat, tried to focus on saying the right words without sounding offended. He really couldn't be faulted for the way he viewed the world. Not with all the material privilege he'd been afforded. She understood that better now after the conversation they'd just had together. Lord, it was hard to concentrate when those deep dark eyes were staring at her so close and so intently.

"If it makes you feel better, the gown can become the property of the royal family eventually. The queen is always looking for donated items to be auctioned off for various charities. I'll have it shipped straight to her afterward. I can pretend I was considerate enough to purchase it for that very purpose."

That cracked her resolve somewhat. Essentially, she'd only be borrowing a dress from him. Or more accurately, from the royal family of Verdovia. That was a bit more palatable, she supposed. Especially if in the end it would result in a charitable donation to a worthy cause.

Or maybe she was merely falling for his easy charm and finding ways to justify all that Ray was saying. Simply because she just couldn't think straight, given the way he was looking at her.

Saleh was already outside, idling on the curb in the SUV by the time Ray reluctantly left the diner. His friend did not look happy.

Ray opened the passenger door only to be greeted by a sigh of exasperation. No, definitely not happy in the least.

"After yesterday, maybe I should drive," Ray said before entering the car, just to further agitate him.

It worked. "You have not been answering your phone," Saleh said through gritted teeth.

"I was busy. The ladies treated me to an authentic New England breakfast. You should try it."

Saleh pulled into the street. "If only I hadn't already eaten a gourmet meal of warm scones made from scratch and fresh fruit accompanied by freshly squeezed orange juice at my five-star hotel."

Ray shrugged. "To each his own. I'm happy I got to try something a little different." Who would have thought that there were parts of the world where people had baked beans for breakfast?

"Is breakfast the only thing you tried?" Saleh removed his hands from the steering wheel long enough to place air quotes on the last word.

"What you're alluding to is preposterous, my friend. I simply wanted to make sure the young lady was all right after the accident. Nothing more."

Saleh seemed satisfied with that answer. "Great. Now

that you've made sure, can we move on and forget all this unpleasantness of the accident?"

Ray shifted in his seat. "Well, not exactly."

Saleh's hands gripped the steering wheel so tightly, his knuckles whitened. "What exactly does 'not exactly' mean, my prince?"

"It means I may have made a commitment or two to Miss Osmon."

"Define these commitments, please."

"I'll be taking her shopping at some point."

"Shopping?"

"Yes. And, also, I'll be accompanying her to the Boston mayor's holiday charity ball on Saturday."

Saleh actually hit the brake, eliciting a loud honk from several cars behind them. "You will do what?"

"Perhaps I should indeed drive," Ray teased.

Saleh took a breath and then regained the appropriate speed. "If you don't mind my asking, what the hell has got into you?"

"I'm simply trying to enjoy Christmastime in Boston."

"There are countless ways you can do that, Prince Rayhan. Ways that don't involve risking embarrassment to Verdovia and the monarchy behind it."

"I've already committed. I fully intend to go."

"But why?" the other man asked, clearly at a loss. "Why would you ever risk your identity being discovered?"

Ray pinched the bridge of his nose. He didn't want to have to explain himself, not about this. The truth was he wasn't sure even how to explain it. "I'll be careful to avoid that, Saleh. I've decided the risk is worth it." Mel was worth it.

"I don't understand. Not even a little."

Ray sighed, searched for the perfect words. If he

couldn't confide in Saleh, there really was no one else on this earth he could confide in. He had to try. "I'm not sure how to put it into words, Saleh. I felt something when I lifted her into my arms after she was hurt. The way she clung to me, shivering in my embrace. And since this morning, the more time I've spent with her, the more I want to. You must understand that. You must have felt that way before."

Saleh bit the inside of his cheek. "My wife and I were seven when we met."

Okay. Maybe Saleh wasn't the person who would understand. But he had to see where Ray was coming from.

"I just don't understand how this all came about. How in the world did you end up agreeing to attend a charity ball of all things? You always complain about having to frequent such affairs back home."

"It's a long story."

"We have a bit of a drive still."

Ray tried to summon the words that would make his friend understand. "It's different back home. There I'm the crown prince. Everyone who approaches me has some ulterior motive." Most especially the ladies, be it a photo opportunity or something more involved. "Or there's some pressing financial or property matter." Ray halted midspiel. He was bordering on being perilously close to poor-little-rich-prince territory.

"So we could have hit a few clubs in the evening," Saleh responded. "I don't see how any of that leads you to your decision to take this Mel to a holiday ball."

Ray sighed. "Also, her ex-husband will be attending. A very nasty man. She had no one to go with. She wants to prove to him that she's content without him."

Saleh nodded slowly, taking it in. "I see. So she has feelings for her former spouse."

"What? No. No, she doesn't." At least Ray didn't think she did.

"Then why would she care about what he thinks?"

It was a possibility Ray hadn't considered. He felt himself clench his fists at his sides. The idea rankled more than he would have thought.

Saleh continued, "I urge you to be careful. This is simply to be a brief reprieve, coupled with a business transaction. Do not forget you still have a duty to fulfill upon your return."

Ray turned to stare out the window. Traffic had slowed down and a light dusting of snow filled the air.

"I haven't forgotten."

CHAPTER FIVE

MEL DIDN'T COME to Newbury Street often. By far one of the ritziest neighborhoods in downtown Boston, it housed some of the city's most premier shops and restaurants, not to mention prime real estate. Many of New England's sports stars owned condos or apartments along the street. High-end sports cars, everything from Lamborghinis to classic Bentleys rolled down the pavement. Being December, the street was currently lined with faux mini Christmas trees, and big red bows adorned the old-fashioned streetlights.

When she did come out this way, it certainly wasn't to visit the type of boutique that she and Ray were about to enter. The type of boutique that always had at least one limousine sitting out front. Today there were two. And one sleek black freshly waxed town car.

When Ray had suggested going shopping, she'd fully expected that they'd be heading to one of the major department stores in Cambridge or somewhere in Downtown Crossing.

Instead his friend Sal had picked her up and then dropped both her and Ray off here, at one of the most elite shops in New England. A place she'd only heard of. The sort of place where a well-heeled, well-manicured associate greeted you at the door and led you toward a sitting area while offering coffee and refreshments.

As soon as they sat down on the plush cushioned sofa and the saleslady walked away, Mel turned to Ray. "This is not what I had in mind. It's totally wrong. We shouldn't be here," she whispered.

Ray lifted one eyebrow. "Oh? There are a couple of other spots that were recommended to me. This was just the first one on the street. Would you like to continue on to one of those stores?"

He was totally missing the point. "No, that's not what I mean."

"Then I don't understand."

"Look at this place. It has to be beyond pricey. This is the sort of place queens and princesses buy their attire."

Ray's face grew tight. Great. She had no doubt insulted him. Obviously he could afford such extravagance or whoever his acquaintance was wouldn't have recommended this to him.

"Please do not worry about the expense," he told her. "We have an agreement, remember?"

"But this is too much. I doubt I'd be able to afford so much as a scarf from a place like this." She looked down at her worn jeans and scruffy boots. It's a wonder the saleslady hadn't taken one look at her and shown her the door. If Ray wasn't by her side, no doubt she would have done exactly that.

"It's a good thing we are not in the market for a scarf today."

"You know what I mean, Ray."

"I see." He rubbed his chin, studied her. "Well, now that we're here, let's see what's available. Don't forget, we are not actually buying you a dress. It will go up for bidding at one of the queen's auctions, remember."

That was right. He had said that yesterday. When one considered it that way, under those conditions, it really didn't make sense for her to argue. Essentially, she was telling Ray how to spend his money and what to present to his queen. Who was she to do that? "I suppose it won't hurt to look."

As soon as she made the comment, the young lady who'd greeted them stepped back into the room.

"Miss, our designer has some items she would have you look at. Come right this way." With no small amount of trepidation, Mel followed her. She wasn't even sure quite how to act in a place like this. She certainly didn't feel dressed for the part. The slim, fashionable employee leading her down an elegant hall looked as if she'd walked straight off a fashion runway. Her tight-fitting pencil skirt and stiletto heels were more stylish than anything Mel owned.

The saleslady must have guessed at her nervousness. "Our designer is very nice. She'll love working with a figure such as yours. I'm sure there are several options that will look great on you."

Mel had the urge to give the other woman a hug. Her kind words were actually serving to settle her nerves, though not by much.

"Thank you."

"I think your boyfriend will be very pleased with the final choice."

"Oh, he's not my boyfriend. We're attending an event together. Just as friends. And I had nothing to wear because I lost my bag. It's why I have this black eye and all this bruising—" She forced herself to stop talking and to take a deep breath. Now she was just rambling. "I'm sorry. I'm not used to seeing a designer to shop for a dress. This is all so unreal." She probably shouldn't have added that last part. Now the poor lady was going to think she was addled in addition to being talkative.

The other woman turned to her with a smile. "Then I think you should pretend."

"I don't understand."

"Pretend you are used to it."

Mel gave her head a shake. "How do I do that?"

She shrugged an elegant shoulder. "Pretend you belong here, that you come here often. And pretend he is your boyfriend." She gave her a small wink before escorting her inside a large dressing room with wall-to-wall mirrors and a big standing rack off to the side. On it hung a dozen dazzling evening gowns that took her breath away. And even from a distance, she could see none of them had a price tag. This wasn't the type of place where tags were necessary. Customers who frequented a boutique like this one knew they could afford whatever the mystery price was.

"Deena will be in to see you in just a moment."

With that, the greeter turned on her high, thin heels and left. All in all, her suggestion wasn't a bad one. Why shouldn't Mel enjoy herself here? Something like this was never going to happen to her again. What if she really was here on one of her regular shopping trips? What if this wasn't a completely novel experience and she knew exactly what she was doing? There was nothing wrong with enjoying a little fantasy. Lord knew she could use a bit of it in her life these days.

And what if the charming, devilishly handsome man sitting in the other room, waiting for her, really was her boyfriend?

Ray stared at the spreadsheet full of figures on his tablet, but it was hard to focus. If someone had told him a week ago that he'd be sitting in a fashion boutique in the heart of Boston, waiting for a woman to pick a gown, he would have laughed out loud at the notion. Not that he was a stranger to being dragged out to shop. He did have two sisters and a mother, after all. In fact, one of his sisters had been the one to suggest this particular boutique. Those two knew the top fashion spots in most major cities. The only problem was, now he was being hounded via text and voice mail about why it was that he needed the recommendation in the first place. He could only hold them off for so long. He would have to come up with an adequate response. And soon.

He felt Mel enter the room more than he heard her. The air seemed to change around him. When he looked up and saw her, his breath caught in his throat. The slim tablet he held nearly slipped out of his hands. Even with a nasty purple bruise on her cheek, she was breathtakingly stunning in the red gown. The color seemed to bring out every one of her striking features to their full effect.

Mel took a hesitant step toward him. She gestured to her midsection, indicating the gown she wore. "I wanted to see what you thought of this one," she said shyly.

He couldn't seem to get his tongue to work. He'd spent his life around some of the most beautiful women in the world. Everything from actresses to fashion models to noble ladies with royal titles. Yet he couldn't recall ever being this dumbstruck by a single one of them. What did that say about his sorry state of affairs?

"Do you think it will work?" Mel asked.

Think? Who would be able to think at such a moment? She could only be described as a vision, perhaps something out of a romantic fairy-tale movie. The dress hugged her curves in all the right places before flaring out ever so slightly below her hips. Strapless, it showed off the elegant curve of her necks and shoulders. And the color. A deep, rich red that not many women would be able to wear without the hue completely washing them out. But it only served to bring out the dark blue hint of her hair and accent the emerald green of her eyes. The fabric held a sheer hint of sparkle wherever the light hit it just so.

Since when had he become the type of man who noticed how an article of clothing brought out a woman's coloring or features?

He'd never felt such an urge to whistle in appreciation. Hardly suitable behavior for someone in his position.

What the hell, no one here actually knew who he was. He whistled.

A smile spread across Mel's face. "Does that mean you like it?"

Someone cleared their throat before Ray could answer. Sweet heavens, he hadn't even noticed the other woman in the room with them. She had a long tape measure hanging from her neck and gave him a knowing smile.

"This one was the top choice," the woman said. "If you're okay with it, we can start the necessary alterations."

He was way more than okay with it. That dress belonged on Mel; there was no way they were walking out of here without it.

"I think it's perfect," he answered the designer, but his gaze was fixated on Mel's face as she spoke. Even with the angry purple bruising along her cheek and jaw and the black eye, she was absolutely stunning.

"Are you sure?" Mel asked. "If you'd like, I can show you some of the other ones."

Ray shook his head. He couldn't be more sure. "I have

no doubt you'll be the most beautiful woman to grace that ballroom with that dress."

Mel ducked her head, but not before he noticed the pink that blossomed across her cheeks. "Even with my black eye?"

"I've never seen anyone look so lovely while sporting one."

"I'll be in the dressing room when you're ready, miss," the designer offered before leaving them.

Ray found himself stepping closer to her. He gently rubbed his finger down her cheek, from the corner of her eye down to her chin. "Does it still hurt very much?"

She visibly shivered at his touch, but she didn't pull away. In fact, she turned her face ever so slightly into his caress. It would be so easy for him to lean in closer, to gently brush her lips with his. She smelled of jasmine and rose, an intoxicating mix of scents that reminded him of the grand gardens of his palatial home.

He'd been trying to deny it, but he'd been thinking about kissing her since having breakfast with her. Hell, maybe he'd been thinking about it much before that. He had no doubt she would respond if he did. It was clear on her face, by the quickening of her breathing, the flush in her cheeks.

The loud honk of a vehicle outside pulled him out of his musings and back to his senses. He couldn't forget how temporary all this was. In a few short days, he would return to Verdovia and to the future that awaited him. One full of duty and responsibility and that would include a woman he wasn't in love with.

Love. For all the earthly privileges he'd been granted by virtue of birth, he would never know the luxury of falling in love with the woman he was to marry. He just had to accept that. He couldn't get carried away with some kind of fantasy while here in the United States. And he absolutely could not lead Mel on romantically. He had nothing to offer her. Other than a fun night celebrating the holiday season, while also proving something to her ex. That was all this whole charade was about.

With great reluctance, he made himself step away.

"You should probably go get the dress fitted and altered. I'll go settle the charge."

It took her a moment to speak. When she did, her voice was shaky. "So I guess we're really doing this, huh?"

"What exactly are you referring to?"

"Going to the ball together. I mean, once the dress is purchased, there'll be no turning back, will there?"

Ray could only nod. He had a nagging suspicion that already there would be no turning back.

Not as far as he was concerned.

CHAPTER SIX

As FAR AS transformations went, Mel figured she'd pulled off a major one. The image staring back at her in the mirror couldn't really be her. She hardly recognized the woman in the glass.

She was in Frannie and Greta's apartment. The two women had spent hours with her in order to get her ready. A lot of the time had been spent camouflaging the discolored bruising on her face. But the effect was amazing. These ladies knew how to use makeup to cover up flaws. Even upon close inspection, one would be hard-pressed to guess Mel had met the broadside of a set of steel handlebars only days before.

As far as soreness or pain, she was way too nervous to take any notice of it at the moment.

Her bosses had also helped do her hair in a classic updo at the crown of her head. Greta had found some sort of delicate silver strand that she'd discreetly woven around the curls. It only became visible when the light hit it just so. Exactly the way the silver accents in her dress did. Frannie had even managed to unearth some antique earrings that were studded with small diamond chips. They provided just enough sparkle to complement the overall look. All in all, the older women had done a notable job helping her prepare.

It was like having two fairy godmothers. Albeit very chatty ones. They'd both gone on incessantly about how beautiful Mel looked, how she should act flirty with Ray in order to get under Eric's skin and because they thought Ray was the type of man who definitely warranted flirtatious behavior. Mel had just stood silently, listening. The butterflies in her stomach were wreaking havoc and made it hard to just breathe, let alone form a coherent sentence.

She was trying desperately not to think about all the ways this night could turn into a complete disaster. Someone could easily ask a fairly innocuous question that neither Ray nor she had an adequate answer to. They'd never even discussed what story to tell about how they'd met or how long the two of them had known each other. The whole scenario was ripe for embarrassing mistakes. If Eric ever found out this was all some elaborate pretend date merely to prove to him that she'd moved on, he'd never let Mel live it down.

His fiancée would also have an absolute field day with the knowledge. Not to mention the utter embarrassment it would cause if her other acquaintances found out.

"I believe your ride is here," Frannie declared, peeking around the curtain to look outside.

Greta joined her sister at the window. She let out a shriek of appreciation. "It's a stretch."

"Not just any stretch," Frannie corrected. "A Bentley of some sort."

Greta gave her sister's arm a gentle shove. "Like *you* would know what a Bentway looks like."

"Bentley! And I know more than you, obviously."

The butterflies in Mel's stomach turned into warring pigeons. He was here. And he'd gone all out apparently, hiring a stretch limo. He so didn't need to do that. She'd never been quite so spoiled by someone before—certainly not by a man. If she wasn't careful, this could all easily go to her head. There would be no recovering from that. She had to remind herself throughout the night how unreal all of it was, how temporary and short-lived it would all be. Tomorrow morning, she'd go back to being Mel. The woman who had no real plans for her future, nothing really to look forward to until she managed to get back on her feet somehow. A task she had no clue how to accomplish just yet.

Taking a steadying breath, she rubbed her hand down her midsection.

"How do I look?"

The sisters turned to her and their faces simultaneously broke into wide grins. Was that a tear in Greta's eye?

"Like a princess."

The buzzer rang just then. "I guess I should head downstairs."

"I say you make him wait a bit," Frannie declared. "In the diner. It's not often our fine establishment gets a chance to entertain such an elegant, handsome gentleman in a well-tailored tuxedo."

"Not often?" Greta countered. "More like never."

That comment earned her a scowl from her sister. Mel slowly shook her head. "I think I should just get down there, before I lose all my nerve and back out completely." It was a very real possibility at this point. She wasn't sure she could actually go through with this. The more she thought about it, the more implausible it all seemed.

"Not a chance we would let you do that," both sisters said in unison with obvious fear that she actually might do such a thing.

Mel willed her pulse to steady. Slowly, she made her high-heeled feet move to the door. Without giving herself a chance to chicken out, she yanked it open to step out into the stairway. Only to come face-to-face with Ray.

"I hope you don't mind. The street door was open so I made my way upstairs." He handed her a single red rose. "It matches the color of your dress."

Mel opened her mouth to thank him but wasn't able to. Her mouth and tongue didn't seem to want to work. They'd gone dry at the sight of him. The dark fabric of his jacket brought out the jet-black of his hair and eyes. The way the man looked in a tuxedo could drive a girl to sin.

What had she got herself into?

The woman was a stunner. Ray assisted Mel into the limousine waiting at the curb as the driver held the door open for them. He had no doubt he'd be the most envied man at this soiree from the moment they entered. If he thought she'd looked beautiful in the shop, the completed product was enough to take his breath away. He would have to find a way to thank his sisters for recommending the boutique; they had certainly come through.

He had half a mind to ask the limo driver to turn around, take them to an intimate restaurant instead, where he could have Mel all to himself. And if that didn't make him a selfish cad, he didn't know what would. He had no right to her, none whatsoever. By this time to-morrow, he'd be walking out of her life for good. A pang of some strange sensation struck through his core at the thought. A sensation he didn't want to examine.

Within moments, they were pulling up to the front doors of the Boston World Trade Center grand auditorium. The aromatic fishy smell of Boston Harbor greeted them as soon as they exited the car. An attendee in a jolly elf hat and curly-toed shoes greeted them as they entered through the massive glass doors.

Mel suddenly stopped in her tracks, bringing them both to a halt.

"Is something the matter?" She'd gone slightly pale under the bright ceiling lights of the lobby. The notes of a bouncy rendition of "Jingle Bells" could be heard from the ballroom.

"I just need a moment before we walk in there."

"Take your time."

"I know this is no time to get cold feet," she began. "But I'm nervous about all that could go wrong."

He took her gently by the elbow and led her away from the main lobby, to a more private area by a large indoor decorative fountain. "I know it's not easy right now, but why don't you try to relax and maybe even have a good time?" She really did look very nervous.

"I'll try but… Maybe we should have rehearsed a few things."

"Rehearsed?"

"What if someone asks how we met? What will we say? Or how long we've known each other. We haven't talked about any of those things."

Ray took in the tight set of Mel's mouth, the nervous quivering of her chin. He should have been more sensitive to her possible concerns under these circumstances. He hadn't really given any of it much thought himself. As prince of Verdovia, he was used to being questioned and spoken to everywhere he went. As a result, he'd grown masterful at the art of delivering nonanswers. Of course, someone like Mel wouldn't be able to respond so easily.

He gave her elbow a reassuring squeeze. "I find that under situations like these, the closer one sticks to the truth, the better."

She blinked at him. "The truth? You want to tell them the truth?"

"That's right. Just not all of it. Not in its entirety."

"I'm gonna need an example of what you mean."

"Well, for instance, if someone asks how long we've known each other, we can tell them we've only met very recently and are still getting to know one another."

The tightness around her eyes lessened ever so slightly. "Huh. And if they ask for details?"

"Leave that part up to me. I'll be able to come up with something."

That earned him a grateful nod. "What if they ask about how we met?" She thought for a moment and then answered her own question. "I know, I can tell them I was knocked off my feet before I'd barely laid eyes on you."

He gave her a small laugh. "Excellent. See, you'll do fine." He offered her his arm and motioned with his head toward the ballroom entrance. When she took it, her grasp was tight and shaky. Mel was not a woman accustomed to even the slightest deception. But some of the tension along her jawline had visibly eased. Her lips were no longer trembling. Now, if he could just get her to smile, she might actually look like someone about to attend a party.

He slowly walked her to the ballroom. The decor inside had been fashioned to look like Santa's workshop in the North Pole. Large replicas of wooden toys adorned various spots in the room. A running toy train traveled along a circular track hanging from the ceiling. Several more staffers dressed up as elves greeted and mingled with the guests as they entered. Large leafy poinsettias served as centerpieces on each table.

"How about we start with some Christmas punch?" he asked Mel as he led her toward a long buffet table with a huge glass punch bowl in the center. On either side was a tower of glass flutes.

"I'd like that."

Ray poured hers first and handed her the glass of the bubbly drink. After grabbing a glass for himself, he lifted it in a toast. "Shall we toast to the evening as it's about to start?"

She tapped the rim of her glass to his. To his happy surprise, a small smile had finally graced her lips.

"I really don't know how to thank you for this, Ray. For all of it. The dress, the limo. That was above and beyond."

"It's my pleasure." It surprised him how true that statement was. They'd only just arrived and already he was having fun and enjoying all of it: the bouncy music, the fun decor. Her company.

"I wish there was some way I could really thank you. Aside from a diner meal, that is," she added, clearly disturbed. Ray had no doubt that even now she was racking her brain to come up with ways to "repay" him somehow. The concept was clearly very important to her.

He wanted to rub his fingers over her mouth, to soften the tight set of her lips with his touch. He wished there was a way to explain that she didn't owe him a thing. "Look at it this way, you're helping me to enjoy Boston during Christmastime. If it wasn't for you, Sal and I would just be wandering around, doing the same boring old touristy stuff I've done before."

Complete with a droll official tour guide and the promise of hours-long business meetings afterward. No, Ray much preferred the anonymity he was currently enjoying. Not to mention the delight of Mel's company.

"You have no idea how refreshing this all is," he told her.

Before Mel could respond, a grinning elf dressed all in green jumped in front of them. She held her hand whimsically above Mel's head. In her grasp was a small plant of some sort.

Mistletoe.

"You know what this means," the young lady said with a cheery laugh.

A sudden blush appeared on Mel's skin. She looked at him with question. "You needn't—" But he wasn't listening.

Ray didn't hesitate as he set his drink down and leaned closer to Mel. As if he could stop himself. What kind of gentleman would he be if he didn't kiss her under the mistletoe at a Christmas party?

They were no longer in a crowded ballroom. Mel's vision narrowed like a tunnel on the man across from her, the man leaning toward her. Ray was about to kiss her, and nothing else in the world existed. Nothing and no one. Just the two of them.

How would he taste? What would his lips feel like against hers?

The reality was so much more than anything she could have imagined. Ray's lips were firm against hers, yet he kept the kiss gentle, like a soft caress against her mouth. He ran his knuckles softly down her cheek as he kissed her. She reached for him, ran her free hand along his chest and up to his shoulder. In response, he deepened the kiss. The taste of him nearly overwhelmed her.

But it was over all too soon. When Ray pulled away, the look in his eyes almost knocked the breath from her. Desire. He wanted her; his gaze left no doubt. The knowledge had her off balance. He was looking at her like he was ready to carry her off to an empty room somewhere. Heaven help her, she would let him if he tried. She gulped in some much-needed air. The mistletoe-wielding elf had left, though neither one of them had even noticed the woman walk away. How long had they stood there kissing like a couple of hormonal teenagers?

"Mel." He said her name like a soft breeze, his breath still hot against her cheek. She found herself tilting her head toward him once more. As foolish as it was given where they were, she wanted him to kiss her again. Right here. Right now.

He didn't get a chance. A familiar baritone voice suddenly interrupted them.

"Melinda? Is that you?"

Her ex-husband stood less than a foot away, staring at her with his mouth agape. He looked quite surprised. And not at all happy. Neither did the woman standing next to him. Talley, his new fiancée.

"Eric, hello." Mel flashed a smile in Talley's direction. "Talley."

Eric unabashedly looked her up and down. "You look nice, Mel." It was a nice enough compliment, but the way he said it did not sound flattering in the least. His tone was one of surprise. Ray cleared his throat next to her.

"Excuse my manners," Mel began. "This is Ray Alsab. He's visiting Boston on business."

Talley was doing some perusing for herself as the men shook hands. She seemed to appreciate what she saw in Ray. But who wouldn't? The man looked like something out of *Billionaire Bachelors* magazine.

"Is that so?" Eric asked. "What kind of business would that be?"

"Real estate." Ray answered simply.

"Huh. What exactly do you do in real estate, Ray?"

Mel wanted to tell him that it was none of his business, and exactly where he could go with his questions. But Ray gave him a polite smile. "I work for the royal government of Verdovia. It's a small island nation in the Mediterranean, off the Greco-Turkish coast. His Majesty King Farood is looking to expand our US holdings, including in Boston. I've been charged with locating a suitable property and starting the negotiations on his behalf."

Eric's eyebrows rose up to near his hairline. He gave a quick shake of his head. "I'm sorry, how does someone in that line of work know Mel?"

The condescension in his voice was so thick, Mel wanted to throw her drink in Eric's face.

But her date merely chuckled. "We met purely by accident." Ray turned to her and gave her a conspiratorial wink, as if sharing a private joke only the two of them would understand. Her laughter in response was a genuine reaction. The masterful way Ray was handling her ex-husband was a talent to behold.

"We'll have to tell you about it sometime," he continued. He then took Mel's drink from her and set it on the table. "But right now, this lady owes me a dance. If you'll please excuse us."

Without waiting for a response, he gently took Mel by the hand and walked with her to the dance floor.

Talley's voice sounded loudly behind them. "I wouldn't mind a dance, Eric. Remember, you promised."

"Nicely done, sir," Mel giggled as she stepped into Ray's arms. The scent of his skin and the warmth of his breath against her cheek sent tiny bolts of lightning through her middle.

"He's still staring. At you. The way he looks at you…" He let his sentence trail off, his hand on her lower back as he led her across the dance floor.

Mel could hardly focus on the dance. She was still enjoying how he'd just handled Eric. But the grim set of Ray's lips and the hardness in his eyes left no question that he was upset. Interactions with her ex often had that effect on people.

"He's just arrogant. It's one of his defining traits."

He shook his head. "It's more than that. He looks at you like he still has some sort of claim," Ray bit out. "As if you still belong to him." His tone distinctly told her that he didn't like it. Not in the least.

Mel had never been much for dancing, but she could hold her own with the steps. Plus, she'd done her fair share of clubbing in her university days. Having Ray as her partner however was a whole new experience. She felt as if she was floating on clouds the way he moved her around the dance floor, perfectly in tune with whatever beat the current song carried.

"You're a man of many talents, aren't you? Quite the talented dancer."

He tilted his head to acknowledge her compliment. "I started taking lessons at a very young age. My parents were real sticklers about certain things they wanted me to be proficient at. It's expected of the pr—" He suddenly cut off whatever he was about to say.

Mel didn't bother to ask for clarification. Whatever the reason, he was the most fluid dance partner a woman could ask for. Whether classic ballroom dances or modern holiday music, he moved like a man who was comfortable with himself. As the kids who ate at the diner would say, the man had the rhythm and the moves.

The impact of the unpleasant encounter with Eric was slowly beginning to ebb, and she decided to throw herself into this experience fully. Remembering what the assistant in the store had told her helped. Sometimes it was all right just to pretend.

And it wasn't exactly difficult to do just that as she

leaned into his length once a slower song had begun to play. He was lean and fit, the hard muscles of his chest firm and hard against hers. It took all her will to resist leaning her head against his shoulder and wrapping her arms around his neck.

And she couldn't help where her mind kept circling back to: the way he'd kissed her. Dear heavens, if the man kissed like that while out in public in front of a crowd of partygoers, what was he like in private? Something told her that, if they hadn't come to their senses, the kiss might very well have lasted much longer, leading to a thrilling experience full of passion. Her mind went there, to a picture of the two of them. Alone. Locked in a tight embrace, his body up against hers. His hands slowly moving along her skin. A shiver ran all the way from her spine down to the soles of her feet.

Stop it!

That train of thought served no purpose. The man lived thousands of miles away, never mind the fact that he was part of a whole different world. Women like her didn't date millionaire businessmen. She had him for this one evening, and she'd make the most of it before he walked out of her life for good.

But someone had other plans. Eric approached from the side and tapped Ray on the shoulder. "May I cut in?"

Ray gave Mel a questioning look, making sure to catch her eye before answering. Mel gave him a slight nod. If she knew anything about her ex, he wasn't going to take no for an answer, not easily anyway. The last thing she wanted was some sort of scene, even a small one. Ray didn't deserve that. And neither did she.

"I'll just go refresh our glasses," Ray told her before letting her out of his arms and walking to the beverage table. "Come find me when you're ready."

Reluctantly, she stepped into the other man's embrace, though she made sure to keep as good a distance as possible. "This was one of your favorite Christmas carols," Eric commented as soon as Ray was out of earshot. "I remember very well."

He remembered wrong. The song currently in play was "Blue Christmas," one she wasn't even terribly fond of. He was confusing it with one she did like, "White Christmas." She didn't bother to correct him. She just wanted this dance to be over.

It was ironic really, how this evening was supposed to be about proving something to the man who currently held her in his arms. But right now, she didn't even want to give him a moment of her attention. In fact, all of her attention was currently fully focused on the dark, enigmatic man, waiting alone for her by the punch bowl. A giddy sense of pride washed over her at the thought. Authentic date or not, Ray was here with her. She could hardly wait to be dancing in his arms again.

Though judging by the looks several ladies were throwing in his direction, he might not be alone for long.

"So is he your boyfriend?" Eric asked with characteristic disregard for any semblance of propriety.

"We are getting to know each other," she answered curtly.

"Right. Is that what you were doing when we first walked in? It looked like you were getting to know his face with your lips."

That was more than enough. "Honestly, Eric. I don't see how it's any of your business. We are divorced, remember?"

He winced ever so slightly. "Don't be that way, Mel. You know I still care about you. I don't want to see you get hurt."

"That's rich. Coming from you."

Eric let out a low whistle. "Harsh. But fair. You've grown a bit…let's say *harder*, in the past several months."

"I've had to grow in all sorts of ways since we parted."

"Just be careful, all right. That's all I'm saying." He glanced in Ray's direction. "Where's he from anyway? Exactly? *Vanderlia* doesn't ring a bell."

"Verdovia," she corrected. "We haven't really had a chance to discuss it." A sudden disquieting feeling blossomed in her chest. She really didn't know much about Ray's homeland. Why hadn't she thought to ask him more about where he was from?

"Why does it even matter, Eric?"

He shrugged. "Just trying to discover some more about your friend." He let go of her just long enough to depict air quotes as he said the last word. "He who's here to investigate potential properties and begin negotiations," he uttered the sentence in an exaggerated mimic of Ray's accent. Mel felt a surge of fury bolt through her core like lightning. Even for Eric, it was beyond the pale. Boorish and bordering on straight elitism.

"Are you actually making fun of the way he speaks?"

"Maybe."

Tears suddenly stung in her eyes. More than outrage, she felt an utter feeling of waste. How could she have given so much to this man? She wasn't even thinking of the money. She was thinking of her heart, of the years of her youth. He'd made it so clear repeatedly that he hadn't deserved any part of her. How had she not seen who he really was? She'd been so hurt, beyond broken, when he'd betrayed her with another woman and then left. Now she had to wonder if he hadn't done her an immense favor.

She pulled herself out of his grasp and took a steadying breath, trying to quell the shaking that had suddenly overtaken her. "I think I'm ready to go back to Ray now. I hope you and Talley have a great time tonight."

Turning on her heel, she left him standing alone on the dance floor. She wouldn't give him anything more, not even another minute of her time.

"You look like you could use some air," Ray suggested before she'd even come to a stop at his side. The grim expression in her eyes and the tight set of her lips told him her interaction with her ex-husband hadn't been all that pleasant. Not that he was surprised. He didn't appear to be a pleasant man in any way.

Which begged the question, how had someone like Mel ever ended up married to him in the first place? He was more curious about the answer than he had a right to be.

She nodded. "It's quite uncanny how well you know me after just a few days."

The comment was thrown out quite casually. But it gave him pause. The truth was, he *had* begun to read her, to pick up on her subtle vibes, the unspoken communications she allowed. Right now, he knew she needed to get away for a few minutes. Out of this ballroom.

"But first—" She reached for the drink he held and downed it all at once.

"It went that well, huh?"

She linked her arm with his. "Let's go breathe some fishy Boston air."

Within moments they were outside, behind the building, both leaning on a cold metal railing, overlooking the harbor. She'd certainly been right about the fishy smell. He didn't mind. He'd grown up near the Mediterranean and Black Sea.

And the company he was with at least made the unpleasant stench worthwhile.

The air held a crisp chill but could be considered mild for this time of year. Still, he shrugged off his jacket and held it out to her.

She accepted with a grateful nod and hugged the fabric around her. She looked good wearing his coat.

Mel drew out a shaky breath as she stared out over the water. "Hard to believe I was ever that naive. To actually think he was good husband material."

"You trusted the wrong person, Mel. You're hardly the first person to do so." His words mocked him. After all, here he was leading her to trust *him*, as well. When he wasn't being straight with her about who he was, his very identity. The charade was beginning to tear him up inside. How much longer would he be able to keep up the pretense? Because the longer it went on, the guiltier he felt.

"I should have seen who he really was. I have no excuses. It was just so hard to be alone all of a sudden. All my friends have moved away since graduation. On to bigger and better things."

He couldn't help but reach for her hand; it fitted so easily into his. Her skin felt soft and smooth to the touch. "What about extended family?"

Her lips tightened. "There's no one I really keep in touch with. Neither did my parents. It's been that way for as long as I can remember."

"Oh?"

"My father had no one. Grew up in foster homes. Got into quite a bit of trouble with the law before he grew up and turned his life around."

"That sounds quite commendable of him."

"Yeah. You'd think so. But his background is the reason my mother was estranged from her family. She came from a long line of Boston Brahmin blue bloods, who didn't approve of her marriage. They thought my father was only after her for their money. They never did come around. Not even decades of my parents being happy and committed could change their minds. Decades where neither one asked for a single penny."

Her declaration went a long way to explain her feelings about the hospital fee payment. No wonder she'd insisted on paying him back. It also explained her pushback and insistence on donating the dress, rather than keeping it.

"I never met any of them," she continued. "Supposedly, I have a grandmother and a few cousins scattered across the country."

He gave her hand a gentle squeeze. "I believe it's their loss for not having met you," he said with sincerity. It sounded so trite, but he wholeheartedly meant it.

"Thank you, Ray. I mean it. Thank you for all you've done tonight. And I'm sorry. I realize you haven't even had a chance to do any of the networking you had planned."

"I find myself caring less and less about that," he admitted.

She tilted her head and looked at him directly. "But it was your main reason for wanting to come."

"Not any longer."

She sucked in a short breath but didn't get a chance to respond. A commotion of laughter and singing from the plaza behind them drew both their attention. Several male voices were butchering a rendition of "Holly Jolly Christmas."

Ray turned to watch as about a dozen dancing men

in Santa suits poured out of a party van and walked into one of the seafood restaurants.

He had to laugh at the sight. "You saw that, too, right? I haven't had too much of that champagne punch, have I?"

She gave him a playful smile and a sideways glance. "If it's the punch, then there's some strange ingredient in it that makes people see dancing Santas." She glanced at the jolly celebrators with a small laugh.

"Only in Boston, I guess."

She turned to face him directly. "You mentioned you wanted to experience the city, but not as a tourist. I may have an idea or two for you."

"Yeah? Consider me intrigued."

Ducking her chin, she hesitated before continuing, as if unsure. "If you have the time, I can show you some of the more interesting events and attractions. There's a lot to see and do this time of year."

He was more intrigued by the idea than he would have liked to admit. "Like my very own private tour guide?"

"Yes, it isn't much, but it would be a small thank-you on my behalf. For all that you've done to make this such a magical evening."

Ray knew he should turn her down, knew that accepting her offer would be the epitome of carelessness. Worse, he was being careless with someone who didn't deserve it in the least. Mel was still nursing her wounds from the way her marriage had dissolved and the heartless way her ex-husband had treated her. He couldn't risk damaging her heart any further by pursuing this charade any longer. This was supposed to be a onetime deal, just for one evening. To try to make up for the suffering and pain she'd endured after the accident he and Saleh had been indirectly responsible for.

But even as he made that argument to himself, he knew he couldn't turn down her offer. Not given the way she was looking at him right now, with expectation and—heaven help him—longing. He couldn't bring himself to look into her deep green eyes, sparkling like jewelry in the moonlight, and pretend he wasn't interested in spending more time with her. He might very well hate himself for it later, and Saleh was sure to read him the riot act. The other man was already quite cross with him, to begin with, about this whole trip. And especially about attending this ball. But Ray couldn't bring himself to pass on the chance to spend just one more day in Mel's company. Damn the consequences.

"That's the best offer I've had in a long while," he answered after what he knew was too long of a pause. "I'd be honored if you'd show me around your great city."

CHAPTER SEVEN

"I DON'T SEE any frogs."

"You do realize it's mid-December, right?" Mel laughed at Ray's whimsical expression. He was clearly teasing her.

"I don't see any frozen frogs either."

"That's because they aren't here any longer. And if they were, they'd most definitely be frozen." She handed him the rented skates.

"But I thought you said we were going to a pond of frogs. Boston does have a very well-known aquarium."

"I figured you must have already been to the aquarium. And besides, they don't harbor any frogs there."

Okay. She obviously hadn't been very clear about exactly what they'd be doing. Mel had decided an authentic winter experience in Boston wouldn't be complete without a visit to the Frog Pond. It was the perfect afternoon for it: sunny and clear, with the temperature hovering just near freezing. Not a snowflake to be seen. She'd figured they could start their excursion with a fun hour or so of skating, then they would walk around the Common, Boston's large inner-city park, which housed the ice rink in the center.

"I said we'd be going to the Frog Pond."

"So where are the frogs?" he asked, wanting to know.

"They're gone. This used to be a swampy pond years ago. But now it's a famous Boston attraction. During the hot summer months, it's used as a splashing pool. In the winter, it turns into an ice-skating rink. I figured it would be fun to get some air and exercise."

"I see." He took the skates from her hands and followed her to a nearby park bench to put them on. "Well, this ought to be interesting."

An alarming thought occurred to her. "Please tell me you know how to skate."

He sat down and started to unlace his leather boots. "I could tell you that. But I'd be lying to you."

Mel would have kicked herself if she could. Why had she made such an assumption about a businessman from a Mediterranean island? She'd planned the whole day around this first excursion, neglecting to ask the most obvious question.

"Oh, no. I didn't realize. I'm so sor—"

He cut her off with a dismissive wave of her hand. "How difficult could it be? I'm very athletic, having played various sports since I could walk. I almost turned pro, remember?"

There was no hint of bragging or arrogance in his tone; he was simply stating a fact.

He motioned toward the rink with a jut of his chin. "If those tiny tots out there can do it, so can I."

Ray quickly proved he was a man of his word. After a couple of wobbly stumbles, where he managed to straighten himself just in time, he was able to smoothen his stride and even pick up some steam.

"Color me impressed," she told him as they circled around for the third time. That was all it took for Ray to complete a full pass around the rink without so much as a stumble. Just as he said, he'd been able to pick it up and had done so with a proficiency that defied logic. "I don't know if you're quite ready to a triple lutz in the center of the rink, but you seem to have got the hang of it."

He shrugged. "It's not all that different from skiing, really."

"Do you ski often?"

"Once or twice a year. My family owns an estate in the Swiss Alps."

Mel nearly lost her balance and toppled onto her face. An estate. In the Alps.

Not only was Ray a successful businessman in his own right—he would have to be to be working directly for the king of his nation—he came from the kind of family who owned estates. There was no doubt in her mind that there was probably more than just one.

Oh, yeah, she was so far out of her league, she might as well have taken a rocket ship to a different planet.

She was spared the need to respond when a group of school-age children carelessly barreled into her from the side. The impact sent her flying and threw her off balance. Unable to regain her footing, she braced herself for the impact of the hard ice. But it never came. Suddenly, a set of strong, hard arms reached around her middle to hold her steady.

"Whoa, there. Careful, love."

Love. Her heart pounded like a jackhammer in her chest, for reasons that had nothing to do with the startle of her near fall.

For countless moments, Mel allowed herself to just stand and indulge herself in the warmth of his arms, willing her pulse to slow. His breath was hot against her cheek. He hadn't bothered to shave or trim down his goatee this morning. The added length of facial hair only served to heighten his devilish handsomeness. She'd never been attracted to a man with a goatee before. On Ray, it was a complete turn-on. He managed to pull it off somehow in a sophisticated, classic sort of way.

"Thanks," she managed, gripping him below the shoulders for support. It was surprising that her tongue even functioned at the moment.

"Sure thing."

"I guess I should have thought this out more." In hindsight, ice-skating wasn't such a good idea, given that Ray hadn't even done it before and how disastrous it would be if she suffered another stumble. "Maybe I should have chosen a different activity."

He glanced down at her lips. "I'm very glad you did choose this. I'm enjoying it more than you can imagine."

She couldn't be misreading his double meaning. They were standing still in the outer ring of the rink, with other skaters whisking by them. The same group of kids skated by again and one of them snickered loudly as they passed. "Jeez, get a room."

Mel startled back to reality and reluctantly removed her hands from Ray's biceps. A quick glance around proved the kids weren't the only ones staring at them. An elderly couple skating together gave them subtle smiles as they went by.

How long had they been standing there that way? Obviously, it had been long enough to draw the attention of the other skaters.

"Just be careful," he said and slowly let go of her, but not before he tucked a stray strand of her hair under her knit cap. "We can't have you falling again. Not when your bruises appear to be healing so nicely."

She wanted to tell him it was too late. She was already off balance and falling in another, much more dangerous way.

* * *

They decided they'd had enough when the rink suddenly became too crowded as the afternoon wore on. Ray took Mel by the elbow and led her off the ice. In moments, they'd removed their skates and had settled on a park bench. Someone nearby had a portable speaker playing soulful R & B. Several middle school–age children ran around the park, pelting each other with snowballs.

All in all, it was one of the most relaxing and pleasurable mornings he'd spent. No one was paying the slightest attention to him, a rare experience where he was concerned. Mel sat next to him, tapping her leather-booted toe in tune with the music.

"Those kids have surprisingly good aim," he commented, watching one of the youngsters land a clumpy snowball directly on his friend's cheek. Mel laughed as the "victim" made an exaggerated show of falling dramatically to the snow-covered ground. After lying there for several seconds, the child spread out his arms and legs, then moved them up and down along the surface of the snow. He then stood and pointed at the snow angel he'd made, admiring his handiwork.

"I haven't made a snow angel in years," Mel stated, still watching the child.

"I haven't made one ever."

She turned to him with surprise clearly written on her expression. "You've never made a snow angel?" She sounded incredulous.

He shrugged. "We don't get that much snow in our part of the world. And when we're in the Alps, we're there to ski."

She stood suddenly, grabbing him by the arm and pulling him up with her. "Then today is the day we rectify that sad state of affairs."

Ray immediately started to protest. Anonymity was one thing, but he couldn't very well be frolicking on the ground, in the snow, like a playful tot. He planted his feet, grinding them both to a halt. "Uh, I don't think so."

Her smile faded. "Why not? You have to do it at least once in your lifetime! What better place than the snow-covered field of Boston Common?"

He gave her a playful tap on the nose. "Making a snow angel is just going to have to be an experience I'll have to forgo."

She rolled her eyes with exaggeration. "Fine, suit yourself."

To his surprise, she strolled farther out into the park and dropped to the ground. She then lay flat on her back. He could only watch as she proceeded to make an impressive snow angel herself.

Ray clapped as she finished and sat on her bottom. "That's how it's done."

He walked over, reached out his hand to help her up.

And realized too late her sneaky intention. With surprising strength, she pulled him down to the ground with her.

"Now that you're down here, you may as well make one, too," she told him with a silly wiggle of her eyebrows.

What the hell? Ray obliged and earned a boisterous laugh for his efforts. By the time they stood, they were both laughing like children.

Suddenly, Mel's smile faltered and her eyes grew serious. She looked directly at him. "You didn't grow up like most boys, did you? Making snow angels and throwing snowballs at friends."

Her question gave him pause. In many ways, he had

been a typical child. But in so many other aspects, he absolutely had not. "Yes. And no."

"What does that mean?"

"It means I had something of a very structured upbringing."

She studied him through narrowed eyes. "That sounds like you never got in any kind of trouble."

He shook his head. "On the contrary. I most definitely did."

"Tell me."

Ray brushed some of the snow off his coat as he gathered the memories. "Well, there was the time during my fifth birthday party when an animal act was brought in as the entertainment."

"What happened?"

"I insisted on handling the animals." Of course, he was allowed to. People didn't often turn down the request of the crown prince, even as a child.

"That doesn't sound so bad."

He bit back a smile at the memory. "There's more. See, I didn't like how the poor creatures were confined, so I set them free. Just let them loose in the garden. Several reptiles and some type of rodent."

Mel clapped a hand to her mouth and giggled at his words. Ray couldn't bring himself to laugh, for he vividly recalled what had happened in the immediate aftermath.

His father had pulled him into his office that evening as soon as he'd arrived home from a UN summit. Ray distinctly remembered that event as his first lesson on what it meant to be a prince. He was expected to be different from all the other children, to never make any mistakes. To never break the rules. He would always be held to a higher standard, as the world would always be watching him. It was a lesson that had stayed with him throughout the years. On the rare occasions he'd forgotten, the repercussions had been swift and great.

"What about as a teen?" Mel asked, breaking into his thoughts.

The memory that question brought forth was much less laughable. "I got into a rather nasty fistfight on the field, during one particularly heated ball game. Walked away with a shiner that could compete with the one you've recently been sporting."

Mel bit her lip with concern.

"But you should have seen the other guy," he added with a wink.

Again, he wouldn't tell her the details—that the mishap had led to a near-international incident, where diplomats were called in to discuss at great length what had essentially been a typical teen tantrum over a bad play. As expected, the press had gone into a frenzy, with countless speculative articles about the king's lack of control over his only son and whether said son even had what it would take to be a competent king when the time came. His father had been less than happy with him. Worse, he'd been sorely disappointed. Yet another memorable lesson that had stayed with Ray over the years. Suddenly, the mood in the air had turned heavy and solemn.

"Come," Mel said after a silent pause, offering him her hand. "I think we could both use some hot cocoa."

He took her hand and followed where she led.

He hadn't been quite sure what to expect out of today. But Ray could readily admit it had been one of the most enjoyable days he'd ever spent. Now he stood next to Mel on the second level of Faneuil Hall, one of the city's better-known attractions.

"So this is Faneuil, then," he asked. He'd heard about

the area several times during his research on Boston and on previous visits to Massachusetts. But he'd never actually had the chance to visit for himself. Until now.

"The one and only," Mel answered with a proud smile.

Ray let his gaze wander. He'd be hard-pressed to describe the place. It was an outdoor plaza of sorts, with countless shops, restaurants and pubs, all in one center area. But it was so much more. Several acts of entertainment performed throughout the square while adoring crowds clapped and cheered. Music sounded from every corner, some of it coming from live bands and some from state-of-the-art sound systems in the various establishments. Holiday decorations adorned the various shop fronts and streetlights. The place was full of activity and energy.

He and Mel had the perfect view of it all from above, where they stood.

"You're in for a real treat soon," Mel announced. "And we're in the perfect spot to see it." Even as she spoke, several people began to climb up the concrete steps to join them. Before long, a notable crowd had gathered.

"What kind of treat?"

She motioned with her chin toward the massive, tall fir tree standing on the first level. Even at this height, they had to look up to see the top of it. "They're about to light it in a few minutes. As soon as it gets dark."

They waited with patient silence as the night grew darker. Suddenly, the tree lit up. It had to have been decorated with a million lights and shiny ornaments.

Several observers cheered and clapped. Mel placed her fingers in her mouth and let out an impressive whistle.

"So what do you think?" she asked him after they'd simply stared and admired the sight for several moments.

"I know Faneuil can be a bit overwhelming for some people."

Quite the opposite—he'd found it exciting and invigorating. "Believe it or not, it reminds me of Verdovia," he told her.

She glanced at him sideways, not tearing her gaze from the majestic sight of the tree as lights blinked and pulsed on its branches. "Yeah? How so?"

"In many ways, actually. We're a small country but a very diverse people. Given where we're located in the Mediterranean, throughout the years, settlers from many different cultures have relocated to call it home. From Central Europe to Eastern Europe to the Middle East. And many more." He motioned toward the lower level. "Similarly, there appears to be all sorts of different cultures represented here. I hear foreign music in addition to the English Christmas carols and American pop music. And it's obvious there are visitors here from all over the world."

Her eyes narrowed on the scene below in consideration of what he'd just told her. "I never thought of it that way. But you're right. I guess I just sort of took it all for granted. I've been coming here since I was a little girl."

"From now on, when you come, you can think about how it's a mini version of my home country."

Her smile faltered, her expression growing wistful. "Maybe I'll be able to see it someday."

Taking her hands, he turned her toward him. "I'd like that very much. To be able to show you all the beauty and wonder of my nation. The same way you've so graciously shown me around Boston."

"That'd be lovely, Ray. Really."

A wayward snowflake appeared out of nowhere and

landed softly on her nose. Several more quickly followed, and before long, a steady flurry of snow filled the air.

Thick white flakes landed in Mel's hair, covering her dark curls. Ray inadvertently reached for her hair and brushed the snow off with his leathered fingers. He heard her sharp intake of breath at the contact.

Then she leaned in and surprised him with a kiss.

Stunned, he only hesitated for a moment. He wasn't made of stone, after all. Moving his hands to the small of her waist, he pulled her in closer, tight up against his length. She tasted like strawberries and the sweetest nectar.

He let her set the pace—she'd initiated the kiss, after all—letting her explore with her lips and tongue. And when she deepened the kiss and leaned in even tighter against him, he couldn't help but groan out loud. The touch and feel of her was wreaking havoc on his senses.

This was no way to behave. They were in public, for heaven's sake. What was it about this particular woman that had him behaving so irrationally? This was the second time in one day he'd wanted to ravage her in the plain view of countless strangers.

Grasping a strand of sanity, he forced himself to break the kiss and let her go. Like earlier at the ice-skating rink, they'd managed to attract the attention of observers.

"Mel."

She squeezed her eyes shut and gave a shake of her head. "I know. I'm sorry, I shouldn't have kissed you in public like that. Again. I can't seem to help myself."

"I believe the first kiss was my doing. But I had a mistletoe excuse."

She rubbed her mouth with the back of her hand and it took all his will not to take those lips with his own again. He really had to get a grip.

"Why don't we grab a bite?" he suggested, to somehow change the momentum and where this whole scenario might very well be headed: with him taking Mel behind one of the buildings and plundering her mouth with his. "The least I can do after you've entertained me all day is buy you dinner."

"I know just the place."

Within moments, they were down the stairs and seated at an outdoor eatery with numerous heat lamps to ward off the chill. Mel had chosen an authentic New England–style pub with raw shellfish and steaming bowls of clam chowder for them to start with.

Ray took one spoonful of the rich, creamy concoction and sighed with pleasure. He'd had seafood chowder before, but this was a whole new taste experience.

"This chowder is delicious," he told her.

"It's pronounced *chowdah* around here," she corrected him with a small laugh.

"Then this *chowdah* is delicious." Only, with his accent, he couldn't quite achieve the intended effect. The word came out sounding exactly as it was spelled.

Mel laughed at his attempt and then nodded in agreement. "It's very good. But I have to tell you, it doesn't compare to the chowder they serve in the town where I grew up. They somehow make it taste just a bit more home-style there. Must be the small-town charm that adds some extra flavor."

"You didn't grow up in the city?"

She shook her head. "No. About forty minutes away, in a coastal town called Newford. I moved to Boston for school and just ended up staying. Things didn't exactly turn out the way I'd intended after graduation, though."

The spectacle of her failed marriage hung unspoken in the air.

"Tell me more about your hometown," Ray prompted, in an attempt to steer the conversation from that very loaded topic.

A pleasant smile spread across her lips. "It was a wonderful place to grow up. Overlooking the ocean. Some of the small islands off the coast are so close, you can swim to them right from the town harbor. Full of artists and writers and creative free spirits."

"It sounds utterly charming."

She nodded with a look of pride. "It is. And we can boast that we have more art studios per block than most New England towns. One of which I could call a second home during my teen years, given all the hours I spent there."

That took him back a bit. "Really? At an art studio?" There was so much about her he didn't know.

"We had a neighbor who was a world-renowned sculptor. A master at creating magical pieces, using everything from clay to blown glass. He took me under his wing for a while to teach me. Said I had a real talent."

"Why haven't you pursued it? Aside from studying art history in college, that is."

She shrugged, her eyes softening. "I thought about maybe creating some pieces, to show in one of the galleries back home, if any of the owners liked them. But life got in the way."

Ray fought the urge to pull her chair closer to him and drape his arm around her. Her dreams had been crushed through no fault of her own. "Do you still see this sculptor who mentored you? Maybe he can offer some advice on how to take it up again."

Mel set her spoon down into her bowl. "Unfortunately, he passed away. These days, if I go back, it's only to visit an old friend of my mom's. She runs the only bed-and-breakfast in town. They also serve a chowder that would knock your socks off."

"I've never actually stayed at one of those. I hear they're quite charming."

"I'm not surprised you haven't frequented one. They're a much smaller version of the grand hotels your king probably likes to invest in. Tourists like them for the rustic feel while they're in town. It's meant to feel more like you're staying with family."

He was definitely intrigued by the prospect. A hotel stay that felt more like a family home. He would have to find time to stay in one on his next visit to New England. A pang of sorrow shot through his chest at that thought. He might very well be a married man at that time, unless he could convince the king otherwise. The idea made him lean closer to Mel over the table. He gripped his spoon tighter in order to keep from reaching for her.

Mel continued, "In fact, I should probably check in on her. The owner, I mean. Myrna has been struggling to make ends meet recently. She's on the market for a buyer or investor who'll take it off her hands and just let her run the place."

Ray's interest suddenly grew. The whole concept definitely called to him. But it wasn't the type of property the royal family of Verdovia would typically even take the time to look at. They'd never invested in anything smaller than an internationally known hotel in a high-end district of a major metropolitan city.

Still, he couldn't help but feel an odd curiosity about the possibilities. And wasn't he officially part of the royal family, who made such decisions?

CHAPTER EIGHT

"WHATEVER YOU'VE BEEN up to these past couple of days, I hope you've got it out of your system."

"And a good morning to you, as well." Ray flashed Saleh a wide smile as the two men sat down for coffee the next morning in the main restaurant of their hotel. Not even his friend's sullen attitude could dampen his bright mood this morning. Between the way he'd enjoyed himself yesterday with Mel and the decision he'd made upon awakening this morning, he was simply too content.

"Must I remind you that we're only here for a few more days and we haven't even inspected any of the hotels we've come out all this way to visit?" Saleh asked, pouring way too much cream into his mug. He chased it with three heaping spoonfuls of sugar, then stirred. How the man stayed so slim was a mystery.

"You're right, of course," Ray agreed. "At this point, we should probably split up the tasks at hand. Why don't you go visit two of the hotels on the list? I believe a couple of them are within a city block of each other."

"And what will you be doing, Rayhan? If you don't mind my asking," he added the last part in a tone dripping with sarcasm.

"I'll be visiting a prospect myself, in fact, if all goes as planned."

Saleh released a sigh of relief. "Better late than never, I guess, that you've finally come to your senses. Which one of those on the list would you prefer to check out?"

"It isn't on our list."

Saleh lifted an eyebrow in question. "Oh? Did you hear of yet another Boston hotel which may be looking for a buyout?"

"Not exactly. Though the place I have in mind is indeed interested in locating a buyer. Or so I'm told." He couldn't wait to run the idea by Mel, curious as to what her exact reaction might be. He hoped she'd feel as enthusiastic about the prospect as he did.

Saleh studied his face, as if missing a clue that might be found in Ray's facial features. "I don't understand."

Ray took a bite of his toast before answering, though he wasn't terribly hungry after the large dinner he and Mel had shared the evening before. He'd definitely overindulged. The woman certainly knew what he might like to eat. In fact, after just a few short conversations, she already knew more about him than most people he'd call friends or family. He'd never quite divulged so much of himself to anyone before. Mel had a way of making him feel comfortable enough to talk about himself—his hopes, the dreams he'd once had. Around her, he felt more man and less prince. Definitely a new experience. He knew better than to try to explain any of it to the man sitting across the table. Best friend or not, he wouldn't understand. Ray couldn't quite entirely grasp what was happening himself.

"I'm considering, perhaps, looking at smaller options," he answered Saleh. "Something different than the grand international hotel chains."

"Smaller? How much smaller?"

"So small that the guests feel like they're actually staying with family."

Back to reality. Mel smoothed down the skirt of her waitress uniform and tried to force thoughts of Ray and the time they'd spent together yesterday out of her mind. Her shift would be starting in a few minutes and she had to try to focus. Customers really didn't like it when their orders were delayed, or if they mistakenly got the wrong dish.

It was time to pull her head out of the clouds. She'd done enough pretending these past few days.

"You look different," Greta declared, studying her up and down.

"Probably because my face is almost completely healed."

Frannie jumped in as she approached them from behind the counter. "No, that's not it. Greta's right. You look more—I don't know—sparkly."

Mel had to laugh. What in the world did she mean by that? "Sparkly?"

Both the older ladies nodded in unison. "Yeah, like there's more brightness in your eyes. Your skin is all aglow. You even had a spring in your step when you walked in. Can't say I've seen you do that before."

Frannie suddenly gasped and slapped her hand across her mouth. "Dear sweetmeat! You said you were spending the day with that businessman. Please tell me you spent the night with him, too!"

Mel looked around her in horror. Frannie's statement had not been made in a low voice. Neither woman seemed to possess one.

"Of course not! We simply did some skating, walked

for a bit around the Common and then had a meal together." Try as she might, Mel knew she couldn't quite keep the dreaminess out of her voice. For the whole day had been just that…something out of a dream. "He dropped me off at my apartment at the end of the evening like a true gentleman."

Greta humphed in disappointment. "Damn. That's too bad."

"You two know me better than that."

"We know you're due for some fun and excitement. You deserve it."

"And that you're not an old maid," the other sister interjected. "Not that there's anything wrong with being one."

"I think you should have seduced him!" Again, the outrageous statement was made in a booming, loud voice. Mel felt a blush creep into her cheeks. Though she couldn't be sure if it was from embarrassment or the notion of seducing Ray. A stream of images popped into her head that spread heat deep within her core, intensifying into a hot fire as she recalled how brazenly she'd kissed him on the walkway overlooking the tree above Faneuil.

"He's leaving in a few days, Greta."

Greta waved a hand in dismissal. "Lots of people have long-distance relationships. Think of how much you'll miss each other till you can see one another again."

"Thousands of miles away, along the Mediterranean coast, is quite a long distance," she countered, fighting back a sudden unexpected and unwelcome sting of tears. Just like her to be foolish enough to go and fall so hard for a man who didn't even live on the same continent.

Not that it really mattered. Where they each lived was beyond the concept of a moot point. The fantasy of

Ray was all well and good. But they weren't the type of people who would ever end up together in the long term.

Her family had never owned a European estate. What a laugh. She could barely afford the rent in her small studio apartment on the south side. She could only imagine how elegant and sophisticated Ray's parents and sisters had to be. Mel didn't even want to speculate about what they might think of someone like her. Look at the way her own father had been treated by his wife's family.

"So have some fun in the meantime," Greta argued. "He's still got a few more days in the States, you said."

"And I repeat, you know me better than that. I'm not exactly the type who can indulge in a torrid and quick affair." Though if any man could tempt her into doing so, it would most certainly be the charming man with the brooding Mediterranean looks who'd haunted her dreams all last night.

"Then maybe he should be the one who tries to seduce you," Frannie declared, as if she'd come up with the entire solution to the whole issue. Mel could only sigh. They clearly had no intention of letting the matter drop. She really did have to keep repeating herself when it came to the Perlman sisters.

"I already mentioned he was a gentleman."

The pocket of her uniform suddenly lit up as her phone vibrated with an incoming call.

Her heart jumped to her throat when she saw whose number popped up on the screen. It was as if her thoughts had conjured him. With shaky fingers, she slid the icon to answer.

The nerves along her skin prickled with excitement when she heard his deep, silky voice. Oh, yeah, she had it pretty bad.

And had no idea what to do about it.

"I wanted to thank you again for taking me to so many wonderful spots yesterday." Ray's voice sounded smooth and rich over the tiny speaker.

Mel had to suppress the shudder of giddiness that washed over her. She realized just how anxious she'd been that he might not reach out to her again, despite his assurances last night that he'd be in touch before leaving the United States. "I had a lot of fun, too," she said quietly into the phone. Greta and Frannie were unabashedly leaning over the counter to get close enough to hear her end of the conversation.

"Believe it or not, I'm calling to ask you for yet another favor," Ray said, surprising her. "One only you would be able to help me with."

"Of course," she answered immediately, and then realized that she should at least inquire what he was asking of her. "Um. What kind of favor?"

"You gave me an idea last night. One I'd like to pursue further to see if it might be worthwhile."

For the life of her, she couldn't imagine what he might be referring to. Was she forgetting a crucial part of the evening? Highly unlikely, considering she'd run every moment spent with him over and over in her mind since he'd left her. Every moment they'd spent together had replayed in her mind like mini movies during her sleepless night. She'd felt light-headed and euphoric, and she hadn't even had anything to drink last night.

"I did?"

"Yes. Are you free later today?"

For him? Most certainly. And it wasn't like she had an active social life to begin with. She could hardly wait to hear what he had in mind. "My shift ends at three today, after the lunch crowd. Will that work?" It was impossible to keep the joy and excitement out of her voice. Something about this man wreaked havoc on her emotions.

"It does. Perfectly."

Mel's heart pounded like a jackhammer in her chest. She'd be spending the afternoon with him. The next few hours couldn't go by fast enough.

"I'm glad. But I have to ask. What is this idea I gave you?"

She could hardly believe her ears as he explained. Her off-the-cuff remark about the bed-and-breakfast in Newford had apparently had more of an impact on him than she would have guessed. She'd actually forgotten all about it. Ray's proposal sent a thrill down her spine. By the time she slid her phone back into her pocket, her excitement was downright tangible.

"Well, what was that all about?" Frannie demanded to know. "From the dreamy look on your face, I'd say that was him calling. Tell us what he said."

"Yeah. Must have been something good," Greta added. "You look like you're about ready to jump out of your skin."

All in all, it was a pretty apt description.

"Why, Melinda Lucille Osmon, let me take a look at you! How long has it been, sweetie?"

Ray watched with amusement as a plump, short older woman with snow-white hair in a bun on top her head came around the check-in counter and took Mel's face into her palms. "Hi, Myrna. It's been way too long, I'd say."

"Now, why have you been such a stranger, young lady?"

"I have no excuses. I can only apologize."

"Well, all that matters is that you're here now. Will you be staying a few days?"

It was endearing how many little old ladies Mel had in her life who seemed to absolutely adore her. She might not have any more living blood relatives, but she seemed to have true family in the form of close friends. Ray wondered if she saw it that way.

Right now, this particular friend was making a heroic effort to avoid glancing in his direction. No doubt waiting for Mel to introduce him and divulge what they were doing there together on the spur of the moment.

Not too hard to guess what conclusion the woman had jumped to about the two of them arriving at the bed-and-breakfast together. The situation was bound to be tricky. Both he and Mel had agreed on the ride over that they wouldn't mention Ray's intentions about a potential purchase. Mel didn't want to get the other woman's hopes up in case none of it came to fruition.

Mel hesitantly cleared her throat and motioned to him with her hand. "This is a friend of mine, Myrna. His name is Ray Alsab. He's traveling from overseas on business. He wanted to see an authentic bed-and-breakfast before leaving the States."

"Why, I'm honored that mine is the one he'll be seeing," the other woman said with a polite smile.

Ray reached over and took her hand and then planted a small kiss on the back, as was customary in his country when meeting older women. "The honor is all mine, ma'am."

Myrna actually fanned herself. "Well, you two happen to have great timing. It's the night of the annual town Christmas jamboree. To be held right here in our main room."

Ray gave Mel a questioning look. "It's a yearly get-together for the whole town," Mel began to explain. "With plenty of food, drink and dancing."

"Another ball, then?"

Myrna giggled next to him. "Oh, no. It's most definitely not a ball. Nothing like it. Much less fancy. Just some good old-fashioned food and fun among neighbors." She turned to Mel, her expression quite serious. "I hope you two can stay."

This time it was Mel's turn to give him a questioning look. She wasn't going to answer without making sure it was all right with him. *Why not*, Ray thought. After all, the whole reason he was here was to observe the workings and attraction of a small-town lodge. To see if it might make for a worthwhile investment.

Yeah, right. And it had absolutely nothing to do with how it gave him another excuse to spend some more time with Mel. He gave her a slight nod of agreement.

"We'd love to stay and attend, Myrna. Thank you."

Myrna clasped her hands in front of her chest. "Excellent. Festivities start at seven o'clock sharp."

"We'll be there."

"I'm so happy you're here. Now, let's get you two something to eat." She laid a hand on Mel's shoulder and started leading her down the hall. "Ruby's thrown together a mouthwatering beef stew, perfect for the cold evening." She turned to Ray. "Ruby's our head cook. She does a fine job."

Ray politely nodded, but his mind was far from any thoughts of food. No, there was only one thought that popped into his head as he followed the two women into a dining area. That somehow he was lucky enough to get another chance to dance with Mel.

* * *

"So, what do you think of the place?" Mel asked him as he entered the main dining room of the Newford Inn with her at precisely 7:00 p.m.

"It's quite charming," Ray answered truthfully. The establishment was a far cry from the five-star city hotels that made up most of his family's resort holdings. But if he was to deviate from that model, the Newford Inn would be a fine choice to start with. It held a New England appeal, complete with naval decor and solid hardwood floors. And the chef had done an amazing job with the stew and fixings. He still couldn't believe just how much of it he'd had at dinner. But Myrna had put bowl after bowl in front of him and it had been too good to resist.

"I'm so glad to hear it." She gave him a genuine smile that pleased him much more than it should have.

"Mel? What are you doing here?"

They'd been approached by a tall, lanky man who appeared to be in his thirties. He had a fair complexion and was slightly balding at the top of his head. The smile he greeted Mel with held more question than friendliness.

"Carl," Mel answered with a nod of her head. Her smile from a moment ago had faded completely.

"Wow, I wasn't expecting to see you here tonight."

"It was something of an unplanned last-minute decision."

The other man looked at Ray expectedly, then thrust his hand in his direction when Mel made no effort to introduce them. "I'm Carl Devlin. Mel and I knew each other growing up."

"Ray. Nice to meet you."

Carl studied him up and down. "Huh. Eric mentioned

you were seeing someone," he said, clearly oblivious to just how rude he was being.

Mel stiffened next to him. "You and Eric still talk about me?"

Carl shrugged. "We talk about a lot of things. We're still fantasy-ball buddies."

Yet another American term Ray had never really understood the meaning of. It definitely didn't mean what it sounded like. As if American sports fans sat around together fantasizing about various sports events. Though, in a sense, he figured that was how the gambling game could be described.

Mel gave him a sugary smile that didn't seem quite genuine for her part either. "I'm so terribly happy that the two of you have remained friends since I introduced you two at the wedding. After all this time."

"Yeah. I'm really sorry things didn't work out between you two."

Ray felt the ire growing like a brewing storm within his chest. The blatant reminder that Mel had once belonged to a man who so completely hadn't deserved her was making him feel a strange emotion he didn't want to examine.

Luckily, Mel cut the exchange short at that point. She gently took Ray's arm and began to turn away. "Well, if you'll excuse us then, I wanted to introduce Ray to some friends."

Ray gave the other man a small nod as they walked away.

"I'm sorry if that was unpleasant," she said as she led him toward the other corner of the room. "I should have remembered that he and Eric still keep in touch."

"No need to apologize," he said and put his arm around her waist. "Though it occurs to me that we have the same predicament as we had the other evening at the holiday ball."

Her eyebrows lifted in question. "How so?"

"Looks like we'll have to put on a good show for your old friend Carl." He turned to face her. "Shall we get started?"

She responded by stepping into his embrace and giving him just the barest brush of a kiss on the lips.

CHAPTER NINE

"THIS MIGHT VERY well be the silliest dance I've ever done."

Mel couldn't contain her laughter as Ray tried to keep up with the line dance currently in play in the main room. Had she finally found the one thing Ray might not be good at? He was barely keeping up with the steps and had nearly tripped her up more than once when he'd danced right into her.

She had to appreciate the lengths he was going to simply to indulge her.

"You'll get the hang of it," she reassured him. "You're used to dancing at high-end balls and society events. Here at the Newford Inn, we're much more accustomed to doing the Electric Slide."

"It appears to be more complicated than any waltz," he said with so much grim seriousness that she almost felt sorry for him.

The song finally came to an end before Ray had even come close to mastering the steps. The next song that started up was a much slower love ballad. The dancers on the floor either took their leave and walked away, or immediately started to pair up. Ray reached for her hand. "May I?"

A shiver meandered down her spine. With no small amount of hesitation, she slowly stepped into his arms.

She wasn't sure if her heart could handle it. The lines between pretending to be a couple for Carl's benefit and the reality of her attraction to him were becoming increasingly blurry.

She had no doubt she was beginning to feel true and strong emotions for the man. But for his part, Ray's feelings were far from clear. Yes, he seemed to be doing everything to charm her socks off. But how much of that was just simply who he was? His charm and appeal seemed to be a natural extension of him. Was she reading too much into it all?

And that kiss they'd shared the night before while they'd watched the tree lighting. She'd felt that kiss over every inch of her body. She wanted to believe with all her heart that it had meant something to him as well, that it had affected him even half as much as it had affected her. The way he'd responded to her had definitely seemed real. There had been true passion and longing behind that kiss—she firmly believed that. But she couldn't ignore the fact that she'd initiated it. How many men wouldn't have responded? She didn't exactly have the best track record in general as far as men were concerned. Look at how badly she'd read Eric and his true intentions. In her desire to belong to some semblance of a family again, she'd gone ahead and made the error of a lifetime.

She couldn't afford to make any more such mistakes.

At the heart of it, there was only one thing that mattered. Ray would be gone for good in a few short days. She had to accept that. Only, there was no denying that he'd be taking a big part of her heart with him.

How foolish of her to let that happen.

Even as she thought so, she snuggled her cheek tighter

against his chest, taking in the now-familiar, masculine scent of him. It felt right to be here, swaying in his arms to the romantic music.

Any hope she had that he might feel a genuine spark of affection died when he spoke his next words. "We definitely seem to have your friend Carl's attention. He seems convinced I can't keep my hands off you. If Eric asks, I'm sure he'll get the answer that we're very much enamored with each other."

Something seemed to snap in the vicinity of her chest. She yanked out of his arms, suddenly not caring how it would look. To Carl or anyone else.

"I don't care."

He blinked at her. "Beg your pardon?"

"I don't care what Eric thinks anymore. It was childish and silly to go through so much trouble just to prove a point to a selfish shell of a man." She swallowed past the lump that had suddenly formed in her throat. "A man I should have never fallen for, let alone married."

There was a sudden shift behind his eyes. He reached for her again and took her gently by the upper arms. "Come here."

Mel couldn't allow herself to cry. Since they'd walked into the room, all eyes had been focused on them. There was zero doubt they were being watched still. It would be disastrous to cause a scene right here and now. The last thing she wanted was gossip to follow her on this visit.

She couldn't even explain why she was suddenly so emotional. Only that her heart was slowly shattering piece by piece every time she thought of how temporary this all was. A month from now, it would be nothing more than a memory. One she would cherish and revisit daily for as long as she lived. More than likely, the same could not be said for how Ray would remember her.

Or if he even would.

The thought made her want to sob, which would definitely cause a scene.

"Please, excuse me," she pleaded, then turned on her heel to flee the room. She ran into the outer hallway, making her way past the desk and toward the small sitting area by the fireplace. Ray's footsteps sounded behind her within moments. He reached her side as she stood staring at the crackling flames. She wasn't quite ready to turn and face him just yet.

"What's the matter, Mel?" he asked softly, his voice sounded like smooth silk against the backdrop of the howling gusts of wind outside.

She took too long to answer. Ray placed a gentle hand on her shoulder and turned her around. The concern in his eyes touched her to her core.

"Nothing. Let's just get back and enjoy the dancing." She tried to step to the side. "I guess I'm just being silly."

He wasn't buying it. He stopped her retreat by placing both hands on either side of her against the mantel. Soft shadows fell across his face from the light of the fire and the dim lighting in the room. With the heat of the flames at her back and that of his body so close to hers, she felt cocooned in warmth. Ray's warmth. Her stomach did a little quiver as he leaned closer.

"*Silly* is the last word I would use to describe you."

She wanted to ask him how he would describe her. What were his true, genuine thoughts as far as she was concerned?

The sudden flickering of the lights, followed by a complete blackout, served to yank her out of her daze. Now that the music from the other room had stopped, the harsh sound of the howling wind sang loudly in the air.

She'd been a New Englander her whole life and could

guess what had just happened. The nor'easter storm forecast for much later tonight must have shifted and gained speed. The roads were probably closed or too treacherous to risk. Attempting the forty-minute ride back into Boston would be the equivalent of a death wish.

They were almost certainly snowbound for the night.

"I'm sorry, dear. Unfortunately, the one room is all I have. Between the holidays, the storm warnings and this annual holiday jamboree, we've been booked solid for days now. I only have the one small single due to a last-minute weather-related cancelation."

Mel had been afraid of that. She stood, speaking with Myrna in the middle of the Newford Inn's candlelit lobby. Most of the partygoers had slowly dispersed and headed back to their rooms or to their houses in town. Ray stood off to the side, staring in awe at the powerful storm blowing outside the big bay window. The power wasn't expected to come back on in the foreseeable future and Myrna's backup generators were barely keeping the heat flowing. "I understand. I'm not trying to be difficult. I hope you know that."

Myrna patted her hand gently. "Of course, dear." She then leaned over to her and spoke softly into her ear so that only Mel could hear her. "Are you scared in any way, dear? To be alone in a room with him? If you are, even a little bit, I'll figure something out."

Mel felt touched at her friend's concern. But fear was far from being the issue. She didn't know if she had the emotional stamina to spend a night alone in a small room with Ray.

She shook her head with a small smile. "No, Myrna.

I'm not even remotely in fear of him. It's just that we haven't known each other that long."

"I'm so sorry, Mel," Myrna repeated. "Why don't you sleep with me in my room, then? It will be tight, but we can make do."

That offer was beyond generous. Mel knew Myrna occupied a space barely larger than a closet. Not to mention she looked beyond exhausted. Mel knew she must have been running around all day to prep for the jamboree. Then she'd had to deal with the sudden power outage and getting the heat restored before it got too cold. All on top of the fact that Mel and Ray hadn't been expected. She felt beyond guilty for causing the other woman any inconvenience.

Ray suddenly appeared at her side and gently pulled her to the corner of the room. "Mel, I must apologize. I feel responsible that you're stranded here. With me."

The number of people suddenly apologizing to her was beginning to get comical. All due to a storm no one could control or could have predicted.

Ray continued, "Please accept whatever room the inn has available for yourself. I'll be perfectly fine."

"But where will you sleep?"

He gave her hand a reassuring squeeze. "You don't need to concern yourself with that."

"I can't help it," she argued. "I am concerned." The only other option he had was the SUV. "You're not suggesting you sleep in your car, are you?"

"It won't be so bad."

"Of course it will. You'd have to keep it running all night to avoid freezing. You probably don't even have enough gas to do that after our drive here."

"I can handle the cold," he told her. "I have roughed it in the past."

She quirked an eyebrow at him.

Ray crossed his hands in front of his chest. "I'll have you know that military service is a requirement in my country. I spent many months as a soldier training and surviving in worse conditions than the inside of an SUV during a storm. I can survive a few hours trying to sleep in one for one night."

He'd been a soldier? How much more was there about this man that she had no clue about?

Nevertheless, they had more pressing matters at the moment.

Mel shook her head vehemently. She couldn't allow him to sleep outside in a car during a nor'easter. Especially not in a coastal town. Plus, she felt more than a little responsible for their predicament. She was the native New Englander. If anything, she should have been prepared for the storm and the chance that it might hit sooner than forecast.

"Ray, setting aside your survival skills learned as a soldier, making you sleep outdoors is silly. We can share a room for one night."

He studied her face and then tipped his head slightly in acceptance. "If you insist."

She turned back to Myrna, glad to be done with the argument. What kind of person would she be if she allowed herself to sleep in a nice, comfortable bed while he was outside, bent at odd angles, trying to sleep all night in a vehicle? Military service or not.

"We'll take the room, Myrna. Thank you for your hospitality."

The other woman handed her an old-fashioned steel key. "Room 217. I hope you two stay warm."

"Thank you," she said with a forced smile, trying to convey a level of calm she most certainly didn't feel.

"Have a pleasant sleep," her friend added, handing her two toothbrushes and a minuscule tube of toothpaste.

That was doubtful, Mel thought as she motioned for Ray to follow her. It was highly unlikely she'd get much sleep at all. Not in such close quarters with a man she was attracted to like no one else she'd ever met.

Not even the man she had once been married to.

Ray placed his hand on Mel's as she inserted the key to open the door to what would be their room for the night. "My offer still stands," he told her, giving her yet another chance to be certain. "I can go sleep outside in the vehicle. You don't need to do anything you're not completely comfortable with."

He'd never forgive himself for the predicament he'd just put Mel in. Who knew the weather along the northeastern coast could be so darn unpredictable? He wasn't used to accommodating unexpected whims of the forecast where he was from.

"I appreciate that, Ray. I do." She sighed and turned the key, pushing open the wooden door. "But we're both mature adults. I've spent enough time with you to know you're not a man to take advantage. Let's just get some sleep."

"You're sure?"

She nodded. "Yes. Completely."

Grateful for her answer—he really hadn't been looking forward to being sprawled out in the back seat of an SUV for hours in the middle of a storm—he followed her in. The room they entered wasn't even half the size of one of his closets back home in his personal wing of the castle. But the real problem was the bed. It was barely the size of a cot.

Mel must have been thinking along the same lines.

Her eyes grew wide as they landed on it. He could have sworn he heard her swear under her breath.

"I'll sleep on the floor," he told her.

She immediately shook her head. "There's only the one comforter. That wouldn't be much better than sleeping in the car."

He took her by the shoulders and turned her to face him. "Again. I'm sorry for all of this. I can assure you that you can rest easy and fall asleep. I won't do anything to make you uncomfortable. You don't have to worry about that."

She gave him a tight nod before turning away. Again, she muttered something under her breath he couldn't quite make out.

Despite his unyielding attraction to her, he'd sooner cut off his arm than do anything to hurt her. It was hard to believe how much he'd come to care about her in just the short time since they'd met. She had to know that.

They both got ready for bed in awkward silence. Mel climbed in first and scooted so close to the wall she was practically smashed up against it. Ray got into bed and lay on his side, making sure to face the other way.

"Good night, Mel."

"Good night."

Wide-awake, he watched as the bedside clock slowly ticked away. The wind howled like a wild animal outside, occasionally rattling the singular window. Had Mel fallen asleep yet? The answer came when she spoke a few minutes later.

"This is silly," she said in a soft voice, almost near to whispering. "I'm close to positive you aren't asleep either. Are you?"

Just to be funny, he didn't answer her right away. Several beats passed in awkward silence. Finally, he heard Mel utter a chagrined "Oh, dear."

He allowed himself a small chuckle, then flipped over onto his other side to face her. "Sorry, couldn't resist. You're right. I'm awake, too."

"Ha ha. Very funny." She gave him a useless shove on the shoulder. The playful motion sent her body closer against him for the briefest of seconds, and he had to catch his breath before he could speak again.

"I've never experienced a New England snowstorm before," he told her.

"It's called a nor'easter. We get one or two every winter, if we're lucky. If not, we get three, maybe even four."

"They're pretty. And pretty loud."

He felt her nodding agreement in the dark. "It can be hard to fall asleep, even if you're used to them."

"Since neither of us is sleeping," he began. "I was wondering about something."

"About what?"

"Something you said tonight."

"Yes?"

"When you told me you no longer cared about what Eric thought. Did you mean it?"

The sensation of her body so near to his, the scent of her filling his nostrils compelled him to ask the question. He realized he'd been wanting to all night, since she'd spoken the words as they'd danced together earlier.

He felt the mattress shift as she moved. "Yes. I did mean it. And I realize I haven't cared about his opinion for quite a while."

He wanted to ask her more, was beyond curious about what had led to their union. She seemed far too good for the man Eric appeared to be—she was too pure, too selfless. But this was her tale to tell. So he resisted the urge to push. Instead, he waited patiently, hoping she would continue if she so chose.

She eventually did. "I honestly don't know exactly what drew me to Eric. I can only say I'd suffered a terrible loss after my parents' passing. It's no excuse, I know."

"A person doesn't need an excuse for how they respond to grief," he told her.

"You speak as if you're someone who would know." She took a shaky breath. "Have you lost someone close to you?"

That wasn't it. He wouldn't be able to explain it to her. As the heir to the crown, he'd been to more ceremonial funerals than he cared to remember. Words had always failed him during those events, when confronted with the utter pain of loss that loved ones experienced.

"I haven't," he admitted. "I've been quite fortunate. I never knew my grandparents. Both sets passed away before I or my sisters were born."

She stayed silent for a while. "I lost the two most important people in the world to me within a span of a few months," she said, reminding him of their conversation from the other day. "I guess I longed for another bond, some type of tie with another person. So when Eric proposed…"

"You accepted." But she'd gone above and beyond the commitment of her marital vows. "You also put him through school."

"I never wanted finances to be an issue in my marriage. Money was the reason I had no one else after my parents died."

"And you never fought to get any of it back? To get your life back on track or even to pursue your own dreams?"

He felt her tense up against him. Maybe he was getting too personal. Maybe it was the effect of the dark and quiet they found themselves in. Not to mention the tight and close quarters. But he found he really wanted to understand her reasoning. To understand *her*.

"It's hard to explain, really. I didn't have the stomach to fight for something I readily and voluntarily handed over."

"Is that the only reason?"

"What else?"

"Perhaps you're punishing yourself. Or maybe trying to prove that you can be independent and rebound. All on your own."

He felt her warm breath on his chest as she sighed long and deep. "I thought I was in love. To me, that meant a complete commitment. Materially and emotionally." The statement didn't really answer his question. But he wasn't going to push.

She didn't need to explain anything to him. And he suddenly felt like a heel for making her relive her grief and her mistakes. Gently, softly, he rubbed his knuckles down her cheek. She turned her face into his touch and he had to force himself not to wrap his arms around her and pull her closer, tight up against him. As difficult as it was to do so, he held firm and steady without moving so much as a muscle. For he knew that if he so much as reached for her, it would be a mistake that could only lead to further temptation.

Temptation he wasn't sure he'd be able to control under the current circumstances.

Mel couldn't believe how much she was confiding about herself and her marriage. To Ray of all people—a man she'd just recently met and barely knew. But somehow she felt more comfortable talking to him than anyone else she could name.

She was curious about things in his past, also.

"What about you?" she asked, not entirely sure she really wanted to know the answer to what she was about to ask him. "There must have been at least one significant relationship in your past. Given all you have going for you."

"Not really. I have had my share of relationships. But none of them amounted to anything in the long run. Just some dear friendships I'm grateful for."

"I find that hard to believe."

He chuckled softly. The vibration of his voice sent little bolts of fire along her skin. "You can believe it."

"Not even at university? You must have dated while you were a student."

"Sure. But nothing that grew serious in any way."

She had no doubt the women he was referring to would have much rather preferred a completely different outcome. Ray seemed to have no idea the trail of broken hearts he must have left in his wake. Her eyes stung. She'd soon be added to that number.

After pausing for several moments, he finally continued, "I never really had much of a chance to invest any kind of time to cultivate the kind of relationship that leads to a significant commitment. As the oldest of the siblings, familial responsibilities far too often fell solely on my shoulders. Even while I was hundreds of miles away, studying in Geneva."

Ray sounded like he bore the weight of an entire nation on those shoulders. "Your family must be very important in Verdovia."

That comment, for some reason, had Ray cursing under his breath. "I'm sorry, Mel," he bit out. "For all of it."

He had to be referring to all the pain and anguish of

her past that she'd just shared. Mel couldn't help but feel touched at his outrage on her behalf. The knowledge that he cared so deeply lulled her into a comfortable state of silence. Several moments went by as neither one spoke.

She wasn't sure how she was supposed to sleep when all she could think about was having Ray's lips on hers.

So it surprised her when she opened her eyes and looked at the clock, only to see that it read 7:30 a.m. A peaceful stillness greeted her as she glanced outside the window at the rising sun of early morning. The only sound in the room was the steady, rhythmic sound of Ray breathing softly next to her.

At some point, the winds had died down and both she and Ray had fallen asleep.

The air against her face felt frigid. Her breath formed a slight fog as she breathed out. The generators must not have been able to quite keep up with the weather, as the temperature in the room had gone down significantly. She came fully awake with a start as she realized exactly how she'd fallen asleep: tight against Ray's chest, snuggled securely in his arms. She hadn't even been aware of the cold.

CHAPTER TEN

THE AWKWARDNESS OF their position was going to be unbearable once Ray woke up. Mel racked her mind for a
possible solution. She didn't even know what she would
say to him if he woke to find her nestled up against his
chest this way.

There was no doubt she'd been the one to do the nes-
tling either. Ray remained in exactly the same spot he'd
been when they'd got into the bed. She, on the other hand,
was a good foot away from the wall.

She did the only thing she could think of. She pretended to snore. Loudly.

At first he only stirred. So she had to do it again.

This time, he jolted a bit and she immediately shut her
eyes before he could open his. Several beats passed when
she could hear him breathing under her ear. His body's
reaction was nearly instantaneous. Heaven help her, so
was her response. A wave of curling heat started in her
belly and moved lower. Her fingers itched to reach for
him, to pull him on top of her. Electricity shot through
her veins at the images flooding her mind. She didn't
dare move so much as an inch.

Mel heard him utter a soft curse under his breath.
Then he slowly, gently untangled himself and sat up on
the edge of the mattress. She felt his loss immediately.

The warmth of his skin, the security of his embrace—if she were a braver, more reckless woman, she would have thrown all caution to the wind and reached for his shoulder. She would have pulled him back toward her and asked him for what she was yearning for so badly.

But Mel had never been that woman. Especially not since her divorce and the betrayal that had followed. If anything, the fiasco had made her grow even more guarded.

Ray sat still for several more moments. Finally, she felt his weight leave the mattress.

She wasn't proud of her mini deception, but what a relief that it had worked. The sound of the shower being turned on sounded from behind the bathroom door. There was probably no hot water. But Ray probably didn't need it.

She rubbed a shaky hand down her face. Hopefully he would take his time in there. It would take a while for her heart to steady, judging by the way it was pounding wildly in her chest.

Before long, the shower cut off and she heard him pull the curtain back.

Mel made sure to look away when Ray walked out of the bathroom, wearing nothing but a thick terry towel around his midsection. But it was no use, she'd seen just enough to have her imagination take over from there. A strong chiseled chest with just enough dark hair to make her fingers itch to run through it. He hadn't dried off completely, leaving small droplets of water glistening along his tanned skin. She had to get out of this room. The tight quarters with him so close by were wreaking havoc on her psyche. Not to mention her hormones. She sat upright along the edge of the mattress.

"You're awake," he announced.

She merely nodded.

"I…uh… I'll just get dressed."

"Okay." She couldn't quite meet him in the eye.

He began to turn back toward the bathroom.

"Do you want to take a walk with me?" she blurted out.

"A walk?"

"Yes. The wind and snow has stopped. We won't be able to start driving anywhere for a while yet. The salt trucks and plows are probably just now making a final run to clear the roads."

"I see. And all that gives you a desire to walk?" he asked with a small smirk of a smile gracing his lips.

"The aftermath of a snowstorm in this town can be visually stunning," she informed him. "I think you'd enjoy the sight of it."

He gave her an indulgent smile. "That sounds like a great idea, then."

She gave him a pleasant smile. "Great, you get dressed. I'll try to scrounge us up some coffee from the kitchen and meet you up front."

"I'll be there within ten minutes," he said with a dip of his head.

It was all the cue Mel needed to grab her coat and scarf, and then bolt out of the room.

As soon as she shut the door behind her, she leaned back against it and took several deep breaths. A walk was definitely an inspired idea. The air would do her good. And she knew just where to take him. Newford was home to yet another talented sculptor who put on a stunning display of three or four elaborate ice statues every year, right off the town square. At the very least, it would give them something to talk about, aside from the strange night they'd just spent in each other's arms.

But first, caffeine. She needed all the fortitude she could get her hands on.

Ray made sure to be true to his word and took the center staircase two steps at a time to find Mel waiting for him by the front doors. They appeared to be the only two people up and about—in this part of the hotel anyway.

"Ready?" she asked and handed him a travel mug of steaming hot liquid. The aroma of the rich coffee had his mouth watering in an instant.

He took the cup from her with a grateful nod and then motioned with his free hand to the doors. "Lead the way."

He saw what she'd meant earlier as soon as they stepped outside. Every building, every structure, every tree and bush was completely covered in a thick blanket of white. He'd never seen so much snow in a city setting before, just on high, majestic mountains. This sight was one to behold.

"It looks like some sort of painting," he told her as they started walking. The sidewalks still remained thick with snow cover, but the main road had been plowed. He was thankful for the lined leather boots he was wearing. Mel was definitely more accustomed to this weather than he was. She maintained a steady gait and didn't even seem to notice the cold and brisk morning air. He studied her from the corner of his eye.

Her cheeks were flushed from the cold, her lips red and ripened from the hot brew she was drinking.

His mind inadvertently flashed back to the scene this morning. He'd awoken to find her snuggled tight in his embrace. Heaven help him, it had taken all the will he possessed to disentangle her soft, supple body away from his and leave the bed.

In another universe, upon waking up with her that way, he would have been the one to put that blush on her cheeks, to cause the swelling in those delicious ruby red lips.

He blinked away the thoughts and continued to follow her as she made her way to what appeared to be the center of town.

"Do we have a destination?" he asked, trying to focus on the activity at hand and not on the memory of how she'd felt nestled against him earlier.

"As a matter of fact, we do," she replied. "You'll see soon enough."

As he'd thought, they reached the center of town and what seemed to be some sort of town square. The sound of the ocean in the near distance grew louder the farther they walked. There was nothing to see in the square but more snow. How in the world would all this get cleaned up? It seemed an exorbitant amount. Where did it all go once it melted?

Verdovia's biggest snowstorm in the past decade or so had resulted in a mere light covering that had melted away within days.

"This way," Mel said.

Within moments, she'd led them to a small alleyway between two long brick buildings, a sort of square off to the side of the main square. In the center sat a now quiet water fountain of cherubic angels holding buckets.

But the true sight to behold was the handful of statues that surrounded the cherubs. Four large ice sculptures, each an impressive display of craftsmanship.

"Aren't they magnificent?" Mel asked him with a wide smile.

"Works of art," Ray said as they walked near to the closest one. A stallion on its hind legs, appearing to bray at the sky.

"They certainly are," Mel agreed. "This spot is block-aded enough by the buildings that the sculptures are mostly protected from the harsh wind or snow, even during nasty storms like the one last night," she explained.

True enough, all four of them looked none the worse for wear. He couldn't detect so much as a crack in some of the most delicate features, such as the horse's thick tail.

After admiring the statue for several moments, they moved on to the next piece. A mermaid lounging on a rock. The detail and attention on the piece was astounding. It looked like it could come to life at any moment.

"One person did all these?"

Mel nodded. "With some minor help from assistants. She does it every year. Arranges for large blocks of ice to be shipped in, then spends hours upon hours chiseling and shaping. From dusk till dawn. Regardless of how cold it gets."

He smiled at her. "You New Englanders are a hearty lot."

"She does it just for the enjoyment of the town."

"Remarkable," he said. Mel took him by the arm and led him a few feet to the next one.

"Take a look at this piece. This one's a repeat she does every time," she told him. "It's usually my favorite." She ducked her head slightly.

It was a couple dancing. That artist's talent was truly notable, she had managed to capture the elegance of a ballroom dance, even depicting an expression of sheer longing on the faces of the two entwined statues. With remarkable detail, the man's fingers were splayed on the small of the woman's back. She was arched on his other arm, head back atop a delicately sculpted throat. Icy tendrils of hair appeared to be blowing in the wind.

"She's really outdone herself with this one this year," Mel said, somewhat breathless as she studied the frozen couple.

Ray was beyond impressed himself. And he knew what Mel had to be thinking.

They'd danced that way together more than once now. He couldn't help but feel touched at the thought of it.

Mel echoed his thoughts. "It sort of reminds me of the holiday ball. I think you may have dipped me just like that once or twice."

Mel hadn't exaggerated when speaking of the artistic talent of her small town. These pieces were exquisitely done, even to his layman's eye. He'd never seen such artwork outside of a museum. Yet another memory he would never have gained had he never met the woman by his side.

He turned to her then. "I don't know how to thank you, Mel. This has truly been the most remarkable holiday season I've spent."

She blinked up at him, thrill and pleasure sparkling behind her bright green eyes, their hue somehow even more striking against the background of so much white. "Really? Do you mean that?"

"More so than you will ever know."

"Not even as a child?"

"Particularly not as a child."

She gripped his forearm with genuine concern. "I'm really sorry to hear that, Ray."

He took a deep breath. How would he explain it to her? That Christmas for him usually consisted of endless events and duties that left no time for any kind of appreciation for the holiday. By the time it was over, he was ready to send the yuletide off for good.

In just the span of a few short days, she'd managed to show him the excitement and appeal that most normal people felt during the season.

He was trying to find a way to tell her all of that when she surprised him by speaking again. She took a deep breath first, as if trying to work up the courage.

"If you end up buying the Newford Inn," she began, "do you think you'll come back at all? You know, to check on your investment?"

The tone of her question sounded so full of hope. A hope he would have no choice but to shatter. He'd allowed this to happen. Mel was conjuring up scenarios in her head where the two of them would be able to meet up somehow going forward. Scenarios that couldn't have any basis in reality. And it was all his fault.

What had he done?

Ray might not have spoken the words, but his stunned silence at her question was all the answer Mel needed.

He had no intention of coming back here, regardless of whether he purchased the property or not. Not to check on an investment. And certainly not to see her. His expression made it very clear. Another thing made very clear was that he was uncomfortable and uneasy that she'd even brought up the possibility.

She'd done it again.

How much battering could a girl's pride take in one lifetime? If there was any way to suck back the words she'd just uttered, she would have gladly done so.

Foolish, foolish, foolish.

So it was all nothing but playacting on his part. She no longer had any doubt of that. Both at the ball and last night at the party. He'd never told her otherwise. She'd gone and made silly, girlish speculations that had no basis in reality.

"Mel," Ray uttered, taking a small step closer to her.

She held a hand up to stop him and backed away. "Please. Don't."

"Mel, if I could just try to ex—"

Cutting him off again, she said, "Just stop, Ray. It's really not necessary. You don't have to explain anything. Or even say anything. It was just a simple question. I'm sorry if it sounded loaded in any way with an ulterior motive. Or as if I was expecting anything of you with your answer."

Something hardened behind his eyes, and then a flash of anger. But she had to be imagining it. Because anger on his part would make no sense. He was the one rejecting her, after all.

"I didn't mean to imply," he simply stated.

"And neither did I."

She lifted her coffee cup and took a shaky swig, only to realize that the beverage had gone cold. The way her heart just had. Turning it over, she dumped the remaining contents onto the white snow at her feet. It made a nasty-looking puddle on the otherwise unblemished surface. Matched her mood perfectly.

"I appear to be out of coffee. I'd like to head back and get some more, please."

He bowed his head. "Certainly."

Suddenly they were being so formal with each other. As if they hadn't woken up in each other's embrace earlier this morning.

"And we should probably make our way back into Boston soon after. With our luck, another storm might hit." She tried to end the sentence with a chuckle, but the sound that erupted from her throat sounded anything but amused.

For his part, Ray looked uncomfortable and stiff. She had only herself to blame. The forty-minute ride back into the city was sure to be mired in awkward silence. So different from the easy camaraderie they'd enjoyed on the ride up. How drastically a few simple words could change reality overall. Words she had no business uttering.

The walk back to the hotel took much less time than the one to get to the statues, most of it spent in silence. In her haste, she almost slipped on a hidden patch of ice in the snow and Ray deftly reached out to catch her before she could fall. Tears stung her eyes in response to his touch, which she could feel even through her thick woolen coat. It was hard not to think of the way he'd spent the night touching her, holding her.

"Thanks," she uttered simply.

"You're welcome."

That was the bulk of their conversation until they reached the front doors of the bed-and-breakfast. Ray didn't go in; instead, he pulled the car keys out of his pocket. "I'll just go start the car and get it warmed up. Please, go get your coffee."

"You've seen all you need to see of the hotel, then?"

He nodded slowly. "I believe I have. Please thank Myrna for me if you see her. For all her hospitality and graciousness."

"I'll do that. It might take me a few minutes."

"Take your time. Just come down when you're ready."

Mel didn't bother to reply, just turned on her heel to open the door and step into the lobby. So it was that obvious that she needed some time to compose herself.

Clearly, she wasn't as talented at acting as Ray appeared to be.

CHAPTER ELEVEN

RAY REALLY NEEDED a few moments alone to compose himself.

He knew she was angry and hurt. And he knew he should let it go. But something within his soul just couldn't let the issue drop. He hadn't misread her intention when she'd asked about him returning to the United States sometime in the future. He couldn't have been that mistaken.

Regardless, one way or another, they had to clear the air.

Ray gripped the steering wheel tight as Mel entered the passenger seat and shut her door. Then he backed out of the parking spot and pulled onto the main road. It was going to be a very long ride if the silent awkwardness between them continued throughout the whole drive back.

She didn't so much as look in his direction.

They'd traveled several miles when he finally decided he'd had enough. Enough of the silence, enough of the tension, enough of all the unspoken thoughts between them.

He pulled off the expressway at the next exit.

"Where are we going?"

"I'd like a minute, if you don't mind."

She turned to him, eyes wide with concern. "Is everything all right? I can take over the driving if you'd like to rest your legs. I know you're not used to driving in such weather." Even in her ire, she was worried about his state. That fact only made him feel worse.

"It's not my legs," he said, then turned into an empty strip mall. The lone shop open was a vintage-looking coffee stop. "Did you mean what you said back in Newford? That you really don't expect anything of me?"

Mel stared at him for several beats before running her fingers along her forehead.

"Yes, Ray. I did. You really don't need to concern yourself." She let out a soft chuckle. "It really was a very innocuous question I asked back by the ice statues."

He studied her face. "Was it?"

"Absolutely."

He could prove her wrong so easily, he thought. If he leaned over to her right now, took her chin in his hand and pulled her face to his. Then if he plunged into her mouth with his tongue, tasted her the way he'd so badly wanted to this morning, it would take no time at all before she responded, moaning into his mouth as he thrust his fingers into her hair and deepened the kiss.

But that would make him a complete bastard.

She deserved better than the likes of him. The last thing he wanted was for her to feel hurt. Worse, to be the cause of her pain.

Instead, he sighed and turned back to look out the front windshield. "Well, good," he said. "That's good."

A small hatchback that had seen better days pulled up two spots over. The occupants looked at him and Mel curiously as they exited their car. It occurred to Ray just how out of place the sleek, foreign SUV must look in such a setting. Especially with two people just sitting inside as it idled in a mostly empty parking lot.

"Fine," Mel bit out.

She certainly didn't sound as if she thought things were fine. He inhaled deeply. "I'd like to clear the air, Mel, if I could. Starting with the bed-and-breakfast."

"What about it?"

"I should have been clearer about Verdovia's potential investment in such a property. Please understand. A small-town bed-and-breakfast would not be a typical venture for us. In fact, it would be a whole different addition to the overall portfolio of holdings. I would have to do extensive research into the pros and cons. And then, if the purchase is even feasible or even worth the time and effort, I'd have to do some real convincing. I haven't even run the idea by my fa—" He caught himself just in time. "I haven't run it by any of the decision makers on such matters. Most notably, the king and queen."

"I understand. That sounds like a lot of work."

"Please also understand one more thing—I have certain responsibilities. And many people to answer to." An entire island nation, in fact. "A certain level of behavior is expected of me. With a country so small, even the slightest deviation from the norms can do serious damage to the nation's sovereignty and socioeconomic health."

He refrained from biting out a curse. Now he sounded like a lecturing professor. To her credit, Mel seemed to be listening intently, without any speculation.

He watched as she clenched her hands in her lap. "You can stop trying to explain, Ray. See, I do understand. In fact, I understand completely," she told him through gritted teeth. "You mean to say that I shouldn't get my hopes up. About the Newford Inn, I mean." Her double meaning was clear by the intense expression in her blazing green eyes and the hardened tone of her voice. "I also understand that Verdovia is much more accustomed to making bigger investments, and that nothing gets decided without the approval of the royal couple. Who have very high expectations of the man who obtains property and real estate on their behalf. Does that about sum it all up?"

Ray had to admire her thought process. It was as clear as day. She had just given him a perfect out, a perfect way to summarize exactly what he needed to say without any further awkwardness for either of them. He couldn't decide if he was relieved, annoyed or impressed. The woman was unlike anyone he'd ever met.

"I'm sorry." He simply apologized. And he truly was. She had no idea. The fate and well-being of an entire nation rested on his shoulders. To do what was best for Verdovia had been ingrained in him for as long as he could remember. He couldn't turn his back on that any more than he could turn his back on his very own flesh and blood. Verdovia needed a princess, someone who had been groomed and primed for such a position.

Even if he could change any of that, even if he turned to Mel and told her the complete truth about who he was at this very moment, then called his father and asked him to scrap the whole marriage idea, what good would any of it do?

Mel wasn't up to withstanding the type of scrutiny that any association with the Verdovian crown prince would bring into her life. Not many people could. If the international press even sniffed at a romantic involvement between Rayhan al Saibbi and an unknown Boston waitress, it would trigger a worldwide media frenzy. Mel's life would never be the same. He couldn't do that to her. Not after all that she'd been through.

He resisted the urge to slam his fist against the steering wheel and curse out loud in at least three different languages. The real frustration was that he couldn't explain any of that to her. All he had left were inadequate and empty apologies.

Mel finally spoke after several tense beats. "Thank you, but there's no need to say sorry. I'll get over it."

She turned to look out her side window. "And Myrna will be fine, too. The Newford Inn will find a way to continue and thrive. You said it yourself this morning. We New Englanders are a hearty lot."

Again, her double meaning was clear as the pure white snow piled up outside. With no small degree of reluctance, he pressed the button to start the ignition once more.

"I should get you home."

He had no idea what he would say to her or do once he got her there.

Mel plopped down on her bed and just stared at the swirl design on the ceiling. She felt as if she'd lived an entire year or two in the last twenty-four hours. Ray had just dropped her off and driven away. But not before he'd looked at her with some degree of expectation. She suspected he was waiting for her to invite him up so they could continue the conversation that had started when he'd pulled over to the side of the road.

She couldn't bring herself to do it. What more was there to discuss?

Not a thing. Once Ray left, she would simply return to her boring routine life and try to figure out what was next in store for her.

Easier said than done.

It occurred to her that she hadn't bothered to look at her cell phone all day. Not that she expected anything urgent that might need her immediate attention. Frannie and Greta weren't expecting her at the diner and no one else typically tried to contact her usually.

But this time, when she finally powered it on, the screen lit up with numerous text messages and voice mail notices. All of them from one person.

Eric.

Now what?

Against her better judgment, she read the latest text.

Call me, Mel. I'd really like to talk. I talked to Carl last night.

That figured. She should have seen this coming.

She had to admit to being somewhat surprised at his level of interest. He'd wasted no time after speaking with Carl to try to get more information out of her about the new man he thought she was seeing. What a blind fool she'd been where Eric was concerned. The man clearly had the maturity level of a grade-schooler.

No wonder she'd fallen for Ray after only having just met him.

But that was in itself just as foolish. More so. Because Ray wasn't the type of man a lady got over. Mel bit back a sob as she threw her arm over her face. Ray had certainly put her in her place during the car ride. He'd made it very clear that she should harbor no illusions about seeing him again.

She'd managed to hold it together and say all the right things, but inside she felt like a hole had opened up where her heart used to be.

She might have been able to convincingly act unaffected in front of Ray, but she certainly wasn't able to kid herself. She fallen head over heels for him, when he had no interest nor desire in seeing her again once his business wrapped up in the States.

She couldn't wallow in self-pity. She had to move on. Find something, anything that would take her mind off the magical days she'd spent with the most enigmatic and attractive man she was likely to ever meet.

She hadn't done anything creative or artistic in nearly two years. This might be an ideal time to ease herself back into using her natural talent for sculpting and creating something out of a shapeless slab of raw material. The idea of getting back into it sent a surge of nervous anticipation through the pit of her stomach.

She called up the keypad and dialed the number of the glass studio in Boston's Back Bay. A recorded voice prompted her to leave a message. She did so, requesting a date and time for use of the studio and materials. Then she made her way to the bathroom and hopped in the shower.

Studio time wasn't much in the way of adventurous, but at least it gave her some small thing to look forward to.

Her cell rang ten minutes later as she toweled off. Mel grabbed the phone, answering it without bothering to look at the screen. The studio had to be returning her call.

Mel realized her mistake as soon as she said hello. The caller wasn't the studio at all. It was her ex-husband.

"Mel? I've been calling you all day."

"What can I do for you, Eric?"

She had an urge to simply disconnect and hang up on him. She really was in no mood for this at the moment. But he'd simply keep calling and hassling her. Better to just have it out and get this over with.

"Carl called me last night. He mentioned you were visiting Newford. And that you weren't alone."

Well, he'd certainly gone and cut to the chase. Mel released a weary sigh. "That's right. I don't see how it's any of your business. Or Carl's, for that matter."

"I told you, Mel. I still care about you. We were man and wife once. That has to mean something."

"As much as it did the day you took off with your dental assistant, Eric?"

He let out an audible, weary sigh. "That's kind of why I'm calling. I've been giving this a lot of thought. I messed up, Mel. I shouldn't have walked away from our marriage."

What?

She nearly lost her grip on the phone. She had no idea where all this was coming from. But she had to nip it in the bud without delay. The whole idea of faking a pretend boyfriend in front of her ex-husband had backfired big-time. She'd simply meant to prove she'd moved on, and that she could attend a yearly event, even though he'd left her. The disaster happening right now hadn't even occurred to her as a remote possibility. Her ex-husband had made it more than clear two years ago that he had moved on and would be spending his life with another woman.

Or so Mel had thought.

She gripped the phone tight and spoke clearly. "Eric, you don't know what you're saying. I'm guessing you and Talley had a fight. And now you're simply overreacting."

He chuckled softly. "You're right about one thing."

"What's that?"

"We had a fight, all right. She became upset because I couldn't stop talking about you. And why you were with that businessman."

Mel had been ready to tell him the complete truth about Ray—she really had. If only just to end this nightmare of a phone call and return Eric's wayward thoughts back to where they belonged, to his wife-to-be.

But the way he said it, with such an insulting and derisive tone, made her change her mind. She didn't owe this man anything, not an explanation, not any comfort. Nothing. Eric wasn't even worth her anger. He simply wasn't worth her time. No, she didn't owe him anything. But the truth was, he did owe *her.*

"Please, Mel. Can we just get together and talk?"

Ray's words from last night echoed in her mind. "Actually, maybe there is something we can talk about."

"Anything."

Mel figured he wouldn't be so enthusiastic once she brought up the subject matter. But Ray was right. She needed to stand up for herself and ask for what was rightfully hers. "I think we need to discuss some ways for you to pay me back, Eric. At least partially."

A notable silence ensued over the speaker. She'd shocked him.

She continued before he could say anything, "Other than that, you really need to stop concerning yourself with me and go resolve things with your fiancée. Now, if you'll excuse me, I'm waiting for an important phone call."

She didn't give him a chance to respond before continuing. "I wish you well, Eric," she said and meant it.

Then she disconnected the call.

CHAPTER TWELVE

MEL HUNG UP her apron and reached for her handbag atop the freestanding cabinet in the back kitchen. It had seemed a particularly long shift. Probably because she hadn't been able to focus on a thing to do with her job. Her mind kept replaying scenes from the past week over and over. Scenes which starred a handsome, dark-haired businessman who sported a shadow of a goatee on his chin and a smile that could charm a demon.

Hard to believe three days had gone by since Newford and the nor'easter that had stranded them overnight. It didn't help matters that she relived the entire experience every night in her dreams, as well as several times during the day in her imagination.

Suddenly Greta's scratchy voice sounded from the dining area. "Well, lookie who's here."

Mel's mouth went dry and her blood pounded in her veins. She wasn't sure how, but she knew who her friend was referring to. *Ray.* He was here.

The suspicion was confirmed a moment later when Greta yelled yet again. "Mel, you should come out here. Someone to see you."

Mel threw her head back and closed her eyes. Taking a steadying breath, she grasped for some composure. She could do this. Even if the chances were high that he was simply here to tell her goodbye. For good.

Masking her emotions as best she could, she pushed open the swinging door and went out of the kitchen. Her breath stopped in her throat when she saw him. Again, he hadn't bothered with a coat. A crisp white shirt brought out the tanned color of his skin and emphasized his jet-black hair. His well-tailored dark gray pants fitted him like a glove.

She smoothed down the hem of her unflattering wait-ress uniform and went to approach him, her bag still clutched in her hands and a forced smile plastered on her face.

"Ray, I didn't expect to see you."

He jammed his hands in his pockets before speaking. "I took a chance you may be at work. I was going to try your apartment if you weren't here."

"I see. Did you want to sit down?" As luck would have it, the only clean booth was the one they'd sat at together for breakfast that morning not so long ago—though now it seemed like another lifetime.

She'd been well on her way then, but hadn't yet quite fallen in love with him. Because that was exactly what had happened. She could no longer deny it. She'd fallen helplessly, hopelessly in love with Ray Alsab.

"I came to tell you that I've come to a decision. And it looks like we'll be moving forward."

She had to rack her brain to figure out exactly what he was talking about. Then it occurred to her. The bed-and-breakfast.

"You'll move forward with buying the Newford Inn, then?"

He nodded with a smile. "I wanted to tell you myself. We haven't even contacted Myrna yet."

Her heart fluttered in her chest, though whether it was the result of hearing the good news or seeing Ray's dashing smile again, she couldn't be sure.

"I've been speaking to all the appropriate people for the past three days," he added. "We've all decided to move ahead. The attorneys are drawing up the paperwork as we speak."

She was happy to hear it, she really was. Particularly for Myrna, who would have so much of the burden of owning the inn taken off her shoulders. But she couldn't just ignore the fact that all she wanted to do right now was to fling herself into his arms and ask him to take her lips with his own. Did he feel even a fraction the same?

It didn't appear so. Because here he was, and all he could talk about was the business deal he'd come to Boston for in the first place.

"It wouldn't have happened without you, Mel. I mean that. And this is just the start."

"The start?"

"That's the best part of it all. I told you the inn was much too small compared to Verdovia's hotel holdings. So we've decided to make it part of something bigger. We'll be investing in several more. A chain of resorts and inns throughout New England, all bearing the royal name. And you were the catalyst for it all."

She didn't know what to say. As much as she appreciated the credit he was giving her, all she could think about was how much she'd missed him these past few days, how she hadn't been able to get him out of her mind. There was no way she was going to tell him that, of course. But, dear heavens, she had to say something.

The words wouldn't form on her tongue, so she just sat there and continued to smile at him stupidly.

"Well, what do you think?" he finally prompted.

If he only knew.

"I think it's wonderful news, Ray. Really. I'm so glad it will work out. Sounds like your business trip will be a success. I'm happy for you."

His eyes suddenly grew serious. He reached across the table and took her hand in his. "There's something else I need to talk to you about."

Mel's pulse quickened and her vision suddenly grew narrow, her only focus at the moment being Ray's handsome face.

"I need to return home to get some things settled once and for all."

Mel felt the telltale stinging behind her eyes and willed the tears not to fall. She was right. This was simply a final goodbye. But his next words had her heart soaring with renewed hope.

"But then I'm going to call you, Mel. Once the dust is settled after I take care of a few things."

That was it, she couldn't hold back the tears, after all. He wasn't giving her the complete story, clearly, but neither was he shutting the door on the two of them. She would take it. With pleasure. She swiped at her eyes with the back of her arm, embarrassed at the loss of control.

He let out a soft chuckle and gripped her hand tighter. "Why are you crying, sweet Mel?"

She didn't get a chance to answer. Ray's phone lit up and vibrated in his front shirt pocket. With a sigh of resignation, he lifted it out. "I have to take this. I'm sorry, but it's about the inn and we're right in the middle of setting up the deal."

She nodded as he stood.

"I'll be right back."

Something nagged at the back of her mind as she watched Ray step outside to take the phone call. She'd got a brief look at the screen of his phone just now as his call had come through. The contact had clearly appeared on the screen as a call from someone he'd labeled as *Father*.

But he'd just told her the call was about the offer he was making to buy Myrna's bed-and-breakfast.

Why would his father be involved in a deal he was doing for the king?

Ray had never mentioned his father being in the same line of work. It didn't make any sense.

She gave her head a shake. Surely she was overthinking things. Still, the nagging voice continued in the back of her mind. The fact was, she'd had the same curious sense before. There seemed to be too many holes in the things Ray had told her about himself. Too many random pieces that didn't quite fit the overall puzzle.

She'd resisted looking at the questions too closely. Until now.

With trembling fingers, she reached into her handbag for the mini electronic tablet she always carried with her to work and logged on to the diner Wi-Fi. Ray was still outside, speaking on the phone.

Mel clicked on the icon for the search engine.

Ray rushed back to the booth where Mel still sat waiting for him, anxious to get back to their conversation.

Something wasn't right. Mel's fists were both clenched tight on the table in front of her. Her lips were tight, and tension radiated off her whole body. One look at the screen on the tablet in front of her told him exactly why.

"Mel."

She didn't even bother to look up at him, keeping her eyes fixed firmly on what she was reading. Ray had never considered himself to be a violent man, save for that one youthful indiscretion on the ball field. But right now, he had a near-overwhelming desire to put his fist through a wall. The gossip rags never failed to amaze him with the unscrupulous ways they so often covered his life.

Mel had gone pale. She used her finger to flip to another page on the screen. Ray didn't need to read the specific words to know what she was seeing. The international tabloid Mel currently stared at was a well-known one. One that featured him just often enough. Ray didn't bother lowering his voice as he bit out a vicious curse.

"Mel. Hear me out."

She still refused to look at him, just continued to read and then clasped a shaky hand to her mouth. Her gasp of horror sliced through his heart.

"Oh, my God," she said in a shaky whisper. "You don't just work for the royal family. You *are* the royal family."

"Mel." He could only repeat her name.

"You're the prince!" This time she raised her voice. So loud that the people around them turned to stare.

"It's what I was trying to explain." Even as he spoke, Ray knew it was no use. Too much damage had just been done. She was going to need time to process.

"When?" She pushed the tablet toward him with such an angry shove, it nearly skidded off the table before he caught it. "When exactly were you going to explain any of this?"

One particular bold headline declared that the Verdovian prince had finally chosen a bride and would be married within months. Somehow they'd snapped a picture of him with a young lady Ray didn't even recognize.

Damn.

"What's there to explain anyway?" she bit out through gritted teeth. "You lied to me. For days."

She was right. He'd been fooling himself, telling himself that not telling Mel the complete truth was somehow different from lying to her.

That itself was a lie.

He had no one to blame but himself. He rammed his hand through his hair and let out a grunt of frustration.

"Is it true?" she demanded to know. "That you're due to be engaged soon?"

He refused to lie yet again. "Yes."

"I need to get out of here," Mel cried out and stood. Turning on her heel with a sob that tore at his soul, she fled away from the table and toward the door.

Ray didn't try to chase after her. He didn't have the right.

And what would he tell her if he did catch up to her? That what she'd seen was inaccurate? The fact was he *was* the crown prince of Verdovia. And he had deceived her about it.

Greta and Frannie stood staring at him from across the room with their mouths agape. For that matter, the whole diner was staring.

"You'll make sure she's not alone tonight?" he asked neither sister in particular. They were both giving him comparably icy glares.

"You bet your royal patootie."

"Don't you worry about it," Frannie added. At least he thought it was Frannie. Not that it really mattered. All that mattered was that Mel was looked after tonight. Because of what he'd done to her.

As he left, Ray heard one of the diner patrons behind him.

"Told you this place was good," the man told his dining companion. "We got dinner and a show."

Ray was the prince. The actual heir to the crown. An heir who was due to marry a suitable, noble young woman to help him rule as king when the time came for him to take over the throne. Mel felt yet another shiver of shock and sorrow wash over her. Greta rubbed her shoulder from her position next to her on the couch. Frannie was fixing her a cup of tea in the kitchen. She didn't know what she'd do without these women.

"How could I have been so clueless, Greta?" she asked for what had to be the hundredth time. "How did I not even guess who he might have been?"

"How would you have guessed that, dearie? It's not every day a prince runs you over in the middle of a busy city street, then insists on buying you a dress to make up for it."

Mel almost laughed at her friend's summary. In truth, that accident had simply been the catalyst that had set all sorts of events in motion. Events she wasn't sure she would ever be able to recover from.

Her doorbell rang just as Frannie set a tray of cookies and steaming tea on the coffee table in front of them.

All three of them looked up in surprise. "Who could that be?"

Greta went over to look through the peephole. She turned back to them, eyes wide. "It's that fella that was with your prince. The one who was at the hospital that day."

Her prince. Only, he wasn't. And he never would be.

Mel's heart pounded at the announcement. "What could he possibly want?"

"Only one way to find out," Greta declared and then pulled open the door without so much as checking with Mel.

The gentleman stepped in and nodded to each of them in turn. He pulled an envelope out of his breast pocket. "Sal?"

He gave her a slight bow. "My full name is Saleh. Saleh Tamsen."

Okay. "Well, what can I do for you, Mr. Saleh Tamsen?"

"It's more what I'm here to do for you," he informed her. What in the world was he talking about?

"The kingdom of Verdovia is indebted to you for your recent service in pursuing a business contract. This belongs to you," he declared and then stretched his hand out in her direction.

Mel forced her mouth to close, then stood up from the couch and stepped over to him. He handed her the envelope. "What is it?"

"Please open it. I'm here to make sure you're satisfied and don't require a negotiation."

Negotiation? Curiosity piqued, Mel opened the envelope and then had to brace herself against Greta once she saw what it contained.

"Yowza!" Greta exclaimed beside her.

She held a check in her hand for an exorbitant sum. More money than she'd make waitressing for the next decade.

"I don't understand."

"A finder's fee. For bringing the prince to the Newford Inn, which he is in the process of acquiring on behalf of the king and the nation of Verdovia."

"A finder's fee? I hardly found it. I grew up near it." None of this made any kind of sense. Was this some type of inspired attempt on Ray's part to somehow make things up to her? That thought only served to spike her anger. If he was trying to buy her off, it was only adding salt to her wounds.

"Nevertheless, the check is yours."

Mel didn't need to hesitate. She stuck the check back in the envelope and handed it back to Saleh. "No, thank you."

He blinked and took a small step back. "No? I assure

you it's standard. We employ people who do the very thing you accomplished. I can also assure you it's no more or less than they receive. Take it. You've earned the fee."

She shook her head and held the envelope out until he reluctantly took it. "Nevertheless, I can't accept this. Thank you, but no."

Saleh eyed her up and down, a quizzical gleam in his eye. "Fascinating. You won't accept the money, even though you've earned it."

"No, I won't. And please tell His Royal Highness I said it's not necessary."

Saleh rubbed his chin. "You know what? Why don't you just tell him yourself? He's waiting downstairs for me to return."

CHAPTER THIRTEEN

To HIS CREDIT, Ray looked pretty miserable when he walked through her door. Though she doubted his misery could even compare to the way she was feeling inside—as if her heart had been pulled out of her chest, torn to shreds and then placed back inside.

Greta and Frannie had gone into the other room in order to give them some privacy. No doubt they had their ears tight against the wall, though, trying to hear every word.

Ray cleared his throat, standing statue still. "Mel. I didn't think you'd want to see me."

She didn't. And she did.

She gave him a small shrug. "It just didn't feel right. You know, leaving a prince waiting alone in a car. The last time I did that, at the inn, I didn't actually realize you were a prince. So you'll have to forgive me," she added in a voice dripping with sarcasm.

"You have every right to be upset."

If that wasn't the understatement of the century. "How could you, Ray?" She hated how shaky her voice sounded. "How could you have not even mentioned any of it? After all this time?"

He rubbed his forehead in a gesture so weary that it nearly had her reaching for him. She wouldn't, of course. Not now. Not ever again.

"It wasn't so straightforward. You have to understand. Things seldom are for someone in my position."

"Not even your name? You're Rayhan al Saibbi. Not Ray Alsab."

"But I am. It's an anglicized version of my name. I use it on business matters in North America quite often." He took a hesitant step toward her. "Mel, I never purposely lied to you."

"Those are merely semantics and you know it, Ray." She wanted to sob as she said the last word. She wasn't even sure what to call him now, despite what he was telling her about anglicized business aliases.

"It would have served no purpose to tell you, love. My confiding it all would have changed nothing. I'm still heir to the Verdovian throne. I still have the same duties that came with my name. None of my responsibilities would have changed. Nor would the expectations on me."

Mel had to gulp in a breath. Every word he uttered simply served to hammer another nail into her wound. She felt the telltale quiver in her chin, but forced the words. "The purpose it would have served is that I would have preferred to know all that before I went and fell in love with you!" Mel clasped a hand to her mouth as soon as she spoke the words. How could she have not contained herself? How could she have just blurted it out that way? Well, there was no taking it back now. And what did it matter anyway? What did any of it matter at this point?

Ray took a deep breath, looked down at his feet. When he tilted his head back up to gaze at her, a melancholy solace had settled in the depths of his eyes. "Then allow me to tell you the honest truth right now. All of it."

Mel wanted to run out of the room. She wasn't sure if she could handle anything he was about to tell her. Nothing would ever be the same again for her. No matter what he said right now. Her broken heart would never heal.

Ray continued, "The truth is that I completely enjoyed every moment you and I spent together. In fact, it might very well be the first time I actually spent a Christmas season having any fun whatsoever. In a different universe, a different reality, things would be very different between you and me. You are a bright light who also lights up everyone you're near. You certainly lit a light inside me. You should never forget that, Mel." He stepped over to her and rubbed the tip of his finger down her cheek in a gentle caress. "I assure you that I never will."

She couldn't hold on to her composure much longer. Mel knew she would break down right there in front of him if he said so much as one more word.

"I think you should leave now," she whispered harshly, resisting the urge to turn her cheek into his hand.

He gave her a slight tilt of his head. "As you desire."

She held back her tears right up until the door closed behind him. Then she sank to the floor and simply let them fall.

"Well, that went about as well as could be expected."

Ray slid into the passenger side of the car and waited as Saleh pulled away and into traffic.

"Your lady is definitely not a pushover, as the Americans say."

Ray didn't bother to correct his friend. Mel certainly couldn't be referred to as his lady in any way. But he so badly wished for the description to be accurate.

"Did you even convince her to take the fee?" Saleh asked.

"No. I know there's no use. If she refused it from you, she will most definitely refuse it from me."

Saleh clicked his tongue. "Such a shame. The young lady is being stubborn at her own expense and detriment."

Ray nodded absentmindedly. He couldn't fully focus on Saleh's words right now. Not when he couldn't get Mel's face out of his mind's eye. The way she'd looked when she'd told him she'd fallen in love with him. What he wouldn't give to have the luxury of saying those words back to her.

But his friend kept right on talking. "Sometimes one should simply accept what he or she is owed. Or at least be adamant about asking for what they're owed, I would think. Don't you agree?"

Ray shifted to look at the other man's profile. "Is there a point you're trying to make?"

Saleh shrugged. "I simply mean to remind you that you are a prince, Rayhan. And that your father is the current ruling king."

"I think you should have taken the money!" Greta declared and popped one of the now-cold cookies into her mouth. The whole cookie. She started chewing around it and could hardly keep her mouth closed.

Frannie turned to her sister. "Why don't you go make us tea, Greta? It's your turn."

Greta gave a grunt of protest but stood and walked to the kitchen.

"You doin' all right, kid?" Frannie asked, taking Greta's place on the couch.

Mel leaned her head against the back of the couch and released a long sigh. "I don't know, honestly. It feels like there's a constant stabbing pain around the area of my heart and that it will never feel better." She sniffled like a child who'd just fallen and skinned her knee.

"It will. Just gonna take some time, that's all." Frannie patted Mel's arm affectionately. "Tell me something?"

"Sure."

"What's makin' you hurt more? That he didn't tell you who he was? Or that you can't have him?"

Mel blinked at the question. A friend like Frannie deserved complete honesty. Even if the question was just now forcing her to be honest with herself.

"I think you know the answer to that," she replied in a low, wobbly voice. Now that she was actually giving it some thought, she realized a crucial point: it was one thing when there had still been a chance for her and Ray, regardless of how miniscule. When she thought he was a businessman who might change his mind and return to the States because he couldn't bear to live without her. But he was a prince. Who had to marry someone worthy of one. Someone who was the polar opposite of a divorced, broke waitress who now lived in South Boston. It was almost exactly how her parents' relationship had started out. Only without the happy ending and loving marriage they'd shared.

"You didn't tell him that," Frannie declared. "You didn't even ask him how he felt. Don't you think you deserved to know? From his own mouth and in his own words, I mean?"

Mel closed her eyes. This conversation was making her think too hard about things she just wanted to forget. In fact, thinking at all simply made the hurt worse. "Well, as he pointed out himself, Frannie, none of it would have made any sort of difference." She knew her voice had taken on a snarky tone, but she couldn't summon the will to care. Hopefully the older woman would just drop the subject.

No such luck. Frannie let out a loud sigh. "Not so sure about that. Now, I may be old but I can count to two."

Mel gave her friend a confused look. "Is that some sort of South Boston anecdote?"

"All I'm saying is there appears to be at least two instances in your adult life where you didn't come out and ask for what was rightfully yours. Damn the consequences."

Mel couldn't be hearing this right. "You can't be including my ex-husband."

"Oh, but I am."

"Are you suggesting that I shouldn't have walked away from Eric? That I should have fought for him, despite his betrayal?" The question was a ridiculous one. She'd sooner have walked through the tundra in bare feet than give that man a second chance. Especially now, after these past few days with Ray.

Frannie waved her hand dismissively. "Oh, great heavens, no. Getting away from that scoundrel was the best thing that could have happened to you."

"Then what?"

Frannie studied her face. "He took your money, dear. Just took it and walked away with another woman."

"I gave him that money, Frannie. It was my foolish mistake."

"Your biggest mistake was trusting that he would honor his vows and his commitment. He didn't."

Of course, the older woman had a valid point. But this train of conversation was doing nothing for her. She loved both Frannie and Greta, and she was beyond grateful for all the support and affection they'd consistently shown her. But Frannie had no idea what it was like to come home one day and find that your husband wouldn't be returning. That he'd found someone else, another woman he preferred over you. Frannie was a widow, whose husband had adored her right up until he'd taken his last breath. They'd had an idyllic marriage, much like her own parents'. The type of union that was sure to elude Mel, given her track record with men so far.

"Well, it just so happens I did ask Eric for the money back. At least some of it." Though she wasn't going to admit to her friend that it had been a half-hearted effort that was meant more to just get Eric off the phone the other night. And to make sure he didn't start harboring any illusions about the two of them reuniting in any way.

But Frannie had her figured out pretty well. Her next words confirmed it. "But you're not really going to fight for it, are you?"

Mel didn't bother to answer. She couldn't even think about Eric or what he owed her right now. Her thoughts were fully centered on Ray and the hurt of his betrayal.

"It's a cliché, but it's true," Frannie went on. "Some things are worth fighting for."

Mel clenched her hands. "And some fights are hardly worth it. They leave you bloodied and bruised with nothing to show for it."

"You might be right," Frannie admitted. "Matters of love can be impossible to predict, regardless of the circumstances. I'm just saying you should at least fight for what belongs to you." She nodded toward the door, as if Ray had just this instant walked out, rather than over two hours ago.

"And that man's heart belongs to you."

CHAPTER FOURTEEN

RAY COULDN'T REMEMBER the last time he'd tried to sleep in. He wasn't terribly good at it. But he felt zero incentive to get out of bed this morning. For the past few days, he'd awoken each morning with the prospect of seeing or at least speaking with Mel.

That wasn't the case today. And wouldn't be the case from now on. Hard to believe just how much he would miss something he'd only experienced for a short while.

His cell phone rang and his father's number flashed on the screen. He had half a mind to ignore it but couldn't quite bring himself to do so. In all fairness, he was way past the point where he owed the king a status report.

He picked up the phone. "Hello, Father."

"Good morning, son."

"Morning."

"Is there anything you'd like to tell me?"

So it was clear his father had heard something. Ray rolled onto his back with the phone at his ear. "Which tabloid should I be looking at?"

"Take your pick," his father answered. "There's some American man who claims to have been at something known as a 'jamboree,' where you were in attendance. Apparently, he took plenty of photos and is now selling them to whoever will pay."

Ray pinched the bridge of his nose. "I apologize, Your Majesty. I was conducting myself with the utmost discretion. But I failed to anticipate an unexpected variable."

"I see. I hope you've resolved the matter with the young lady in question."

"I'm working on it, sir."

His father paused for several beats before continuing, "You do realize the depth of your responsibilities to Verdovia, don't you, Rayhan? Don't lose sight of who you are. Loose ends will not be tolerated, son."

Ray felt a bolt of anger settle in his core. The way his father referred to Mel as a loose end had him clenching the phone tight in his hand.

He hadn't wanted to do this over the phone, but he'd come to a few decisions over the past few days. Decisions he wasn't ready to back away from.

"With all the respect you're due, Your Majesty, I feel compelled to argue that the lady in question is far from a loose end."

The king's sharp intake of breath was audible across the line. Ray could clearly picture him frowning into the phone with disappointment. So be it.

"I'm not sure what that means, son. Nor, frankly, do I care. I simply ask that you remain mindful of who you are and of your duties."

Ray took a deep, steadying breath. He'd been hoping to wrap things up here and have this conversation with his father in person. But fate appeared to be forcing his hand.

"Since we're discussing this now, Father, I wondered if we might have something of a conversation regarding duty and responsibility to the sovereign."

Silence once again. Ray couldn't remember a time

he had tested the king's patience in such a manner. Nor his authority.

"What kind of conversation? What exactly is it you would like to communicate with me about responsibility and your honor-bound duties as prince?"

His father was throwing his words out as a challenge. Normally Ray would have been the dutiful, obedient son and simply acquiesced. But not this time. This time he felt the stakes too deeply.

"Thank you for asking, sir," Ray replied in his sincerest voice. "I'm glad to have an opportunity to explain."

His father sighed loudly once again. "If you must."

"I've been going over some numbers, sir."

"Numbers? What kind of numbers exactly?"

"I've been looking at our nation's holdings and overall wealth and how it impacts our citizens. Particularly since the time you yourself took over the throne. Followed by the growth experienced once I graduated university and began working for the royal house as a capitalist."

"And?" his father prompted. He sounded much less annoyed, less irritated. The discussion about figures and wealth had certainly gained his attention, just as Ray had known it would.

"And a simple analysis easily shows that the country has prospered very nicely since you started your reign, sir. And it continued that growth once I started acquiring investments on behalf of Verdovia. As a result, we've seen increased exports, higher wages overall for our citizens and extensions of most social benefits."

His father grunted, a sure sign that he was impressed. "Go on. Is there a point to all of this, son?"

"A simple point, sir. Maybe our duty shouldn't need to go any further than such considerations—to further the quality of life for our citizens and nationals. And that maybe we even owe a duty to ourselves as well, to ensure our own fulfillment and happiness. Despite being members of the royal house of al Saibbi."

Ray wouldn't blame her if she didn't open the door. He'd texted her last night to say he wanted to stop by this morning. She hadn't replied. Well, he was here anyway. On the off chance that she would give him one more opportunity and agree to see him.

The possibility of that seemed to lower with each passing second as he braced himself against the blowing wind, while standing on the concrete stoop outside her door.

He was just about to give up and turn around when he heard shuffling footsteps from the other side of the wood. Slowly, the lock unlatched and Mel opened the door.

She stepped aside to let him in.

"Thank you for seeing me, Mel. I know it's short notice."

She motioned toward the sofa in the center of the room. "I just brewed a pot of coffee. Can I get you some?"

"No. Thank you. I won't take up much of your time."

She walked over to the love seat across the sofa and sat as well, pulling her feet underneath her. Ray took a moment to study her. She looked weary, subdued. He saw no hint of the exuberant, playful woman he'd got a chance to know over the past week. He had no one but himself to blame for that.

"So you said you wanted to talk about a business matter? Do you have questions about the Newford Inn? If so, you could have called Myrna directly."

He shook his head. "This business matter involves you directly."

Her eyes scanned his face. "I hope you're not back to

offer me another check. I told your associate I'm not interested in taking your money. Not when I didn't really do anything to earn it."

Ray leaned forward, braced his arms on his knees. "Well, we'll have to agree to disagree about whether you earned that money or not. But that's not why I'm here."

"Then why?"

"To put it simply—I'd like to offer you a position."

Mel's eyes narrowed on him, her gaze moving over his face. "Come again? Aren't you a royal prince, who'll eventually become king? What kind of position would someone like that offer a waitress?"

It was a valid question. "I am. The royal house is the largest employer in Verdovia. And a good chunk of the surrounding nations, in fact."

"Okay. What's that got to do with me? I'm a waitress in a diner."

At that comment, he wanted to take her by the shoulders and give her a mild shake. She was so much more than that.

"I mentioned to you earlier, that day at the diner, that we were looking to purchase several New England inns and B and Bs. I'd like to charge you with that. Your official title would be project manager."

Mel inhaled deeply and looked off to the side. "You're offering me a job? Is that it?"

He nodded. "Yes, I think you'd be perfect for it. You know the way these establishments operate and you know New England. The first part will be to get the Newford Inn purchased and renovated. That will give you a chance to slowly get your feet wet. What better way to ease into the job?"

When she returned her gaze to his face, a hardened

glint appeared in her eyes. "It sounds ideal on the surface."

"But?"

"But I'm not sure what to tell you, Ray. What if you'd
never accidentally met me that day? Would I be the person you would think of to fill such a position?"

Ray gave her a small shrug. "It's a moot point, isn't
it? The fact that we met is the only reason these deals
are happening."

"I guess there's a certain logic in that," she agreed.

He pressed his case further. "Why worry about what-
ifs? I need someone to assist with these acquisitions, and
I think you'd do well."

She chewed the inside of her lip, clearly turning the
matter over in her mind.

"Please, just think about it, Mel."

"Sure," she said and stood. "I'll think about it."

Something in her tone and facial expression told him
she was simply humoring him. But he'd done what he
could.

She walked him to the door.

He turned to her before she could open it. "Mel, please
understand. Cultural changes don't happen quickly. Especially in a country so small and so set in its ways."

"You don't have to explain, Ray. I understand the reality of it all. You're here to offer me the only thing you
feel you can. A job in your employ."

Damn it, when she put it that way…

"Thank you for stopping by. I promise to give your
proposal a lot of consideration." She cracked an ironic
smile that didn't quite reach her eyes. "After all, it's not
like I'm all that great a waitress."

Mel watched through the small slit in her curtains as
Ray walked down her front steps to the vehicle wait-

ing for him outside. He hesitated before pulling the car door open and turned to stare at her building. It would be so easy to lift the window and yell at him to wait. She wanted to run out to him before he could drive away, to accept his offer, to tell him she'd take anything he was willing to give her.

But the self-preserving part of her prevailed and she forced herself to stay still where she was. Eventually, Ray got in and his car pulled away and drove off. She didn't even have any tears left; she was all cried out. In hindsight, she had to admit to herself that none of this was Ray's doing. She was responsible for every last bit of it.

Melinda Osmon alone was responsible for not guarding her heart, for somehow managing to fall for a man so far out of her league, she wasn't even in the same stratosphere. To think, she'd believed him to be out of reach when she knew him as a businessman. Turned out he was a real live prince.

He'd had a point when he'd told her that he'd never lied to her outright. He'd never led her on, never behaved inappropriately in any way.

And he'd just shown up at her apartment with the offer of a job opportunity because he knew she was disappointed and defeated.

Mel leaned back against the window, then sank to her knees.

No. She had no one to blame but herself for all of it.

So now there was only one question that needed to be answered. What was she going to do about it? A part of her wanted so badly to take what she could get. To do anything she could to at least inhabit a spot in his orbit, however insignificant.

But that would destroy her. She wasn't wired that way. To have to watch him from a distance as he performed the duties of the throne, as he went about the business of being king one day.

As he committed himself to another woman.

And what of much later? Eventually, he would start a family with the lucky lady who ended up snaring him. Mel could never watch him become a father to someone else's children without shattering inside. Bad enough she would have to see it all from a distance.

Even the mere thought of it sent a stab of pain through her heart. She wouldn't survive having to watch it all from a front-row seat.

She knew Ray thought he'd found a workable solution. He'd offered her the only thing he could.

It just simply wasn't enough.

Ray sat staring at the same column of numbers he'd been staring at for the past twenty minutes before pushing the laptop away with frustration. He'd never had so much trouble focusing.

But right now, all he could think about was if he'd done the right thing by offering Mel a job. He might very well have crossed a line. But the alternative had been to do nothing, to walk out of her life completely. At least as an employee of Verdovia's royal house, he could be confident that she was being taken care of, that she had the backing of his family name and that of his nation. It was the best he could do until he figured out what to do about everything else.

One thing was certain. He wasn't going to go along with any kind of sham engagement. If there was anything he'd learned during these past few days in the States, it was that he was unquestionably not ready. If that meant upsetting the council, the king and even the constituency, then so be it.

The sharp ring of the hotel phone pulled him out of his reverie. The front desk was calling to inform him there was some sort of package for him that they would bring up if it was a convenient time. Within moments of him accepting, a knock sounded on the door.

The bellhop handed him a small cardboard box. Probably some type of promotional material from the various endeavors he was currently involved in. He was ready to toss it aside when the return address caught his eye.

Mel had sent him something.

With shaky fingers, he pulled the cardboard apart. He couldn't even begin to guess what the item might be. She still hadn't given him any kind of answer about the job.

The box contained a lush velvet satchel. He reached inside the bag and pulled out some type of glass figurine. A note was tied to it with a red satin ribbon, almost the identical color of the dress she'd worn the night of the mayor's charity ball. He carefully unwrapped the bow to remove the item.

And his breath caught in his throat.

A blown-glass sculpture of a couple dancing. It wasn't quite a replica of the one made of ice they'd seen in the town square after the storm. She'd put her own creative spin on it. This couple was wrapped in a tighter embrace, heads closer together.

Her talent blew him away. She'd somehow captured a singular moment in time when they were on the dance floor together, a treasured moment he remembered vividly.

He gently fingered the smooth surface with his thumb before straightening out her note to read it.

Ray,
Though I can't bring myself to accept your offer,
I hope that you'll accept this small gift from me.
I didn't realize while creating it that it was meant

for you, but there is no doubt in my mind now that you were the intended recipient all along.

I hope it serves as a cherished souvenir to help you to remember.

As I will never forget.

M

Ray gently set the figurine and the note on the desk and then walked over to the corner standing bar to pour himself a stiff drink. After swallowing it in one swig, he viciously launched the tumbler against the wall with all the anger and frustration pulsing through his whole being.

It did nothing to ease his fury.

CHAPTER FIFTEEN

RAY STILL HADN'T cleaned up the broken glass by the time room service showed up the next morning with his coffee tray. The server took a lingering look at the mess but wisely asked no questions.

"I'll get Housekeeping to clean that up for you, sir," the man informed him as Ray signed off on a tip.

"There's no rush. It can wait until their regular rounds."

"Yes, sir."

So he was surprised when there came another knock on the door in less than twenty minutes.

Ray walked to the door and yanked it open. "I said there was no hur—"

But it wasn't a hotel employee standing on the other side. Far from it.

"Mother? Father? What are you two doing here?"

His mother lifted an elegant eyebrow. "Aren't you going to invite us in, darling?"

Ray blinked the shock out of his eyes and stepped aside. "I apologize. Please, come in."

The queen gave him an affectionate peck on the cheek as she entered, while the king acknowledged him with a nod.

He spoke after entering the room. "Your mother grew

quite restless with the girls away on their performance tour of Europe and you here in the States. She wanted to surprise you. So, surprise."

That it certainly was.

"How are you, dear?" his mother wanted to know. "You look a little ragged. Have you been getting enough sleep?"

Ray couldn't help but smile. Shelba al Saibbi might be a queen, but first and foremost she was a mother.

"I'm fine, Mother."

She didn't look convinced. "Really?"

"Really. But I can't help but think there must be more to this visit than your boredom or a simple desire to spring a surprise on your son." He looked from one to the other, waiting for a response.

"Very well," his mother began. "Your father has something he needs to discuss with you. After giving the matter much thought."

The king motioned to the one of the leather chairs around the working desk. Ray waited until his father sat down before taking a seat himself. The queen stood behind her husband, placing both hands on his shoulders.

"What's this about, Your Majesty?"

"Saleh called me a couple of days ago," his father began. "He wanted to make sure I was aware of certain happenings since you've arrived in the US."

Ray felt a throb in his temple. Why, the little snitching…

His mother guessed where his thoughts were headed. "He did it for your own good, dear. He's been very concerned about you, it seems."

"He needn't have been."

"Nevertheless, he called and we're here."

"Does this have anything to do with your impending engagement?" his father asked.

Ray bolted out of the chair, his patience stretched taut beyond its limits. Perhaps Saleh was right to be concerned about him. He'd never so much as raised his voice around his parents. "How can there be an engagement when I don't even really know the women I'm supposed to choose from? How can I simply tie myself to someone and simply hope that I grow fond of them later? What if it doesn't work out that way?" He took a deep breath before looking his father straight in the eye and continuing, "I can't do it. I'm sorry. I can't go forward with it. Even if means Councilman Riza continues to rabble-rouse, or that Verdovia no longer has the specter of a royal engagement to distract itself with."

"And what of your mother?" the king asked quietly, in a low, menacing voice.

Ray tried not to wince at the pang of guilt that shot through his chest. "Mother, I'm sorry. Maybe we can hire some more assistants to help you with your official duties. I can even take over of the international visits myself. But I'm simply not ready to declare anyone a princess. I'm just now starting to figure out what type of relationship I might enjoy, the kind of woman I might want to spend my days with. It's not anyone back in Verdovia, I'm afraid."

His father stared at him in stunned silence. But to his utter shock, his mother's response was a wide, knowing grin.

"Well, goodness. You should have just told us that you've met someone."

Ray blinked at her. How could she possibly know that? Saleh might have called his parents out of concern, but Ray knew the other man would have never betrayed that much of a confidence.

"Is that so?" his father demanded to know. "Is all this

turmoil because of that woman you were photographed dancing with?"

Ray forced himself to contain his ire. Not only were these people his parents, they were also his king and queen. "That woman's name is Melinda Osmon. And she happens to be the most dynamic, the most intriguing young lady I've ever met."

"I see." His father ran a hand down his face. "Is that your final say, then?"

Ray nodded. "I'm afraid so."

"You do realize that this will throw the whole country into a tailspin. Entire industries have been initiated based on speculation of an upcoming royal engagement and eventual wedding. Also, Councilman Riza will pounce on this as a clear and damning example of the royal family disappointing the people of Verdovia. A royal family he believes serves no real purpose and which is part of a system he believes should be abolished."

Ray swallowed and nodded. "I accept the consequences fully."

His mother stepped around the table to face her husband. "Farood, dear. You must think this through. We cannot have our only son bear the full brunt of this simply because he has no desire to be engaged. And we certainly can't have him miserable upon his return home."

She turned back to her son. "Do not worry about me, I can handle my duties just fine. Frankly, I'm getting a bit tired of all the fuss over my health. I'm not a fragile little doll that needs anyone's constant concern," she bit out, followed by a glare in her husband's direction.

Ray couldn't hide his smile. "I believe I've come across stone blocks more fragile than you are, Mother."

The queen reached over and gave her son an affectionate pat. "I believe there's someone you need to go see, no?" She indicated her husband with a tilt of her head. "Do not worry about what this one will have to say about it."

For several moments, none of them spoke. A thick tension filled the air. Ray clenched his hands at his sides. The king had never been challenged quite so completely before. But he refused to back down.

It was what the Americans liked to call a "game of chicken." Finally, his father threw his hands up in exasperation. "I don't know what the two of you expect me to do about any of this."

The queen lifted her chin. "May I remind you, dear, that you are in fact the king?"

The statement echoed what Saleh had said to him all those nights ago.

His mother then added in a clipped tone, "I'm sure you'll think of something."

Mel tried not to turn her nose at the morning's breakfast special as she carried it out to the latest customer to order it. Lobster-and-cheese omelet. It appeared to be a big hit among the regulars, but for the life of her, she couldn't fathom why.

The holiday shoppers supplied a steady flow of patrons into the diner, despite the wintry cold. The forecasters were predicting one of the whitest Christmases on record. Though she'd be remembering this year's holiday herself for entirely different reasons. How would she ever cope with the Christmas season ever again when everything about it would forever remind her of her prince?

The door opened as several more customers entered, bringing with them a brisk gust of December wind and a good amount of snow on their covered boots and coats.

She nearly dropped the plates she was carrying as she

realized one of those customers happened to be a hand-some, snow-covered royal.

Mel couldn't help her first reaction upon seeing him. Though she hadn't forgotten the hurt and anguish of those few days, she'd realized she missed him. Deeply. She set her load down quickly in front of the diners before making a complete mess. Then she blinked to make sure she wasn't simply seeing what her heart so desperately wanted to see. But it really was him. He really was here.

Ray walked up to her with a smile. "Hey."

"Hey, yourself."

He peeled his leather gloves off as he spoke. "So I was hoping you could help me order an authentic New England breakfast. Any recommendations?"

She laughed, though she could barely hear him over the pounding in her ears. "Definitely not the day's special."

He tapped her playfully on the nose. "Should you be discouraging people from ordering that? You're right, you're not that great a waitress."

"What are you doing here, Ray? I thought you'd be heading back home. Myrna mentioned that the deal has already been settled and signed."

"I came to offer you a proposition."

Mel's heart sank. The happiness she'd felt just a few short moments ago fled like an elusive doe. He was simply here to make her some other kind of job offer.

"I'm afraid I'm still not interested," she told him in a shaky voice. "I should get back to work."

He took her by the arm before she could turn away. The touch of his hand on her skin set her soul on fire. She'd give anything to go back to the morning when she'd woken up in his arms at the inn. And to somehow suspend that moment forever in time.

She tried to quell the shaking in the pit of her stomach. Seeing him again was wreaking havoc on her equilibrium. But she refused to accept his crumbs. She'd made that mistake once already to avoid being alone, and she wouldn't do it again. Not even for this man.

"I can't do it, Ray. Please don't ask me to work for you again. I don't want your job opportunity."

He steadfastly held on to her arm. "Don't you want to hear what it is first?" he asked with a tease in his voice.

Something about the lightness in his tone and the twinkle in his dark eyes gave her pause. Ray was up to something.

"All right."

He tapped the finger of his free hand against his temple. "I've come up with it completely myself. A brand-new position, which involves a lot of travel. You'll be accompanying a certain royal member of Verdovia to various functions and events throughout the world. Maybe even a holiday ball or two."

He couldn't mean… She wouldn't allow herself to hope. Could she? "Is that so?"

He nodded with a grin. "Definitely."

Oh, yeah, he was definitely up to something. "What else?" she prompted, now unable to keep the excitement out of her voice. Was he really here to say he wanted to spend time with her? That he wanted to be with her? Or was it possible that she had not actually woken up yet this morning and was still in the midst of the most wonderful dream.

Ray rubbed his chin. "I almost forgot. There'll be a lot of this—" Before she could guess what he meant, he pulled her to him and took her lips with his own. The world stood still. Her hands moved up to his shoulders as she savored the taste of him. It had been so long.

She couldn't tear herself away, though a diner full of people had to be watching them. This was all she'd been able to think about since the moment she'd first laid eyes on him on that Boston street.

Someone behind them whistled as another started a steady clap. Mel knew Greta and Frannie had to be the initiators of the cheers, but pretty soon the whole diner had joined in.

In response, Ray finally pulled away with a small chuckle and then twirled her around in a mini waltz around one of the empty tables in the center of the room.

"I miss dancing with you," he whispered against her ear and sent her heart near to bursting with joy.

The applause grew even louder. Catcalls and whistles loudly filled the air. But she could hardly hear any of it over the joyous pounding of her heart.

Ray dipped Mel in his arms in an elaborate ending to their mini waltz and gave her another quick kiss on the lips.

He turned to where Frannie and Greta stood over by the counter, grinning from ear to ear. He gave them both a small nod, which they each returned with an exaggerated curtsy that almost had Greta toppling over.

"If it's not all that busy, would you mind if my lady here takes the rest of the day off?"

Their answer was a loud, resounding "Yes," which was said in unison.

Mel laughed in his arms as he straightened, bringing her back up with him.

"Get your coat and come with me before I have to carry you out of here."

Behind them, Ray heard a voice that sounded vaguely

familiar. "I'm telling you, these guys should sell tickets. It's better than going to the movies."

The man was right. This was so much better than any movie. And Ray knew without a doubt there'd be a happy ending.

EPILOGUE

"THOSE TWO MAKE for the most unconventional brides-maids in the history of weddings," Ray said, laughing, motioning across the room to where Greta and Frannie sat with his two sisters at the bridesmaids' table.

Mel returned his chuckle as she took in the sight of the four of them.

"One would think those four have known each other for years."

"They certainly don't seem to mind the vast age difference," Mel added with a laugh of her own.

Ray took her hand in his on top of the table and rubbed his thumb along the inside of her palm. A ripple of arousal ran over her skin and she had to suck in a breath at her instant reaction. The merest touch still set her on fire, even after all these months together.

"They're pretty unconventional in lots of ways," she said with a smile, still trying to ignore the fluttering in her chest that was only getting stronger as Ray continued his soft caress of her hand.

Verdovia's version of a rehearsal dinner was certainly a grand affair, a sight straight out of a fairy tale—with a string quartet, tables loaded with extravagant foods and desserts, and even a champagne fountain. In fact, Mel felt like her whole life had turned into one big fantasy. She was actually sitting at a table with her fiancé, the crown prince, as his parents, the king and queen, sat beaming on either side of them.

Mel cast a glance at her future mother-in-law, who returned her smile with a wide one of her own. She looked the perfect picture of health and vibrancy. The king was equally fit and formidable. It didn't look like she and Ray would be ascending any throne anytime soon. A fact she was very grateful for. No one would ever be able to replace her real parents, Mel knew. But her future in-laws had so far shown her nothing but true affection and kindness. In fact, the whole country had received her with enthusiasm and acceptance—a true testament to the regard they felt for their prince and the royal family as a whole. And all despite Mel's utter unpreparedness for the rather bright proverbial spotlight she'd suddenly found herself in once her and Ray's engagement had been announced to the world.

Her fiancé pulled her out of her thoughts by placing a small kiss on the inside of her wrist. A sensation of pure longing gripped her core.

"I can't wait to be alone with you," he told her.

"Is that so?" she asked with a teasing grin. "What did you have in mind?"

He winked at her. "To dance with you, of course."

Mel gave in to the urge to rest her head against his strong shoulder. "There's no one else I'd rather dance with," she said, her joy almost too much to contain.

"And there's no one else I'd rather call my wife."

His words reminded her that the true fantasy had nothing to do with the myriad of parties being held for them over the next several weeks or even the extravagant wedding ceremony currently being planned. All that mattered was the complete and unfettered love she felt for this man.

Her husband-to-be was a prince in many more ways than one.

* * * * *

A STONECREEK CHRISTMAS REUNION

MICHELLE MAJOR

To the True Love readers—
thank you for inviting me into your reading lives.
It's a great honour.

Chapter One

"More lights."

Maggie Spencer surveyed the work taking place in the town square, a mix of confidence and anxiety spiraling through her. Her small town of Stonecreek, Oregon, was about to be thrust into the national spotlight.

Or at least the social media spotlight. LiveSoft, a wildly successful software and mobile app development company, was searching for a new location for its company headquarters. The over-the-top lifestyle in Los Angeles, their current location, clashed with the app's branding and corporate culture. LiveSoft was all about using technology to slow down and simplify life. LA wasn't a great place for that.

So in conjunction with a request for proposals, the company had launched a marketing campaign during which its social media followers would help determine which Pacific Northwest city would be the best fit for a company move.

As Stonecreek's recently reelected mayor, Maggie was determined to make sure her town was chosen and had been working around the clock since the election to that end. Stonecreek had arrived late to the proverbial party, finding out about the proposal deadline only a week before submissions were due. But she'd been thrilled to learn just before Thanksgiving that her town had been short-listed by the company's CEO.

And why not? Stonecreek was only an hour south of Portland and she liked to think the community boasted the potential workforce, opportunity for growth and work-life balance LiveSoft had outlined in their preferences. The company was best known for its mobile app that claimed to "balance internal life with the outer world." Of course, she had yet to download the app herself, but it was on her to-do list along with a million other items.

"We've already added two dozen extra strands." Jacob Snow, head of the town's maintenance department, had been coordinating the town's holiday decorations for the past two weeks. "At this rate you're going to be able to see this place from the moon."

"There's no such thing as too festive," Maggie told him.

"You ever seen that National Lampoon Christmas movie?" Jacob asked with a soft chuckle. "I feel like Clark Griswold out here."

Maggie frowned, looking around at all the activity with fresh eyes. The entire town square was draped with lights while a huge, elaborately decorated fir tree stood in the center of the park waiting for tonight's tree-lighting ceremony. An almost fifteen-foot tall menorah had been given pride of place in front of the main archway into the square, ready to be lit on each of Chanukah's eight nights. Wreaths had been draped over every lamppost and nearly life-size nutcrackers lined the main path. In addition to a makeshift stable that had been built to house the nativity-scene animals, there was a display of Santa riding his sleigh, complete with reindeer painted by the high school's art department, and all the planters situated through the park burst with oversize ornaments and colorful dreidels.

"Oh, my." She clasped a hand to her chest when her heart started beating out of control. "Is it too much? Our theme is winter wonderland. I don't want it to be gaudy. Are we trying too hard? It has to look effortless, like the holidays in a TV movie. Charming and quaint, not over-the-top. Should we take down some of the lights? What about the live manger? I knew those goats would cause trouble."

Jacob stared at her for several seconds then climbed down from the ladder. He'd been working for the town since Maggie was a girl, hired when her grandmother had been mayor.

He'd never married and rarely dated as far as Maggie knew. In fact, Jacob Snow was a bit of a mystery, keeping the town running smoothly but rarely participating in the myriad of festivals and fairs that delineated the seasons in Stonecreek throughout the year. Other than his silver-white hair, he looked very much like he had twenty years ago when Maggie first met him.

"Slow down. It will be beautiful," he said, awkwardly patting her shoulder like he knew she needed comfort but wasn't sure how to offer it. "Like it always is."

"This year is different," Maggie whispered. "It matters more."

"Because of that new company thinking of coming here?" He reached for another strand of lights.

She nodded. "LiveSoft is one of the fastest-growing technology companies in the region. It would mean new jobs and increased tax revenue for the town. We could fund programs for impacted kids in the school district. Some of those maintenance requests you've put in would be approved."

"Like a new snowplow?" he suggested with a wink.

"Exactly." She drew in a slow breath. "I'm freaking out."

Jacob smiled. "I hadn't noticed."

"There's no reason for me to freak out, right?"

"None at all."

"But there's so much I want to do for Stonecreek. Now that I'm mayor—"

"You've been the mayor for two years," he reminded her. "You were *re*elected by a landslide last month."

She sighed. "Yes, but it feels different now. I feel like the town elected me and not Vivian Spencer's granddaughter. It changes everything."

Maggie had finally stepped out from behind the long shadow her grandmother cast. The Spencers had been one of Stonecreek's most powerful families since the town was founded in the mid–eighteen hundreds. But Maggie's grandma had taken their leadership to a whole new level. As soon as Grammy married into the family, she'd made it her mission to ensure the Spencer name was synonymous with Stonecreek.

Grammy had been the biggest force in Maggie's life, especially after she'd stepped in to help when Maggie's mother died eleven years ago. Maggie owed Grammy so much—they all did—but she also wanted a chance to make her own mark on the town. She loved this community.

Although she'd won the election, the months leading up to it had been tumultuous to say the least. Her opponent had been Jason Stone, cousin of her ex-fiancé Trevor who she'd left at the altar last spring when she'd discovered he'd been cheating on her.

As if that didn't complicate things enough, she'd then fallen for Trevor's brother Griffin, the black-sheep of the Stone family, who'd returned to town to work on the vineyard the family owned and operated outside town. When Griffin broke her heart a little over a month ago, it had made her question everything.

Everything except her dedication to the town, which was why she had to do an amazing job as mayor. Her work was everything to her now. She might be a dismal failure at love, but she could succeed at this.

"Maybe you're the one who's changed," Jacob told her gently. "I've known you since you were a wee girl, Ms. Maggie. You were always the apple of your grandmother's eye. She wouldn't have encouraged you the way she did if she didn't think you could handle it. I see how hard you're working for the town. Everyone around here does, and we appreciate it."

"Thanks, Jacob." Emotion clogged Maggie's throat. "I'm going to go check on Dora Gianelli at the bakery. It's the first business we're spotlighting as part of the campaign. What says holidays more than hot chocolate and a Christmas cookie?"

"Cocktail weenies and a beer?" he suggested.

She nudged his arm, the tension in her shoulders relaxing as she grinned. "When are you going to come to Christmas with our family? There's plenty of room."

"Vivian likes to keep things private," he said, scrubbing a hand over his whiskered jaw.

"Grammy would love to have you join us," Maggie countered, even though she'd never discussed the matter with her grandmother.

"She never mentioned it to me."

Maggie rolled her eyes. "She gets busy around this time of year. I'm not going to force you, but keep it in mind, okay?"

"Okay," he agreed. "I've got one more string of lights to hang." He held up a hand when she opened her mouth to comment. "Trust me on this. One more strand will be the perfect amount."

She nodded. "I'll see you later tonight at the tree lighting."

"The whole town will be here to make you look good." He rubbed a hand over his jaw once more. "I may even shave for the occasion."

She leaned in and bussed him on the cheek. "I'm lucky to have you."

Maggie watched for another minute as he climbed the ladder, feeling marginally better that she could accomplish her goal. There was no reason LiveSoft wouldn't want to come to Stonecreek. Nestled in the heart of Central Oregon's Willamette Valley, the town had great restaurants, outdoor activities, a fantastic school system and tight-knit community.

Groaning softly, Maggie realized she was becoming a bit too obsessed with work when even her internal thoughts made her sound like a billboard for the town.

She turned to head across the town square toward the bakery only to find Griffin Stone blocking her path.

He looked as handsome as ever, the bright afternoon sunlight shining off his dark blond hair. He wore a flannel button-down, faded jeans and work boots. She couldn't see his green eyes because of the sunglasses perched on his nose, but the set of his jaw and the way his broad shoulders remained rigid told her this wasn't going to be an easy conversation.

Fine. Maggie wasn't in the mood for easy when it came to Griffin. She'd had plenty of time to get over him. She *was* over him so she could certainly manage a few words without losing her mind.

"I'm busy," she said and started down the path that would take her out the west gate of the town square. Stonecreek Sweets was on the north end, but she told herself she needed the exercise walking around the block would give her. Just because she *could* handle talking to Griffin didn't mean she wanted to handle it.

"You can't avoid me forever," came his rough reply from behind her.

"I can try," she said over her shoulder and quickened her pace. It didn't matter. Griffin caught up with her in a few long strides.

"Maggie, stop." He reached for her arm, but she yanked away.

"Do. Not. Touch. Me."

He held up his hands, palms out. "Fine. Okay. Sorry."

Her eyes narrowed.

"I'm so sorry," he whispered.

"It's fine," she lied.

"I called you." He ran a hand through his hair, looking past her. "Eventually."

She sniffed. "I blocked your number. Take a hint."

"This isn't you," he said, glancing back at her.

"Oh, yes," she shot back. "This is me. You know how I'm sure of that? Because I never left. I've been here the whole time. Some of us don't have the luxury to take off when things get too real, Griffin."

"That's not what happened. It's complica—"

"Don't say *complicated*. That word is off-limits with us," she told him. "Along with apologies. Remember?"

"I remember everything."

Despite her resolve to hate this man, his words felt like a caress against her skin, a secret promise and one she knew he could fulfill with remarkable skill. All the more reason to hold tight to her willpower.

"Go away," she said, not bothering to try to hide

the pain from her voice. Let him understand he hurt her. That was all on him.

He sighed. "Give me a chance to explain."

"I don't need an explanation. You ran off to your ex-girlfriend. Sends a pretty clear message, you know?"

"I called," he repeated.

"Almost two weeks after you left."

"Things were crazy and I—"

"You said you loved me," she blurted, and it felt like sandpaper coated her throat. "Here's some advice for next time. Don't say 'I love you' if it doesn't mean anything." She took a step closer to him, ignoring the tears that sprang to her eyes. So much for being unaffected. Maybe what she needed to truly move on was to get this out of her system. "If you love someone, you tell them everything. Not weeks later or when it's convenient. I don't know what happened between you and Cassie, and I don't care. Go to her again if that's what she needs. We're finished, Griffin."

"She died."

Maggie drew in a sharp breath and watched as Griffin pulled off his sunglasses and tucked them into his shirt pocket. His eyes were sad, almost hollow, and darn it all if she didn't want to reach out to him, offer whatever comfort she could.

But no. It was too late for that.

"I'm sorry," she said softly. "I know you loved her."

"I cared about her," he corrected. "I *love* you."

She shook her head. "Not in the way I needed you to."

There was the truth of it, and when he took a small step back like she'd hit him, she knew he felt the impact as much as she did.

He lifted a hand and used his thumb to wipe a stray tear from her cheek.

"Are you staying in Stonecreek?" she asked, because she had to know.

"I'm not sure yet." He cleared his throat. "There are extenuating circumstances."

She huffed out a humorless laugh. "I imagine one might even call them 'complications.'"

"One might," he conceded with a nod.

"Good luck with wherever life takes you." It was difficult to get the words out, but she even managed a small half smile to go with them.

"This can't be the end."

"We were naive to think it ever would have worked out between us."

He shook his head. "You know that's not true. Maggie, please."

"Please what, Griffin?" She threw up her hands. "What exactly do you want from me at this point?"

"I want another chance."

"No." She fisted her hands at her sides, her fingernails digging into the fleshy center of each palm until it hurt. Physical pain to mask another emotional hit. Of course, a part of her wanted to give in. It would be so easy. She could take one step forward and be in his arms again.

Except he was still holding back. She didn't know what it was or understand why, but she could almost see the barrier that surrounded him.

"I've got to go," she told him. "The tree lighting is tonight and it's a big deal this year."

"I heard about LiveSoft. I'm sure you'll put on quite a show for them."

"Yes, well…the show must go on and all of that. Goodbye, Griffin."

His jaw tightened. "I won't say goodbye," he whispered.

"That doesn't change me leaving," she said and walked away without looking back.

Griffin returned to the vineyard, his mood as black as a starless sky at midnight. He wasn't sure what he'd expected from Maggie. He thought he'd understood how mad she was, but other than that one moment when tears had filled her eyes, she'd been cold more than anything.

It had been like talking to some kind of vintage automaton, and the ice in her eyes when she looked at him made frustration curl along the base of his spine.

He kicked a piece of loose gravel in the driveway in front of his mother's house. The air was thick with the scent of wet earth from the rain that was so typical this time of year. He drew in a deep breath, hoping the earthy smells would ground him, as they always had in the past.

When he'd left home at eighteen after that final, awful fight with his father, Griffin had never expected to return. As much as he loved the vineyard, Dave Stone had made it clear that his oldest son would never be worthy of having any place in the family business.

Griffin still didn't understand the animosity that

had simmered between him and his dad back then. Yes, his mother had given him an explanation about his dad feeling trapped by her unexpected pregnancy and taking out his frustration on his older son. But Griffin couldn't imagine punishing a child for the things in life that didn't work out the way his dad wanted them to.

Especially now.

He'd been home only a day and had yet to talk to Marcus Sanchez, Harvest Vineyard's CEO, who'd announced plans to step away from his position right before Griffin left for Seattle. Griffin had no idea if Marcus still wanted him to take over the business, or if his abrupt departure had burned bridges with more than just Maggie.

As much as he wanted to get his former life back on track, he understood nothing would ever be the same. With another glance at the fields stretching out below the hillside, he headed for the house.

His mother, Jana, greeted him at the door, one finger lifted to her lips.

"Is he okay?" Griffin whispered, unfamiliar panic making the hair on his arms stand on end.

"Sleeping," she mouthed then motioned him into the house.

They walked through the foyer, and she stopped at the edge of the dining room.

Griffin's eyes widened as he took in the antique cherry table, covered with various blankets and sheets.

"In there?" he asked.

She gave him another strident finger to her mouth then led the way toward the back of the house and the big farmhouse kitchen that had been remodeled when he and his brother, Trevor, were in high school.

"I checked on him about ten minutes ago," she said, her delicate brows furrowing. "He was fast asleep, clutching that ratty blanket he carries everywhere."

"He calls the thing Chip," Griffin told her. "You never would have let Trevor and me cover the dining room table with blankets. As I remember, that room was strictly off-limits."

"I had to keep one room sacred from you heathens," she said with an equal mix of humor and affection. "Besides, neither you nor your brother dealt with anything near the trauma that boy has." She pulled a pitcher of iced tea from the refrigerator and glanced over her shoulder. "I heard him last night."

Griffin nodded, his gut tightening at the memory. "The nightmares are a regular thing since the funeral. He has to be exhausted."

"What are you going to do?" She poured two glasses of tea.

If he had a quarter for every time he'd asked himself the same question over the past few weeks…

When his ex-girlfriend and longtime friend, Cassie Barlow, had paid him a surprise visit in early October, she'd given no indication she was secretly interviewing him for the role of guardian for her four-year-old son, Joey. According to what she'd told him when he arrived in Seattle over a month ago, she hadn't known either.

Treatment for the breast cancer diagnosis she'd received over the summer had seemed straightforward, a course of chemo and radiation and she'd been donning her own pink ribbon as a survivor. Then they'd discovered the cancer had metastasized throughout her body and within weeks, her prognosis had gone from sunny to "put your affairs in order."

Being an eternal optimist, Cassie had still believed she could beat the disease. It wasn't until hospice intervened that she'd called Griffin. He'd arrived at her bedside only to find out about her wishes for Joey.

The boy was polite and respectful but hadn't warmed to Griffin at any point. Not that Griffin blamed him. He'd tried to convince Cassie there must be someone more appropriate for Joey than he was, but she'd been adamant. He'd managed to have her moved home with round-the-clock care at the end and then spent four agonizing weeks sitting by her bed and helping the nurses care for her before she'd slipped away peacefully late one night. He'd hoped the peace of her death might make things easier for Joey.

Could anything lessen the pain and trauma of a young child watching his mother die?

The night of the funeral had been the first time Joey had woken screaming and thrashing in his bed. The episode had taken years off Griffin's life, but now he was used to the unsettling incidents. He'd wake within seconds of hearing the boy and bound to his bedside to comfort him. It was the only time Joey allowed himself to be touched.

It made Griffin's heart break to feel that small body trembling in his arms and damned if he had any idea how to help the boy.

"I called Dr. Cunningham earlier," he told his mother, massaging his hand against the back of his neck. "To say he was surprised to hear from me would be the understatement of the year."

She smiled. "The thought of you calling your former pediatrician for advice is fairly shocking."

"I get it. He gave me the names of a couple of child psychologists to call. I'll try them on Monday morning. I think it would help if Joey had someone to talk to. I know it would help me."

"You're doing a good job," she said, placing a comforting hand on his arm.

"Only you could say that at this point." He laughed. "I've managed to muck up every part of my life once again. Maggie is done with me, and I can't imagine how Marcus took my absence."

Jana leaned one hip against the counter. "It would have helped if you'd let me talk to him about why you left."

Griffin shook his head. "I couldn't deal with people knowing when I wasn't sure what exactly was going to happen with Joey."

"Would you have stayed in Seattle if he'd put up a fight about coming here?"

"Of course. At least for a while. Hell, I almost wish he had resisted. Or showed any kind of emotion. It was like the sicker Cassie got, the more Joey retreated into his shell. I should have done more to bond with him, but I was so focused on her."

"She was lucky to have you," his mother told him.

"It's so unfair," he muttered. "She seemed happy and healthy when she came to visit in the fall. Maybe I'm not the right person to judge. Cassie and I were both a bit of a mess when we were together."

"Which is perhaps why the relationship didn't

work?" She sipped her tea. "You never talked much about her."

He shrugged. "We dated for six months when we were in our early twenties. To be honest, we were too much alike to be together in that way. I was drinking a lot and Cassie…" He closed his eyes as he remembered some of the wild times they'd had together. The memories were hazy and left him with a sick pit in his stomach. "Cassie had other vices. But she finally had her life on track, and she was a great mom."

"He's a sweet boy."

Panic tightened like a noose around Griffin's chest. "Am I going to screw him up, Mom? Should I have stayed in Seattle?"

"What do you think?" she asked softly.

"I don't know." He downed the glass of tea then set in on the counter, but the cool liquid did nothing to ease the burning in his chest. "Actually, I do know. He'll be better here, or at least I will, and that has to be better for him." He met his mother's gentle gaze. "I don't know how I could face this without you."

"I'm here for whatever you need."

Before Cassie's summons, Griffin had been staying in the efficiency apartment above the barn on the property. He'd planned to rent a place in town so that he and Maggie could have more privacy. Now he was back in his childhood bedroom, with Joey across the hall in Trevor's room. It had made the most sense logistically so that his mom could help with the boy.

"I want to be a part of Harvest," he told her. "This is my home. The grapes are in my blood."

"I know," she murmured.

"But Joey has to be my first priority."

"Yes," his mother agreed without hesitation.

"What does that mean for the CEO position?"

She lifted the pitcher and refilled his glass. "Your dad managed the company and his family. Being a father doesn't mean you can't run the vineyard as well if that's what you want."

"A father," Griffin repeated, a little stunned at the words.

"That's what you'll be to him. We're his family now."

Griffin nodded. Cassie had told him she didn't know who Joey's father was. She'd been an only child and her parents had died in a car crash when she was seventeen. She had no siblings and no relationship with any extended family.

"I need to talk to Trevor," he said, almost to himself.

"He's still angry at you for leaving." Jana's mouth pulled down at the corners. "At Marcus for wanting to wait for you to take over his job and at me for supporting him in that decision."

"Maybe Trevor has a point."

His mother shook her head. "He'll understand once you explain about Joey. I'm surprised the news didn't sway Maggie."

Griffin looked out the kitchen window. It overlooked the backyard, which included a large flagstone patio, built-in grill, seating area and a stone fire pit. Beyond that was an expansive yard with ornamental grasses and beds of perennials. It was the only part of the property they kept properly manicured.

He'd have to build a play set for Joey, as the one he and Trevor had used had been removed years ago. Maybe a tree house too. He'd always wanted one in the big maple tree in the corner, but his father never had time.

"I didn't mention it," he said, turning his back to his mom.

"Griffin." The word was a soft admonishment.

"I couldn't guilt her into taking me back."

"You hurt her badly."

"I get that." He felt a muscle tick in his jaw and pressed two fingers to it. "Maybe I didn't understand while I was in Seattle, but I do now."

"So you're going to let her go?"

He squeezed shut his eyes then opened them again. "What other choice do I have?"

"You could fight for her."

"What do I have to offer?" He lifted a hand, ticking off all the areas of his life that were in chaos. "I'm the guardian of a boy who just lost his only parent and will barely make eye contact with me. I have no actual job at the moment and I'm back to living with my mom."

"Maggie moved in with her father when she rented her house before the wedding."

"That's temporary."

"So is this," she reminded him. "You have a job if you want it, Griffin. You have a place at Harvest. You always have."

He laughed at the absurdity of that statement. "Not when Dad was alive."

"He would have come around eventually," his mother insisted.

"Doubtful."

"This isn't about your father. You love Maggie."

"Who knows if what I felt was even real. I'm not sure why I thought I'd be able to make a relationship like that work in the first place. My track record is spotty at best."

"You don't give yourself enough credit."

He stepped forward and drew his mom in for a quick hug. "You give me too much."

A faint sound drew his attention to the far side of the room. Joey stood in the doorway, clutching his blanket in one hand with his other thumb shoved in his mouth.

"Look who's awake," Jana murmured with a smile.

"Hey, buddy." Griffin plastered the biggest, brightest smile he could manage onto his face. "Did you have a nice nap?"

The boy shrugged.

"Would you like to make some cookies?" Griffin's mother asked. "I have ingredients for chocolate chip or peanut butter. Which do you like best?"

Joey stared at her for a moment then popped his thumb out of his mouth. "Peanut butter."

Jana let out what sounded to Griffin like a relieved sigh. She'd probably wondered if the boy would even answer her. "Peanut butter it is."

Joey stepped into the kitchen, the corner of his tattered blanket trailing across the travertine tiles. "Are you going to make cookies?" he asked Griffin.

"Um…" Griffin glanced at his mother then back to Joey. "I'd love to, but I need to do a walk-through of the vines before I meet with Marcus…" He paused, then clarified, "He's the man who runs the vineyard right now and I'm going to help with his job now that we're here to stay."

"I'm so glad to hear that," his mother whispered, squeezing his arm on the way to the pantry.

"I want to come with you," the boy mumbled.

Jana stilled.

"Are you sure?" Griffin scrubbed a hand across his jaw. "I'm just walking through fields, checking on rows of grapevines. Your... My... Ms. Jana here is offering an amazing afternoon filled with sugar and chocolate chips and—"

"I like it outside," Joey said simply.

Griffin glanced at his mother, who smiled and dabbed at the corner of her eye. "All those years when you'd try to follow your dad around while he worked. Who would have ever thought you'd be in his shoes?"

She meant the words as a compliment. A fond reminiscence of her late husband. Because of that, Griffin didn't correct her. But he wanted to. He wanted to shout and rail that he was nothing like his dad. If Joey wanted to shadow him in the fields, he'd let him and the afternoon wouldn't be filled with lectures and admonishments.

"Do you have boots?"

"Nope," came the boy's answer.

"Your gym shoes will suffice for now, but you'll need something sturdier as the weather gets colder."

"What's sur-fice?" the boy asked, his little brows furrowing.

"They'll be okay until we get you new shoes," Griffin clarified.

"Can the new ones have basketballs on them?"

"We'll see what we can do."

"Does that mean yes or no?"

Jana laughed then covered it with a cough. Griffin shot her a glare then returned his attention to Joey.

"It means I'll try," he told the boy.

Joey cocked his head, like a puppy studying his owner after being told to sit for the first time. The seconds ticked by, but Griffin didn't dare move. Somehow this moment felt like a test, and he'd never been great at tests.

"Okay," his new ward answered finally, and the tightness in Griffin's chest eased slightly.

Maybe trying really would be good enough.

"I'll have cookies waiting when you get back," his mom promised.

"Thanks," he told her and hoped she realized it was for so much more than just the promise of cookies.

His first instinct was to take Joey's hand, but he worried that would cause the boy to shut down. So he inclined his head toward the door. "Follow me and pay attention. Today is your first lesson as an apprentice vintner."

Joey fell into step a pace behind him. "What's a vintner?"

"Someone who makes wine."

"What's wine?"

Griffin shook his head as he led the way out the front door and started toward the hill that would take them down to the estate field, Inception, the first his father had planted. "It's grape juice for adults."

"I like chocolate milk," Joey reported.

"Of course you do." The boy had no idea what

he was talking about, but he was *talking*. The mere fact made Griffin smile for the first time in weeks.

With a little luck, he'd get his life back on track sooner than later.

Chapter Two

Maggie glanced around the illuminated town square later that night. Just as Jacob promised, everything looked perfect. She was relieved and grateful that so many residents had attended the lighting of the town Christmas tree and were now taking part in the Winter Wonderland festival. Sometimes it was hard to keep track of which event was happening on what night. Stonecreek's community calendar was as jam-packed as a socialite's in the middle of the Season.

But they were a small town without any big industry or corporation to anchor them. Tourism was a huge deal, all year round. The popularity of Harvest Vineyard helped with that, especially during the fall. That fact didn't make her breakup with Griffin any easier, just as it had complicated calling off the wedding to Trevor in the spring. Somehow she and their mother had managed to keep a friendly working relationship. Jana Stone had even become something of a mentor to Maggie, although they hadn't spoken much in the weeks since Griffin left for Seattle.

She hoped that could change now that he'd returned, whether or not he chose to stay. Maggie liked having an experienced woman to talk to and bounce ideas off since she was trying to pull back from discussing town business with her grandmother.

Grammy meant well but it was often difficult for her to remember that she'd retired from the position of mayor, and although Maggie loved her, she wouldn't be a puppet to her grandmother's whims regarding how the town should be run.

"Everything looks beautiful."

Maggie whirled around to find her grandmother standing directly behind her, Christian Milken, the CEO of LiveSoft, at her side.

Grammy frowned. "Mary Margaret, are you blushing?"

Maggie pressed a hand to her cheek and smiled at them both. "No, of course not. I think it's the cold."

"It's still nearly fifty degrees," her grandmother pointed out. "Unseasonably warm for December."

"I'm wearing a coat," Maggie said, even though the light jacket she'd worn over her red fit-and-flare dress offered little warmth, as it was more for fashion than function. She shrugged out of it anyway.

"That's a lovely dress," Christian said.

"Thanks."

"I'm curious to know what you were thinking of just then." Grammy shook her head and lowered her voice to a whisper. "No time to sit on your laurels, girly. We started off the competition with a bang but we'll need to keep up the full-court press if we're going to convince LiveSoft to choose Stonecreek."

"Right." Maggie offered an awkward smile to Christian. Even Grammy's quiet voice had a way of carrying. Now she really was blushing, embarrassed that her grandmother had so quickly and carelessly reduced an evening of holiday cheer to something almost mercenary in nature.

Yes, she wanted to win the competition—her town could use the influx of revenue and jobs. What town couldn't?

But tonight was also about having fun and kicking off the holiday season. Maggie loved Christmas. Some of her fondest memories from childhood, before her mother's death, were of how special the holidays had been. They'd cut down a real tree out in the woods every year, strung popcorn as garland and sung carols around the fire. Her mom had been a fantastic baker, and Maggie had been so proud to deliver cookies to neighbors and friends.

She'd tried her best to keep some of the family traditions alive once her mom died, but it hadn't been easy. Then she'd gotten busy with her own life and it felt like her family had lost something precious. She'd moved back to her house two weeks ago when the tenants she'd rented it to had decided to return to Alabama a few months early. But she'd vowed to make this Christmas extra special for her younger siblings, Morgan and Ben, and their father. Along with her extra work on the town's campaign for

LiveSoft, she hoped to keep herself so busy she wouldn't have any time to miss Griffin.

"I need to talk to Dora about the uneven icing on her cookies," Grammy said, already looking past Maggie. "Mary Margaret, entertain Christian please." Without waiting for an answer, Vivian walked away, much like Maggie imagined the queen would after giving an order to one of her faithful servants.

"I used to know how to juggle," she told Christian with a shrug. "But I'm pretty rusty and fresh out of props."

"Know any magic tricks?" he asked, raising a thick brow. "Or a good knock-knock joke?"

Maggie laughed and shook her head. "Unfortunately, no. But I do know the ladies over at the high school boosters' booth make the best hot chocolate in town. Would you like to join me for a cup?"

"That sounds perfect."

She glanced at Christian out of the corner of her eye as they got in line at the booth. He was handsome in a country-club sort of way, short blond hair and piercing blue eyes. He was always clean-shaven from what she'd seen and favored tailored shirts and pressed jeans with expensive-looking loafers.

She'd done her research on the CEO, born and raised in Boston to a former senator and his homemaker wife. Christian had attended private schools and then graduated from Harvard before moving to the West Coast to start LiveSoft. He'd been one of the company's founders, although she remained fuzzy on his role in developing the app. However, he'd become the face of the brand and was thought to be responsible for much of the company's meteoric growth.

In fact, social media and marketing were his specialties. The public campaign to help choose the company headquarters had been his idea.

"I hope you enjoyed tonight," she said, inclining her head toward the towering Christmas tree in the center of the square. "And not just because of the competition, despite what Grammy would have you think."

"It was great," he said. "Very Norman Rockwell."

"We're all community spirit around here," she said, then cringed. "I hate that everything I say to you sounds like I'm selling Stonecreek."

"I don't mind," he insisted. "We were in Timmins last night and they tried to manufacture snow and ended up causing a minor flood in the elementary school gym."

"Oh, my," she breathed. They stopped at the back of the long line for hot chocolate. "At least we didn't go that over the top." She arched a brow. "Unless you like over-the-top and I'll make sure to ramp things up."

"Move aside, people!"

Maggie glanced sharply toward the covered booth in front of them as the crowd parted. Grady Wilson, who ran the only locally owned gas station in town, made his way forward, elbowing people out of the way as he did. Grady's grandson was the quarterback for the high school football team, so he and his wife were very involved in the boosters.

Grady grinned at Maggie. "Our beloved mayor and potential beloved town savior shouldn't have to wait for a hot drink."

"It's fine," Christian called, waving a hand. "I don't mind waiting my turn."

"Town savior?" Maggie muttered, shaking her head. "I guess we've got over-the-top covered after all."

Grady approached them with a wide smile, a steaming cup in each hand. "Nonsense," he insisted. "I gave you both extra whipped cream too. Our Maggie here's a big fan of whipped cream."

Christian raised a brow in her direction, a small smile playing at the corner of his mouth.

She felt color rise to her cheeks again. Grady certainly didn't mean his comment to sound like a sexual innuendo, but somehow it came out that way.

As she thanked him for the hot chocolate, she noticed the assistant who'd filmed the lighting of the town tree earlier standing a few feet to the side, her phone held aloft like she was taking a video of this episode.

"You stick with Maggie," Grady told Christian. "She'll make sure you're in good hands."

Maggie darted another look at the camera then forced a bright smile. "Everyone in Stonecreek is excited about this opportunity," she announced. "Aren't we, folks?"

The people in line gave an enthusiastic round of applause—bless them—and Christian toasted Maggie's cup of hot chocolate. "To new opportunities," he said, making his voice loud enough to carry and earning more clapping.

As they turned to head back toward the center of the square, he leaned in closer. "And to extra whipped cream," he whispered, his voice teasing.

"That did not mean what you might have thought it meant," she said, looking over her shoulder. "Are we still on camera?"

He shrugged but kept his gaze forward. "Danielle was going to get some extra footage in case she needed filler, but I doubt it will be used and there's no audio with it."

"Okay, good. I'm not used to my every move being documented."

"Aren't you on social media?" he asked, brows pinching.

"Yes, but I'm not active. It doesn't come naturally to me."

"That's why you need LiveSoft," he told her. "The app can organize everything for you in a way that makes it less overwhelming and more streamlined." He pressed the heel of his palm to his forehead. "Now I sound like a walking advertisement for my own company. Sorry."

"No need to apologize. You have a great product. I do plan to use the app, although I'm horrible with technology."

"I could give you a tutorial," he offered. "Maybe over dinner one night next week? I'm heading out early tomorrow to get ready for a meeting on Monday, but I'll be back by the end of the week."

"Dinner?" she said, her voice coming out in a squeak.

"You've heard of it, right?" His smile was teasing and more than a little flirty.

Christian Milken was flirting with her. She fought the urge to check on the camera again. How was it possible that she'd just sworn off men, and suddenly, in the span of twenty-four hours, Griffin had reappeared and Christian was asking her out? Okay, wait. Maybe she was reading too much into this. If Stonecreek was chosen as LiveSoft's headquarters, he'd be relocating here. He probably was just being friendly...neighborly even.

"Of course," she said with forced cheer. "Dinner would be lovely."

"Not as lovely as you," he murmured and lifted his hand to trace a finger along her jaw.

So much for being neighborly.

A throat cleared behind Maggie, and she whirled around to find Griffin standing there, a wine bottle in each hand. His expression was dark as midnight, his green eyes intense on her.

"I hope I'm not interrupting," he said through clenched teeth.

She shook her head, swallowing down the lump of emotion that welled in her throat at the sight of him.

"Have you met Christian Milken?" she asked stepping back to include the CEO in the conversation.

"That's why I'm here." Griffin's voice was tight but he gave Christian a friendly smile. "I'm Griffin Stone from Harvest Vineyard. We donated a few bottles of wine for the silent auction earlier, and I thought you might like to add a couple to your collection."

Christian took one of the bottles Griffin held out and studied the label. "Pinot Noir. That's my preferred type."

"I heard." Griffin flicked a glance toward Maggie then back to Christian. "We're all excited about the potential of having you make Stonecreek your new headquarters. I can tell you it's a fantastic place for a growing business. The town does its best to make sure the business community is taken care of."

Maggie's fingers tightened around her cup of hot chocolate. Here was one more example of a perfectly innocuous comment sounding vaguely suggestive to her ears. Like she was personally responsible for servicing local business owners. She knew Griffin didn't mean it that way, any more than Grady had, and hoped Christian understood it too.

"I'm coming to appreciate what Stonecreek has to offer more with each moment," Christian said, inclining his head toward her.

Griffin's broad shoulders went even stiffer, if that was possible. Not that Christian would notice. Griffin wore faded jeans, another thick flannel shirt and a baseball cap with the Harvest Vineyard logo stitched on the front. To the casual observer, he'd appear to be relaxed and easy-going, just another resident helping to make a good impression.

But Maggie could feel the tension radiating from him.

"The business owners around here support each other," she said with patently fake cheer. "It's one of the things that make us stand out."

"Among others," Christian murmured softly.

"Harvest is a great example of that," she continued as if he hadn't spoken. "Griffin's father founded the vineyard. From the start, and especially in the past few years, they've become a leader in the Oregon wine industry."

Christian adjusted the scarf wound around his

neck and nodded. "I met your brother last week," he told Griffin. "He has some big plans for expansion."

"Yes, he does," Griffin agreed almost reluctantly. "But we're also focused on environmental steward-ship and the type of community we create. Our en-tire team contributes to the end product. We want to make our company healthy for the land and the people who work for us."

"I like the sound of that." Christian's blue eyes lit with interest. "Work-life balance is one of the tenets LiveSoft was founded on."

Maggie drew in a steadying breath as the two men discussed company culture as well as environ-mental building practices. She also had a moment to observe the two of them, both attractive but so dif-ferent in looks and temperament. Despite his obvious enthusiasm for the topics, Christian remained almost aloof as he spoke with Griffin, every inch the tall and lean corporate executive. Griffin was earthy and raw, gesturing with his hands, his brows furrowing as he considered the other man's ideas. And when he scrubbed a hand over the stubble that shadowed his strong jaw, Maggie's insides tightened.

Would she ever not have that kind of visceral re-action to him?

"I'd like to set up a time to visit your operation," Christian said. "I was only planning on staying in town for a day next week, long enough to shoot foot-age for the next installment of the social media story. But if you could carve out an afternoon, I can push the next stop on my small-town tour?"

"Sure," Griffin said, glancing at Maggie. "Happy to show you around. Anything for Stonecreek."

She knew he wasn't happy to spend any more time with LiveSoft's polished CEO than was absolutely necessary. The look he shot her was brief, a slight raise of his brows and a flash in his green eyes. In that moment she understood the only reason he was being the least bit cordial was to help her.

What was she supposed to make of that after she'd just cut him out of her life a day earlier?

"Thank you," she told him.

"You should come out too, Maggie May," he answered with a far too innocent smile. "Our plans at Harvest might interest you, as well."

She opened her mouth to argue but Christian put a hand on her back. "Great idea. We can talk more about how LiveSoft might fit into the current community and what our employees are looking for with regard to the balance between work and their personal lives."

"Sure," she answered, her cheeks aching from so much fake smiling. "Um…text me."

"I will." Both men answered at the same time, only adding to the awkwardness of the moment, at least for Maggie.

She turned up the wattage on her smile, surprised her cheeks didn't begin to crack. "Sounds good," she answered both of them at once. "Right now I'm going to go help with cleanup."

"Doesn't Jacob Snow usually handle that?" Griffin asked.

"I'm here to support *everyone*," she said sweetly. "You fellas have a great evening." Without waiting for a response from either of them, she turned and walked away.

After tossing her empty hot chocolate cup into a nearby trash can, she massaged her fingers against her temples. Was it possible she'd sworn off men only to find herself torn between two of them?

Griffin stalked into O'Malley's Tavern after finally ditching Christian Milken. The man might run one of the hottest app-development companies in the industry, but he seemed like a total tool to Griffin. His distaste had plenty to do with Milken's obvious infatuation with Maggie.

Griffin had come to the Winter Wonderland festival under the pretense of checking on the Harvest wine donation, but he'd also hoped to see Maggie. His life might be an unholy mess at the moment, but he wasn't ready to give up on her. He understood the way he'd left had hurt her, and he wasn't ready to talk to her about Joey, but he'd returned to Stonecreek and planned to stay. Now he just needed Maggie to let him back into her life.

Granted, she wasn't aware of either of those revelations yet. In fact, Griffin had just made the commitment to himself earlier in the day. It was walking the fields with Joey that had done it. The boy had been fascinated by the rows of vines, reaching out to touch the curving stalks and listening intently as Griffin explained the growing cycle of the grapes. As his mother noted, the boy's interest had reminded Griffin of himself when he was a kid. No matter what had been going on in his life and how bad things had gotten with his dad, he'd always found solace in the fields.

He understood that Joey's grief from the loss of his

mother couldn't be easily overcome, but he believed with his whole heart that being in Stonecreek would be a help rather than a hindrance to the boy's healing.

As it had become for Griffin.

Maggie and her unfailing dedication to the community were a big part of what had helped him feel connected to the town again. She had every right not to trust him, but he was bound and determined to convince her he deserved another chance. He'd be the kind of man who deserved her.

Even if that meant helping to convince that far-too-slick-for-Griffin's-taste CEO to relocate his company there.

After just a few minutes in the guy's presence, Griffin needed a beer. He'd texted his mom and she'd confirmed Joey was sound asleep. One quick drink before heading back couldn't hurt.

He waved to Chuck, the bartender and longtime owner of the pub then slid onto one of the wooden stools in front of the bar.

"Fancy meeting you here," a familiar voice said, and Griffin suppressed a groan as he turned to see his brother, Trevor, in one of the booths that ran along the wall next to the bar.

"I called you earlier," Griffin answered, slapping down a crisp bill on the bar when Chuck placed a beer in front of him.

"You two plan to meet up like this?" the bar owner asked with a knowing wink.

"Lucky coincidence," Griffin muttered.

So much for a few minutes to unwind. He picked up the beer and moved to the booth, slipping in across from Trevor.

"To Christmas in Stonecreek," his brother said, raising a glass of amber liquid for a toast.

"I thought you only drank wine," Griffin told him.

"I'm making an exception for the holidays." He lifted his glass and drained it. "One more, barkeep," he shouted.

"Fine," Chuck called back. "But I'm cutting you off after that."

"I can walk home from here," Trevor protested.

"Understood, but your mom will kill me if you end up sleeping on the sidewalk. I'm not convinced you won't pass out on the way home."

"I'll make sure he gets there safely," Griffin said, looking back toward the bar owner.

Trevor gave a loud chuckle. "That's right. My big brother has my back. Ask anyone." His bleary gaze settled on Griffin. "Like Maggie."

"I thought we were past that." Griffin adjusted his ball cap then took a long drink of beer.

"Me too." Trevor shrugged. "You left again, and it hurt her."

"That's my problem," Griffin said through clenched teeth.

"It's not right," Trevor continued as if Griffin hadn't spoken. "You get to come and go whenever the mood suits you."

"It wasn't like that. Not this time or when I left years ago. You know that."

"Do I?" Trevor flashed a grateful smile at the waitress who set his drink on the table. "Thanks, sweetheart."

"I'm off in an hour," the young blonde told him

with a subtle wink. "If you need an escort home, I'm happy to oblige."

"Much appreciated," Trevor told her. "But this night is all about brotherly love."

The woman made a face.

"Not that kind of love," Griffin clarified. "He's too drunk to make any sense."

"I make perfect sense," Trevor countered. "You just don't want to hear the truth." He leaned forward across the table. "You can't handle the truth," he said, doing a really pathetic Jack Nicholson impression.

The waitress laughed then turned away.

"What the hell is going on with you?" Griffin demanded. "You never drink like this."

"I got offered a job today," Trevor blurted then sucked in a breath. He lifted the glass then set it down again. "I turned it down."

"What kind of job?"

"Marketing director for Calico Winery."

Griffin whistled softly. "That's huge, Trev. Calico is the biggest and the best when it comes to Sonoma vineyards."

"Don't remind me," his brother whispered.

"You didn't even consider taking the job?"

"How could I when I'm going to have so much fun working for you?" Trevor held out his hands. "You can take off for over a decade, show up for a few months then disappear again and still…" He pointed an angry finger at Griffin. "Still Mom and Marcus want you to take the helm. I've been here toiling away, trying to make a name for Harvest and no one even gives a rip."

"That's not true."

"I have plans for the vineyard," Trevor continued. "Plans to make us the biggest organic-certified producer in the Oregon wine industry. All I get is pushback for any idea I bring forward."

Griffin dragged a hand along his jaw, unsure of the best way to have this conversation with his brother, especially in Trevor's current state. They'd never been exactly close, not with their father's affection and approval so clearly favoring Trevor.

Dave Stone hadn't done either of his boys any favors with his preferential treatment of his younger son. Instead, he'd subtly pitted one brother against the other. Griffin had loved the vines, but Trevor had been the company's heir apparent.

Now that things were changing, Griffin understood it was a difficult pill to swallow. He also appreciated Trevor's dilemma. As angry as Griffin had been when his dad had all but kicked him out of their lives, it ultimately had been something of a blessing. He'd had a few years to make his own way in the world. He'd joined the army and then worked in construction around much of the Pacific Northwest. When he finally made his way back to Stonecreek, despite his varying emotions about this place, he knew in his heart the choice to stay would be his.

Trevor never had that choice.

"Maybe your plans are bigger than what Harvest can hold," he suggested quietly.

"Because you want to get rid of me?" Trevor's lip curled into an angry sneer.

"Because I want you to be happy."

Trevor's head snapped back like Griffin had punched him. "Why do you think Dad acted the way he did with the two of us?" he asked after a long moment.

Griffin sighed. He'd only recently learned the whole truth around the start of their parents' marriage. "Mom got pregnant with me to trap him into marrying her." It pained him to say the words, both because of the shadow it cast over his mother's character and what it said about how wanted he'd been as a baby. Which was not very much, at least by his dad.

"But he loved her," Trevor said, shaking his head and looking suddenly far more sober than he had a few minutes earlier. "Why would it matter how things started? And you had nothing to do with any of that."

"I don't quite understand it," Griffin admitted, "and Dad isn't saying much from beyond the grave."

"Damn, Grif," Trevor muttered.

"It wasn't easy for Mom to share it with me." He took another drink of beer then laughed. "Although it was better than the explanation I'd come up with on my own, which basically boiled down to questioning whether Dad was my real father."

Trevor made a face. "You look like Mom, but you're a chip off the old paternal personality block."

"Maybe, but I'd had fantasies as a kid of some Clint Eastwood–type guy showing up and claiming me as his own." He shrugged. "I could imagine every moment up until the point where I had to leave Harvest. Then it got fuzzy."

"You left anyway."

"Dad and I would have torn each other apart if I'd stayed." He blew out a long breath. "I'm sorry you felt like you didn't have a choice in the path your life took, Trev."

His brother massaged two fingers against his forehead. "It seemed like one rebel in the family was enough."

"You *do* have a choice." Griffin sat up straighter. "I'm not trying to push you out. If you want to stay at Harvest, we'll find a way to run the business together. But Calico might be a once-in-a-lifetime opportunity. No one would blame you for wanting to do something for yourself at this point."

"You want to check with Mom before you start making promises?"

"I don't need to," Griffin insisted. "She's not like Dad. You know that. She wants you to be happy, no matter how that looks or where it takes you."

Trevor leaned back, crossed his arms over his chest. "I always figured the family business was my only option. Dad made it clear—"

"He's gone," Griffin interrupted then shook his head. "The old man did a number on both of us, but I have to believe he meant well in his own narcissistic way. You can't let everything that came before dictate what comes next for you. You have big ideas and you're damn good at what you do."

"I love it," Trevor said softly. He looked down at the drink in front of him then added, "But I want more. I want to take the job."

Griffin nodded. "We'll talk to Mom in the morning, explain what's going to happen. She'll understand. We'll make sure of it."

"Thank you." Trevor's gaze lifted to Griffin's and there was a mix of anticipation and relief in that familiar gaze that made Griffin's chest ache. Why hadn't they talked like this before now? They'd lost so many years… Griffin had wasted so much time on anger and resentment. He hated himself for it, but all he could do now was vow to change.

"You ready to head home?"

Trevor rolled his eyes. "I'm not going to end up passed out on the sidewalk."

"Let me walk with you anyway. I have some big brothering to catch up on."

"Fine," Trevor grumbled but he didn't seem upset by Griffin's insistence. "I'm holding you to the offer to be there when I talk to Mom. She's going to freak out."

Griffin thought about their mother's calm reaction when he brought Joey home with him. "I think she'll handle it okay," he told Trevor with a smile.

They each climbed out of the booth, waved to Chuck and headed out into the cold December night.

Chapter Three

Jana opened the front door the following morning and felt her jaw go slack. Instead of her younger son, who Griffin had told her would be stopping to discuss something with both of them, Jim Spencer stood on the other side.

Her hand automatically lifted to smooth the hair away from her face. She wore no makeup and was afraid she looked every day of her fifty years. Joey'd had another nightmare at three in the morning. She and Griffin had spent over an hour trying to get him back to sleep, resulting in very little rest for Jana after that.

She stepped onto the porch and closed the door behind her. Griffin was working in the office that had been her late husband's, a room off the kitchen, while Joey remained asleep. Although she didn't approve of Griffin keeping Joey a secret from Maggie, she respected that the decision was his. Obviously, he wouldn't want Maggie's father discovering the boy before he was ready to share the news himself.

"What are you doing here?" she demanded, her tone harsher than she meant it to be.

Jim frowned, inclining his head to study her. He'd always had a contemplative air about him, the soul of an artist even before he became the renowned sculptor he was today.

"Are you okay, Jana?" he asked softly, reaching out a finger to gently trace the frown line between her eyes. A fat lot of good that would do. One of her friends had recently suggested a dermatologist in Portland who was known to be an expert with Botox. Jana had smiled and said she liked that her face told a story. Now she wished she'd called for an appointment.

"Fine," she answered, shifting away from his touch, which still elicited a tingling along her spine, much as it had when they'd been teenagers. Only she was nowhere near the naive girl she'd once been. "Griffin is on a call," she lied, "so he needs quiet."

Jim nodded, although the excuse was lame even to her ears. The old farmhouse was plenty big to accommodate the two of them without disturbing her son.

"We'd scheduled a meeting to discuss your commission," he said, holding up a slim file folder. "I did initial sketches and pulled some ideas into a file for you to review."

Right. The commission for a sculpture she'd discussed with him at the hospital fund-raiser she'd chaired over a month ago. What had she been thinking?

That she wanted something for herself.

That she wanted to feel alive again.

That she wanted another chance with the man who'd broken her heart over three decades earlier.

Jana kept her features placid even as panic and embarrassment washed over her in equal measure. She'd like to blame her impulsive request that he create a sculpture for the vineyard on the emotional highs and lows of menopause. What else could explain reaching out to Jim?

She'd moved on from her first lost love. For heaven sakes, they'd lived in the same town for years and she hadn't revisited her feelings.

"I'm sorry," she said coolly. "I know we agreed to meet after the Thanksgiving holiday, but I've been busy." She licked her dry lips. "Griffin had a rough time while he was away."

Jim's gentle eyes hardened as he shook his head. "I can't bring myself to have any sympathy for him. Not after what he did to Maggie."

"I know he feels terrible for hurting her."

"He's a scumbag."

"Jim."

"You'd think the same if our positions were reversed."

"Like when Maggie walked out on Trevor minutes before the wedding?"

One thick eyebrow lifted. "Because she discovered he was cheating on her. I hardly think it's the same thing."

She shook her head. "I hate that my sons have hurt your daughter."

"I'm afraid Maggie is somehow paying the karmic price for how I hurt you once upon a time."

"That isn't how karma works," she whispered, not trusting her voice to manage anything steadier. It was the first time he'd acknowledged the pain he'd caused. "We both moved on a long time ago, made our own lives."

He turned, looked out toward the view of the fields below. She'd always loved how the old farmhouse was situated so that from every window she could see the rows of vines thriving in the rich, loamy soil of Central Oregon's Willamette Valley. Her late husband had resented the farm and everything it stood for. Even though Dave had made a success of the land he'd inherited, he'd never been truly happy here. He'd longed for adventure and excitement, not the relentless life of a vintner.

But Jana was content, at least as much as she could be with the turmoil that had always brewed between Dave and Griffin, slowly escalating until she couldn't seem to find a way to bridge the chasm between her husband and their older son.

"I still think about you," he said, although the words were almost swallowed by the cold winter wind that suddenly whipped up from the valley. His graying hair blew across his face as he stared at her, his eyes still the color of the sand where it met the sea. God, those eyes had mesmerized her when she'd been younger. He'd mesmerized her.

"I think about us," he continued. "You're as beautiful as the day we first met, Jana."

She laughed out loud at that bit of ridiculousness. "I'm old, Jim."

"Not to me."

"I hate to break it to you," she said with another laugh. "But you're old too."

The breeze blew again, and she shivered, as much from the cold air as the intensity of his gaze on hers.

"You shouldn't be out here without a coat. Can I come inside?" He stepped closer, his big body blocking the brunt of the wind. He was well over six feet tall, and while the height had made him gangly as a young man, he now seemed perfectly comfortable in his own skin. She found it undeniably attractive. "It's business." He paused then added, "For now."

The door opened behind her, and she turned to find Joey standing at the entrance to the house. He rubbed his eyes with one hand while the other clutched the worn blanket he took everywhere.

"Good morning, sweetheart," she said, stepping away from Jim with a furtive look in his direction.

"It's cold," the boy observed. "You need a coat."

"So I've been told," she murmured. "I'll be inside in a minute. Griffin's in the office next to the kitchen. Do you remember how to get there?"

Joey nodded then said, "I dreamed about Mommy last night. She was an angel."

A lump formed in Jana's throat. "Your mommy is an angel," she confirmed. "She'll always be with you that way."

"I gotta pee." Joey looked around her to where Jim stood, his jaw slack.

"That happens in the morning," Jim confirmed, a confused half smile curving one side of his mouth.

The boy disappeared into the house, slamming shut the door.

"Right now isn't the best time for me," Jana said, reluctantly meeting his curious gaze. "Is it okay if I text you later in the week?"

"Who's the boy?"

She bit down on her lower lip. "It's complicated, Jim, and I'm not sure Griffin wants anyone to know about Joey. He hasn't even told Trevor yet. I'm the only one—"

"Who is he?" The question was more insistent this time.

"The son of Griffin's ex-girlfriend, the one he left town to see." She shook her head. "*See* isn't the right word. Cassie was dying. She asked Griffin to become Joey's guardian."

She watched as Jim sucked in a sharp breath, his expression going blank. It wasn't like him. Normally every emotion he felt played across his strong features. At least that's how she remembered him. What did she really know at this point?

"Surely he's told Maggie about the boy?" He ran a hand through his hair. "She hasn't mentioned anything but—"

"She doesn't know," Jana confirmed. "Like I said—"

"I can't keep this from her. She has a right to—"

"No." Jana crossed her arms over her chest, wishing the ruby-colored turtleneck she wore was thicker. "You can't tell her anything."

"I won't lie to her."

"Then don't say anything."

"A lie of omission," he muttered.

"Please, Jim." She placed a hand on his arm. She could feel the warmth of his skin under his thick jacket. For several moments, they both stared at her hand. She wasn't sure who was more surprised that she'd touched him.

"This has turned Griffin's world upside down," she continued.

"As his leaving did to Maggie's," he insisted.

She squeezed his arm, feeling the muscles under her hand go taut. "He cares about her very much, and I know he wants to make things right. He needs time."

He continued to study her hand, and she pulled it away, self-conscious of the veins that threaded through the top of it. She'd been infatuated with Jim Spencer from the first day she'd arrived in Stonecreek, as a girl of seventeen. He'd been the most intoxicating combination of James Dean cool and Paul Newman sophistication, the scion of the most powerful family in town but also the artistic rebel. For an awkward girl from a barely blue-collar family who just wanted to fit in with the kids at her new high school, he'd been fascinating. Jim didn't care what anyone thought about him. His confidence had drawn her in, and when he'd finally noticed her, she'd been a goner.

"I can't forgive him for hurting her," he whispered, "even if he thinks he had a good reason for it."

"That's understandable. You're a good father."

He glanced up at her, his brows quirking and an almost remorseful look flashing in his eyes. "Not really, but I'm trying."

"It's never too late."

Her breath caught as he took her hand in his, the rough callouses on his palms making heat pool low in her belly.

"I hope you mean that," he whispered.

She yanked her hand away, fisting it at her side. "I need to check on Joey," she said on a rush of air. "And Trevor will be here any minute."

As if on cue, a sleek Porsche appeared around the bend in the long gravel driveway that led to the house.

"Text me later," Jim said. He held the file folder out to her and then turned away once she took it.

Jana swallowed, emotions she'd thought long buried bubbling up inside her as if from a dormant spring brought to life.

She waved to her younger son then took a step back and opened the front door. Griffin appeared in the entry. "Joey's having breakfast. I'd like to tell Trevor about him before they meet." He looked to where Jim was climbing in his old Volvo station wagon and frowned. "Why was he here?"

"I'm commissioning a sculpture for the flower garden next to the tasting room," she said, forcing her voice to come out in a measured tone. "We discussed it before you went to Seattle."

"What did you tell him about Joey?"

"Enough."

"Mom, he can't—"

"He won't say anything to Maggie until you talk to her." She turned to him, cupped his cheek with her palm. "You have to tell her, Griffin."

"You trust him?" His jaw tightened. "He has no reason to keep this secret."

"He will," she said, as sure of Jim's confidence as she was of her own name. "I'm going to sit with

Joey. Talk to Trevor. Make sure he's calm before you two come in again."

Griffin nodded, and Jana walked past him into the house. She closed the door behind her, drew in a shuddery breath and dabbed at the corner of her eye.

It had been a spontaneous decision to invite Jim Spencer back into her life, and now she wondered if she'd opened herself to a second chance or simply unlatched a Pandora's box of renewed trouble and possible heartache.

Maggie jumped at the knock on her door a few nights later. She stood in the kitchen, the only light coming from the glow of her cell phone screen.

The electricity had gone out almost an hour ago, and although it was only eight at night, her house was almost completely dark. The glow of lights from her neighbors' homes shone from beyond the window. Bright strands of Christmas lights outlined the houses, which told her she was the only one affected by the loss of electricity.

But she'd checked the breaker box multiple times and could find nothing wrong.

Whoever was at her door knocked again. She hit the flashlight button on her phone and made her way to the front of the house.

To her shock, Griffin stood on the other side of the door.

He lifted a hand to shade his eyes when she shone the flashlight at him.

"How did you find me?" she asked, lowering the light and casting them both into shadows.

"Don't sound so ominous," he said with a soft laugh.

"I'm serious."

"Morgan was out at Harvest after school today. She mentioned that you'd moved back in here."

"Oh, she and I are going to have a talk," Maggie muttered.

"Was it a secret? It's a small town, Maggie May. I was bound to find out."

"I guess," she agreed reluctantly.

"So…um…" He glanced past her into the house. "I came to bring you a house-rewarming gift." From behind his back, he pulled a ceramic pot that held a Christmas cactus. "Had you gone to bed extra early tonight?"

"My power's out." She took the plant from him, her heart skipping a beat. She'd been so happy to move back to her house, but she was the only one who seemed to think it was a big deal, a step in reclaiming her life.

The fact that Griffin understood made her sad for everything they'd lost.

"Did you check the electrical box?"

"I can't find any tripped breakers," she said with a nod.

"Want me to take a look?"

No. If she let him into her house, she was a little worried she'd end up climbing him like a spider monkey. She might tell herself that she wanted nothing to do with Griffin Stone, but her body clearly hadn't gotten the memo.

It was difficult not to notice how handsome he was in the canvas coat that made his shoulders appear even broader than normal. Stubble darkened his jaw, and although his eyes were still in shadow, she could feel the intensity of his gaze.

"Sure. That would be great."

She lifted the light again and he followed her into the house, through the narrow hall to the staircase that led to the basement.

"Careful, it's steep," she advised, starting to reach out a hand for the railing only to realize she was still holding the plant Griffin had given her.

Turning around, she ran right into the solid wall of his chest.

"I'm going to leave the plant upstairs," she told him, her voice annoyingly breathless.

"Good idea," he murmured and she heard rather than saw his smile.

Between the darkness and her body's reaction to him, Maggie had become totally discombobulated in a matter of minutes. Giving herself an internal lecture on how to not be a ninny, she hurriedly placed the plant on the kitchen table then returned to the top of the stairs.

"I can go down on my own," he offered.

"It's my house." She held her phone up high. "I want to be the one to take care of things."

"Got it." He followed her down the stairs then flipped on the flashlight from his own phone to study the breaker box. "It's a tripped breaker." He flipped the switch, much as she'd done earlier. But now the lights turned back on, leaving Maggie both frustrated and embarrassed.

"I did that," she told him, frowning at the row of switches. "I swear I did that exact thing."

"It hadn't been pushed all the way to the off position before you flipped it on again," he explained. "You'll know for the next time."

"It's still annoying," she grumbled, staring at the breaker box. "But thank you." She glanced up to find Griffin grinning down at her. "What's so funny?"

"You're cute when you're mad." He brushed a strand of hair away from her face. "Actually, you're beautiful all the time. I miss that about you, along with everything else."

Maggie stepped back, flustered as color rushed to her cheeks. "You'll get used to it," she told him and whirled around to escape up the basement steps.

She reached the kitchen and turned off her flashlight then stepped forward to get a better look at the plant he'd brought. It was a perfect size, with delicate red flowers blooming on the ends of several stems.

"I thought you had renters until the spring."

Griffin stood on the opposite side of the kitchen, slowly closing the door to her basement.

"The husband got a job offer in Alabama, where they were from, and the wife wanted to move back there. I was happy to let them break the lease, although I think my dad's actually disappointed I moved out before Christmas."

"He wanted to have the whole family under the same roof for the holidays?"

"I guess." She smoothed a hand along the butcher-block counter she'd loved since childhood. The house had belonged to her grandmother before Maggie bought it, so she'd spend hours here as a girl. In the four years she'd owned it, she'd done little to update things, but that was about to change.

As if reading her mind, Griffin moved toward the oak table, holding up a sample of subway tile. "Remodeling?"

"It's my Christmas present to myself. I'm starting with the bathroom upstairs. It still has the pink toilet my grandma installed when she moved in."

"Who's doing the work?" Griffin asked absently.

"Me," she reported, trying not to fidget when his gaze sharpened on her. "I've checked out lots of tutorials on YouTube and read about a million DIY blogs."

"You're going to renovate a bathroom based on what you've read on the internet?"

She made a face. "Don't be so old-fashioned. You'd be surprised what you can learn online. Plus there's HGTV. Based on the hours of renovation shows I've watched, I'm pretty much an expert."

"Clearly. It's a big job, Maggie."

"I can handle it," she told him. "I have extra time now that the election is over and could use something to keep me..."

He lifted a brow.

"...busy," she finished, crossing her arms over her chest.

"What about the competition for LiveSoft?" he asked, thankfully ignoring the fact that she had so much time on her hands in part because he was no longer in her life.

"I'll manage both."

"Maybe the stuffy CEO will want to help."

"Christian isn't stuffy, and why would he want to help me remodel a bathroom?"

"I got the impression he'd be happy to help you

change a lightbulb or watch paint dry or whatever…" He scrubbed a hand over his jaw. "He's interested in you, Maggie."

"He might be moving his entire company here, Griffin. Of course he's interested in me. I'm the mayor."

"Not because you're the mayor."

"That's none of your business."

"Maggie."

"I mean it." She threw up her hands. "I told you we're over. If I want to date someone else…Christian Milken or Mikey at the barbershop, you have nothing to say about it."

He shrugged. "Mikey's wife might have an opinion."

"You know what I mean."

"Don't date the CEO," he said softly, and the edge of desperation in his tone shocked her.

"I'm not planning on it," she admitted after a long moment.

Griffin walked toward her.

"I'm not planning on dating anyone," she said, pressing a hand to his chest when he'd closed the distance between them.

"I had to leave." His heartbeat was steady under her hand as he spoke. Although touching him had the usual effect of spinning her senses out of control, she couldn't force herself to pull her hand away. "But I came back."

"For how long?" she asked then pressed her lips together. She told herself it didn't matter, but that wasn't true and they both knew it.

"Forever."

He said the word with such conviction it made her heart break all over again. She'd thought she and Griffin were on their way to forever. Then he'd disappeared, and it had taken every bit of strength she had not to fall apart completely.

How could she open herself up to that kind of pain again, no matter how much she wanted to believe he meant it this time?

"You should go," she told him, dropping her hand to her side.

"Maggie." The word was a whispered plea on his lips as he leaned in, his nose almost grazing the sensitive skin of her neck.

"Thank you for the plant," she said, shifting away from him. "And for helping with my breaker." She moved to the kitchen table. "I'm starting demo this weekend, so I need to pack up that bathroom and make sure I have all the tools I need."

"More blogs and YouTube on the docket?"

"Tonight I'm updating my Pinterest board," she told him, earning a small smile.

"I did have something I wanted to talk to you about."

She frowned. In the span of a few seconds, his entire demeanor had changed. He looked sheepish and contrite as he shifted his gaze to the plant he'd brought, like he couldn't quite stand to look her in the eye.

Once again, the urge to offer comfort for whatever was plaguing him rolled through her. But she ignored it. That was simply her being weak, and she was done with weakness.

"Whatever it is won't change things," she said before he could speak.

He was silent for what seemed like an eternity. "Alright then," he said finally, his voice rough. He stepped away from her, and she drew in a deep breath. "Call if you need anything. I understand you want space, but I'll be here if that changes. Always, Maggie."

She inclined her head and he walked out of the kitchen. It took every bit of willpower she possessed not to run after him, but she didn't move. Only lifted a hand to her cheek to wipe away the tears that once again fell.

Chapter Four

For Maggie, the following few days were a whirl-wind of balancing her normal life with managing the aftermath of the latest video uploaded to LiveSoft's social media platforms. The remodeling project had taken a backseat as most of her time was spent answering questions about her particular involvement in the decision about a new headquarters. Christian Milken's assistant, who'd filmed the tree lighting, had edited the footage so that it hinted at a possible spark igniting between Christian and Maggie.

While more unwanted attention on her personal life was embarrassing, Maggie had to admit that LiveSoft's followers seemed to love it. Stonecreek had been named one of the two top contenders for the new headquarters. She'd spent the better part of the morning reviewing and responding to comments on the town's Facebook page and Twitter feed, many of which talked about what a cute couple she and Christian would make.

Elsie German from Blush Salon had brought her a basket of skin-care products, to "liven up your complexion" for the next time she'd be on camera. Several other business owners had stopped by to see her, with advice ranging from the length of her skirts to how much lipstick to apply.

In fact, her office had become a revolving door of well-meaning members of the community, all of them excited by the town's chances of winning and annoyingly supportive of her pursuing the charismatic CEO.

"You might want to go shopping for a new bra or two," Irma Cole from The Kitchen restaurant suggested, her smile gleeful. Irma and Grammy had come to talk about plans for the weekend's big event, the annual Stonecreek Christmas pageant. Irma had offered to donate food for the reception after the pageant. She didn't want anyone to be "hangry" while on camera.

Grammy harrumphed from where she sat in the chair across from Maggie's desk. "Don't be ridiculous," Grammy told her longtime friend. "Maggie isn't selling her body to solidify the win."

"Of course not," Irma said with an eye roll. "That would make her a prostitute. Maggie is far too classy for that." She adjusted her own ample cleavage. "But if she likes him, there's no reason she shouldn't have matching lingerie for when things go to the next level. I may be old, but I know men still like some fancy bits when the clothes come off."

"I'll admit you have a point." Grammy pinned Maggie with a stony look. "Do you have nice underwear?"

"I'm not discussing that with either of you," Maggie answered through clenched teeth.

"Even if she didn't get anything new when she was with Griffin," Irma said, ignoring Maggie's affronted tone, "I'm sure she bought nice things for her honeymoon." She glanced at Maggie. "Isn't that right?"

"Still not talking about it," Maggie whispered.

"But you like him," Grammy said, as if it were a predetermined fact. "You agreed to have dinner with him this week."

"We're going to talk about the town," Maggie clarified for what felt like the fiftieth time since she'd mentioned her plans to have dinner with Christian.

"That can't be the only topic you'll discuss," Irma insisted.

"Maybe he'll want to talk about how strange and inappropriate it is that everyone in Stonecreek seems so interested in the two of us dating." She picked up one of the bottles of fancy moisturizer then set it down again.

She couldn't imagine what he thought of the spotlight on his personal life.

"People are excited that we could win," Irma explained, almost apologetically. "And for you to have a new man in your life, of course."

"There's no new man in my life."

How could Maggie consider a new man when she couldn't seem to get over the old one? She'd spent almost every night since Griffin had come to her house dreaming of him. It was as if her heart couldn't let go of him, despite what her brain instructed.

"She's right," her grandmother agreed, rising from her chair. "Mary Margaret's love life is no one's concern but her own. Stonecreek is the best choice for LiveSoft regardless of whether she's dating the CEO or not."

"Thanks, Grammy," Maggie whispered.

Vivian nodded as she walked to the door, gesturing to Irma to follow. "But wear that navy dress with the scoop neck to dinner, dear," she called over her shoulder. "The color makes you look not so washed-out."

Maggie swallowed a shocked laugh. Her grandmother giveth support and her grandmother taketh away.

She should be angry but couldn't quite muster the emotion, understanding why everyone was so invested in Stonecreek winning. It was also difficult to deny that Christian's interest in her was more than simply professional. He'd been texting her regularly, messages that appeared innocuous on the surface but contained a flirty undertone that Maggie wasn't certain how to handle.

It would be easy to fall for a guy like Christian—smart, powerful, handsome and wealthy. Yet even if Maggie hadn't sworn off dating, Christian wouldn't be the man she'd pick.

She had to make it clear that all she could offer was friendship and the promise of life in an amazing town. Surely he'd be fine with that. They barely knew each other. Whatever chemistry people saw between them on social media was a trick of the camera.

Stonecreek would win the competition because it was the right choice, not due to anything she did or didn't do with the CEO.

She opened the drawer to her desk and shoved her new skin-care products into it. Christian and Griffin were meeting at Harvest Vineyard today to discuss environmental sustainability and corporate culture—two subjects they both seemed to find fascinating. Christian had asked her to attend, and although she'd tried to offer excuses, he'd been insistent.

The drive to the vineyard made her heart ache. The last time she'd been out there had been for the hospital gala and after she'd spent the night in Griffin's arms. The landscape looked totally different now, cold and grim and nearly barren. A gray sky loomed above her, perfectly matching her mood. Had Griffin heard the gossip about her and Christian?

She tried to tell herself that she didn't care about his reaction, but that was too big of a lie even for her to swallow.

Panic crested like a wave inside her as she got out of her car. It crashed over her, and she took a step back. The hulking black SUV Christian drove while he was in town sat in the parking lot outside the winery's main office along with Griffin's vintage Land Cruiser.

She thought about the two men, what each might want—what she wanted for herself. The town's expectations and the pressure of making sure everything went according to plan over the next few weeks. It was too much.

Was she really equipped to deal with any of it? She wanted to believe she could handle things. Yet she had difficulty having that kind of confidence in herself. What had she done to earn it?

Instead of heading toward the office where she was due to meet Griffin and Christian, Maggie started down the hill that led to the massive estate vineyard. The temperature had dropped at least ten degrees since she'd left downtown. A fog was quickly descending over the fields, and she could feel the cold to her bones. Zipping up the parka she wore over her wool sweater dress, she kept moving until she was making her way down the rows of dormant vines.

Her tension propelled her forward, like she could outrun her nerves or freeze them from her system. Central Oregon in December was typically rainy, but she could tell from the low-hanging clouds and the fact that she could barely feel her nose that any precipitation they got today would be in the form of snowfall.

As if on cue, a few flakes appeared in the air in front of her. Snow was unusual, so she stopped and tipped up her face, holding out her tongue to feel the snow on it.

"It doesn't taste like nuffin'."

Maggie gave a sharp cry and whirled, shocked to find a solemn-faced boy staring at her from the row next to the one where she stood.

"Snow tastes like water," she said, clasping a hand to her chest.

"My mommy told me snow tasted like cotton candy," he reported, tiny slashes of dark brows furrowing.

Maggie shook her head. "Not so much."

"She also told me she wasn't gonna die," the boy

said, his small voice never wavering. "That was a lie too."

"Oh." Maggie's heart lurched. The pain she felt on this child's behalf chased away her panic more quickly than anything else could have. "I didn't know your mommy, but I bet what she told you was more of a hope than a lie. My mom died when I was fifteen and my sister was only a little older than you at the time. I know it was her greatest hope that she'd find a way to keep living."

"How do you know how old I am?" he asked, ducking under a branch and then between two vines to stand directly in front of her.

"It's the sign on your forehead," she told him then winked when he lifted a hand to his face. "Just kidding. I'm actually pretty good with ages and I'd guess you're around four."

He nodded. "My birthday was in August."

"Mine's in March," she told him. "It's kind of cold today."

"That's why there's snow," he confirmed, kicking a dirt clump with his toe.

"I'm sorry about your mommy. You must miss her very much."

The boy nodded and wiped his nose with the back of one sleeve.

"It's really cold out here, huh?"

Another nod.

"I'm Maggie." She held out her hand. After a moment the boy shook it, his fingers icy cold. "What's your name?"

"Joey," he told her, barely above a whisper.

"Do you live near the vineyard, sweetie? Is your daddy home right now?"

His brow scrunched. "I don't have a daddy." He drew back his hand. "I have Griffin. Mommy gave me to him."

"Oh, my—" Maggie pressed a hand to her mouth. She should have realized it earlier. Griffin had told her he'd gone to Seattle and Cassie had died. Of course, he'd forgotten to mention that he'd become the guardian of his ex-girlfriend's young son.

She straightened as she heard a deep voice calling the boy's name. "Does anyone know you're out here?" she asked.

Joey shook his head. "They were busy."

"Right now they're busy looking for you."

"I like it out here," he told her, kicking the dirt again. "Even when it's cold."

"I understand." She crouched down in front of him. "When my mom died I liked being outside too. The quiet helped me talk to her."

"Yeah," the boy murmured, his eyes seeming to flash with relief at being understood.

"But you have to let a grown-up know where you're going when you leave the house. They get worried otherwise."

Joey seemed to think about that for a moment. "Okay," he agreed, nodding.

"Let's let them know you're okay." She smiled. "Okay?"

"Yeah."

Maggie turned in the direction of the loudest of the voices. "Over here, Griffin," she shouted, taking Joey's hand in hers to begin walking toward the end of the row.

A moment later, Griffin appeared, silhouetted against the creeping fog. "Joey," he shouted and ran forward.

The boy gripped Maggie's hand tighter. "Griffin's mad," he whispered.

"Not exactly mad," Maggie assured him. "He's worried."

"Where the hell have you been?" Griffin demanded of the boy as he came to a stop in front of them.

Joey looked up, giving Maggie an "I told you so" glance that would have made her grandmother proud.

"No swearing," she told Griffin, arching a brow.

His eyes narrowed. "Are you joking right now?"

She squeezed Joey's hand. "We'll talk to Jana about getting a swear jar for the house. Every time he curses, that's a dollar in the swear jar. You get to use the money for whatever you want."

"Really?" Joey asked, his mouth curving into a small smile.

"I promise."

"What are you talking about?" Griffin shook his head. "Joey, you scared Ms. Jana half to death."

The boy's lower lip trembled. "I don't want her to die."

"Griffin." Maggie kept her voice soft but widened her eyes so Griffin would get her message. "You're scaring him," she mouthed above the boy's head.

Griffin closed his eyes and drew in a deep breath. "Joey, I'm sorry." He ran a hand through his hair, making the thick tufts stand on end. He looked wild and desperate and absolutely unsure of what to do next. It melted Maggie's frosty heart.

"I told you," Maggie said to the boy, crouching down again. "Griffin and Ms. Jana were worried. That's why you have to tell someone when you leave the house. In fact, a grown-up needs to go with you if you want to come down to the fields."

"They bury the canes so they don't get cold," the boy said matter-of-factly, reaching out a hand to touch one of the exposed vines.

"I can tell who he's been spending time with," she said, lifting her gaze to Griffin.

His face softened and the glimpse of vulnerability she saw in his eyes there struck to her core.

A gust of wind whipped down the row of vines, making the boy shiver. "Let's get you back to the house," Griffin said, closing the distance between them and lifting the boy into his arms.

Maggie noticed that Joey stayed stiff, unsure of how to relax in Griffin's arms.

She trailed along behind them, trying to wrap her mind around the idea of Griffin as a father figure.

The snow came down heavier, blanketing the fields with a coat of pristine white.

"Will there be enough for a snowman?" Joey asked, unaware of the tension simmering between Griffin and Maggie.

"Maybe," Griffin answered, glancing around at the literal winter wonderland surrounding them. At least a wonderland compared to what they normally experienced in this part of Oregon. "This is what I wanted to talk to you about the other night," he said to Maggie.

Before she could answer, a relieved cry sounded from the top of the hill they were climbing.

"Joey," Jana called on a choked sob as they made their way up. Griffin's mother looked beside herself with worry. She wore a cream-colored turtleneck sweater, dark jeans and worn work boots that came up to her knees. The boots didn't mesh with Jana's otherwise polished appearance, and it made Maggie remember that this woman was tougher than she looked.

Maggie respected Jana for it and liked to think they had that inner strength in common. She drew in a breath, thinking of her near breakdown when she'd first arrived at the vineyard. A few minutes of doubt were manageable. Maybe even normal.

But she'd proven she could handle whatever life handed her. She was infinitely blessed but had also dealt with losses, setbacks and challenges. Each one she'd overcome and she was determined to continue in that vein.

"Maggie found him in the estate vineyard," Griffin reported to his mother as she took the boy from his arms.

"You must be freezing," Jana murmured. Joey wrapped his arms around her neck and buried his face into the soft fabric of her sweater. It was so different from how he'd reacted when Griffin held him.

A quick glance at Griffin's stony features and Maggie realized he was well aware of the boy's contrasting reactions.

"I wanted to check on the grapes," Joey said softly to Jana.

Griffin closed his eyes for a moment. "We should

get him to the house to warm up," he said, his dispassionate tone belying the emotions Maggie could almost see swirling inside him.

"I'll take him," Jana said. "Joey and I can have hot chocolate while he tells me about his adventure. You finish the meeting."

At that last word, Maggie looked toward the office to see Christian moving toward them, a scowl marring his perfect features. The snow had already stopped, although the air was still bitterly cold for the valley. She knew most of what Griffin planned to show Christian was inside the winery, but she still thought that between the scare with Joey and the weather, the time wasn't right for the kind of attention the CEO needed.

"We can reschedule," Griffin told his mother.

"He's fine," Jana said gently.

"I want hot chocolate," Joey announced.

"Cancel if you want," Christian called, his hands shoved deep in his coat pockets. "But this is the only day I have available." He paused then added, "I'm heading to Timmins to talk to the city planner over there. LiveSoft is interested in their environmental initiatives. Did you know Timmins has the most environmentally certified buildings per capita than any other city in Oregon?"

Griffin gave a sharp shake of his head.

Christian glanced toward Maggie. "The town council has offered to donate a tree to every one of my employees to increase the community's overall canopy. Impressive, right?"

"Sure." Maggie grimaced inwardly even as she tried to keep her emotions from showing on her face. She understood that Christian was a busy man and LiveSoft had to be his priority, but his reaction seemed insensitive at best.

Going forward with today's meeting had to be the last thing Griffin wanted to do.

"Maybe we could reschedule for next week," she offered, moving to stand next to Griffin. She didn't want him to think she expected him to carry on like he hadn't just had a huge scare.

Christian shook his head, suddenly looking like a petulant schoolboy. "It's now or never."

She swallowed. "Well, then—"

"We'll go over our sustainability initiatives now," Griffin interrupted. He turned to his mother, who was setting Joey on his feet. The main house was situated across a wide swath of snow-covered lawn. "Call if you need anything."

"We'll be fine," she repeated in the way of an experienced mother. Maggie had no doubt Jana would be able to handle Joey with no issues.

Griffin ruffled the boy's hair. "If you want to visit the vines, tell me next time. I'll take you down."

"You were busy," the boy answered, his eyes trained on the ground in front of him.

Crouching down until he was almost at eye level with Joey, Griffin placed a finger under the boy's chin and tipped it up. "I'm never too busy for you. Never."

The boy tilted his head, studying Griffin as if to discern whether he meant the words. After a moment he nodded. "Okay."

Jana took the boy's hand as Griffin straightened again, and they walked toward the house.

"Are you and the kid's mom divorced?" Christian asked when it was just the three of them again.

"Not exactly," Griffin said tightly.

"I get it." Christian nodded. "It's complicated."

Griffin glanced at Maggie. "I hate that word."

She ignored him and instead smiled at Christian. "Did you know Harvest was the first vineyard in Oregon to be certified organic?"

A bit of the impatience in his gaze disappeared. "What made you decide to go that route?"

Griffin was silent for several seconds, and Maggie wondered if he was going to answer the question. Christian might not realize it, but it was clear to her that Griffin couldn't stand the successful CEO.

She cleared her throat and after another moment he said, "This valley is a special place. We want our fields to flourish in harmony with the land and the people who live here. Environmental stewardship is more than just planting trees. Would you like to see the bottling operation?"

"That sounds great."

"Let's head over to the winery."

Maggie hung back, and Griffin turned to her. "Are you coming with us?"

"I'm going to stop in and see Brenna for a minute," she said, forcing a bright smile. "I'll catch up with you."

Griffin's eyes narrowed but his smile remained fixed in place. "Don't be too long." He leaned closer and added in a whisper, "Or I might throttle your CEO boyfriend."

"He's not my—" She shook her head. "Never mind. I won't be long."

She turned and walked into the Harvest office, breathing in the warm, vanilla-scented air. Brenna rose from behind the receptionist desk and walked toward Maggie. "I'm so glad you found Joey. Jana was really worried."

"You knew about him?" Maggie asked, pressing a hand to her stomach. Her shock at finding the boy and gratitude that he was safe were beginning to wear off, anger taking their places inside her heart.

Brenna shook her head, her big brown eyes filled with sympathy. "Of course not. Not until Jana came rushing in here a few minutes before you showed up. I was about to get my coat on to help with the search."

"But he lives in the main house," Maggie whispered. "Marcus runs the vineyard. Did he know?"

Marcus Sanchez was the Harvest Vineyard's CEO. Jana had given him the leadership position after her husband, Dave, died four years ago. Marcus was a soft-spoken man in his late forties. He'd worked at the vineyard for years and had more than earned his place in the business. He had a gift for working the land. Apparently he'd also had a serious crush on Maggie's best friend, Brenna Apria, since she'd come to work in the Harvest office two years ago. It was only after Maggie's aborted wedding that the two of them had connected romantically.

Brenna had known about Trevor's infidelity but hadn't admitted as much to Maggie until the day of the wedding, and her friend's silence had felt like an additional betrayal on top of Trevor's cheating. Maggie had eventually found a way to forgive Brenna, as well as Trevor, and she was sincerely happy Brenna and Marcus were such a perfect fit for each other.

Marcus was sweet and attentive to Brenna. He clearly loved and respected her with his whole heart. Plus he doted on her daughter, Ellie. In fact, much of the reason for him leaving his position at the vineyard was to devote more time to Brenna and Ellie.

"According to Marcus, Griffin didn't tell anyone outside the family. I don't know why."

Maggie tried not to let the pain she felt show on her face, but Brenna wrapped her in a tight hug anyway. "Don't take it personally," her friend whispered.

"How am I supposed to react?" Maggie pulled back. "I tell a man I love him and a few days later he ghosts me then returns and asks for another chance but doesn't bother to mention that he's now the guardian to a four-year-old boy."

"Yikes," Brenna murmured. "When you say it like that, it's not so great."

"It's worse than that." Maggie sighed. "I need to get out there. Griffin doesn't like Christian—"

"Because Christian likes you."

"Among other reasons," Maggie admitted. "But let's take my mind off my mess of a life for a quick second and talk about your wedding." Brenna and Marcus were getting married on New Year's Eve then leaving on an extended honeymoon through Europe, taking Ellie along with them.

"Your dress will be in tomorrow if you can squeeze in a fitting."

"Squeeze being the operative word with all of the catered holiday events I've been attending lately." Maggie smiled. "I'm so excited for you, Brenna."

"Me too." Brenna beamed, happiness radiating from her. Maggie was only a teensy bit jealous and reminded herself that Brenna had been through so much before finding her happily-ever-after.

"I'll text you in the morning and we can meet at the dress shop if that works?"

Brenna nodded. "Ellie will want to come too. She's so excited that the two of you are going to be in matching dresses."

"I'm going to be upstaged by a kid," Maggie said with a laugh then glanced at her watch. "I need to go."

"Are you really going to join their meeting? Can you imagine the amount of testosterone flying through the winery at the moment?"

"That's the plan but..." Maggie pressed the heel of her palm to her forehead. "I'm not sure if I can face either of them."

"I'll handle it," Brenna said, squeezing her hand. "I can tell Griffin you got an emergency call about something in town and had to drive back."

"Thank you," Maggie whispered. "I need a little time to process...well...everything."

Brenna hugged her. "It's fine, sweetie."

Maggie walked out into the cold, glancing toward the winery. The Craftsman-style building looked tranquil in the snow. A central corridor drawing visitors toward the tasting room situated to the west and overlooking the main vineyard separated two wings that contained barrel storage. Looks could be deceiving, Maggie thought as she headed for her car. It might be wimpy of her to take off, but she'd have plenty of time to deal with both Griffin and Christian over the next couple of weeks. An escape was exactly what she needed right now.

Chapter Five

"Maybe I'll just wait out here." Griffin eyed the dress boutique then met Marcus's amused gaze. "Seriously. I'm fine to wait."

"Don't be a chicken," Marcus told him, making little squawking noises.

"That's rude," Griffin muttered.

"It's freezing. The dress shop is warm."

That much was true. The weather had stayed in the high twenties and yesterday's snowfall had yet to melt off.

"Besides," Marcus continued, "Ellie will want you to see her dress."

Griffin smiled even as he shook his head. Marcus's soon-to-be stepdaughter was an adorable bundle of energy. The girl had been a regular visitor to the Harvest office ever since Marcus and Brenna became an official couple. Griffin hoped that one day Joey would be as lively and outgoing as Brenna's six-year-old daughter, although it seemed doubtful with everything the boy had been through.

They'd had another rough night of sleep so Joey was napping now. Griffin's mom had been happy to stay at the house while Griffin drove into town. He'd met with two preschool directors, trying to determine the best fit for Joey, who would start attending school in the New Year. Both had advised him that a routine would be good for the boy, although panic speared through Griffin at the thought of leaving Joey with anyone but Jana. Did all parents have these kinds of nerves? Could Griffin really consider himself the boy's parent?

His heart stammered at the thought.

"It's a dress boutique," Marcus said, giving him a curious look. "Not a torture chamber."

"Understood." Griffin followed him into the store. The little bells above the door jingled and it was like entering an alternate universe. He'd grown up in Stonecreek and thought he knew the town like the back of his hand, but he'd managed to avoid Something New Boutique for all of his thirty years on the planet.

A world dominated by a million shades of white enveloped him. From the racks of dresses lining the walls to painted furniture that looked so delicate he'd be afraid to sit down, to the decorative chandeliers and oversize mirrors and a huge vase of flowers in the center of a table that seemed to serve as the store's register counter, everything was white or off-white or cream colored or… How could there be so many white hues?

"Wow," Marcus murmured.

"You're rethinking the torture aspect, aren't you?" Griffin asked under his breath.

"Marcus, look at me." Ellie's gleeful shout broke the quiet as she came dashing out from behind a heavy curtain. She was a shooting star of color, her dress a deep ruby that looked almost brilliant against the store's neutral palette. It was shiny satin with lace cap sleeves and an overlay studded with tiny crystals. She looked adorable and ecstatic to be showing off her gown.

"You're a princess," Marcus told her, grinning widely. The girl jumped into his arms. "The most beautiful girl I've ever seen."

"Is that so?" Brenna followed her daughter, one brow quirked.

"And you're the most beautiful woman," Marcus answered without hesitation.

"Smooth," Griffin muttered. He turned to greet Brenna and froze, his mouth going dry as his heart began to gallop in his chest.

She'd opened the curtain all the way to reveal Maggie standing in front of a full-length mirror, wearing a dress the same color as Ellie's but in a far more mature style. It was strapless, the rich hue making her skin look luminous, and seemed to highlight the rich color of her dark hair. The dress was fitted to her waist and the curve of her hips before flaring near the hem.

Her gaze met his in the mirror, and her cheeks went bright pink. She sucked in a breath and for a moment he saw every emotion that raced through her reflected in her gray eyes. Pain…need…hope…desire…disappointment. The last one pierced his heart. He'd never wanted to hurt her, but there was no denying he had.

"Something you forgot to mention?" he asked Marcus.

"Someone actually," his friend corrected. "You can thank me later."

Brenna put a hand on his arm. "I haven't had a chance to talk to you since we learned about Joey."

Griffin's gaze darted to Maggie, who quickly pulled shut the curtain.

"I meant to tell everyone." He met Brenna's sympathetic gaze once again. "It was wrong, but I didn't know how to talk about it."

"I understand," she told him with a gentle squeeze. "Maggie will get there too."

He bit off a gruff laugh. "Are you sure?"

She shook her head. "No, but I'm hopeful."

"Yeah," he said with a sigh. "Hope isn't something I'm used to relying on."

"Don't give up." She smiled again as she looked over to where Marcus was dancing with Ellie, the girl laughing as he swung her around. "Selfishly, I'm glad you're back. Marcus feels a lot better about stepping away from the day-to-day operations at the vineyard with you on board to take over."

"It's still hard for me to believe. My dad is probably rolling over in his grave."

"From what your mom has told me, I doubt that's true."

Griffin gave a good-natured eye roll. "She's a fan of hope, as well."

"Ellie, time to change back into your regular clothes."

"I like the dress," her daughter said, crossing her arms over her thin chest.

"The child has good taste." An older woman, who Griffin assumed must be the saleslady or owner of the boutique, emerged from behind the curtain, the dress Maggie had been wearing draped over her arm. "Just like her mother."

"Not another word." Marcus held up his hands. "I don't want to know anything about my beautiful bride's dress until our wedding day."

"Mommy's going to look real pretty," Ellie told him.

"Of course she is," he agreed without reluctance.

His phone rang and he pulled it out of his pocket. "I need to take this call. Ellie, if you take off the dress, we'll stop for ice cream on the way to the vineyard."

The girl squealed her agreement then followed Brenna behind the curtain. Marcus stepped outside to take his call and the saleslady walked into a back room with Maggie's dress. That left Griffin alone to—

"How's Joey?"

He drew in a breath as Maggie appeared and closed the distance between them.

"He has nightmares and sometimes I hear him crying when he's supposed to be brushing his teeth. We're seeing a therapist tomorrow." He shrugged. "On the plus side, he has a great appetite."

"It will get better."

"I'm sorry you found out that way," he said quietly.

"What happened to no apologies?" Her fingers played with the delicate amber pendant around her neck.

"That was a stupid suggestion on my part." He lifted a hand to reach for her then thought better of it. He hadn't earned the right to touch her again, no matter how much he wanted to. "Along with the belief that I could get through life without complications."

"I can guarantee that's not going to happen when you're raising a child," she said with a sad smile.

"It wasn't going to happen anyway," he answered. "But Joey is way more than a complication."

"I'm sure it meant a lot to Cassie that you were willing to take him."

"She didn't give me much of a choice," he admitted ruefully. "I tried to convince her she could find someone more suited for the task, but at this point he belongs to me. He's been through too much and needs some stability."

"Griffin Stone offering stability," Maggie murmured. "Who would have ever thought it?"

"I'm not sure I would have known I'm capable of handling it without these past few months and you in my life."

She dropped her gaze, the corners of her gorgeous mouth turning down into a slight frown. "Don't say that."

"It's true, Maggie. I can't imagine how I'll keep going without you."

"You already are."

"Have I told you today that I miss you?"

She shook her head, snagging her bottom lip between her teeth.

"That you're beautiful and smart and I don't deserve another chance but want one so much it hurts."

"Stop," she whispered. "It doesn't change anything. You can't use the boy to manipulate my emotions."

"Ouch." Griffin massaged the back of his neck, trying to absorb the sting of her words. "I'm not trying to do that. Joey is here. He's mine. My life has been turned upside down this past month. You're the only part of it that I never questioned."

"Except you did." She met his gaze and he hated that he'd been the one to put the shadow in her eyes.

"I've messed things up. I get that. But I can change." He cleared his throat. "I *have* changed."

"Griffin."

"Can we at least be friends, Maggie? Don't shut me out completely."

Her full lips pressed into a thin line but after a moment she nodded. "Friends."

Before he could thank her, the door to the boutique opened and Marcus came back in. "Maggie, I hear things are going well with LiveSoft."

She smiled. "We're in the finals. It will be a whirlwind before the holidays, but everyone is pitching in. We have the pageant and the historic home tour this weekend. Christian and a few key employees from the company will be here. The hope is that they fall in love with the town and see their futures here."

"No pressure," Marcus said with a laugh.

"Right?" She shook her head, glancing at Griffin, her brows pinching slightly.

"With you leading Stonecreek, there's no doubt the town will win," he told her.

She sighed. "I wish I had your confidence. But if we aren't chosen, it won't be for lack of trying. Actually, I'm late to meet Miles to talk about available real estate. Would you tell Brenna and Ellie I said goodbye?"

"You bet," Marcus answered.

"I can walk you to his office," Griffin offered, already moving toward the door.

"I know the way," she said, shaking her head. "I'll talk to everyone later."

He watched her leave, pain splitting his chest.

"She'll come around," Marcus said, sounding much like Brenna had earlier.

"I messed up royally," Griffin muttered. "You have no idea."

Marcus inclined his head toward the dressing room. "Those two gave me back my heart. After my divorce, I went on autopilot and lived like that for years. I'd given up on life having meaning outside of work. One look at Brenna and everything changed. Then I met Ellie and there was no going back." He shrugged. "She didn't want to take a chance on me, but I knew we were meant to be together. She was my one."

Griffin drew in a deep breath. "Maggie is the only woman I've ever truly loved. I won't find anyone else. I don't want to try."

"Be patient with her."

"Not my strong suit."

"Is she worth it?"

"Yes," Griffin answered, an unfamiliar sense of

peace settling in his chest. Maggie was worth waiting for no matter how long it took. And if she never gave him the chance he yearned for, he'd find a way to be grateful for the time he'd had with her.

Ellie ran out from the dressing room and Marcus automatically bent to scoop her up once again. After everything Joey had been through, Griffin wondered if he'd ever see that kind of pure joy on the boy's face. He had his doubts but knew for certain he'd do everything in his power to make it so.

"Hello?" Jana pushed open the door to the detached studio that sat behind the Spencer house on a tree-lined street north of downtown Stonecreek. "Jim?"

There was no answer so she walked in without an invitation. His Volvo was parked in the driveway and they'd scheduled a time to meet so he must be around somewhere.

Her heart leaped to her throat when she caught sight of him, a pair of wireless headphones over his ears which explained why he hadn't heard her knock.

The studio was bright, if cluttered, with high windows and skylights on the north side. The ceiling was vaulted, and in addition to the door she'd entered, there was a wide warehouse-type door at the far end. The walls were cream colored and mostly unadorned. Along with the main studio space, she could see two other smaller rooms, one that looked like an office and another that appeared to function as a storage room.

Jim stood in front of a large stand that held an enormous hunk of clay, using his hands and metal tools he grabbed from a nearby tool chest to shape his creation. The scene reminded Jana of the first time she'd seen him. Her family had just moved to Stonecreek so she'd been new to the high school, trying to navigate her way through a student population who had, for the most part, known each other since grade school. At that time, the town was smaller and the community even more tight-knit. She'd gone looking for her English teacher after school, needing to get caught up on a reading assignment. In the empty classroom, she'd stumbled upon a boy at the chalkboard—back in the day when they still relied on old-fashioned chalk.

He was tall and lanky, his thick brown hair grazing his shoulders in a way that was both rebellious and ultrasexy. He'd been sketching on the board, swirling shapes and geometric designs. The chalk squeaked and clicked as he worked, his arm moving at a furious pace like he was possessed by some fiery need to release the creativity bottled up inside him.

She'd been mesmerized, moving closer, drawn toward him by some invisible string. Then she'd tripped over the leg of a desk chair and the stack of books in her arms had tumbled to the floor.

The boy turned, his arm still lifted, and his gaze crashed into hers. She'd never seen anything like the mix of passion and desperation in his eyes. In that moment, Jana had fallen hopelessly in love with Jim Spencer.

Although decades older now, his body remained muscled. He'd moved on from sketching and painting to sculpture. The change in medium suited him.

She could tell he was in his element as he concentrated on the work in front of him.

He wiped at his brow with the back of one arm then stilled and slowly turned toward her.

She pointed a finger at her ear and he stripped off the headphones, the tinny sound of classical music filling the studio.

"Sorry," she said automatically. "I didn't mean to interrupt." He tapped on the phone sitting on top of the tool chest, and the music stopped. "I swear I didn't make a sound."

"White musk," he said, flipping on the water at the utility sink to wash his hands.

"Excuse me?"

"Your perfume," he clarified. "It's the same one you've worn for years."

She felt color rise to her cheeks. When was the last time she'd blushed? "I read somewhere that a woman needs a signature scent so I've never deviated." She laughed, surprised at how breathless she sounded. "Or perhaps I'm just boring."

"Not boring," Jim told her with a half smile. The curve of his lips had always made her knees go weak, but it had been years since he'd smiled at her like that. They'd both done a bang-up job over the years of being civil but never really interacting. It hadn't been difficult. Jana spent most of her time at the vineyard, and Jim tended to become consumed with whatever piece of art he was working on at the moment.

"I like your space," she said when the weight of his stare became too much for her to bear.

He glanced around the room as if seeing it through her eyes. "Things are a mess." He pointed to stacks

of papers shoved into one corner. "I need to organize
and catalog but it's not my priority."

"I could help," she blurted then immediately re-
gretted it when Jim gave her a look of pure shock.
"You probably don't want help. It's not a big deal."

"It is," he countered softly. "I never let anyone
help in the studio. My art is the most personal thing
I have." He shrugged. "It sounds petty now, but this
place was the only thing I ever had that felt like it
truly belonged to me. When the kids were little, I
kept the door locked because I didn't want them to
mess with anything. Even Charlotte rarely came in
here."

Jana drew in a breath at the mention of Jim's de-
ceased wife. She hadn't known Charlotte Spencer
well. The other woman had been a couple of years
younger than Jana and part of the "in crowd," unlike Jana. Charlotte's father was a prominent surgeon
in town. The family ran in the same country-club
crowds as the Spencers. Unlike Jana. It was hard to
believe that a town the size of Stonecreek would have
such a social hierarchy, but it did then just as it did
now. Charlotte had always been at the top of it and
because of that, Vivian Spencer had thought her to
be the perfect wife for her beloved only son.

Unlike Jana.

Of course, none of Jana's uncharitable feelings toward Charlotte were actually founded. She'd always
been kind, if quiet. An introvert happy to devote her
life to raising her three children and taking care of
her absentminded husband.

"I understand." Jana forced a smile even though
she felt like a naive little fool for suggesting he'd want

her intrusion into this private space. "Honestly, I'm just looking for something to fill my time. Joey is going to start preschool after the break and I want to give Griffin space as he takes over at Harvest. Nothing like having Mom looking over your shoulder when you're a grown man and—"

"I'd like for you to help," Jim interrupted.

She placed a hand on her heated cheek. "So I stop babbling?"

He chuckled. "You're looking at the new and improved Jim Spencer. I'm trying hard to change from the selfish jerk I've been for years."

"You were never that," she whispered.

"We both know I was." His brows furrowed. "Although you know me more as spineless. A man who couldn't stand up to his mother."

"You were still a boy back then."

"It doesn't excuse how I treated you." He took a step closer. "I'm sorry, Jana."

She forced a laugh, waved a hand in front of her face as if to brush off his comments then pulled it to her side when it was clear her fingers were trembling. "There's no reason for you to apologize. We were young. Things didn't work out. We've both gone on to have great lives."

"Yes," he agreed but his gaze remained intense on hers. "But do you ever think about what might have been?"

"Oh, no." She took a step away from him, needing more distance. Wanting to turn tail and run. "That wouldn't be helpful to anyone. I loved Dave and you were happy with Charlotte. Things worked out the way they were meant to." She nodded, trying to convince herself as much as him. "We can be friends now, Jim, but we aren't the people we used to be."

"Thank God for that in my case," he muttered.

"You're too hard on yourself." She inched closer again, the invisible pull between them drawing her in. "You have a career, three wonderful children—"

"Maggie practically raised Morgan and Ben after Charlotte died. I retreated into myself and it's taken me years to come out of that."

"Everyone deals with grief in their own way."

"You never would have ignored your boys the way I did my kids. It's my deepest regret."

His voice was hollow yet filled with so much pain. She reached for him, placing her hand on his arm. "I made plenty of mistakes. I might have been present for my sons, but I also stood by and watched my husband and Griffin try to tear each other apart. I could have—should have—stepped in to stop it, but I didn't. Maybe Dave would have gotten past his anger, or at least stopped taking out his resentment on our son."

"That was on him," Jim told her. "Not you."

"I could have made it better if—" She broke off as guilt and regret swamped her. Jim wrapped his strong arms around her and she rested her head against his chest, taking comfort in his steady heartbeat.

"We're quite a pair," he whispered.

She glanced at him from under lashes, and the tenderness in his gaze chased away all the pain encircling her heart.

Then he kissed her. Her breath caught in her throat as his lips brushed across hers, both soft and firm. The kiss felt new and at the same time familiar, a homecoming to a place she'd never been before. She splayed her hands across his chest, reveling in the moment. His heat enveloped her, and she could smell a heady mix of his soap and the earthy scent of clay.

She wanted to stay like this forever, but Jim pulled away suddenly. She reached out a hand to steady herself then went stiff at the sound of Maggie's voice behind her.

"Dad? Jana? What's going on?"

Jim blinked, opened his mouth to explain but no words came out. So Jana schooled her features and turned with a smile.

"Hey, Maggie. Your dad and I were meeting about the commission he's doing."

Maggie crossed her arms over her chest. "Really?"

Jana licked her lips and nodded. "Yes. I'm also going to help him clean up the studio a bit." She grabbed a small stack of papers from a bookshelf situated on one wall. "Organization is my strong suit."

"That should make you happy, Mags," Jim said. "You've been wanting me to take care of the mess in here for years."

"True," Maggie agreed with a slow nod. "Although I'm surprised you've finally agreed to it."

"Jana is very convincing," Jim murmured, and Jana felt color flood her cheeks again. She was blushing in front of the woman who'd dated both of her sons.

Maggie glanced between the two of them a few more seconds then said, "Do you remember we're going to the junior high band concert tonight?" She looked at Jana. "It's Ben's first year in the jazz ensemble."

"Good for him," Jana said quickly. "Trevor was in the band. I used to love the holiday programs."

"You're welcome to join us," Jim offered, stepping forward and pressing a hand to the small of her back.

She saw Maggie's eyebrows go up.

"I appreciate the offer, but I should be getting back to home. Griffin took Joey with him on some errands. I'd like to be there when they return."

Jim nodded. "How's he doing?"

"You know about the boy?" Maggie's tone was rife with accusation. "I never mentioned it."

Jana closed her eyes for a moment and heard Jim sigh. "Your father came to the vineyard last week for a meeting. It was only a few days before you met Joey."

"By accident," Maggie said.

"My introduction was about the same." Jim ran a hand through his hair, the same nervous gesture he'd had since they were young.

"Don't be angry with your dad," Jana pleaded. "I made him promise not to say anything until Griffin had a chance to tell you."

"Had a chance," Maggie muttered. "We both know that isn't how it went."

"You have to understand how difficult this has been for him."

"Perhaps if he'd told me about—" Maggie stopped, shook her head. "It's fine. Griffin made his choice, and I made mine."

"I love my son," Jana told her. "But he's made some doozy-level mistakes. How he left things with you was the biggest. I had such a great time working with you on the hospital benefit. I hope that what's between—or no longer between—you and Griffin doesn't change our…" she paused, offered a smile "…our friendship."

To her relief, Maggie returned her smile. "Of course not. I'm sure Griffin and I will end up friends of a sort, eventually. Stonecreek is too small a town to have a breakup rule your life."

Jim's hand dropped from her back, but Jana kept her smile in place. "You're way smarter than I ever was, Maggie," she said. She glanced up at Jim but didn't his gaze. "We seem to keep getting distracted, but I'm looking forward to talking to you about the commission."

"How about lunch tomorrow in town?" he asked.

Not a date, she reminded herself, when her heart seemed to skip a beat. A business lunch. "That would be fine. I'll meet you at The Kitchen at noon."

Without waiting for an answer, she said goodbye to Maggie and walked out, suddenly overwhelmed by both the present moment and the feelings she'd buried for so long that rose up inside her.

Chapter Six

Griffin pulled up outside Maggie's house just before midnight on Friday, glancing into the backseat of his Land Cruiser as he turned off the ignition.

"You should be asleep."

Joey blinked at him, his dark eyes bright and wide. "I'm not tired."

The boy had gone to bed almost two hours earlier, after a bath and several stories. Griffin had congratulated himself on mastering a bedtime routine and had gone into his father's old office to continue reviewing vineyard files after his mom went to her room to read. He still had so much to catch up on as far as running Harvest.

He'd been shocked to see Maggie's number pop up on his phone, both due to the late hour and because she'd been so sure when she told him she needed space.

Her frantic voice at the other end of the line had made his gut tighten, although thankfully the emergency had just been a broken pipe. He'd instructed her on turning off the main water supply to her house over the phone then immediately offered to come by and help her fix the issue.

It was obvious she didn't want his assistance but had reluctantly agreed when he'd insisted, reminding her that she was going to have a hard time finding a local plumber to come before morning. He'd walked out of the office to gather his tools and tell his mom he was heading out, only to find Joey sitting in the hallway, his bony knees gathered to his chest.

So much for mastering bedtime.

Griffin had tried to convince the boy to go to bed—using every trick he'd learned in the dozens of parenting articles he'd read since Cassie died.

Joey could have cared less about Griffin's armchair expertise.

He'd thought about simply walking out, but after the little disappearing act in the fields he figured that wasn't a great idea. The last thing he needed was a search party at midnight with the temperatures hovering near freezing.

His mom hadn't blinked an eye when he'd explained the situation, proving that he'd indeed turned their lives so totally upside down that very little could shock her at this point.

Clearly he'd done the same to Maggie, whose face went slack for only a moment before she smiled down at Joey and stepped back to allow them both into her house. She wore faded jeans and a damp and dusty University of Oregon T-shirt, her long hair pulled back into a messy bun. It was the polar opposite of how she appeared recently, poised and polished in her role as mayor. The glimpse behind her public mask did crazy things to his insides.

"Joey couldn't sleep," Griffin said under his breath. "I tried to convince him but—"

Joey turned and gave him a look that could only be described as withering. "I can hear you."

"Would you like a glass of warm milk or something to eat?" Maggie asked the boy, helping him out of his winter coat.

"I'm going to watch Griffin," Joey answered. "I don't know whether I'm going to be a winemaker or a plumber when I grow up." He paused then added, "Or maybe a firefighter."

Maggie ruffled his hair. "All noble professions." She hung the coat on a rack in the corner of the entry then held out a hand to Griffin. "May I take your coat as well?"

He shrugged out of the heavy canvas jacket and handed it to her, shifting his toolbox from one hand to the other.

"Does it stink?" Joey asked, stepping forward and pressing his nose to the sleeve of Griffin's coat.

"No, of course not," Maggie said quickly. "I just…"

"You smelled it," Joey told her. "A big whiff."

Griffin frowned as color rose to her cheeks.

"It smells like Griffin," she whispered after a moment.

"He doesn't stink," Joey reported. "Unless he's gone for a run."

"That's true," she agreed then gave Griffin a tight

smile. "Why don't I show you where I'm having the problem?"

He nodded, deciding against commenting on the fact that she'd just sniffed his jacket. But a tiny glimmer of happiness bubbled up inside him. She might not want to like him at the moment, but she still liked the way he smelled. He was desperate enough to see that as a win.

Besides, she'd called him and agreed to let him come over to help. He couldn't imagine Captain CEO handling a busted pipe.

He followed her and Joey up the stairs and through her bedroom. The room was decorated in shades of pale blue and off-white, soothing colors for a space that seemed like a sanctuary. The furniture was crafted from blond wood and looked antique, but the thick cover on the bed and the white plantation shutters that adorned the window offset it with a modern feel.

"Whoa," Joey breathed as they walked into the adjoining bathroom. "This place is a mess."

"I was doing demo," Maggie explained then added, "I'm behind on my timeline so I might have gotten a little overzealous."

"I'd say so." Griffin stepped into the space behind Joey, sliding a hand across his jaw as he surveyed the damage. The bathroom was a decent size, especially for a house that was at least fifty years old. It looked like she'd started with the walls, as piles of crumbling tile littered the floor. "Not a fan of salmon-colored tile I take it?"

"It's like they stuck it to the walls with super glue.

I couldn't get the tiles to come off, and it made me really mad."

"The adhesive is meant to last."

"After a while, I thought it would be easiest to take down the whole wall. Even when I managed to pry off a tile, the wall behind it was damaged so..."

"Not a bad idea," Griffin said with a nod. "But you have to be careful not to hit the water lines."

"Great tip." Maggie rolled her eyes. "Thanks to you I managed to turn off the water to the house before I flooded the whole place. But now I can't even flush the toilet."

"Don't go number two then," Joey advised. "That's gross."

Griffin laughed softly and was happy to see Maggie smile at the boy's comment. Then she pressed a finger to the corner of one eye with a sniff, and he realized how upset the mistake had made her.

"We'll figure it out," he promised.

Her smile went slightly brittle at the edges. "I can stay with my dad again if I need to. He doesn't even know I'm tackling the remodeling on my own."

Griffin stepped over the piles of fragmented tile and cracked plaster.

"It looks like you hit the hot water supply line for the shower. I'll need to cut the pipe and we're going to cap it off so you can turn the water back on to the rest of the house. You'll need a plumber to repair the shower before it's able to be used again."

Her chin trembled slightly as she stared at the broken pipe. "Thank you," she whispered. Griffin couldn't quite understand her reaction to the mistake. Her dismay seemed out of proportion for how simple it would be to fix.

"Can I have a snack now?" Joey asked, lifting a hand to cover his yawn. "And watch TV? I don't think I want to be a plumber. I forgot about number two."

Maggie nodded, her smile firmly back in place. "Sure, sweetie."

"I need to grab a few things from the Land Cruiser." Griffin ruffled the boy's hair. "I won't be long."

They filed out of the bathroom and Griffin headed for the front door as Maggie led Joey to the kitchen.

By the time he returned from gathering the rest of the tools he needed, she was settling Joey on the couch, a cartoon playing on the flat-screen television.

"I can handle it if you want to change into clean clothes," he told her when she met him at the bottom of the stairs.

"It's my house," she said firmly. "I want to learn how to take care of it."

He wanted to grin at the determined glint in her gray eyes but had a feeling she wouldn't appreciate that at all. Her resolve only made him admire her more.

Admire. What an insufficient word to describe everything he felt for Maggie. Admiration, yes. Desire. Need. Longing. Lov—

No. He wouldn't allow himself to go there again. Not yet. He understood how badly he'd messed up. He needed to earn his place in her life. Tonight was an opening that he'd gladly take. He wouldn't push her.

"That's a smart idea," he said and turned to the stairs.

"You think I'm in over my head," she said quietly when they were surveying the debris once more. "I can't do it on my own."

"I never said that."

"But you're thinking it." She gave a humorless laugh. "Heck, *I'm* thinking it. With everything else going on right now plus Christmas around the corner, this wasn't the time for a home renovation project. Especially when I know nothing about home renovations."

"What inspired the remodel?" He arched an eyebrow. "Too many binge sessions of HGTV?"

"Maybe," she admitted with a genuine smile then shrugged. "Those people get a lot done in an hour, even with commercials."

"True," he agreed, handing her a pipe cutter. "I brought everything you need based on how you explained the problem over the phone. You're going to cut out the damaged ends of the pipe and then we'll solder on a copper cap."

"With a blow torch?"

He lifted the welding tool. "We're not making crème brûlée with this thing."

She looked dubious but followed his instructions and within a half hour and one check-in on Joey, the pipe had been capped.

"That was kind of awesome," she said as she stepped back to survey her work.

"You did great."

"I started this to have something of my own." She bit down on her lower lip, sending another shockwave of awareness through Griffin. He tamped it down.

This was the friend zone, and he wasn't going to let his lust muck it up.

"You bought the house from your grandmother," he pointed out. "It belongs to you."

Maggie nodded then shook her head. "Yes, but in the four years I've owned it, nothing has changed. I haven't made anything personal. Most of the furniture, other than the bedroom, belonged to her. It's just like my job."

"Being mayor?"

"I followed in her footsteps, and although I was elected to that first term, it felt more like I'd inherited the position."

He put away the tools. "Your re-election changed that?"

"I thought so. During the campaign, I stepped out of her shadow. So much happened this year. I wasn't very popular when I walked away from my wedding."

"Trevor wasn't the most well-liked guy after it came out that he'd cheated."

"But we both shook off some of the expectations of our families and this town after the scandal. I had big plans for Stonecreek. I still do." She sighed. "Instead of working on those goals, my focus has been smiling and playing hostess for the LiveSoft campaign."

"Are you having second thoughts about trying to bring the company here?"

"Not at all. It's a growing company with tons of potential that's a perfect fit for the town. It would be a huge win for Stonecreek, but it feels like the competition is more about me doing a song and dance for Christian. No one is focusing on the substantive piece—the town as a whole is the right choice."

"I don't spend much time on social media, but from what I've seen substance is in short supply."

"It's all part of the game." She ran her hand along the edge of the vanity's pink marble top. "I get that. This town means so much to me. I'd do almost anything for Stonecreek, but tearing out old tile was for me. Does that make sense?"

"Yes," he said slowly, "although some people would argue a pedicure or sitting down with a good book would also be a way to treat yourself."

She picked up a tiny piece of broken tile and lobbed it at him, sticking out her tongue. "Some women get pedicures. I knock down walls."

"Good to know," Griffin said with a chuckle. "The town is lucky to have you, Maggie May."

"Thanks," she whispered.

"I was lucky to have you." He cursed himself when she looked away.

"Tell me about Joey coming with you tonight." She brushed at the front of her T-shirt like that would take care of the dust and grime covering it.

"Nighttime is tough for him. Sometimes the nightmares wake him, but tonight he couldn't fall asleep. I could have forced him to stay with my mom but he's my responsibility."

She looked up at him and flashed a small smile. "He's lucky to have you."

Suddenly the air between them was charged with the same electric connection he'd felt the moment he'd laid eyes on her hurrying along the sidewalk in a wedding dress six months ago. He could never have imagined the changes that had occurred in his life since returning to Stonecreek and what an important part of it Maggie would become.

She licked her lips, and he nearly groaned. Instead of letting his body take the lead, Griffin picked up his toolbox and shrugged. "I should go check on him."

Maggie blinked several times then nodded. "Sure."

She led the way back downstairs, and they found Joey curled up on the sofa, fast asleep.

"He's really adorable," she murmured. "I hate what he's been through."

"Me too." Griffin ran a hand through his hair. "Cassie was a great mom. It's still difficult for me to believe she's gone. I can't imagine how he feels. The therapist says we need to address his anxiety and keep giving him love and reassurance so he begins to feel safe again."

"You're taking him to see someone?"

"Cassie already had a therapist in Seattle. She and the pediatrician here both recommended the same person. Do you know Lana James? She's a few years older than my mom so I think she's been around for a while."

Maggie put a hand to her chest. "She's who Morgan, Ben and I saw after Mom died. Grammy set it up. She'd just started her practice. There were only a few sessions, but it helped. She helped."

"I didn't think about the fact that you and Joey had that kind of loss in common. You were fifteen when your mom died, right?"

She nodded and looked up at him, her beautiful eyes sad but clear. "He and I talked about it when I found him in the fields. Morgan was his age. If you think it would help, I'm sure she'd be happy to talk to him. She's on a better path now and is great with kids."

"Really?" The viselike band that'd had Griffin's heart in a stranglehold for the past six weeks loosened the tiniest bit. He knew he wasn't alone in all this, but for Maggie to get involved gave him a different kind of hope. "I should probably talk to Dr. James first, make sure she thinks Joey could handle it."

"Of course."

"Thank you, Maggie. That…um…" He cleared his throat when his voice cracked. Griffin wasn't used to feeling…well…this much emotion. The woman standing next to him had changed everything. "That means a lot."

She reached out and placed a hand on his arm, a gentle touch that he felt to his core. "If you're going to stay in Stonecreek," she told him, "you better get used to accepting help. I know that lone wolf thing is all hot and sexy, but we're a pack community around here." She inclined her head toward the boy sleeping on the sofa. "And you're raising a child. You're going to be coaching little league in a year or two if you don't watch out."

He leaned closer and nudged her shoulder. "You might need to repeat that last bit. I got caught on the part where you think I'm hot and sexy."

She laughed, poking him in the ribs before stepping away. "And incorrigible."

"In case I haven't mentioned it before, I find five-syllable words vociferously sexy."

"You have an indefatigable spirit," she said with a wink.

"Six?" He held up his hands, palms out. "Now you're just showing off."

She touched the bun on the back of her head and grimaced. "Look at me. I'm about the least sexy I've ever been."

"Eye of the beholder," he whispered, reaching out to tuck a loose lock of hair behind one ear.

Her eyes darkened and that crazy charge between them sparked to life again. She swayed toward him, and Griffin cupped her cheek with his palm. "Maggie?"

"Hmmm."

"Tell me to kiss you." He leaned closer but resisted the urge to press his mouth to hers. "Please."

She stared into his eyes for several long seconds. "I'm not going to say that," she whispered after a moment.

Disappointment lashed at him, but when he started to pull away, she covered his hand with hers. "Remember what I told you about wanting to feel in control." She shifted so that only inches separated them, and her breasts grazed his shirtfront. "This is me taking control."

Then she kissed him.

Her lips were soft and she tasted like mint gum and Maggie. He'd missed this. Missed her.

Desire and emotion swirled through him, mingling so that it was difficult to know whether it was his body or his heart so overwhelmed by the moment.

He didn't wrap his arms around her or try to deepen the kiss. She was in control and her soft exploration was the most erotic thing he'd ever experienced.

Because it was Maggie. Because it gave him hope.

She made a sound, a barely audible hum of need but it seemed to break her out of the moment. She pulled back, her eyes clouded with desire, and raised a hand to her lips.

"I didn't mean that," she said, shaking her head.

He wanted to pull her to him, cover her mouth with his and prove that she not only meant it, but she wanted more. She wanted him, even if she wouldn't admit it.

He gave her what he hoped was a gentle smile. "I'll take it, just the same. Thank you." Before she could answer, argue with him or find a way to shore up the opening in the wall she'd erected around her heart, Griffin walked into the family room. He scooped up Joey, relieved when the boy's eyes remained closed.

"Call Andy Mason. He's the best plumber in town and an old friend of mine. If you need any more help, let me know."

She nodded, brushing the hair from Joey's forehead. "Thanks for coming over tonight. I hope the rest of it is peaceful."

"Good night, Maggie."

"Good night," she echoed, opening the front door to let them out.

The air was cold and smelled of snow. He walked to the SUV, a newfound hope making warmth spread across his chest. He wasn't giving up on her yet. Not by a long shot.

Chapter Seven

Saturday night, Maggie once again had a smile affixed to her face, only this time it was natural. She stood to one side of the sanctuary in the church where she'd once planned to be married, waiting for the audience to take their seats.

The Stonecreek Christmas Pageant was a holiday tradition that had been part of the town's busy December calendar since before Maggie was born. In fact, she'd played Mary twice, an unprecedented honor that her grandmother still reminded her of each Christmas season.

This year she had the responsibility of introducing the play since the event was being filmed for LiveSoft. She smiled at the kids who stood waiting behind the makeshift stage curtain they'd erected to one side of the pulpit. The group consisted of Mary,

Joseph, shepherds and the wise men and women plus
various barn animals played by children ranging in
age from six to eleven. A few years ago they'd tried
to use real animals for the pageant, but one of the
sheep had relieved itself in front of the altar, leading to general pandemonium and a whole lot of tears.
The building custodian put a moratorium on animals
after that fiasco.

But tonight would be perfect.

The sanctuary was standing room only. The pageant was universally loved in town. Whether or not
people had a child or grandchild participating now,
everyone crowded in to see the current production.
There'd be talk for days over coffee and at the local
hardware store about the delivery of lines and how
cute Mary and Joseph had been together. At least a
half dozen of the holy couples from years past had
gone on to date in real life when they reached high
school. Trevor had been Maggie's Joseph one year,
although thankfully no one had reminded her of that
recently.

Christian sat in the front row, sandwiched between
his assistant Allyson on one side and Grammy on
the other.

Griffin and Joey were behind them with Brenna
and Marcus. Brenna's daughter Ellie was making
her pageant debut as a lamb. Trevor sat a few pews
away. Despite his betrayal during their relationship,
she still considered him a friend. They'd spent a lot
of these December evenings together over the years.
She'd gone to coffee with him before he left for his
trip and was glad to see him so happy at the prospect
of his new venture.

Suzanne Bayer, the youth minister overseeing the pageant, gave Maggie her cue from the other side of the stage. Maggie walked out, shielding her eyes slightly as one of the student volunteers working the lights shone a spotlight directly on her face.

"Welcome," she said when she reached the microphone stand, "friends both old and new to Stonecreek and our annual Christmas pageant." She inclined her head toward Christian, who winked and flashed what felt like a suggestive smile at such a public event. Maggie cleared her throat, ignoring Griffin's narrowed eyes in the row behind the CEO. He couldn't possibly have seen how Christian looked at her.

"This is one of my favorite events of the season," she told the crowd. "In the craziness that often accompanies December, let's take an evening to remember what Christmas is really about. The kids have worked hard this year and they have a special performance planned for you. Without further ado, I give you our Nativity play."

She moved the stand to one side of the stage and lowered the microphone so that Lila Moore, the sixth grader who was narrating the pageant this year, could speak directly into it. As the girl spoke about the star of wonder appearing to the shepherds in the field, the kids in homemade robes tied with rope sashes filed onto the stage, along with a few floppy-eared donkeys and fluffy sheep.

Maggie watched from the shadows as the boy playing the star poked his head through the black curtain, only one star spoke getting stuck in the fabric. There was hushed laughter from the audience when a lamb sat back on his haunches and shoved a thumb in his mouth.

She glanced at the audience to see Christian watching the pageant with a look of bemused confusion on his face. It was almost as if he'd never seen children act before. He didn't seem bored, so that was one thing in their favor at least.

Maggie'd watched the footage from his most recent visit to their rival town Timmins. He'd had a difficult time feigning attention at the gingerbread house contest where he'd been an honorary judge.

Behind him, Griffin leaned down to whisper something to Joey, who smiled broadly. Maggie's heart stuttered as Griffin placed an arm around the boy's small shoulders. Then he looked up and met her gaze. Her breath caught at the emotion he allowed her to see in his green eyes.

She turned her attention back to the pageant as Lila described Mary and Joseph's journey and search for a place to stay with baby Jesus. The girl who was playing Mary, a tiny wisp of a thing with dark hair and big eyes made her entrance and the crowd applauded.

Mary was accompanied by a taller boy in the role of Joseph and another husky boy, who was acting as a donkey based on the floppy felt ears attached to the headband he wore and his gray sweatshirt and sweatpants. Someone had come up with the idea for Mary to ride in on the donkey so the kid with the ears was on all fours with the girl, who looked like she wanted to throw up from nerves, straddling his back, holding tight to the baby doll in her arms. At least they'd decided to forgo the actual birth of the baby and gone with a scenario where the Christ child had already been born as they traveled to the stable.

A hush fell over the audience as the trio made their procession across the stage. Even Maggie held her breath, wondering if the donkey was going to make it to the manger. The boy was quite a bit bigger than the girl playing Mary, but Maggie could see him wheezing for breath. Then a loud trumpeting noise broke the silence.

Maggie clasped a hand to her mouth. That couldn't have been—

"You farted on me," the donkey shouted, rearing up.

Mary tumbled from his back, smacking against the tile floor. "Did not," she yelled back, scrambling to her feet.

"Jessica. Braden." Mrs. Bayer leaned out from the other side of the church's nave. "Stay in your roles."

"She farted." Braden threw up his hands. "I *felt* it."

Laughter rang out from the audience and the other children let out a chorus of disgusted groans.

"Farting Mary," one of the shepherds called, holding his staff in front of him like a shield.

"Shut up," the girl, Jessica, hissed at the same time Mrs. Bayer hurried forward. But before she reached the pair, Jessica whacked Braden on the shoulder with the doll she held in her arms.

"She hit him with baby Jesus," a girl dressed as a goat—or maybe a cow—yelled.

"It's not baby Jesus," the teacher said. "It's my daughter's doll. Everyone stay calm." Her gaze darted to Maggie and she mouthed the words *help me*.

Right. Maggie needed to do something. Allyson

was still avidly videoing the whole fiasco as the rest of the audience seemed to look on with a mix of horror and fascination.

"Close the curtain," Maggie whispered to the volunteer standing behind her, then walked—with purpose she hoped—onto the stage. Suzanne Bayer was busy calming the donkey, who was furiously wiping at his back and complaining loudly about "fart juice."

Maggie took Mary's hand and lifted the doll out of her arms, doing her best to reswaddle it as she cradled the baby to her shoulder. She stepped closer to Lila, who was crying softly as she stared out at the crowd.

"It's going to be fine, girls," she murmured then bent toward the microphone. "We're going to take a short break due to some technical difficulties. Please sit tight for a few minutes and—" she ratcheted up her smile a few notches "—in the meantime, would anyone like to lead us in a few Christmas carols?"

The audience murmured amongst themselves, and there were a few guffaws of laughter from the high schoolers in the back row. When no one began to sing, an awkward silence descended.

"Anyone?" she asked. "Trust me. You don't want to hear me."

Her eyes darted to Griffin, and she felt color flood her cheeks as she remembered the first date they'd gone on where he'd gently teased her about her singing voice. As if reading her mind, his mouth lifted at one corner and a moment later he began humming the first few notes of "O Holy Night."

A few people turned to look at him, including

Christian and the LiveSoft assistant. Then he began to sing.

She knew his voice was amazing, but at the moment it sounded like Andrea Bocelli and Marvin Gaye had a vocal love child in Griffin. Maggie squeezed Jessica's hand when a few more people started singing. Maggie felt her shoulders relax ever so slightly as the entire audience seemed to join in the popular carol.

Her father, Morgan and Ben sang along, and Grammy looked vaguely pleased as she glanced around from her seat next to Christian.

Maggie tugged on Jessica's hand and led her and Lila off stage, where Mrs. Bayer was giving the other students a pep talk about the magic of Christmas and how the show must go on.

The woman flashed a grateful smile as Maggie approached. "Great thinking on the carol," she said. "Jessica, we're going to put everyone in their places around the manger."

The little girl shook her head. "I don't want to go back out." She sniffed. "It was an accident."

"Why don't you get everyone else in place," Maggie suggested to the harried youth minister. "I'd like to talk to Jessica for a minute. I think I understand a bit about what she's feeling."

Suzanne nodded and Maggie led the girl to a quiet corner.

"Have you ever farted on someone?" Jessica asked, swiping at her cheeks.

Maggie hid her smile. "No, but a few months ago I was really embarrassed in front of most of the town."

Jessica studied her for a long moment then nodded. "You were the runaway bride. My mom and grandma talked about you."

"Everyone did," Maggie agreed grimly. "It made me want to hide away forever."

"You aren't hiding now," Jessica said with a sniff.

"No, sweetie. I decided the best way to make people—myself included—forget about what happened was not to hide. As hard as it was, I held my chin high and went on with life." She smoothed the hair out of Jessica's face. "I think you can do the same thing with the Christmas pageant. Head over to the manger and be the best Mary this town has ever seen."

"Even better than you?"

"Way better than me." Maggie handed the doll to the girl.

Jessica held it tight to her chest. "Okay," she whispered.

Suzanne Bayer approached, giving Jessica an encouraging smile. "Is our Mary ready?"

The girl nodded and took her teacher's outstretched hand while Maggie breathed a sigh of relief.

"Thank you."

She turned as a frazzled-looking woman stepped out of the shadows.

"I'm Jessica's mom, Christine." Maggie shook the mom's outstretched hand. "She was so nervous about playing Mary anyway. I came back because my husband and I were sure she'd be in hysterics after what happened."

"She's handling it well." Maggie smiled. "Once she gets through the rest of the pageant, I hope she'll feel better."

"You helped. I thought it would upset her more to know I was here, and you did a great job of calming her. Thank you again."

"I've definitely been in her shoes." Maggie made a face. "Although not with…"

Christine chuckled. "I get it."

"Maggie," Suzanne called in a stage whisper. "We're ready to begin again."

"I'm going back to my seat," the mom said, "so I don't miss anything."

Maggie nodded and headed out into the spotlight. The audience finished the final chorus and fell quiet.

"Thanks for your patience," Maggie said into the microphone, gesturing for Lila to join her. "Let's continue with our story. Mary and Joseph arrived at the inn and found the only place available to house them is the stable. So the child has been placed in a manger and our lovely narrator is going to finish recounting the events of that night for you."

She backed away as the curtain opened. The crowd applauded loudly and one of the wise men waved to his parents. The rest of the pageant went off without a hitch, and the kids got a standing ovation at the end.

As soon as the play was finished, Maggie made her way through the crowd toward Christian and his assistant.

"That was quite a production," he said with a laugh.

"Yeah," she agreed. "About that." She looked between the two of them. "Any chance you could not post the first part of the pageant? I think people could get the spirit of the town just from the last bit and the kids taking their bow so—"

"Are you joking?" Allyson looked up from her phone. "I uploaded a snippet, and the video is already trending. 'Farting Mary.'" The woman, who couldn't have been more than a couple years younger than Maggie, gave a harsh laugh. "It's going to be an instant classic."

"It's going to embarrass an innocent girl," Maggie said firmly. "I'd like you to take it down." She moved closer to Allyson and tapped a finger on the top of her phone. "Now."

"Maggie, come on," Christian crooned. "You signed off on having us post content from our visits to Stonecreek. It's part of the contest."

"I understand," she said, keeping her features neutral. Most of the audience had dispersed but enough people still milled around the sanctuary that she didn't want to look like she was making a scene. Heaven forbid. "But this is different, Christian. It's personal to our community."

"Your community is part of a national promotion to become the location for LiveSoft's new headquarters," Allyson insisted. "Do you know how much tax revenue is on the line with this deal?"

"Yes," Maggie answered through clenched teeth. This woman had the heart of a grinch. "We're a small town. So I also know how embarrassing it could be for the girl to have the video splashed across social media. People in town will already be talking. I'm sure there are plenty of videos taken by parents in the audience. But public humiliation on a national stage is different than in a school auditorium."

"I'm sorry." Allyson shook her head. "But I won't—"

"Take it down," Christian interrupted, his gaze remaining on Maggie. "We don't need the footage."

"But it's hilarious," the assistant protested.

"That's not the point of the campaign."

Maggie breathed a sigh of relief. "Thank you so much."

"But," he continued, his blue eyes almost cunning, "we'll need something else to upload in place of the pageant."

"You can't use the second half from when the carols began? That was lovely, right?"

He gave a noncommittal shrug. "It might seem odd without the entrance of Mary and Joseph."

"Okay, it's down." Allyson looked up from her phone, adjusting her tortoiseshell glasses. "I can't control the previous views. But the content is no longer available from any account associated with LiveSoft."

"Thanks," Maggie said. "What do you think about using the later footage?"

Allyson nodded. "I should be able to—"

"It won't work," Christian insisted.

"Not at all," the assistant immediately agreed.

"I don't understand." Maggie clenched her fists at her sides. "Does this mean Stonecreek doesn't have anything to show for this week?"

"We can film something new tonight." Christian smoothed a hand over his shirtfront. "One of the things people are responding to is your success at attracting a younger, vibrant demographic to the town. It's a benefit for my employees, as well."

"I guess." At this point, Maggie was simply trying

to keep her head above water. But if he'd gotten the impression she'd been successful on any front, she wasn't about to disabuse him of that notion.

"You're the face of Stonecreek."

"Um…"

"I think we should use that to the town's advantage."

A frisson of unease slipped down her spine. "Um… use it how?"

"More focus on you."

She smiled and the familiar ache in her cheeks returned. "But the *focus* is the town. We want your employees to want to come here."

"You want *me* to want to come here," Christian countered. "Corporate relocations track closely with where the CEO lives. The board wants us in a smaller community, but I like my life in the city. I need a reason to relocate, if you know what I mean?"

"How about dinner and a carriage ride?" Allyson suggested cheerily. "We'll have the Christmas lights as a backdrop and can ask the store owners to stay open later. Maggie can give you a personal tour and really sell you on living here."

The words themselves were innocent, but somehow Allyson sounded like a bright-eyed and bushy-tailed pimp saying them.

Christian nodded. "Perfect. We've never had a chance for some time to ourselves."

"I'm n-not sure," Maggie stammered. "People are so busy this time of year. It's a lot to ask for shop owners to—"

"It's free publicity," Allyson said with an airy

laugh, suddenly as perky as Barbie after a double shot of espresso now that Christian seemed happy.

More like satisfied in the way of the cat that ate the canary, Maggie thought.

He tried to look innocent but Maggie could tell Christian Milken was a man who wanted to get his way in everything. Right now he wanted her. She'd managed to avoid going out with him up until this point and didn't appreciate being put on the spot now. She'd already had more than her fair share of notoriety in her personal life.

But the opportunity to house LiveSoft's headquarters was still the best chance she had to ensure Stonecreek's future. It was her chance to prove people had made the right choice in electing her.

To prove it to herself.

"It will be fun," Maggie said, refusing to admit, even to herself, how far she'd go to make sure Stonecreek won this competition. "Pick me up at six?"

"We'll be there," Allyson said then held up a hand when Christian frowned. "He'll be there. I mean, I'll be there to film, but I won't be part of the date because that would be weird and—"

"She gets the point," Christian said tightly. He turned so that he was blocking Allyson and placed his hands on Maggie's shoulders. "I'm looking forward to having an evening with just the two of us."

And all of LiveSoft's social media followers, Maggie wanted to add but smiled instead. "Me too."

He gently squeezed her shoulders, as if he were reluctant to let her go, but then turned and led Allyson out of the auditorium.

Maggie glanced around, thankful that the few

people still there seemed focused on cleaning up and breaking down the set. She left through a side door, needing time to collect herself before tonight.

Chapter Eight

"One other great thing about Stonecreek is you can see the stars at night." Maggie pointed to the sky above them then took a long sip of her hot chocolate, wishing Dora had laced the drink with a healthy swig of liquor. "You don't get that in the big city."

"Add it to the list," Christian said with the same winsome smile he'd been giving her all night. She wondered if his facial muscles ached as much as hers did. "It's clear you love this town."

"Yeah," she agreed, trying not to let her gaze dart to Allyson, who was snapping photos and taking videos every few minutes or whenever they entered a new shop.

Maggie had asked Brenna to call the business owners along Main Street and explain the idea for tonight. All of them had been happy to stay open and a couple had even enlisted "customers" to shop during their late hours.

Christian had been charming during dinner, peppering her with questions about her family and her interests outside her job. He was easy to talk to, although Maggie realized she still knew very little about him other than what she could find on his corporate bio. It seemed odd to have spent so much time with him in the last few weeks and still feel like he was a stranger.

She wondered how Griffin and Joey were doing? This morning her doorbell rang while she was still in her pajamas. A tiny part of her hoped he'd returned to check on her water but Andy the plumber had greeted her instead. He'd explained that Griffin had insisted he get to her house first thing to fix the pipe, even though he'd had emergency jobs already scheduled for the day.

"We have one more stop," she told Christian, trying her best to sound normal and not like this whole evening had been staged.

"Oh, drat." Allyson hopped down from the park bench she'd been standing on to film them as they walked along the sidewalk. "My phone is dead. Christian, can I use your camera and send everything to my phone to post?"

"I have a better idea," he answered, placing a hand on Maggie's back. "Let's take the rest of the night off from the competition."

Maggie noticed a split-second flash of disappointment in the other woman's eyes before she pocketed her phone and nodded. "Sure. I'm going to head back to the inn so…"

"Great. I'll see you tomorrow morning," Christian offered. "What time do we leave?"

"Nine," Allyson said quietly. "I'll have breakfast sent to your room at eight thirty. Two eggs over medium, just like you like them."

Christian was already turning to face Maggie. "Where to next?"

"Um…okay…" Allyson called with a limp wave. "Have a great rest of the night, you two."

"Do you want us to walk you to the hotel?" Maggie looked around Christian to smile at the assistant. "It's kind of late."

"I can't imagine any place safer than Stonecreek," Christian answered before Allyson could speak. "She'll be fine."

Maggie's stomach tightened as Allyson's mouth pressed into a thin line. Maggie had a suspicion the woman had a crush on her boss and didn't relish the idea of leaving Maggie alone with him. "I'm fine," the assistant repeated and quickly headed across the street.

She needed to find a way to communicate that she liked Christian as a friend but nothing more without offending him. She could tell him she didn't want a relationship, but it was only partly true.

As much as she tried to convince herself she was happier alone, her heart remained stubbornly fixated on Griffin. But she could ignore her heart. Easy-peasy.

"What are you thinking about?" Christian tipped his head to study her. "You look lost in thought."

"Toilets," she blurted then grimaced.

He chuckled. "A surprise answer. Good idea saving that revelation for off camera."

"Sorry. I need to stop by the hardware store and order a toilet for the bathroom I'm renovating. I keep forgetting to do it. I hope you don't mind the practical errand as part of your holiday tour of Stonecreek?"

"Not at all." She started to move forward but he quickly bent and brushed his lips across hers before falling into step next to her.

A sick feeling opened in the pit of her stomach as she glanced around to see if anyone had witnessed the kiss. Brief as it had been, tongues would be wagging all through town if word got out that LiveSoft's CEO had kissed her on the street.

"No reaction?" he asked, reaching down to take her hand as they walked.

She forced air in and out of her lungs. "That was a surprise, as well."

"I like you, Maggie." His voice had taken on a suggestive edge. "You have to know that."

"I like you, too, but we'd be crossing some boundaries we shouldn't if things got personal during the competition."

"Like I said earlier, the decision about a new headquarters *is* personal. I grew up on the East Coast. I'm used to big cities and nightlife. I understand why the board wants a change. A move to a smaller town for the new headquarters might be best for the company, but it's a stretch for me." His fingers tightened on hers. "I need to know I'm making the right choice."

A nervous laugh escaped her lips as she tugged her hand away under the guise of opening the door to Meyer's Hardware and Lumber. Certainly he wasn't insinuating that she should be that reason? Saying he liked her was a far cry from moving his entire company to a town because of her. Yes, she'd had concerns about his expectations, but part of her wanted to believe she was overreacting because of feedback from so many people in town. Now she wondered…

"Hey, Maggie," Kurt Meyer, the store's owner, called from the front counter. "What brings you in?"

"Toilets," she replied trying to muster another smile but finding it difficult.

"We have many fine types of bathroom fixtures at Meyer's Hardware and Lumber," Kurt continued, holding out his hands like he was giving a sermon. "As well as other tools and supplies a person new to town might need."

Maggie frowned. Kurt said the words in a staccato rhythm like he was a bad actor rehearsing lines for a play. And she'd lived in this town all her life. She wasn't new to Meyer's so why—

"Oh, Kurt, no." She waved her hands in front of her. "They're not taping right now. It's just Christian and me."

"Shopping for toilets," the CEO added drily.

Kurt wiped a hand across his brow and sighed. "What a relief. I've always had horrible stage fright. Worse than poor little Jessica tonight."

He leaned over the counter and touched a spot on the back of his head. "Feel this," he commanded.

"What the…" Christian muttered as Maggie stepped forward. Kurt had always been eccentric, but he was a decent person.

She reached out two fingers and rubbed them

against his scalp. The scent of wood shavings and Old Spice drifted toward her. "There's a bump."

He nodded, straightening. "I fell off the risers during our spring recital when I was in third grade. Passed out and knocked my head against the corner of the metal. I had a concussion and eight stitches. The bone never healed quite right."

"That explains a lot," Christian said under his breath as he joined Maggie at the counter.

She darted him a quelling look. She liked Kurt and wouldn't have anyone making fun of him.

"I'm sorry I didn't mention it right away." She patted the older man's rough hand. "We certainly don't want to stress you out. I forgot that everyone was staying open tonight for filming. I can stop in tomorrow during my lunch break."

Kurt waved away her concern. "Might as well look now. I'm here, and I'd much rather have you shopping than making me into some kind of Clark Gable wannabe."

"I bet you would have given him a run for his money back in the day."

A small snort from Christian had her glaring at him again.

"You're not my only customer, anyway," Kurt continued, oblivious to any judgment coming from the man next to her. "I might need to extend my hours on a regular basis."

"Although I'm not in the market for something as exciting as a new toilet," a deep voice said from down one of the aisles.

Griffin appeared at the endcap, wearing a thick down jacket over a dark sweater and jeans.

"Hey, man." Christian immediately moved forward, shaking Griffin's hand enthusiastically. "What are you doing here?"

"Great question," Maggie added, lifting a brow even as butterflies flitted across her stomach. The last thing she needed adding another complication to this night was Griffin, although she couldn't deny how happy she was to see him.

Griffin smiled as the CEO shook his hand. Christian's palm felt as smooth as a baby's bottom, another mark against him as far as Griffin was concerned. "Brenna called and said they were looking for extras for filming tonight. I needed a few things from here, anyway, so it will save me a trip into town tomorrow."

"Don't tell me that a trip to the hardware store is the most excitement this town has to offer on a Saturday night," Christian said with a groan. "Throw me a bone."

"You should grab a drink at O'Malley's across the street," Griffin answered, faking enthusiasm. "Chuck pulls in a decent crowd."

He knew Maggie had spent the evening with Christian. Hell, it was the reason Griffin had agreed to an after-hours trip into town. As far as he could tell, the whole town was buzzing about Maggie going on a date with the CEO. He wanted to believe she was doing it for the competition but had to see for himself.

He glanced over at her now, and his heart squeezed when she gave him a quick, private smile.

"Yeah," Kurt agreed from behind the counter. "And they've got karaoke on Thursday nights with a professional machine. Irma Cole can belt out Lady Gaga like nobody's business."

"Fantastic," Christian said with an eye roll.

"It's fun." Maggie stepped forward, placing a hand on the other man's arm. Griffin felt his eyes narrow. "We should all go sometime."

"Um...okay." Griffin had never known Maggie to show up for karaoke night and he sure as hell wasn't planning on—

"You probably heard Griffin leading the carol tonight," she continued. "He has a great voice. Thanks for that, by the way." Pink colored her cheeks. "It helped keep everyone calm while we figured things out backstage."

"Sure." He tipped his head to study her, trying to figure out what was wrong. Her eyes were too bright and one of her hands was clenched in a tight fist, pressing against her stomach.

"Right now I could use a drink," Christian announced. He draped an arm over Maggie's shoulder, winding his fingers through the ends of her long hair. "Maggie, do you mind holding off on the bathroom shopping until tomorrow? I'd like to get out of here."

She shifted away slightly, but when the other man didn't let go seemed to settle into the embrace. "That's fine." She glanced over her shoulder. "Kurt, I'll stop by in the morning."

The older man held up a hand. "I'll plan on having a bran muffin for breakfast so I'm ready to talk toilets." He laughed at his own potty-humor joke. "If you know what I mean?"

"Unfortunately, I do," Maggie answered with a nod.

"You want to join us?" Christian asked, but Griffin shook his head, not trusting himself to speak when the guy was hanging on to Maggie like she belonged to him. "Fine then. I'll give you a call when I'm coming to town next. I'd like to talk more about the sustainability of your new tasting room construction. If LiveSoft ends up in Stonecreek, the board is going to want to implement some of those initiatives in building the headquarters."

"Fine then." Griffin echoed Christian's words when it was clear he had to say something.

He turned without saying goodbye to Maggie and headed back down the aisle to pick up a new blade for his miter saw. Kurt didn't seem like he was in any hurry to lock up for the night, so Griffin took his time. There was no way he wanted to take a chance on running into Maggie and Christian walking through town arm in arm.

By the time he got to the counter, snow fell outside the window, coming down in thick, heavy flakes that almost created a whiteout effect.

"Mind if I come back in the morning for the wood?"

Kurt glanced from the flatbed cart stacked with boards then behind him at the sudden storm. "No problem." He used the scanner to ring up Griffin's purchase. "Maggie's doing us a solid, you know?"

"Know what?" Griffin tapped an impatient finger on the counter.

"That CEO guy is obviously smitten and she's going above and beyond to make sure he's happy in Stonecreek."

He had no interest in knowing what Kurt meant by "above and beyond."

"The town can sell itself. If the company picks Stonecreek, great. If not, we'll be fine."

Kurt shrugged. "The tax money would go a long way around here."

Griffin waited while Kurt bagged his purchases, trying not to think of Maggie and Christian together—and failing miserably.

"I guess we'll see what happens in a few weeks. Have a good night, Kurt. Enjoy your muffin tomorrow."

"The wife puts extra raisins in them," Kurt said, "because that's how I like it."

"You're a lucky guy." With a final wave, Griffin left the store and was immediately covered in snow. The flakes were fluffy and cold on his heated skin, and he could almost hear them sizzle as they landed. It had been a stupid idea to come to town tonight. Maggie made it clear she'd accept his friendship and nothing more. Now he had an ill sensation in his gut to accompany him on the way back to the vineyard. His car was parked around the corner. As he approached, he saw the outline of a woman sitting on his back bumper.

Maggie.

Her head was bent forward, her hands folded in her lap. A dusting of white snow covered her, giving her almost an ethereal quality. He guessed she'd been there at least five minutes.

The streets were empty as most of the town would be home at this hour. Unless there was an event, Stonecreek rolled up the sidewalks early.

So why was Maggie here waiting for him?

His boots crunched in the wet snow as he approached, but she didn't look up. There was something about a heavy snowfall that made the world close in on itself. It felt like they were the only two people for miles. The air was already cold, and he could feel the temperature dropping quickly.

"Hey," he said when he was directly in front of her. Her eyes remained closed, dark lashes resting against her pale skin. Griffin crouched down in front of her, dropping his bag to the ground and covering her hands with his. "Maggie, what's going on?"

Her fingers were like ice, and he suddenly realized she was shivering madly. He brushed the snow out of her lap and off her shoulders as she blinked and focused her gaze on him, seeming almost surprised to find him in front of her.

"You're freezing," he said, pulling her to her feet. "Let's get in the car."

"I'm messing it all up." She let herself be led to the passenger side of the Land Cruiser. He unlocked the door and she climbed in.

"I want to hear everything," he promised. "But we need to reheat you first."

He plucked the bag off the ground then got into the car, placing his purchases in the backseat. Turning the key in the ignition, he prayed for the heat to kick in quickly as he adjusted the vents to aim at Maggie.

"I'm going to take you home," he told her, already pulling onto the street. "I don't know what's going on but you're in no shape to drive in this weather. We can pick up your car wherever it's parked tomorrow."

She shook her head. "Chr-christian picked m-me up," she said through chattering teeth.

"The date," he muttered. "I heard. Where is he

now?" He glanced at her huddled in the seat next to him and then cursed when he felt the vents, which were still blowing cool air. "Why didn't he take you home?"

"H-he wanted me t-to come to h-his hotel," she said and Griffin wished he could transfer some of the heat raging through his body to hers.

"I'll kill him," he whispered automatically.

She shook her head. "N-not for that. A d-drink. That's all."

Right. Griffin could only imagine how the amorous CEO wanted only to share a nightcap with Maggie. In his hotel room. Because that's just how powerful men worked.

Luckily Maggie lived in the neighborhood adjacent to downtown, and he was pulling into her driveway within minutes.

As he came around the front of the car, she started to climb out. He scooped her into his arms and slammed shut the door, stalking toward the house.

Maggie laughed into his coat. "Th-this is like m-my wedding d-day. I c-can walk."

"I'm well aware," he said under his breath but didn't put her down until they were on the front porch. In truth, it was difficult to force himself to release her even then.

Yes, he'd carried her to her house after she'd twisted her ankle fleeing from the church and her impending marriage to his brother. But six months ago felt like a lifetime in the past. At that point, he'd felt sorry for Maggie. Before he'd even known the details, it was clear Trevor had hurt her. He'd appreciated her spunk and the way she'd tried to be brave but now…

Now he loved her.

Something about her interaction with Christian Milken tonight had forced her out into a snowstorm and clearly messed with her head.

Truly, he was going to destroy the man, if not literally then he'd find a way to wreck him for hurting Maggie.

No one hurt Maggie.

He inwardly cringed as he watched her struggle to unlock the front door with trembling fingers. The only thing that stopped him from taking the key from her was the knowledge that he'd hurt her—probably far worse than whatever Christian had done.

Griffin should see her safely inside then leave. She was stronger than she realized. He had no doubt she'd find a way to make right whatever it was she thought she'd "messed up."

But he wouldn't leave. He couldn't.

The door clicked open and he followed her in, watching as she flipped on lights and cupped her hands in front of her mouth to breathe warm air onto them.

"You should get out of those clothes."

She gave him a dubious look. "And you're upset about Christian asking me for a drink?"

"Into something warm and dry," he clarified. "I'll heat water for tea."

She studied him a moment longer then sighed. "Thank you."

He ran a hand through his hair as he watched her disappear up the stairs. On the way to the kitchen, he texted his mom to tell her something had happened with Maggie and he might not be home until later. She confirmed that Joey was sleeping soundly and that she could handle things if the boy woke.

For years, Griffin had prided himself on the fact that he didn't have messy attachments to people. Any attachments, really. He'd been estranged from his family and although he would have done anything for his army buddies, now he felt completely enmeshed in the lives of the people he cared about. Downright domesticated if he faced the truth.

It suited him, much to his surprise.

He heated water on the stove and opened cabinets until he found a container of chamomile tea bags. He dropped one into a mug and waited for the kettle to whistle.

A few pieces of sample tile and paint swatches were spread across the counter. Maggie was taking control of her life, and pride flooded him at her determination.

That determination filled her gray eyes as she walked into the room wearing a thick fleece pullover and black yoga pants. Were yoga pants supposed to be sexy? Probably not, but the fact that he found them seriously arousing said a lot about his state of mind at the moment.

"Thank you for getting me home tonight," she said, her tone crisp. "I overreacted."

"To Christian putting the moves on you?" He shook his head. "I doubt it."

A keening whistle sounded from the teapot and he flipped off the burner then poured steaming water into a mug.

"You aren't joining me?" she asked, stepping closer.

"Tea isn't really my thing."

"A beer?"

"If you have one."

She opened the refrigerator and pulled out a bottle. He dunked the tea bag several times then they traded—tea for her and a microbrew for him.

"You could lace it with whiskey," he suggested as he lifted the bottle to his lips.

She smiled and shook her head. "I had wine with dinner. I'm kind of a lightweight."

"Only when it comes to alcohol," he reminded her.

She sipped the tea, spreading her fingers around the mug. "This is perfect. I thought I'd never be warm again. Probably not in the best interest of the town if I let myself freeze before the competition is over."

"The town will be fine." He repeated his earlier words to Kurt then held up a hand when her eyes widened. "Without LiveSoft," he clarified. "Not you. We need you."

"I appreciate that, especially after tonight."

His grip tightened on the beer bottle. "What happened with Christian?"

"Nothing." She bit down on her lower lip. "Yet."

"Remember when I punched Trevor in the sanctuary after you walked away from the wedding?"

She nodded and rolled her eyes. "I don't need—"

"If I decked that sanctimonious CEO," he interrupted, "it would be as much for me as for you. That guy rubs me the wrong way."

"He likes me," she blurted.

"He's human," he countered, earning another eye roll.

"It's going to mess up everything. He basically told me that I'd be his biggest reason for choosing Stonecreek as the headquarters."

"I thought the social media followers voted and the board makes the final decision."

"Well, yes, but Christian's assistant edits all of the content. She directs the narrative, and apparently they want me to be part of it."

"What do you want?" he forced himself to ask.

"To take care of the town."

"By dating our potential rainmaker?"

"I don't want to date Christian," she insisted with more conviction than he would have expected after she'd spent the evening with the guy.

"But you went out with him tonight."

She set the mug onto the counter then pressed her palm against her forehead. "I asked them to delete the footage of Jessica's embarrassing moment at the pageant."

"Good for you."

"He suggested I go to dinner with him in return—just the two of us. Well, the two of us and a camera. They needed replacement content." She shook her head. "Brenna called everyone about staying open late. I thought it would be an easy way to get additional publicity for some of the local businesses."

"The town is doing great on its own."

"There are still struggles. Budget constraints that most people don't see. With an influx of tax revenue, I could do so much. The community deserves more. Everyone thinks we're going to win the competition."

"We could," he said quietly.

"Christian needs an incentive to give up the big city for small-town life."

"How is it that you don't want me to kill him?"

"I want to believe he means it as a compliment."

"Maggie, come on."

"Okay," she said, throwing up her hands. "But I can't be rude about it."

"Hell, yeah, you can."

"I'll mess up our chances," she protested.

"It doesn't matter."

"You don't understand."

"I understand that you aren't going to be bullied into dating or whatever else with some powerful corporate honcho to win. You aren't part of the bargain. Not even your grandmother would expect that."

She gave a small laugh. "Have you met her?"

He placed the beer on the counter and moved closer, reaching out a hand to cup her cheek. "How can I help?"

She stared up at him as if seeing him for the first time.

Damn, he hoped that was true. He wanted her to see him for the man he could become. The kind of guy who deserved to be a part of her life.

Chapter Nine

Who was this man standing in front of her?

Maggie leaned into Griffin's touch, loving the warmth of his hand. Yes, he'd hurt her but he'd also been a consistent support in these past few months. Every time she needed him or asked him for anything, he made himself available.

It was more than physical attraction, although wanting him remained a palpable force in her life. He was a friend, maybe the best friend she had.

"I want to make this town look so good that LiveSoft will have no choice but to pick Stonecreek. I'm not sure exactly how to do that…how to add anything more than what we've already got."

"He's interested in spending more time at the vineyard. To be honest, I've been blowing him off since the last meeting because I'm already so busy getting up to speed with everything before Marcus leaves and adding Joey into the mix."

"How are things with him?"

Griffin's handsome features didn't change, but she could feel the tension in him as he thought about the boy. "It changes on a daily, and sometimes hourly, basis. I guess that's normal for kids in general, and especially with what he's been through."

"Yes," she agreed.

"Parenting is damn hard."

She smiled. "A universal truth."

"It doesn't help that he has to face Christmas so soon after his mom died. He actually really enjoyed the pageant tonight, and not just because of Mary and the donkey. I'm trying to figure out how Cassie handled the holidays and honor the traditions he already knows. But my mom has her own way of doing things too. We tried to decorate the tree last night and Joey threw a fit because it's artificial."

"A fit? Surely you're exaggerating."

He shook his head. "Apparently Cassie had something against artificial trees. I don't get it but he insisted it's not Christmas without a real tree."

"What did your mom say?"

"She told me to get a real tree and we'd wait to decorate until then."

"She's the best."

"Absolutely," Griffin agreed.

"My problems aren't your problem," she reminded him. "You have plenty to deal with right now."

He touched one finger to her lips, gently silencing her. "I want to help. I'll invite Christian back out to the vineyard and make it clear that everyone at Harvest is committed to helping his company transition into the community."

"That would be great," she said, reaching out to spread her hand over his chest. She could feel his heart beating, strong and steady under his shirt.

"I don't want you stressed out by all this," he murmured, running the pad of his thumb across her cheek.

She laughed softly. "Too late."

"You are smart, dedicated and amazing with what you do for this town. No one doubts that."

"I want to win," she told him honestly. "So much."

"Then we'll make sure you do," he promised.

She pulled away and gripped his arm, making a show of looking over his shoulder.

"What's that about?"

"Just checking to see if your hero cape is showing."

"Nah. Costumes aren't really my thing."

"Too bad," she said, tapping a finger on his chin. "I had a couple of superhero fantasies I was hoping to explore."

"Always killing me," he muttered as his eyes went dark with desire.

She wound her arms around his neck. Suddenly the past didn't matter. The pain she'd felt disappeared. In its place, sensual sensation sparked along her skin.

He kissed her, deep and hungry. Maggie loved his mouth, the way it was soft and smooth, a contrast to his stubbled jaw and the hard planes of his body.

She'd missed kissing him, missed being close to him in a way that made this moment all the more precious.

Desire and need flowed through her veins, coalescing at her aroused center. Griffin's hands snaked up between their bodies, skimming under her shirt. She grabbed the hem and lifted it over her head.

"No bra," he murmured with a wicked smile. "I approve."

"No panties either," she told him, her voice raspy with need.

"You've moved past superhero status," he said, tugging on her waistband. "You're a goddess."

She laughed and stepped out of her yoga pants. She'd missed this too—how easy it was to laugh with him when they were together. Maggie wasn't exactly known for her playfulness, but Griffin had a way of making everything more fun. "*You're* overdressed."

"Easily remedied," he said as he toed off his boots. She watched his rapid striptease with a wide smile, her breath catching at the sight of his taut muscles.

But when he reached for her, she held up a hand. "We're in my kitchen."

He made a show of glancing around. "So we are. Is that a problem?"

"Um…not exactly…but…"

"I think we can make it work," he promised, pulling her into his arms.

No sooner had she nodded her agreement than he gripped her waist and placed her on the table. His hands slid from her hips, down her thighs until he reached her knees, gently nudging them apart. He touched her exactly where and how she longed to be touched, and she moaned with need.

At the same time, he claimed her mouth again, his tongue mimicking the movements of his fingers.

Within minutes she'd lost herself in the sensations assaulting her, tiny pinpricks of pleasure cascading through her body. The pressure built until her pounding desire drowned out every doubt she'd had about Griffin.

She tried to remind herself that this was only physical. It couldn't mean what she wanted it to, but her body and heart refused to cooperate.

Then he pulled away and she whimpered a protest, wondering if he'd somehow been able to sense her internal struggle.

She was left gasping for breath, balanced on her elbows as he bent toward his discarded jeans.

A moment later he straightened, holding a silver packet. "I need to be inside you," he said, giving her a lopsided smile. "I can't wait, Maggie."

Tugging her bottom lip between her teeth, she nodded. Her lady parts gave a cheer of delight while the doubts she knew would eventually resurface disappeared into the dark recesses of her heart.

Griffin braced a hand on the table and she held on to his shoulders as he pressed forward and entered her.

It was like finding a piece of herself that had been missing.

He moved, shifting his grip on her to anchor her hips. She wound her legs around his waist and arched into him, relishing his strength and control with each powerful thrust.

Tension tightened her belly, and Griffin grazed his lips over her sensitive earlobe. "Let go," he commanded, and she did, spiraling over the edge of desire without any thought to landing on the other side.

But Griffin was there, holding her tight, groaning his own release into the crook of her neck. She felt limp and boneless, and he continued to cradle her in his arms like she was something precious.

"I'll never look at a bowl of cereal the same way again," she whispered when her breathing had almost returned to normal.

He chuckled and pulled back, only to pick her up and carry her to her bedroom.

"Can you stay?" she asked, too content to worry about the need that threaded through her voice.

"For a while," he whispered and kissed the tip of her nose.

She smiled and welcomed him into her bed, still forcing herself to remain focused on this moment and nothing more.

"What if we get lost?" Joey asked from the back-seat of Griffin's Land Cruiser the following morning.

"I promise we won't get lost," Griffin said, glancing at the boy in the rearview mirror.

"Don't they sell Christmas trees here in parking lots like normal?"

Maggie laughed and turned in her seat. "Joey, I promise we're going to find the best tree ever this way. One for my house and one for yours. I appreciate both of you joining me for this little outing. I haven't cut down a tree in the woods since I was a girl."

"I think Miss Jana was sad to put away her fake tree," Joey observed, his brown eyes solemn. "But Mommy said fake trees were boring."

Maggie saw Griffin grimace. "Miss Jana wants

you to have a great Christmas. If it makes you happy to have a real tree, she'll be happy."

The boy nodded and continued tracing shapes in the condensation on the back window.

As Griffin left late last night, Maggie'd impulsively suggested they take Joey on an outing for a Christmas tree today. Her thoughts had been in sync with Joey's—a quick trip to the local garden center, where they shipped in trees from Washington State. But this morning Griffin had texted to ask if she'd be up for a hike in the woods and cutting down their own trees. He thought it would be something new and different for Joey without having to compare it to how Cassie had handled the tradition.

New traditions. 'Twas the season for that it seemed.

With last night's heavy snow, the drive was slow out of town and into the nearby Strouds Run State Park. Griffin had borrowed one of the vineyard's extended cab pickups so it would be easy to load the trees into the back.

They parked at the trailhead and climbed out. The sky was clear, the air crisp and scented with pine. Maggie pulled three packets of hand warmers from her purse.

"Let's drop these into your mittens," she told Joey, crouching down in front of the boy while Griffin collected a hand saw and ropes from the truck bed. "They'll keep your fingers toasty warm."

"Cool," he whispered, still sounding dubious about their impending adventure in the woods. He gave her the mittens and she slipped a warmer into each one of them then helped him put them on. The boy was adorable bundled up in a thick winter jacket, a wool hat with earflaps and a matching scarf.

"It's going to be fun," she promised, glancing around the frozen forest that surrounded them as she tightened his scarf.

He wrapped his arms around her, giving her a sweet if unexpected hug.

She blinked away sudden tears, overwhelmed that this sweet boy seemed to be trying to comfort her in the same way she was for him.

"Maggie has warmers for your hands," Joey announced to Griffin when he joined them.

"I'll be fine," he said gently. "I appreciate the thought though."

Maggie turned away for a moment to swipe at her eyes.

"It's those little moments that get you," Griffin said under his breath as Joey ran forward to touch an icicle hanging from a tree branch.

"I wasn't expecting it," she admitted. "It makes me think of all the hugs he'll miss giving his mom. All the hugs Morgan and Ben missed."

"Yeah," Griffin breathed. "But they had you. Thanks for being part of this day with us. It means a lot."

She drew in a breath then smiled as she shoved the hand warmers into her own mittens. "I'm not freezing my fingers."

"Don't worry." Griffin stepped closer. "I'll warm you if you need it later."

Heat swirled through her at the intimacy in his tone. "I'll remember that."

They started into the woods, with Joey leading the

way. The overnight snowfall, practically a record in Stonecreek, had left about four inches on the ground, so they moved slowly, which was fine with Maggie. She was grateful to be away from town and all the doubts and worries about the competition swirling through her mind.

The trees were thick in this part of the woods, which was why the parks department issued licenses for the trees. With snow weighing down the branches and sunlight making the crystals sparkle like diamonds, it was like walking through an actual winter wonderland.

"Let me know when you find the perfect tree," Griffin called to the boy.

Joey nodded but continued trudging through the ankle-deep snow. Every few feet he'd reach out a hand to touch one of the low-hanging branches, as if he could feel which tree to choose.

About two hundred yards in he stopped. "This one," he said, pointing to a tree that was not much bigger than a shrub.

"It's kind of small," Griffin said slowly, darting a help-me look toward Maggie.

"As I remember it, Miss Jana has a lot of ornaments to hang on the tree. You might want to look for one that's a tiny bit taller."

Joey wiped his nose with one mitten. "This tree needs us." He raised his arms to indicate the huge pines that surrounded the scraggly pine he'd chosen. "All the other ones are so big that he can't get enough sun. He's not happy being the littlest guy with no friends around. We have to take him so he's not alone for Christmas."

Maggie fluttered her mittens in front of her eyes as tears sprang to them once again. The small tree was indeed receiving only thin shafts of sunlight, even though it was a particularly bright day for Oregon in December.

"I'm going to need to invest in waterproof mascara if I ever have kids," she mumbled. "Who knew I was such a crier?"

Griffin wrapped an arm around her shoulder and pulled her close, kissing the top of her head. "You'll be a great mom." He grinned at the boy. "Your logic makes total sense. Miss Jana has been talking about simplifying her life for years. I think a great place to start is by downsizing her Christmas decorations."

"What's downsizing?" Joey asked as he brushed snow off the tiny tree's branches.

"Getting rid of the stuff you don't need anymore."

"Mommy got rid of all her stuff after she called you to come to Seattle. 'Cause she wouldn't need it in heaven."

Maggie leaned her head on Griffin's shoulder, unsure how her heart would make it through this outing.

"Your mommy took care of things," Griffin confirmed. "I bet it would make her very happy that you chose this tree." With a squeeze to Maggie's shoulder, he stepped forward with his saw. "Plus this little guy will be easy to get back to the truck. Well done, Joey. Well done."

The boy's face lit with pride. "What can I do to help?"

Griffin gave him instructions for helping then knelt in the snow and began sawing the base of the trunk. Because the tree was small, it came down in minutes.

"Hey, Freddie," Joey said, patting one of the branches as if greeting an old friend.

"You're naming it?"

"All living things have a spirit. The tree's spirit is named Freddie."

Maggie expected Griffin to scoff or tell the boy he was being ridiculous. Instead, he straightened, then lifted the tree and set it against the trunk of another larger pine. "Say goodbye to your neighbors, Freddie." He spoke directly to the tree then inclined his head like he was listening to an answer. "That's right. You're the best tree in the forest so you're coming home for Christmas." He paused again then turned to Joey. "Freddie says thank you."

Joey giggled and shook his head. "Trees can't talk."

"His spirit talked to me," Griffin explained.

Joey thought about that for a moment then nodded. "You're welcome," he told the tree.

Griffin winked at Maggie and his smile was so filled with tenderness that her heart melted as fast as a snowball held over an open flame. How had she ever thought she could keep this man out of her life forever?

The pain that had seemed to consume her felt like a lifetime ago, and she couldn't help but believe he'd truly changed since becoming the boy's guardian. It had only been a matter of weeks but he was different than he'd been before, grounded in a way she could never have imagined.

It was deeply appealing, and she could almost feel

her ovaries doing a little happy dance of solidarity. Oh, yes. Every part of Maggie appreciated the new and improved Griffin Stone.

Every cell in her body wanted him.

And her whole, recently patched-up heart loved him.

She was in trouble. Big time.

"We need to find a tree for you." Joey tugged on her sleeve. "Do you want a big one or small?"

She swallowed back the emotions bubbling up inside her and tried to make her voice normal. "How about one that's just the right size?"

"You should get a girl," the boy said, slipping his hand into hers. "Freddie kind of wants a girlfriend."

"Freddie's a little young to be thinking about girls," Maggie answered, squeezing his fingers gently.

They continued through the forest, the boy telling her about the different friends he'd had at his daycare center in Seattle. He explained that Bennie liked race cars, Dante loved dinosaurs and Julian wasn't good at sharing his toys.

"But Emma was my best friend," Joey shared. "Her mommy and daddy got divorced. It's not the same as dying but they don't live together anymore, and she doesn't get to see her daddy very much. I gave her a hug when she was sad."

"She was lucky to have a friend like you." Maggie glanced over her shoulder to find Griffin following them with an incredulous grin on his face.

"I'm going to start preschool after Christmas." Joey wiped his nose again. "Miss Jana said I can pick out a brand-new backpack, even though I already have one with trucks on it. I'm gonna get purple camo this time. Purple's my favorite color."

"Mine too," Maggie told him.

"What's your favorite color, Griffin?" the boy called.

"Blue," Griffin answered.

"That was Mommy's favorite. She wanted to get a puppy and name it Blue."

"Is that so?" Maggie asked but before she could warn him about how much work a puppy would take, Joey let out a small squeal.

"There it is," he called. "It's Freddie's friend."

He kicked up snow as he ran and then stopped in front of a pint-size tree that looked just as pathetic as the one he'd chosen for himself. "Do you love her?" he asked, beginning to brush snow from the branches.

"I hope he's directing that question at me," Griffin said from directly behind Maggie. She whirled around, her cheek brushing the collar of his coat. The way he was looking at her left her breathless as warmth flooded her body.

"He's talking about the tree," she said, pushing at his chest. It was like trying to move a slab of granite. She turned back toward the boy, trying her best to ignore Griffin and the way her body reacted to his nearness. So much trouble.

"I do love the tree," she told Joey. "What do you think we should name her?"

"Fiona," he answered after a moment. "Freddie and Fiona will be best friends like me and Emma."

"You're my best friend," Griffin told her, his

breath tickling her ear. "I don't know how I ever got through life without you."

"You shouldn't say things like that," she admonished, even as her heart skipped a beat.

"But it's the truth." He leaned in and kissed her cheek, the spicy, minty scent of him doing crazy things to her senses. "You're some kind of miracle worker with Joey. I haven't ever heard him talk so much. He sounds happy."

"He is," she assured him. "Or at least he will be again. We have to believe that."

She glanced at the boy, who was having a sincere conversation with the pine tree then turned to face Griffin, lifting a mittened hand to his cheek. "He's been through something terrible, but he has you. It sounds like Cassie was a great mom, so he also has a foundation of love in his life. It won't be easy, but I have faith in you to see him through."

Griffin sucked in a deep breath as he studied her face. "Thank you," he whispered, his eyes crinkling at the corners the way they did when he was truly happy. "This is the first time I've believed that since this whole thing started."

"Griffin, can we cut her down now?" Joey asked, his eyes dancing with delight. "I want to bring her over to Freddie."

"We sure can, buddy." Griffin stepped forward. "After we make the big introduction and load them into the back of the SUV, how about we stop for hot chocolate and a cookie in town?"

"Yes," Joey answered immediately, pumping his fist in the air. "Can Maggie come?"

Griffin raised an eyebrow in her direction then

gave a pretty decent imitation of a courtly bow—at least in Maggie's opinion. "Ms. Spencer, would you care to join Master Joey and I post–tree cutting as we raise a hot chocolate mug in celebration of the honorable Freddie and Fiona?"

She laughed despite her immediate reservation. It would certainly set the gossips on a tear if she was seen with Griffin and his new charge in town. Especially on the night after everyone knew she'd been out to dinner with Christian.

As Griffin studied her face, his smile faded. "If not—"

"Of course I'd love to," she answered. "But only if you promise we can get extra whipped cream."

Joey clapped his hands and Griffin's gaze seemed to soften once again. "As much whipped cream as you can handle."

Chapter Ten

Jana studied her reflection in the mirror above the foyer table that afternoon. The house was empty and the sunlight streaming in from the picture window in the adjacent living room seemed to highlight every one of her wrinkles and laugh lines. She practiced a smile then groaned at the crow's feet fanning out from the edges of her eyes.

Never before had she so appreciated the old adage that youth is wasted on the young.

As a car engine sounded from the drive, she slicked on a coat of lip gloss, furtively wiped at her mouth with the back of her hand then quickly re-applied the subtle shade. It was silly that she wanted to look her best for an outing to the foundry Jim used to cast his sculptures.

She hadn't seen him since the kiss they'd shared in

his studio the previous week, although they'd spoken several times to discuss her ideas for the sculpture. To her surprise, each phone call had lasted close to an hour. She felt like a teenage girl again, sitting on the edge of her bed with butterflies flitting across her stomach as she discussed everything and nothing with the boy she secretly liked.

If Griffin or Marcus noted her preoccupation, neither of them mentioned it. She guessed they were too busy with their own schedules to pay any attention to her. That was the amazing thing about reconnecting with Jim. For the first time in years—maybe decades—Jana felt like someone truly noticed her.

Her marriage to Dave Stone had been mainly a happy one, other than his rift with Griffin. But the vines had driven her husband, made him restless in a way she couldn't seem to satisfy. Although she'd never confirmed it, she was almost certain he'd cheated on her. In their later years together, the marriage was much more a platonic partnership rather than any bit of a love affair.

Jana had been satisfied, or at least she thought she had. Something new was unfurling inside her. She didn't believe in regrets, yet life seemed to be giving her the do-over she hadn't even realized she wanted.

She opened the front door just as Jim started up the steps. "You didn't have to—" She stopped, her gaze catching on the bouquet of red roses and stargazer lilies he held.

"These are for you," he said with an almost bashful smile.

"Oh," she breathed, reaching out a hand to take the lovely blooms from him.

"I had to stop at the hardware store on my way here. These were in the window of the florist. The colors looked so bright against the snow." He shrugged. "It's probably silly, but I thought you'd like them."

"I do," she said, breathing in the sweet scent. "Thank you." She held out the bouquet, which did look especially colorful in contrast with the snow that was just starting to melt. The temperature had risen to almost twenty degrees today, though still nowhere near normal in Stonecreek during December. They rarely got more than a dusting of snow in this part of the state. The unexpected storm made for a festive backdrop the week before Christmas, but the monochromatic color scheme it created was unusual. The flowers were a welcome pop of color.

"Please come in for a minute while I put them in water."

She led him into the house, realizing that this was probably the first time he'd ever been in her home. The house she'd shared with her husband. Although other than her visit to the studio, she'd never been in Jim's house. She could imagine it though—eclectic and a bit cluttered, classic without taking itself too seriously. A lot like the man himself.

"You have a beautiful home," he said, as if reading her thoughts.

She glanced over her shoulder and smiled. "It's only in the past few years that I felt like it belonged to me."

"I thought you and Dave lived here for years."

"We did, but his mother was alive for most of that time. She died only six months before him. Mrs.

Stone had strong views on the decor of her home. Quite strong."

He chuckled. "Even though she no longer lived here?"

She pulled a vase from an upper cabinet. "I imagine Vivian would feel the same way."

"You're right," he admitted. "In fact, Maggie is starting to renovate the old house and it's driving Mom absolutely crazy. She keeps lecturing her on respecting the past, and the quality of workmanship and materials in the good old days." He shrugged. "The problem is she can't give up control."

"No offense to your mother, but Charlotte must have been a saint to deal with her. I can't imagine Vivian making it easy for anyone."

One big shoulder lifted again then dropped. "We managed, but I let my mother have too much influence when I was younger. I'm not proud of that."

Her fingers trembled as she unwrapped the flowers and pulled scissors from a drawer to trim the stems. Of course he was talking about her. About the year they'd dated and how his mother had deemed Jana's blue-collar background inferior for her beloved son. It was old news now. Vivian had to give Jana and all the Stones the respect they deserved, even if it was grudging.

Jana had more than earned her place in this community. Why did it still sting that the first boy she'd given her heart to hadn't fought for her?

"We all make mistakes," she said, and they both ignored the false cheer in her voice.

She turned to the sink and filled the vase with water. As she placed the flowers in the glass container, Jim's arms wound around her from behind. He smelled of clay, even away from the studio, and the scent and the feel of his warmth against her made her knees go weak.

"How many times can I say I'm sorry?" he whispered, nuzzling her ear then gently kissing the side of her throat.

"No more apologies," she said, tipping her head to give him better access. "I don't want to be beholden to the past." She flipped off the faucet then shivered as his calloused fingers grazed her neck.

"Then let's focus on right now," he said against her skin. "I want you so damn much, Jana. I've barely thought of anything else since you walked out last week."

She turned and he immediately captured her mouth with his, kissing her in exactly the way she liked to be kissed. This moment was different than the one they'd shared in his studio. That had been a shock, nerves skittering through her at how he might judge the woman she'd become, no longer young and beautiful.

But his words and the way he held her—like she was the most precious thing in the world—gave her confidence. As quickly as they'd appeared, her doubts vanished. This felt so right and her heart thundered at the turn her life was taking.

She'd relegated herself to the back burner of her own life, but here she was in the blue center of the flame. She couldn't think of anything she wanted more…except maybe leading Jim Spencer up to her bedroom.

Then she heard the front door open. She yanked

away from his embrace, knocking over the flowers with one nervous hand. The vase clattered to the porcelain but didn't break, and she quickly righted it, refusing to glance at Jim, who'd thankfully taken a few steps to the edge of the island.

"Mom?" Griffin's voice rang out from the entry.

"In the kitchen," she called.

The patter of small feet sounded in the hall a moment before Joey ran around the corner into the room. "We got a tree," he shouted, more animated than she'd seen him since he arrived in Stonecreek. "I named him Freddie. Come and see. Come and see."

His cheeks were flushed, his little arms waving in the air as a huge grin lit his face. Jana's heart lifted at this glimpse of a happy, carefree child unencumbered by the tragedy he'd endured.

"Who are you?" he asked Jim, skidding to a stop in his stocking feet.

"My name's Jim."

"Mr. Spencer is Maggie's dad." Griffin entered the room, darting a vaguely suspicious gaze between Jana and Jim, as if he knew what they'd been doing moments ago.

Jana felt her face go hot and spun away from her son, busying herself with righting the flowers.

"We got Maggie a tree too," Joey told him, unaware of the underlying tension that suddenly filled the room. "Its name is Fiona."

"What a clever idea," Jana said, trying to keep her voice steady, "to name the trees."

"Wait until you see them," Griffin said. "Are we interrupting something? Where'd you get the flowers, Mom?"

"Jim brought them." Jana took a breath and turned, raising a brow at her son to let him know she was not open for commentary on the gift. "We're about to head out to visit the foundry that casts his sculptures."

"I want to give your mom an idea of the process as we're working on a final design for the Harvest commission."

Griffin walked to the refrigerator and grabbed a bottle of water. "I bet that's not all he wants to give you," he said, low enough that only Jana could hear.

So much for quelling him with an arched brow.

"Enough," she whispered then placed the vase of flowers on the island. "I'd like to see your tree," she said to Joey, reaching out to wipe a speck of chocolate from his cheek. "Looks like you stopped at the bakery on your way home."

"Maggie and I got extra whipped cream on our hot chocolate," the boy reported.

"She likes whipped cream." Tenderness was clear in Jim's voice. His eyes clouded as he glanced at Griffin. "I didn't realize the two of you were spending time together again."

Griffin lifted the water bottle to his lips, his movements casual. Still, Jana could almost feel him bristling at the subtle accusation in Jim's tone. "Is that a problem?"

Jim straightened his shoulders, transforming from eclectic artist and ardent kisser to overprotective father in an instant. Even with his defensive stance directed at her son, Jana respected him for it. "I don't want to see her hurt."

A muscle jumped in Griffin's jaw, the same way

it had in his father's when Dave was frustrated or angry. But her son only nodded. "I understand." He set the water bottle on the counter. "I promise I won't hurt her again. She means the world to me."

She held her breath as Jim mulled over the declaration. To say Griffin kept his emotions close to the vest was an understatement, so she knew it had taken a lot for him to reveal any bit of his feelings for Maggie.

"See that you don't," he answered finally. Griffin let out a long breath and nodded.

"Freddie is waiting." Joey tugged on Jana's hand.

She smiled at Jim. "Would you like to meet Freddie?"

"Absolutely," he answered and she felt a deep sense of contentment that all the pieces of her life were finally beginning to fit together.

The more time Griffin spent with Christian Milken, the deeper his distaste for the slick CEO became. He'd given him a tour of the bottling operation today, reviewing the environmental practices they employed, including alternative energy and an extensive recycling program. Some of the details weren't applicable to the technology LiveSoft created but much of the construction initiatives could become a blueprint for how the company built their new headquarters.

"You've been doing this your whole life?" Christian asked, taking in the view of the fields from Griffin's new office. It was actually Trevor's old office. Griffin had expected to feel odd in the space. Instead, it gave him a sense of connection with his brother.

Trevor had been traveling back and forth between Stonecreek and Sonoma, and seemed happier than Griffin had ever seen him. He was already talking about a partnership between Calico and Harvest, and it came as a huge shock to both of them that they were excited to work together.

"No," he admitted without reservation. "I left Stonecreek when I was eighteen to join the army. Did three tours then retired from active duty and worked in the construction industry around the region. I returned to Harvest about six months ago."

Christian looked surprised. "You certainly sound like an expert."

"I've kept tabs on the industry and Marcus has been a great teacher since I've been back."

"You think after all you've seen that you can be happy in this tiny part of the world?"

"Without a doubt. Stonecreek is home."

"It's so damn small."

"So is Timmins."

Christian laughed softly. "True enough. I'm not trying to compare the two. They're equally provincial in my mind."

"Are you having reservations about making a choice for the headquarters?"

"Where we have our headquarters is a part of the branding for the company. LiveSoft is all about helping people to slow down and smell the roses. Our employees are like little cult members with all the meditation and mindfulness. So being in a small town makes sense for growing the business and for the corporate culture."

"Why does it sound like the CEO isn't buying into the branding?"

"Dude, you've got to understand. You're here now, but you chose to come back. Look at your brother moving off to greener pastures. I love my life in Los Angeles. There are things to do and people to see twenty-four/seven."

Griffin wasn't sure what he found more annoying—this grown man using the word *dude* or the fact that the company's leader didn't believe in what his product represented.

Christian didn't seem to notice that Griffin wasn't captivated by his musings on the good life in LA. "I can hop a plane and be in Vegas in an hour or Cabo in just a little longer. Up here is a different world. It's like real life."

"Isn't that the point?" Griffin didn't bother to hide his irritation, and Christian blinked like it shocked him that someone didn't agree with his opinion.

"I'm not knocking it…exactly. We all have to settle down at some point. You know I started LiveSoft as a lark, right? My roommate at Harvard was brilliant—makes Zuckerberg look like a slacker. But he wasn't driven, not the way you need to be to make it these days. He ended up dropping out after the first year, went to Costa Rica to run a tree farm or something. I flew down for spring break junior year and he already had a beta version of the app. It was his brainchild, but I saw the potential in it."

"So you partnered with him?"

Christian was still looking out the window so Griffin clicked on his email, not really caring about the genesis of LiveSoft.

"Hell, no." Christian laughed. "I took it from him."

Griffin's fingers stilled on the mouse and he stood. "Took as in stole?"

Christian held up his hands. "Intellectual property rights are tricky to enforce. He had the idea and the software to support it. I traded him shares in the tree farm for rights to bring LiveSoft to market. Grant was happy as a clam until hurricane season last year. His whole property was wiped out. Poor schmuck." He moved toward the desk and lowered his voice. "But do you know what the best part is?"

"No idea."

"As part of the app, users input a ton of vital statistics. It's more than just shopping habits. They enter workouts, grocery lists, sleep cycles, vacation plans and career goals. I know what cars they drive and the value of their homes. It's all in one place, managed by my company. No one bats an eye, and marketing firms pay huge money for that intel."

"Are you allowed to sell it? I thought part of the draw of the app was confidentiality. My brother said he tried to work with you, but there are so many hoops and nondisclosures to be a designated partner."

"That's true." Christian nodded, and Griffin wanted to wipe the self-satisfied look off his face. "Subscribers pay money because they think we're protecting them. Marketing firms pay money to get access to our lists. I'm selling data on the back end. It's a revenue cash cow all the way around."

"What happens when your customers realize it?"

"Dude. Not going to happen."

"You think you can keep something like that secret?"

"I pay my tech guys very well for that secret."

Griffin felt his stomach tighten at the thought that his town was getting mixed up with such a crook. Yes, LiveSoft was on top now but what would happen when its shady practices were exposed? He didn't care how much Christian paid anyone, there was no keeping secrets in this day and age.

"It's your business." Griffin tried not to let his disgust show on his face. "I guess." Maggie wanted to woo this fraudulent jerk and Griffin wanted to support her no matter what. He only wished there was a way to entice the company but leave its CEO far behind.

"Yeah, and the board only cares that I'm making money for them. We're talking about taking the company public once the location for the headquarters is selected. It's going to make me a very rich man."

"Sounds like you could be based in Stonecreek but travel wherever and whenever you want. Best of both worlds."

"That's a good point." Christian nodded. "It could work out fine, especially if I have someone like Maggie Spencer on my arm."

Griffin stepped around his desk. "I don't think so."

"Seriously?" Christian scoffed. "Come on, dude. That woman is hot for me. She's giving off so many signals she's more overworked than a traffic light in NYC."

"It's Maggie's job to make sure you're happy," Griffin said through clenched teeth. "She wants to win the competition. You might not care for small-town life, but LiveSoft is an exceptional opportunity for Stonecreek. It matters and, therefore, you matter."

"Nah. She likes me. Trust me. I can read women."

"What a talent."

"I heard she used to be engaged to your brother?"

Another subject Griffin had no intention of discussing with this man. "Yes."

"Do you think he could give me any tips on how to get in her pants? I thought I was close the other night, but she got cold feet."

I'm going to kill him, Griffin thought. "Trevor and Maggie have been friends for years," he answered instead. "Just because the wedding didn't work out doesn't mean he'll help you take advantage of her."

"Whoa, there. No one's taking advantage. Let's just say…" Christian winked. "A merger between myself and the lovely Ms. Spencer would be mutually beneficial."

"Right."

"You want to go get a drink?"

"Not tonight." Or ever in a million years, he added silently.

"Too bad. Maggie and I are meeting at O'Malley's. Maybe we'll grab dinner after and…" He wiggled his eyebrows. "Who knows where the night will lead."

Wait. What?

"You have a date with Maggie?" he asked and something must have leaked into his tone because Christian frowned.

"Is that a problem?"

Hell, yeah. A big one.

"Nope. But I'm going to take you up on that drink after all. If you don't mind a third wheel?"

"No worries, dude. Just be sure to make yourself

scarce once she gets a little tipsy. If you know what I mean?"

He was pretty sure Christian meant he had plans to get Maggie drunk and take advantage of her. No way in hell would Griffin let that happen.

He still couldn't understand why Maggie was going out with Christian after the night they'd had together. He hadn't told her he loved her but he'd *made* love to her. She had to understand what that meant. Or did she?

Chapter Eleven

Maggie walked into O'Malley's that night, immediately greeted by Chuck and several regulars.

"Your guys are in the back," Chuck told her.

Her tongue suddenly felt too big for her mouth. "My g-guys?" she stammered.

"It doesn't seem fair." Jenna Phillips, one of the bar's longtime waitresses and Maggie's former babysitter from when she was a girl, bumped her hip like they were dancing. "I've been divorced for five years and can barely scrounge up a date on Match and you've got two hot men vying for your attention."

Maggie shook her head. "No one is vying for me."

Jenna laughed, low and husky from decades of Marlboros. "When was the last time you checked the LiveSoft competition page? I wouldn't have guessed you'd become the Stonecreek Siren, but I guess it fits.

Griffin looked like he wanted to strangle that slick CEO when they walked in earlier."

"What is a Stonecreek Siren?" Maggie asked, her head beginning to swim.

"*Who*, you mean," Chuck clarified. "It's you, darlin'. At least according to the comments on social media."

Maggie hadn't actually viewed any of the latest photos or videos uploaded to the LiveSoft site. Work had been crazy and she'd been too busy at night with her renovation project. She also had to admit that she didn't relish the idea of watching herself take center stage. She'd asked Morgan to view it and make sure she hadn't come out looking like a total fool. Her sister reported back that everything was great, but now Maggie realized the teenager probably hadn't even bothered to look.

Great. She was the Stonecreek Siren.

"It's putting us way ahead on likes and follows," Brett Russell, one of Stonecreek's police deputies—off-duty now—reported. "I set it up to get notifications. If we win, we're hoping some of that increased tax revenue will head in the department's direction." He pulled his phone out of his jacket pocket. "We're up to—"

"Don't tell me," Maggie blurted, holding up a hand. "I'm nervous enough already."

"Public voting is only one part of the equation," Chuck said from behind the bar, as if she didn't realize that already. "The board and senior management team have to review our proposal. I assume you did a good job on it?"

Jenna, Brett and the rest of the bar patrons waited for her answer with intense stares.

She laughed at the thought of being put on the spot by the happy-hour crowd, but nodded at Chuck. "I did my best."

No one looked particularly convinced that her best would be good enough, but then Jenna winked. "Did you bring the cameras tonight? Might be some fireworks."

"The cameras aren't mine," Maggie told them, as if they didn't know that already. "Christian is here to meet with the town council and spend some time at Harvest, but they won't film again until Christmas Eve."

"What did you get him for Christmas?" Brett asked.

Maggie rolled her eyes. "I haven't had time to do any shopping, but Christian isn't on my gift list. He's a business colleague."

"You went on a date with him," Jenna pointed out, none too helpfully as far as Maggie was concerned.

"It was a dinner with his assistant filming the whole time. I didn't want them to use the footage of Jessica in the pageant. I'm guessing you already know that."

"Yeah." Jenna shrugged. "But it doesn't go with the Stonecreek Siren bit quite as well."

Maggie blew out a frustrated breath. "Chuck, can I get a glass of pinot grigio?"

The bartender nodded. "On the house, Ms. Mayor. I'm already counting on being the favorite watering hole for the LiveSoft crowd."

"No pressure," Maggie muttered under her breath but gave the burly bar owner a thumbs-up.

He poured a glass of Harvest Pinot Grigio, and Jenna handed it to her.

Maggie walked toward the game room at the back of the bar. Christian and Griffin stood on the far side, facing a dartboard that hung on the back wall. Both of them turned as she came around the corner, and a group of men playing pool at a nearby table waved a greeting.

"Hey," Christian called. "You want to play the winner?"

She shook her head. "I'm not much for darts."

"Come on," he coaxed as she moved closer. "I'll give you some pointers." He wrapped an arm around her waist and pulled her close. She smiled but shifted away, flicking a gaze at the other patrons and then to Griffin, who was watching her with steely eyes.

"I didn't expect to see you here," she said to him.

"I bet."

Anger and frustration warred in his tone. She wished she could explain that she'd agreed to meet Christian tonight to tell him there could be nothing between the two of them other than friendship. Surely Griffin didn't think she was interested in the other man after what they'd shared. But she couldn't cut Christian out of her life in the middle of the competition for his company.

Maggie took a long swallow of wine before smiling again. "Who's winning?"

"Me, of course," Christian said and she saw Griffin roll his eyes behind the other man's back. "I thought he was going to take me, but he whiffed the last shot."

"He outplayed me," Griffin said, deadpan, and Maggie realized he was doing all this for her. The knowledge did funny things to her heart. It couldn't be easy for a man like Griffin to humor a guy he clearly couldn't stand—schmoozing and glad-handing were skills more aligned with Trevor's wheelhouse. But he was making the effort because LiveSoft, and therefore its CEO, were important to Maggie.

"Your Christmas tree looks great," she said quietly, willing him to understand that this evening wasn't at all what it appeared from the outside. He'd texted a photo of Joey in front of the scraggly tree, a huge smile on his face and the tree covered in ornaments and colored lights.

"Thanks."

"I need another beer," Christian announced, oblivious to the tension sparking around him.

"Jenna should be making her rounds in a few minutes," Maggie offered.

"I'll go the bar," Griffin said tightly.

"That's my bro." Christian took out his wallet. "You need me to spot you some cash?"

Griffin shook his head. "This round's on me. Maggie?"

"I'm good," she said, lifting her half-full glass.

"Indeed you are." Christian chuckled, the only one of them amused by the innuendo.

Maggie watched Griffin walk away, wondering why she hadn't thought to tell him about her plans with Christian earlier. It had seemed inconsequential at the time, but now it felt foolish.

She took a fortifying breath, tamping down her

guilt about the expectations of people in the community and stepped toward Christian. "We need to talk."

"That sounds ominous," he said with a wide grin. "You sure you don't want to play a round of darts? I can help with your form." He reached for her, but she stepped back, placing her wineglass on a nearby high-top table.

"This isn't a date," she blurted. "We aren't dating."

His brows drew together. "It feels like a date to me."

"No. This situation is new for both of us. The competition complicates things. I like you, Christian." That wasn't exactly a lie. He was smart and charming and easy to talk to. Before he'd made it clear he wanted more from her, she'd thought they could be friends. Still, as dedicated as she was to the town, she couldn't sacrifice her own happiness to win a competition. "But I'm not part of the incentive package."

He twirled one of the plastic darts between two fingers. "I thought I made it clear I need a good reason to pick Stonecreek."

"Yes," she agreed slowly. "If you take a look at our proposal, we've given you several. Stonecreek is a great fit for your headquarters. We offer low taxes, minimal regulations, a high-quality talent pool, affordable real estate and low living costs. We'd do everything we can to support the entrepreneurial culture at LiveSoft. I hope to get the chance to welcome you to the town." She pursed her lips then added, "But not to my bed."

"Ouch." He scrubbed a hand over his jaw. "Have you seen what they're calling you online?"

She shook her head. "I just heard about it."

"The folks in Timmins did too. They called about an hour ago with an offer for an additional two million in tax breaks and incentives if LiveSoft comes there."

Maggie felt her eyes widen. Timmins was a similar economic makeup to Stonecreek, although with Mount Hood in their backyard, the town relied more heavily on tourism income. Where would they get the reserves to offer that kind of money?

"That's generous," she whispered.

"I was hoping for generosity of a different sort from you," he said coolly.

"That's funny," a deep voice said from behind Maggie. "Because with talk like that, it sounds like you're hoping to get your teeth knocked in."

Maggie looked over her shoulder to find Griffin glaring at Christian, a beer bottle clenched in each fist.

His gaze locked on hers before returning to the CEO. "You need to apologize to Maggie."

"Dude, chill out." Christian transferred the darts to one hand and reached for a beer with the other.

Griffin placed the two bottles on a table then folded his muscled arms over his chest. "Don't call me dude. This isn't Chris and Grif's excellent adventure."

"No doubt," Christian muttered. "Talk about a buzzkill night."

"I think you're done here," Griffin said, his voice ominously quiet.

"Stonecreek Siren?" Christian bit off an angry laugh. She noticed that his eyes looked glassy and wondered how many drinks he'd had tonight. This man was so different than the charismatic company leader she'd met at the beginning of the month. "More like the Stonecreek Tease. I'm disappointed, Maggie. I thought you cared about your town."

"I do," she whispered, glancing around to realize they were beginning to attract the attention of other patrons. Attention Maggie didn't want or need right now.

"Prove it."

"We're trying." She moved toward him so that they hopefully wouldn't be overheard, tucking her hair behind her ears. "If you think about the people you've met in town and the welcome you've received. Please spend some time reviewing our proposal. I'm sure you'll—"

"I'm not talking about the town." He leaned in, so close she could smell the alcohol on his breath, something strong and acrid. Not just a few beers at happy hour. "I mean *you* prove it. I'm going to walk out of this bar right now. My room number is four twenty-three. I'll expect you there in—"

The sound of her open palm smacking his cheek startled her. She gasped as Christian reeled back with a curse. Holding a hand to his face, he lunged forward only to be stopped by Griffin's hand on his chest.

Maggie was jostled into a table, the force knocking over her wineglass.

"Get the hell out," Griffin growled, his voice like granite.

"Come on, dude. I'm playing. If she wasn't so uptight then—"

Griffin closed his fist on Christian's shirtfront, wrinkling the expensive fabric. "Out of respect for what your company means to this town, you have thirty seconds to clear out of O'Malley's. After that, I'm going to escort you out myself. I couldn't give a damn about your tax revenue, and I know for sure this isn't the kind of place that tolerates men who talk to a woman like she's your personal property. I'm sure as hell not going to let you get away with it."

There were a few shouts of agreement from the other side of the game room.

Christian wrenched free from Griffin's grasp and jabbed a finger in Maggie's direction. "Is this how you want it to end?"

"It doesn't have to end," she said, automatically going into damage control mode. She ignored Griffin's snort of derision. "Things got out of hand tonight," she said. "But don't throw out everything that's gone before because of it. We're the right choice for LiveSoft."

She hated the feeling that she was groveling, but what else could she do? She wasn't about to sleep with the CEO to guarantee a win, yet she had to at least try to smooth the waters between them. "Our relationship isn't over."

Christian looked at her and then Griffin as if seeing them with fresh eyes. Understanding dawned and his mouth curled into a sneer. "Think again, sweetheart." He practically spat the words at her before storming past.

The bar was silent other than a classic Bob Seger song playing from the speakers.

Maggie drew in several long breaths then righted the wineglass with trembling fingers.

"Don't worry about that, hon." Jenna was beside her the next moment. "I'll clean it up."

"I'm sorry," Maggie whispered, and she hoped Jenna understood it was for more than the spilled drink.

"It's fine." Jenna's voice soothed some of the ache inside Maggie. "If a rich, powerful guy like that can't find a girlfriend without bribing one, there's got to be something wrong with him." She nudged Maggie's arm with her shoulder. "Like maybe his junk don't work?"

Maggie gave a small laugh. "I don't know about that." She turned, ready to thank Griffin for rescuing her once again, only to find that he'd disappeared.

"He left right after the other one," Jenna told her. "Hopefully not to track him down."

Maggie swallowed and dug in the cross-body purse she wore for her wallet. "I've got to talk to him," she whispered.

"Your drink's on the house," Jenna said. "Or the table more like it. You go after Griffin. Don't let him get away."

With a sharp nod, Maggie walked through the bar, purposely avoiding eye contact with anyone or answering the myriad of comments and questions she received on her way out.

"What happens now?"

"Does this mean Stonecreek lost?"

"Too bad the cameras weren't filming tonight."

The temperature had risen into the low forties earlier today, melting most of last weekend's snow. Right now it dipped closer to thirty degrees, and the cold night air felt good on Maggie's face as she exited the bar.

Quiet enveloped her as the heavy door slammed shut, and she closed her eyes for a moment, trying to calm her racing heart.

"Please tell me you aren't thinking of going to his room."

She turned at the sound of Griffin's voice. He leaned against the brick building on the other side of the bar's entrance.

Her stomach flipped wildly as if she hadn't seen him in months instead of minutes. "You can't be serious."

"The last thing I heard you tell him was 'our relationship isn't over.'" He straightened, running a hand through his hair as he approached her.

"I was talking about the town. You saw me slap him, Griffin. Wasn't that clear enough for you?"

"I don't know what to think anymore. A few days ago I was in your bed and tonight I have to listen to that CEO chump share his plans to get lucky with you after your date. Your *date*, Maggie."

"It wasn't a date. I agreed to meet him to explain that we weren't going to have a relationship. I thought I could make him understand without jeopardizing the town's chances in the competition."

"By going on a date," he muttered.

"It. Wasn't. A. Date."

"You don't know how it killed me to play nice with him."

She laughed despite her mounting frustration. "That was you playing nice?"

"He's not bleeding."

"I'm sorry I didn't talk to you about my plans for tonight," she said softly.

"You don't owe me that," he answered. He moved forward, reached out and cupped her cheeks between his palms. As always, she revelled in the warmth of his touch. The rough feel of his calloused palms sent sparks racing along her spine. Would this electric response to Griffin Stone ever stop? It was part curse and part blessing. She couldn't decide which would weigh out in the end.

"I didn't mean—"

He placed his two thumbs on the seam of her lips. "When Christian told me he was going on a date with you, it ripped at my heart. But I also understand how badly I messed up when I left for Seattle with only a lame text." He shook his head. "I thought I was doing the right thing at the time."

"It's okay."

"I love you, Maggie."

She pulled away, even as the words ricocheted through her heart. "Don't say that."

Griffin's mouth dropped open and she saw pain, raw and unfiltered, in his gaze before the emotional shutter dropped over his eyes. "I thought that's what you wanted."

"I… Yes… No…" She shook her head, wondering how to explain something she barely understood herself. "I've moved on," she lied.

"You haven't." He crowded her, his warmth easily melting the ice she was trying to keep frozen around her heart.

"I don't trust you," she whispered, miserable for both of them.

"You trusted me enough to let me into your bed," he said, his voice a low rasp.

She closed her eyes and shared the truth that would drive the final wedge between them. "But not enough to open my heart again."

"Maggie."

The word was both a plea and a promise.

"You're here now because it's necessary. You have to settle down for Joey. But what if things change?"

"What things?" he demanded, taking a step back like her words were shards of glass stabbing at him.

"I don't know." She threw up her hands. "What if you get sick of the wine business or small-town life in Stonecreek? You could take him anywhere or leave him with your mom while you—"

"I'd never do that."

She knew he wouldn't desert the boy. Unfortunately, she had no such confidence in his devotion to her. She wanted to believe him, but him leaving had damaged something deep inside her. She'd made a decision about the path her life would take and was too scared to change it now.

"I can't, Griffin," she said, letting a finality she didn't feel color her tone.

"What about the other night?"

"It was lovely," she said quietly. "But a mistake."

"A mistake? Good to know how you really feel."

She kept her gaze on the sidewalk. If she looked into his eyes right now she wouldn't be able to let him go.

"Thank you for coming to my defense tonight," she told him. "Even if between the two of us we ruined Stonecreek's chances of becoming the next

LiveSoft headquarters, I appreciate having you on my side."

"I'll always be on your side."

She swallowed back the sob that threatened to escape.

"Goodbye, Griffin."

"Good night, Maggie," he answered and she walked away before he had a chance to notice the tears streaming down her face.

Chapter Twelve

"Did you find out Santa put you on the naughty list?" Marcus asked the following morning.

Griffin lifted the ax high above his head then swung it down hard, the piece of oak splitting with a satisfying crack. "What the hell are you talking about?"

"You're chopping that wood like you have a personal vendetta against it," Marcus said, flexing his gloved hands. "I think your mom could have an actual bonfire every night for the rest of the season and still have a pile of kindling left over."

"It may snow again," Griffin answered. "The temperatures will drop."

"Have you heard of the nifty invention called a furnace?"

Griffin swiped a hand across his brow, rolled his

shoulders against the ache already forming there. "Did you need something, Marcus?"

"My wedding's coming up in a couple of weeks."

"New Year's Eve." Griffin grabbed another log from the pile and set it on the wood block. "It's on my calendar."

"Brenna pointed out to me last night that I don't have a best man. Would you stand up with me?"

Griffin stilled. "Me?"

"Don't sound so shocked," Marcus said with a soft laugh.

"I *am* shocked." Griffin set the ax on the ground and pulled in a deep breath. "I'm honored, but it's not a good idea."

"Why not?"

Heartache clogged Griffin's throat, making it difficult to get the words out. He walked away a few paces and rearranged several logs on the woodpile as Marcus waited for an answer. Griffin had always admired the other man's seemingly endless patience. He wished he had more of it.

"Is Maggie going to be Brenna's maid of honor?" he asked finally, turning back.

"Of course."

"There's your reason."

"I thought the two of you were working things out."

"Yeah, well…" Griffin massaged a hand along the back of his neck. "I thought so, too, but—"

"You can't give up on her."

Both men turned as Brenna walked up the hill toward them. Griffin glanced at his friend, jealousy winging through him at the obvious love that filled

Marcus's dark eyes. He immediately walked forward and wrapped an arm around Brenna's shoulder, the action at once protective and tender, like he couldn't resist his need to touch the woman he loved. The gaping hole in Griffin's chest widened at the thought that he'd lost his chance for that with Maggie.

"It's hard to give up something that was never really mine," he said without emotion.

"I thought you'd changed when you came back. I thought you were going to fight for Maggie." She stepped away from her fiancé's embrace and toward Griffin. "What about the video?"

Griffin shook his head. "What video?"

"The one Ray Sharpe took at the bar last night." She placed her hands on her narrow hips, one foot tapping like she was dealing with a recalcitrant schoolboy. "Christian Milken is a slimeball."

"No argument here." Griffin shrugged. "But what does that have to do with me giving up on Maggie? I told her I loved her, Brenna. She walked away this time."

"She's scared. You hurt her."

"I know, but I can't make her give me another chance. She might be right that I don't deserve one."

"Coward," Brenna whispered then pulled her phone from her coat pocket. "Press Play." She shoved the phone in front of him, and Marcus came to stand next to Griffin as he hit the play button. The same anger he'd felt last night bubbled to the surface as he watched the events in the bar, this time as an observer. It was difficult to hear all of what was being said until the bar gradually went quiet, but the outrage and disappointment in Maggie's eyes were clear. And the murder in his own.

He got to the point where he stepped in front of her to confront the dirtbag CEO and his breath caught in his throat. During the interchange, Maggie's gaze stayed on him, filled with gratitude and…love. All the emotions she tried to keep hidden from him were clear. She looked beautiful and vulnerable and strong as hell all at the same time, an intoxicating combination.

The realization struck that since he'd returned to Stonecreek six months ago, Maggie had continually put herself on the line to show him how much he meant to her. He'd had nothing to lose, the black sheep of the family coming back home with no plan to stay. He'd made no promises or commitments and given her very little reason to believe he had anything to offer.

She hadn't cared. She'd brought a light to his life, helping him to make peace with his past while giving him hope for the future for the first time in ages. She'd grounded him with her love. For that, he owed her more than he could ever repay.

He couldn't imagine his life without her. He'd promised himself that he wouldn't give up, but Brenna was right. He was a coward. Maggie hadn't fallen easily back into his arms, and he hadn't rolled up his sleeves to fight for her.

She deserved a man who would stay no matter what. She'd let him back into her life after he'd hurt her. No wonder she didn't trust him. He still needed to earn that trust.

He muttered a string of curses then handed the phone to Brenna, shocked to find her grinning at him.

"Sorry," he whispered. "I need to watch my language."

"The language doesn't bother me," she said. "It sounds like you're finally ready to pull your stupid head out—"

"I think you made your point, hon," Marcus said, shaking his head.

"Right." Brenna pocketed the phone then lifted a challenging brow at Griffin. "So what are you going to do about it?"

"I just came to the realization I'm an idiot. Give me a minute to figure out how to make things better." His mind raced as he thought about the possibility of winning her back. It was a challenge he'd find a way to overcome, no matter what.

Jana took the glass of wine Jim handed her and downed half of it in one gulp.

"Nervous?" he asked, a smile curving his lips.

"Are you sure it's okay for me to be here?"

He nodded. "Morgan and Ben went to a basketball game at the high school. They won't be back for hours." He traced a rough finger down her cheek. "Even if they were at home, it would be fine for you to be here too. You're important to—"

"You shared this house with your wife," she blurted, setting down the wineglass on the kitchen table and walking to the window. She lifted her hand to the cold glass, looking out to the cheerfully decorated houses up and down the street. Christmas lights twinkled in the darkness, making the neighborhood look even more charming.

"Yes," Jim agreed slowly. "We were happy here. Just like you and Dave made a life at Harvest. But that has nothing to do with now, Jana. Are you going to let the past ruin this chance we have for a future?"

"I don't want to, but I can't seem to let go." She turned, laughing softly. "No wonder Griffin can't move on from everything he went through with his dad. He has a terrible role model in me. I don't know how to get over having my heart broken over thirty years ago."

"You got over it," he said softly. "You created an amazing life for yourself."

"You make me happy," she told him then added, "and I feel guilty because of it." She clenched her hands until her nails dug into the soft flesh at the centers of her palms. "Because it was always you, Jim. I knew it, and Dave knew it. I loved him, but my heart wasn't whole so I could only ever give him half of it. How can I think I deserve to be happy after that?"

"Jana." He moved closer, laced his fingers with hers. "Of course you deserve happiness. Dave would want it for you just like Charlotte would for me."

"I don't know," she whispered.

"Then let me be sure for both of us," he told her, and warmth infused her heart. "I wasn't able to when we were younger, but I'm different now. You fell in love with a boy, but I want to love you the way a man should. The way you deserve to be loved."

She blinked away the tears that sprang to her eyes. Could this truly be happening? Her heart felt so full it was almost bursting. She leaned up on tiptoes to kiss him.

He deepened the kiss and she happily opened for him, their tongues dancing as liquid heat pooled low in her belly.

"Dad?"

At the sound of Maggie's shocked voice, Jana tried to yank away. How had they not heard her come into the kitchen?

But Jim held tight to her, tucking her against his side.

"Hey, Mags," he said, his voice just the slightest bit breathless. "I didn't expect you to stop by tonight."

"Ya think? I left a few sweaters in the closet upstairs. I guess I should have called first."

Jana finally glanced up from the floor. "We didn't hear you," she mumbled, feeling like a teenager who'd been caught making out by a disapproving parent.

"Are you two…?" Maggie shook her head. "How long…?"

"It's new," Jana said quickly. "If you're not comfortable then—"

"We hope you'll get used to it," Jim interrupted. "Griffin isn't the only guy around here who let a good one slip away. I'm not going to make the mistake again."

Maggie stared for another long moment then gave a soft laugh. "My dad is straightening out his life before me. I don't know whether to feel hopeful or more depressed."

"I vote hopeful," Jim answered. "I've had way more time to figure things out."

Jana lifted on her tiptoes to kiss his cheek then moved out of his embrace and toward Maggie. "You aren't messed up, Maggie. To me it seems like you're doing everything right. I haven't seen so much excitement in this sleepy town in years. You're putting us on the map."

"Not for long," she said, and the remorse that flashed in her eyes made Jana's heart hurt. "I think I ruined our chances of winning the competition."

Jana shook her head. "That's impossible. We've all seen how hard you've worked. Stonecreek has never looked so good."

"I slapped Christian Milken at O'Malley's last night," Maggie said dully. "Everyone in the bar saw and he was really upset."

"What did he do?" Jim asked.

Maggie flashed a watery smile, as if grateful her father assumed the CEO had done something to deserve her ire.

"He made it clear I needed to be willing to offer more than a 'proposal' on the town's strengths in order to win his favor."

"I'll kill him," Jim muttered.

"Griffin had the same response. He stepped in when Christian got angry."

Jana swallowed. She could only imagine her son's reaction to Maggie being threatened. "Did he…?"

"They exchanged words," Maggie told her. "No more. But I can't help thinking I could have handled things better. I was friendly with Christian from the start. Maybe too friendly."

"No." Jana took her hand. "Don't you dare blame

yourself for anything that man did or made you feel. You don't owe him anything."

"It's not what I owe him that has me the most upset," Maggie said miserably. "It's what my actions are going to mean for the town."

"Sweetie, no." Jana glanced at Jim, who looked like he was ready to track down the LiveSoft CEO and challenge him to an old-fashioned duel for besmirching his daughter's honor. But Jana knew that wasn't what Maggie needed at the moment. It dawned on her that she could have a place in this house and in this family's life. Despite everything that had gone before, the pain Jim had caused her and the decades of animosity between the Stones and Spencers, she cared about all of them.

She couldn't begrudge Jim the life he'd shared with Charlotte. Yes, he'd hurt her but she'd gone on to find a unique happiness with Dave. She'd raised two amazing sons and now ran a successful business. She had no regrets because there was no way she'd give up any piece of the life she built.

Now she had a second chance with her first love. He'd been through plenty yet was still willing to risk loving her again. For this to work, they'd have to find a way to support the other's children even if they were at odds.

How would her boys have turned out without her? Jana could barely force herself to consider the idea. Maggie lost her mother at fifteen, a difficult age for any girl. She was an amazing woman, and Jana wouldn't let anyone make her feel differently.

"I've seen a lot in my years in this town," she said gently. "No one should expect you to compromise your values or allow yourself to be treated like a commodity."

Maggie bit down on her lower lip. "I hope you're right. I thought I could make it better, smooth things over with Christian without jeopardizing our chances. Instead, I made him angry and I pushed Griffin away in the process."

"Griffin cares about you," Jana said without hesitation.

"He told me he loved me," Maggie said with a sniff. "Again."

"He has a funny way of showing it," Jim muttered and Jana didn't even take offense. She understood how badly her son had hurt Maggie. She'd once felt the same kind of heartbreak.

"Are you going to give him another chance?" she asked, squeezing Maggie's hand.

Maggie shook her head. "I told him I couldn't. I can't risk being hurt like I was before."

"Sometimes…" Jana looked toward Jim then back at Maggie "…you have to risk the hurt to find the happiness."

"Sometimes," Maggie responded, "the risk is too great." She swiped at her cheeks then smiled. "I'm happy for the two of you. Really. It's going to make for some strange family get-togethers, although at this point strange feels like our new normal."

"I love you, Mags," Jim whispered and pulled his daughter in for a tight hug. "You deserve so much happiness."

"I'll find it eventually," she answered but Jana could still see the pain enveloping her. "I'm going to grab the clothes and take off."

"You don't need to go," Jana said quickly. "If you want to spend time with your dad—"

Maggie held up a hand. "You two crazy kids continue with…" She waved a hand. "Well, I don't want to know how you're going to continue. But I would like to be a fly on the wall when you explain this to Grammy."

Jana grimaced and Jim let out a laugh. "Your grandmother will just have to deal."

"Yeah," Maggie agreed with a wink. "Good luck with that."

She turned and walked out of the kitchen. Jana slapped her palm to her forehead. "I'm a middle-aged woman, and I'm terrified that your mother won't approve of me. That's sad."

"She'll approve," Jim assured her, wrapping his arms around her once again. "Mom respects you, and for good reason. You're amazing, Jana. The fact that you can comfort Maggie when she tells you she won't give your son another chance is a testament to your character."

"They're adults." She sighed. "I'm certainly not in a position to judge anyone for the choices they make. I love my son, and I think he truly loves Maggie. I still have hope." She rested her head against his chest, taking solace in the steady beat of his heart. "I'm not giving up on them getting another chance at happiness."

"Thank you," he whispered, kissing the top of her head, "for giving me one." He pulled back, cradling her face in his big hand. "Is it too soon for me to tell you I love you?"

Her heart seemed to skip a beat; an avalanche of

joy tumbled through her. "It's not too soon." The truth was she'd never stopped loving this man. She'd buried the emotion to survive without him. But now love that had lain dormant all these years unfolded inside her like the first bloom of the spring pushing through the dry winter earth.

"I love you, Jana." He kissed her, and she breathed him in, feeling more alive than she had in years.

"I love you too," she whispered. "I always will."

Chapter Thirteen

Griffin looked up from the computer as the door to the home office opened and his mother stepped into the room.

"You're up late," his mom said, inclining her head. "Still trying to get up to speed before Marcus leaves?"

"Not exactly." He glanced at the clock on his computer screen then back at her. "You had a late night, as well. Book club gone wild?"

She smiled and shook her head. "I was with Jim Spencer."

Griffin tried to hide his frown but by the look on his mom's face, he didn't succeed. "How long does it take to design a sculpture? I thought you were going with some kind of homage to the seasons."

"Jim and I are together," she said by way of an answer. "I'm in love with him, Griffin."

Talk about an unexpected punch to the gut. "How is that possible? You barely…" Realization dawned like a painfully bright sunrise after an all-nighter. "He's the guy you dated before Dad?"

She nodded and smoothed a hand over her dark sweater. "It didn't help your father to feel any friendlier toward the Spencers over the years."

"Because Jim hurt you." Griffin pushed back from the desk, folding his arms over his chest. "Dad probably wanted to rip him to pieces."

"We never discussed it," she answered. "But that was a long time ago."

"Who cares how long it's been, Mom? He treated you badly. How can you say you're in love with him now?"

"I'm not sure I ever fell out of love," she admitted. "Which doesn't change or diminish what your father and I had." She held up a hand when Griffin would have argued. "I don't owe you an explanation for the workings of my heart. I love you to pieces and would do anything for you, Griffin. For either you or Trevor, and now Joey too. But this decision belongs to me."

"Jim *hurt* you," he repeated, still remembering the sorrow that had filled his mother's gaze when she'd talked about her past.

"You hurt Maggie," she countered.

He sucked in a breath. Jana Stone with a swift uppercut that left him reeling.

"It's not the same thing."

"Are you sure?"

"No," he admitted, swallowing hard. "At this point, I'm not sure of anything except that I love her and I've lost her."

"Oh, Griffin."

He flicked a hand toward the computer screen. "I'm looking into Christian Milken's history now. The guy seems like the all-American corporate captain of technology, but he's shady."

"Maggie told us about her run-in with him." His mother stepped forward. "And yours."

"You would have been proud." He flashed a quick smile. "I didn't kill him."

"I'm proud of you for so many reasons."

"Brenna called me a coward for not fighting harder to win Maggie back."

"I've always liked that girl."

"I bet." He chuckled. "I don't want to give up on her."

"Then don't."

He rested his elbows on the desk, placing his head in his hands. "I'm so damn scared of failing."

His mother's sharp intake of breath reverberated in the quiet of the room. Griffin didn't look up. He wouldn't be able to say the things he needed to share if he had to meet her gaze.

"I tried with Dad. Not in the way he wanted, but I tried. And no matter what I did, it was never enough. I learned everything I could about the vineyard. I made his passion my passion, and he still wouldn't let me in. At some point, it became easier to disappoint him. If I made that my goal, at least I could succeed at something. I was never enough for him, and part of me thinks I'll never be enough for Maggie."

"You're enough," his mother whispered, her voice filled with tears.

"You have to say that. You're my mom." He was

trying to make a joke because the emotions pouring through him made him anxious, itchy like a junkie craving the needle.

"Maggie loves you," she said, her tone grave. So much for lightening the mood. His heart threatened to beat out of his chest in response to her words.

"Look at what I did to her," he said after several long moments. "I'm worried about you with her father because he hurt you in the same way I hurt Maggie. I wish it could be different."

"You're living in the past," she said. "I know because I spent decades there. But you and Maggie still have a chance, Griffin. It's only too late if you believe it."

"I need to show her I'm worth the risk."

"Then show her."

"Will you help me?"

"Whatever you need." His mom grabbed a ladder-back chair that sat against the wall and pulled it toward the desk. "Do you know the last time you asked me for help was on your fourth-grade science project?"

He laughed for real this time. "I was an idiot even as a kid."

"You're just a slow learner," she said, ruffling his hair like she used to when he was a boy.

"I can't live without her," he whispered and took comfort in his mother's knowing smile.

"I have a feeling you won't have to."

Maggie approached the town square on Christmas Eve with a heavy heart. She knew the video of her slapping Christian had made the rounds through the community, although no one but Brenna had actually mentioned it to her.

It was never a good sign when the town went radio silent. She didn't have the nerve to address it herself, hoping beyond hope the damage hadn't been as bad as she thought.

No one from Christian's team had returned her calls, although she'd gotten a terse text from Allyson that he would honor his commitment to attend the town's annual Christmas Eve caroling event. It was scheduled to be the final activity filmed for the competition.

The community always came together en masse for a public reading of "The Night Before Christmas" and a selection of holiday songs led by the high school chamber choir. It had always been one of her family's favorite traditions. Her mom had loved it especially, and Maggie could still remember that final holiday they'd had together. Her mom had been in a wheelchair, with Ben cradled in her lap. Tears streamed down her face as she sang in her lilting soprano about "little Lord Jesus asleep on the hay."

Both Maggie and her father had been in denial, not willing to admit that they wouldn't have another Christmas together. Miracles happened all the time in movies and television shows. Why not in their little corner of the world?

But there had been no reprieve from cancer. Instead, her mother had died on a cold, dreary afternoon in late January. The following Christmas had been bittersweet and her father had withdrawn into himself. But her mom had made Maggie promise that she'd keep up the traditions they loved so much for Morgan and Ben. She'd forced her dad out of the house, and with Grammy's help, they'd bundled up the two little ones and all of them had attended the Christmas Eve event.

It had been a turning point of sorts. Her father had remained steeped in grief, but after that night there were glimmers of hope in the darkness that had engulfed their lives. For Maggie, the festive occasion had taken on special meaning.

Tonight it felt tainted by her anxiety over the situation with LiveSoft. She wasn't sure how to fix the relationship and still be true to herself. Honestly, she wasn't sure if she wanted to. If Christian believed he could use his position to take advantage of her, would he also abuse his influence in the community if his company moved to Stonecreek? Maggie didn't want to give so much potential negativity any hold in her town, but she couldn't deny the impact headquartering such a growing company would have on the community.

"Come on," her brother called from the sidewalk across the street. "We're going to miss the first part. Grammy's saving us a spot up front."

Maggie smiled as she jogged across the empty street toward Ben, Morgan and their father. This year Morgan's boyfriend, Cole, and Jana Stone joined them.

"Let's hurry then," she said when she got closer, looping an arm over Ben's shoulder as they started walking toward the center of the square. "I don't want you to be late." It made her heart glad that even at fourteen, her brother hadn't outgrown attending these types of events.

Even Morgan looked happy to be there, which probably had a lot to do with the tall, nervous-looking boy holding tight to her hand. In the past couple of months, Morgan had finally released her need to rebel, morphing into a friendly, outgoing young woman with a beautiful spirit to match. She'd gotten a job as an after-school babysitter for one of the neighborhood families and spent much of her free time volunteering at the community center.

Maggie's father looked particularly content as well as he stuck close to Jana's side. Maggie didn't dare ask about Griffin and Joey. It was crazy how much she missed both of them even though the decision to break things off had been hers.

Ben wound around the edge of the crowd gathered in front of the stage that had been erected by volunteers early this morning. The night was clear and cold but not unbearably so. The couples and families standing near the front parted to let Maggie and her group through. She could imagine Grammy barking orders about how she was saving the front row.

She sucked in a breath then plastered on a smile as she realized Christian and his loyal assistant were standing next to Vivian. Allyson turned her ever-present phone toward Maggie to record her arrival, and Christian gave her a terse smile.

"Merry Christmas," Maggie said, hugging her grandma.

"Merry Christmas *Eve*," Grammy corrected, as was her way.

"Of course," Maggie agreed then inclined her head

toward Christian. "We hope you enjoy our town's last official event before Christmas."

"Timmins hosted a parade in my honor. I'm not sure how you expect to compete with a story and a few songs."

Maggie opened her mouth to answer, but her father moved to her side, placing a hand on her arm but addressing Christian. "We don't have to compete," he said, his tone flinty. "Tonight you're a guest in our town, and we're proud of our traditions. We don't have to go overboard for the camera. No one here owes you anything, young man." He pointed a finger at Christian. "You'll do well to remember that."

"Oh, snap," Morgan whispered.

With one last glare thrown at Christian, Jim stepped back to stand next to Jana on the far side of Morgan and Cole.

"Delete that part," Christian muttered to Allyson under his breath.

The young woman gave Maggie an almost sympathetic glance then nodded.

At that point, Chuck O'Malley took the stage. "Welcome everyone," he said into the microphone. "It's an exciting evening and we're glad you took the time out of your busy holiday schedule to join us." He adjusted the red Santa cap perched on his head. "The town has hosted this Christmas Eve event for the past seventeen years, and I've had the honor of reading this special poem each Christmas Eve. I'd like to take a moment to thank the late writer Clement Clarke Moore, who first penned the poem titled, 'Account of a Visit from Saint Nicholas.' We know this beloved tale better as 'The Night Before Christmas.'" There was a round of applause and Chuck made an exaggerated bow.

Then he pulled a pair of wire-rimmed glasses from his shirt pocket and perched them on his nose. "Without further ado," he said with a win, "let's get started. All of you big and little kiddies out there need to hit the hay on time tonight so Santa Claus can make his rounds." He opened a well-worn book and began to recite the poem.

Maggie had always loved the juxtaposition of the burly bar owner showing a sentimental side with his impassioned recitation of the Christmas classic.

This year was no exception and by the time Chuck got to the last line, everyone joined in on a chorus of "Merry Christmas to all, and to all a good night."

Everyone except Christian, who looked bored out of his mind. The man had somehow morphed into Stonecreek's own personal Grinch. Chuck didn't seem to notice as he wiped at the corner of his eye with the edge of one sleeve. "Gets me every time," he whispered into the microphone. "Before we begin with the caroling portion of the evening, there's someone special I'd like to invite to the stage. This young man is relatively new to our community, but we hope he'll be a part of Stonecreek for many years to come."

Out of the corner of her eye, Maggie saw Christian roll his eyes, clearly not relishing taking any part in the evening. She hated that he was going to take center stage for something so personal to her and that meant so much to the town.

"Please join me in welcoming little Joey Barlow and, with him, Griffin Stone."

Christian took a step forward then froze and quickly backed up again, his mouth twisting into a brittle frown.

Joey walked up the steps to the stage, holding tight to Griffin's hand. Chuck ushered Griffin toward the microphone as he patted the boy's head.

"Hey, everyone," Griffin said with a tight smile.

"Hey, Griffin," the crowded shouted back instantly.

His shoulders relaxed ever so slightly. "It's been a few years since I've attended one of these holiday events," he admitted then grimaced. "In fact, I think the last time I was here for Christmas Eve, I indulged in too much eggnog in the alley behind the bakery."

"It took me a month to get the stink out," Dora shouted from the back of the square.

"Sorry about that," Griffin called with a wave of his hand. "But it's a good segue into why I asked Chuck if Joey and I could borrow the mic for a few minutes." He glanced over his shoulder at the burly bar owner. "Just for this year. I promise."

Chuck nodded.

"When Joey heard about the reading of 'The Night Before Christmas,'" Griffin continued, "he was pretty excited because that was his mommy's favorite Christmas story."

Joey tugged on the hem of Griffin's canvas jacket then lifted his arms to be picked up. When Griffin obliged, Joey whispered into his ear. Griffin hugged the boy then spoke into the microphone. "Joey's come

to live in Stonecreek because his mom died this year."
An immediate hush fell over the crowd.

"Yes…well…" Griffin cleared his throat. "Since
it's his first Christmas here, I wanted him to see what
an amazing town we have. I kind of ignored that fact
for a lot of years. It's become clear since I've been
back that there's no place I'd rather be." He shrugged.
"There really is no place like home."

Applause and cheers erupted, and Griffin's gaze
slammed into Maggie's. "I'm here for the long haul,"
he said directly to her, "and you're the reason for it."

Her heart gave a staccato thump in her chest.

"As you might have heard," he told the audience,
"Stonecreek has been participating in a bit of a social
media frenzy for the past couple of weeks. A competition, you might call it."

More applause but it was less enthusiastic. Allyson
held up her camera to take in the crowd behind her.

"I think we can all agree it's been exciting to
showcase the best parts of our community so that
people can see how special this place is. It's been a
good reminder for me, anyway, about what's most
important in my life." He glanced toward Maggie
again, and there was nothing but love in his beautiful green eyes.

No doubt. No defenses. All love and all aimed
at her.

"Damn girl," someone said from the row behind
her. "I wish a fine man would look at me that way."

"I love you, Maggie," he said clearly. "I've let a
lot of things get in the way of that, especially my
own stupidity."

She gave a shuddery laugh and clasped a hand

over her mouth. Never in a million years would she have imagined Griffin professing his love in front of most of the town. Particularly when she'd told him they didn't have a chance. For all he knew, he was putting himself out there for nothing. Risking everything.

"I know I've given you plenty of reasons not to trust me, and I won't blame you at all if you never want to talk to me again after this night." He paused, swallowed then said, "But I will love you forever. I love your passion and your heart and your dedication. I love that you don't let me get away with much. I love that no matter where I am in the world, you will always be my home."

"Oh, my," Grammy whispered next to her. "Oh, my."

Oh, my indeed. Maggie didn't know what to think. Her heart felt like it was going to explode in her chest.

"And here's something else we can all agree on," he said to the crowd in general. "Our mayor, Maggie Spencer, has gone above and beyond in working to make sure Stonecreek is the top contender for the LiveSoft headquarters. She's done everything except—" he held up one finger "—let herself be bullied and harassed by LiveSoft's CEO."

He looked out to the audience. "Is it uploaded, Trevor?"

To Maggie's utter shock, Trevor made his way to the front of the assembled crowd.

"Sure is," he called to Griffin. "With the hashtag 'livesoftnotwrong.'"

"Catchy turn of phrase," Griffin said with a

thumbs-up to his brother. "For those of you who haven't heard, Maggie had an unfortunate incident with Christian Milken a few nights ago where the jerk propositioned her in return for the promise of Stonecreek winning the competition." Griffin held out a hand at the outraged murmurs that snaked through the crowd.

Maggie felt her eyes widen and glanced toward Christian, whose face was turning bright red with anger.

"Now we have someone from LiveSoft filming tonight's event." He focused his gaze on Allyson. "You are still filming, right?"

The woman nodded just as Christian snatched the phone from her hand. "Not very sporting of you, Milken," Griffin said. "But no matter. We've invited a news crew from Portland to attend our Christmas Eve celebration. They've been helpful enough to upload the video taken of Christian harassing our Maggie onto their homepage. So please…" He nodded to the crowd. "Share and retweet and don't forget my brother's clever hashtag." He pointed a finger at Christian. "'Livesoftnotwrong.'"

"This is ridiculous," Christian shouted. "I didn't like this place from the start."

"*You* are ridiculous," Griffin shot back. "Stonecreek is amazing. Maggie is amazing. One of the things that makes this town so special is our community. We aren't going to see anyone disrespected the way you tried to with her. No headquarters is worth compromising our values."

Thunderous applause broke out and Christian stormed past Maggie, Allyson following quickly in his wake. "I'm sorry," the assistant whispered as she passed.

"And now," Griffin said when the applause finally died down. "Let's have our high school choir lead us in a few carols."

Maggie stood stock-still for a few seconds, stunned as friends surrounded her offering words of support and encouragement. As the choir filled the stage, she stepped away from the crowd, trying to catch her breath. What had Griffin done?

"Is this true?" Grammy demanded, making her way to Maggie's side.

"Yes, but…"

"If that man comes near you again," Vivian said, fire in her eyes. "I'll personally shank him."

"Yeah, Grammy," Ben shouted. He and Morgan had followed her, along with their father and Jana.

"I'm sorry about the competition," Maggie whispered to her grandmother. "I tried—"

"No." Grammy shook her head. "Nothing is more important to me than you, Mary Margaret. It doesn't matter what happens in this town as long as my family is safe and happy. You all mean the world to me."

Maggie didn't bother to wipe away the tears that rolled down her cheeks.

"I hate seeing you cry," a familiar voice said from behind her. She turned to where Griffin stood several feet away.

The people around her seemed to fade into the background as she moved toward him until they stood toe-to-toe.

"They're happy tears," she whispered. "That was some speech."

"I meant every word of it." He wiped at her cheeks with the pads of his thumbs, and the familiar fire sparked low in her belly at his touch. Only this time she didn't fight it. "I love you so much, Maggie. I'm sorry I hurt you."

She touched a finger to his lips. "No apologies."

"Then let me—" he wrapped his fingers around hers "—spend the rest of our lives proving that I deserve to be at your side. Give me a chance to make you as happy as you make me."

"I love you," she whispered, and he blew out a breath like those words were a balm to his soul.

To her utter shock, he dropped to one knee and pulled a small black box from his jacket pocket. "I love you, Maggie. I will love you and cherish you forever if you say yes. Will you marry me?"

He opened the box to reveal a beautiful diamond solitaire. Then he crooked a finger and Joey came running over to perch on Griffin's knee. "Will you marry both of us?" Griffin amended and the boy added, "Please?"

"Say yes," someone shouted and she glanced around to realize that the choir had stopped singing and most of the town was watching Griffin propose to her.

"It's our home," he said when her gaze met his again. "I guess it's only fitting that they be a part of this."

"Yes," she said through another round of tears. "Yes, I'll marry you. Yes, I'll give you as many chances as you need. Yes, I'll love you forever."

He slipped the ring onto her finger and then she was in his arms. As she hugged Joey and kissed Griffin, the people she'd known and loved her whole life surrounded them with good wishes. Maggie might not be able to carry a tune, but her heart sang as she finally had everything she'd ever wanted.

Epilogue

"He's dancing." Griffin took Maggie's hand in his and squeezed her fingers. "I can't believe she got him out there."

Maggie smiled as she watched Ellie and Joey twirl to the music amidst the other dancers at Brenna and Marcus's wedding reception. It had been a beautiful ceremony, elegant yet understated with Brenna gorgeous in an off-white sheath dress with a beaded lace overlay. Marcus had seemed almost ready to burst into tears when she'd appeared to walk down the aisle, and Maggie was so happy for her friend. The ceremony had taken place at the small chapel across the street from The Miriam Inn while the reception was being held in the hotel's banquet room.

They'd kept the guest list small, so everyone knew each other. It was turning into a lively celebration of both the marriage and the impending New Year. Maggie smiled in response to the cheeky grin Ellie gave Joey. Although the boy looked more than a little nervous, it was obvious he was having fun with his new best friend.

"How could he say no?" Maggie laughed. "He's smitten."

"I know the feeling," Griffin said, and her heart seemed to skip a beat at the love radiating from his gaze.

"I never imagined I could be this happy," she whispered.

Griffin leaned in and brushed a gentle kiss across her lips. "Just wait until our wedding day."

Tiny shivers of anticipation zipped along her spine. "Do you think we can really get away with inviting only family?"

"We've spent plenty of time in the Stonecreek spotlight recently. We've earned a little privacy."

"At least the national morning shows have stopped calling," she said, cringing slightly.

The fallout from the situation with LiveSoft had been both positive and challenging. The video documenting Christian's treatment of her had gone viral, and he'd been forced to resign from the company. They'd named one of the VPs as acting CEO, but from what Maggie'd heard, the board of directors was trying to woo the man who'd created the original app to come on board with the company.

She couldn't bring herself to feel sorry for Christian. No one should be allowed to abuse their power in that way, and she was proud and grateful that her town had rallied around her.

In the wake of the negative press, LiveSoft had decided to remain headquartered in California for the foreseeable future. But Maggie'd received a call yesterday from a company that manufactured a variety of outdoor-lifestyle products from coolers to apparel. The company had outgrown its original headquarters and was interested in Stonecreek as a possible relocation site. She'd set up a meeting with the owners after the first of the year and felt cautiously optimistic about bringing the business to town.

Either way, she felt confident that Stonecreek would continue to grow and thrive under her leadership. Despite the stress from the LiveSoft competition, she'd learned to believe in herself. Heck, she'd even showered this morning in her brand-new bathroom. Not many people spent Christmas vacation tiling a bathroom, but her family and friends had pitched in to help her finish the job.

"I think we're finally going to return to normal life around here," Griffin told her.

"You won't find normal boring?" she asked, laughing as he tugged her to her feet.

"Life with you could never be boring, Maggie May." He led her to the dance floor, and despite the up-tempo song, wrapped his arms around her waist and slowly swayed to the music.

"Worst dancers ever," Morgan muttered as she shimmied by.

"Come on, Griffin," Cole called as Morgan joined him and Ben on one side of the dance floor. "Let's see that white man's overbite."

Griffin rolled his eyes at the trio. "Maybe later."

"I love your moves," Maggie told him and he held her tighter.

"I love you," he whispered.

She rested her head on his chest and closed her eyes, grateful for everything that had brought her to this moment and to a love she knew would last forever.

* * * * *

COMING SOON!

We really hope you enjoyed reading this book. If you're looking for more romance, be sure to head to the shops when new books are available on

Thursday 29th November

To see which titles are coming soon, please visit **millsandboon.co.uk**

MILLS & BOON